THE
Thief Taker

A Novel

JANET GLEESON

SIMON & SCHUSTER PAPERBACKS

New York   London   Toronto   Sydney

SIMON & SCHUSTER PAPERBACKS
Rockefeller Center
1230 Avenue of the Americas
New York, NY 10020

First Simon & Schuster paperback edition 2006

Originally published in Great Britain in 2004 by Bantam Press,
a division of Transworld Publishers

For information regarding special discounts for bulk purchases,
please contact Simon & Schuster Special Sales at
1-800-456-6798 or business@simonandschuster.com.

Book design by Ellen R. Sasahara

Manufactured in the United States of America

3   5   7   9   10   8   6   4   2

Library of Congress Cataloging-in-Publication Data
Gleeson, Janet.
The thief taker : a novel / Janet Gleeson.—1st Simon & Schuster pbk. ed.
p. cm.
1. Women cooks—Fiction. 2. Silversmiths—Fiction. 3. London (England)—
History—18th century—Fiction. I. Title.
PR6107.L44T47   2006   823'.92—dc22   2006045684

ISBN-13: 978-0-7432-9018-0
ISBN-10:   0-7432-9018-6

For Paul

Chapter One

AGNES MEADOWES first saw the girl one Monday morning, huddled in a doorway in Foster Lane. She was no more than twelve or thirteen; her feet were bare, and apart from a bright crimson shawl wrapped about her head, her costume was ragged, and colorless with dirt.

But there was nothing remarkable about the sight of a beggar loitering in the streets of London in 1750, and Agnes was preoccupied with more important matters. As cook for the Blanchards of Foster Lane, she was thinking about ragout, and where to find the best green angelica for syllabub, and how much the kitchen maid and scullery maid would get done while she was out.

Despite all this, something about the girl, sitting alone surveying the street, struck a chord. The girl was sitting as still as stone, her bony knees pressed up to her pinched face, her eyes fixed on the Blanchards' doorway. Her shawl reminded Agnes of the one her husband had given her on their wedding day, and she felt a moment of sympathy, mingled with suspicion.

A few minutes later Agnes had reached the market and was battling through the throng. She stepped over rotting offal and cabbage leaves to prod breasts of pheasant and partridge. She sniffed oysters and herrings and asked the price of oranges, shouting her requirements over strident cries of "New mackerel!" and

"White turnips and fine carrots, ho!" and "Fine China oranges and fresh juicy lemons!" She watched a juggler with blackened teeth catching knives in his mouth, then sampled a corner of gingerbread so spicy tears welled in her eyes. The street child had slipped from her thoughts.

Within the hour, Agnes had arranged deliveries with half a dozen tradesmen whose goods she could not carry, and jotted every item and its price in her notebook for Mrs Tooley's accounts. In her basket she had carefully stowed sweet oranges, Jordan almonds, two dozen pullet eggs, a pickled salmon, half a pound of angelica, the same of glacé cherries. As she retraced her steps, her mind whirled with all there was to do. At the very least, Rose, the kitchen maid, should have skinned and jointed the hare, plucked and drawn the pheasant, and (provided Philip had not distracted her unduly) begun to grind the sugar for the desserts.

Agnes turned from Cheapside into Foster Lane and approached the railings that lined the steps to her basement kitchen. The beggar girl was exactly where she had been earlier, her eyes fixed on the first-floor windows of the Blanchards' silver workshop. Suddenly, she seemed to sense Agnes's presence, and turned and caught her gaze. Lank strands of hair partially covered her face. Behind them, Agnes detected eyes that were curiously disturbing: upturned and slanted, the whites very white, the pupils large and dark. Instinct told her that the girl was up to no good. She showed every sign of being a cutpurse or some rogue's accomplice. But her limbs were thin as rope, she was plainly in need of nourishment—and Agnes regarded nourishment as a matter of the utmost importance. Moreover, Agnes had a child of her own, Peter, who, owing to her position as cook, she saw infrequently.

The door behind the girl opened and a maidservant darted out. "Get away with you, vermin!" she bellowed, thrusting a broom as if it were a sword, whacking the girl in the small of her back. "Don't think you'll get anything by begging." The girl fell forward, then scrambled to her feet. "I didn't mean no harm," she squawked, rubbing her back. "I wasn't doing nothing wrong."

"You was dirtying my step, and Gawd knows what more besides. So scram, unless you want another feel of the hard end of this," said the maid, waving her broom. The girl raised her hands and sidled away.

"Good riddance." The maid gave the step a brisk once-over before slamming the door.

Agnes understood the maid's concerns, but something in the girl's demeanor, coupled with her own thoughts, impelled her forward. "One moment, if you please," she said, hurriedly rolling three farthings from her purse into her palm.

"What?" said the girl, then, spying the coins in Agnes's hand, she added, more politely, "I ain't done *you* no harm."

"Did someone ask you to wait here?"

The girl looked from Agnes's hand to her face. "No."

"Then what are you doing?"

The girl said nothing, but searched the street. Agnes tentatively offered the coins on the flat of her palm, as if she were feeding a horse that might bite. The girl snatched them away, scratching Agnes's palm slightly in her haste. "My pa's coming," she muttered.

"But you have been here some time. Where is he? Has he employment in the vicinity?" Agnes waved toward the Blanchards' grand shopwindow. Behind stout iron bars was a glittering display of silver salvers, dishes, cups, and candlesticks.

"He does business around here."

Agnes's curiosity was roused. She took an orange from her basket and lifted it to her face to sniff it, regarding the girl from behind the curve of the fruit. "What manner of business?"

The girl considered the orange, then glanced over her shoulder. "He fetches things for people."

The description sounded ominous. Agnes paused. What foolhardy impulse had possessed her to engage such a person in conversation and give her coins? The girl must think her soft in the head. At best, she had shown her that sitting in doorways was a feasible means of making a living. At worst, the girl might even now be signaling to her father to creep up and rob her.

As the girl peered down the street, Agnes observed a sharpening in her expression. Turning apprehensively to follow her gaze, she observed a cluster of foppish gentlemen watching a pair of ladies descend from a carriage. Beyond them was a man clad in a long dun-colored coat and tricorn hat. Agnes pointed at the lurking figure. "Is that your father?"

No sooner had she uttered these words than she felt a grab of surprising swiftness and force. The orange and purse were whisked from her grasp. "Wait!" she spluttered—but the girl had rounded the corner and was gone.

"Trouble, Mrs. Meadowes? Want me to chase after her?" called John, the first footman, loudly, from the top step of the Blanchard residence. A flash in John's eye and a small tick at the corner of his mouth betrayed his amusement at the events. He was sharp-witted, discreet, and generally respectful, and not prone to lewdness—unlike certain others Agnes could mention. But she disliked being the subject of mirth. She prayed that he had not seen the girl take her purse, and thanked heaven that she had been robbed after, rather than before, her trip to market. The purse had had only a shilling and sixpence in it, but this seemed small consolation for the damage to her pride.

She bustled toward the steps, shooting John a reproachful glance. "Thank you, John," she said with what dignity she could muster. "I am in no need of assistance. I was about to give her the fruit, in any case."

He nodded slowly. "'Course you was, Mrs. Meadowes. By the by, would it cheer you to know the post boy just brought a letter for you? I left it with Mrs. Tooley." He tapped the side of his nose as if sharing a secret. "Sender's from Twickenham. Who's that, then? Rare you get correspondence, ain't it?"

Agnes felt her stomach pitch. Twickenham was where her son, Peter, boarded with a certain Mrs. Catchpole, who rarely troubled to write.

At that moment, Nicholas Blanchard appeared on the threshold twirling a silver-topped cane. "Ready, John," he declared. A sudden tightening of his jaw betrayed his disapproval that his first footman was engaged in conversation with his cook. He was poised to pass some remark, but Agnes had no wish to add to her humiliation. She dropped a curtsy, eyes lowered, then, clutching her basket of provisions like a shield, she scuttled down the basement steps.

THE KITCHEN, Agnes's domain, had an uneven flagged floor and was lit by three high-set sash windows that were regularly cleared with vinegar and water. An open iron range with bread ovens and warming cupboards threw out such scorching heat that anyone near it turned redder than cayenne pepper. In a capacious dresser, the tools of Agnes's trade—pots and dishes, utensils and cutlery— were neatly stored. In front stood a long deal table, its ancient surface pitted and scarred by years of use.

Agnes carefully set down her provisions upon this table, next to a dish of jointed hare. She gazed around distractedly, looking for the housekeeper. "Where might Mrs. Tooley be?" she asked.

"Having a lie down—she's been taken strange," said Rose, a comely, buxom, brown-haired maid, as she emerged from the larder bearing a large cod by the gills. "She's got one of her distempers coming."

Doris, the scullery maid, looked up from the bucket of potatoes she was peeling. "She don't wish to be disturbed," she added slowly, as if finding the words cost her considerable effort. "Not 'less it's urgent."

Rose slapped down the fish impatiently at the far end of the table. "And she said to tell you to finish off the dessert. Only the orange cream—there's a jar of plums left out, and the apple pie from yesterday will do."

Agnes suppressed a sigh; it did not do to reveal disgruntlement to those beneath her in case it encouraged them to do the same. "Did she say anything about a letter?"

Doris raised her plump face and tried to puff away a stiff carrot-colored lock. "Don't recall. Did she, Rose?" She shook her head as a question mark of peel fell into her bucket.

"Only that she'd keep it safe till after your duties was finished," replied Rose. "She said you wouldn't have a moment before."

Agnes told herself firmly there was no reason to suppose anything was wrong. The letter might contain nothing more ominous than a list of what Mrs. Catchpole wanted for Peter the next time Agnes visited. She walked to the side of the dresser. Hanging on a hook was a slate, with the menu chalked upon it in her own hand:

First course: almond soup, white fricassee, boiled cod
Second course: chicken patties, jugged hare, roast venison,
     oyster loaves, mushrooms, cauliflower pickle
Dessert: apple tart, orange cream, plums in syrup

Under normal circumstances, Mrs. Tooley took care of the dessert. But at sixty-two, her health was growing fragile. She was prone to sudden contagions and would wash her head with salt, vinegar, and a spoonful of brandy, and lie in her darkened bedchamber, sipping an infusion of aniseed and opium until she fell into a deep sleep. Her condition invariably improved, but it might take several hours. Today, Agnes would have to take on her culinary duties.

Depositing the slate on the table, Agnes opened the middle drawer of the kitchen table and took out a plump volume of handwritten recipes, bound in crimson cloth. She had begun to compile this important record five years ago, when she first came to the Blanchards' as undercook to the French chef. The household was one of middling size and means, with fewer than a dozen servants, but the family aspired to meals that would rival those in grander houses. Agnes had been a competent cook, having run a modest house for her husband, and although she had not had the least knowledge of foreign ways or sauces, she knew that French cooking was greatly superior to traditional fare. Being ambitious and eager to secure her future for her son's sake, she had observed, questioned, and recorded all the chef deigned tell her in his heavily accented English. Written in her meticulous hand, it began with soups, continued with fish, progressed to roasting and boiling, and then branched into all manner of fancy fricandeaus, ragouts, pies, puddings, and desserts.

A year ago, after a barrage of angry shouting, the French chef had been dismissed. A missing half barrel of port had led Mr. Matthews, the butler, to discover a significant discrepancy between the stock in the cellar and the accounts from the vintner. Agnes and Mrs. Tooley had been obliged to make do until a replacement could be found.

But instead of the mayhem Mrs. Tooley had feared, the kitchen ran more smoothly. Pigeon pies, forced calves' heads, and tongues roasted the French way turned out to be all well within Agnes's capabilities. And Agnes was satisfied with a salary of forty pounds a year, whereas a French chef would have demanded twice that sum. After a lengthy conference between Mr. Matthews, Mrs. Tooley, and Lydia Blanchard, Agnes had been promoted permanently to the post of household cook and a new kitchen maid, Rose, engaged to assist her. And Mrs. Tooley, when she was well, turned her hand to making dessert.

Agnes now flicked through the recipes with ease. She knew almost every one from the first two courses by heart, but thought it wise to refer to the one for orange cream so she would make it precisely as Mrs. Tooley would wish. Then her attention returned to the hare. To be properly tender it would need to simmer a good two hours. She told Doris to bring her the stone jug. "Is this seasoned yet?" she inquired of Rose. The girl was haphazard when it came to crucial matters such as pepper, salt, and mace.

"Lord, no, Mrs. M.," said Rose unashamedly. "It slipped my thoughts."

Agnes noticed she had a purplish bruise on her cheek, and her eyes looked feverishly bright. The girl was slicing the cod into uneven steaks. "Not too thick with those," Agnes said sternly. "Try and keep them the same size. And mind you butter the dish well so they don't stick. And wash your hands after, or you'll taint anything else you touch."

Rose raised an eyebrow in the direction of the butler's pantry, where Philip, the second footman, was standing at the lead-lined sink, cleaning knives. "You've no need to tell me that, Mrs. Meadowes," she said pertly. "It's not as if I haven't done it before."

Nettled by this insubordination and Philip's winking reply, Agnes felt herself flush. She shot Rose a look before turning to the hare. She seasoned it, set it in the jug with herbs, bacon, a blade of mace, an onion stuck with cloves, two wineglasses of port, a tablespoonful of currant jelly, and a covering of thin broth, and put it on the heat. Then she moved on to the orange cream. Being fastidious in culinary matters—why estimate and run the risk of being wrong, when you might measure and always be exact?—she took out her balance and weighed the sugar which Rose had ground. As she had suspected, it was a fraction short.

"What delights you knocking up for us today, then, Mrs. M.?" asked Philip, peering over her shoulder. "Something tasty. Make an extra serving for me, will you?" Agnes disliked the feel of Philip's breath on her neck. She sidestepped away from him, pushed the bowl toward Rose, and, managing to keep the tremor from her voice, requested that she grate two ounces more. Rose sullenly stamped off to the larder to fetch the sugarloaf.

Agnes watched her go with a measure of disquiet. Rose's deficiencies were becoming difficult to ignore; she ought to upbraid her more than she did. She ought to find out how she came by that bruise. She was not slow to tick Doris off when she found her work wanting. Why was Rose a different matter?

She knew the unpalatable answer to this question perfectly well, although she disliked admitting it to herself. Six months before she had gone to the larder to fetch a brace of partridge, and found Rose standing between a round of Cheshire cheese and a hogshead of molasses, head thrown back, eyes half closed, skirts and petticoats rucked up, moaning and groaning in ecstasy as Philip, breeches undone, buttocks bare, pressed against her. Both were entirely unconscious of Agnes's arrival. Scalded by embarrassment, Agnes did not know what to do. Should she cough, or shout, or drop something? Should she throw a bucket of water over them? Instead, she tiptoed away before they noticed her and brooded for hours over how to reprimand them. Eventually, having reached no decision, she had said nothing at all.

Agnes knew now that she should chastise the girl for her cheek, yet the memory lingered and she found herself unable to do so.

Chapter Two

THAT SAME MONDAY, Harry Drake rose in his dank cellar home, which was squeezed between a grain store and a ship's chandler, close to Pickle Herring Quay. He was alone. Elsie, his daughter, had risen before dawn and would not return for several hours. Later in the day, he would call on her to ensure all was well and she was doing as he ordered. Without troubling to wash or shave, Harry dressed himself in his finest: a dun cloth coat with pewter buttons snatched from the back of an open carriage; buckskin breeches lifted from the bedchamber of a cove who had taken so much port he never stirred a muscle; and a linen shirt yanked from a washing line in Fetter Lane. He squinted in a shard of looking glass at his swarthy face, with its droopy eyes and crooked nose, then raked his stringy hair with a broken tortoiseshell comb and secured it with a frayed ribbon. Telling himself he looked quite the gentleman, he secreted in various pockets a gold watch, a silver snuffbox, and a notebook containing details of amorous rendezvous between an eminent baron and a lady who was not his wife. This done, he gave his reflection a final admiring glance before emerging from his lair and clambering up a flight of rotten stairs.

Outside, the light on the river was yellowish and the tide was high—choppy brown water lapped over the wharf. Gulls wheeled and cried, gusted by the wind. Harry Drake sniffed the air and felt a drop or two of rain sting his cheek. There was a storm coming, he thought to himself and smiled. Thrusting his hands in his pockets, he prowled into the city streets.

By the time the bells of St. Dunstan's pealed five and the sun sank behind the rooftops of Blackfriars, Harry Drake's business was, by and large, satisfactorily concluded. In place of the valuables, his pockets now contained two gold sovereigns and two silver shillings. The quickening wind flogged his back but the storm had not yet properly arrived, nor had the dark hour for which he waited. Until then, he decided to pass the time pleasurably. First, he required food; a meat pudding and gravy was what he fancied. And afterward, perhaps a sating of a different kind—a visit to Dolly's in Cheapside. With this sequence settled in his mind, Harry Drake headed homeward.

It was twilight by the time he carefully descended the steep stairs so that the rotten wood did not creak and betray his presence. He gently opened the door like a man who wishes to see what lies within before he is observed. There was no window in the cellar. The only light was afforded by three tallow stubs arranged on a wooden board in the middle of a circular table. Through the smoky glow he made out the figure of his daughter, Elsie, with her crimson woolen shawl wrapped about her shoulders. She was sitting by the hearth with a broken wicker basket at her side. The opening door caused a gust, and as the candles flickered, Elsie flinched. Seeing her father's skulking shadow, she nodded mutely and returned to her occupation.

She was building the fire, as she always did at this hour, whatever the season, for warmth never penetrated here. She picked out morsels of coal and wood from her basket, wiped off the worst of the mud, then stacked them in the fireplace as delicately as if she were constructing a house of cards. When the mound was high enough, she ignited it with a splint lit from one of the candles, then puffed until she felt dizzy and the first hesitant sparks caught fire.

Harry Drake took a horsehair blanket from his bed and wrapped it about him. As he watched his daughter's painstaking efforts, his belly growled. The minute Elsie sat back on her heels, he ordered, "Leave off that! I want food—now." He thrust a shilling toward her. "Go to the chophouse. Get me a mutton pudding and a quart of ale. Straight back, no dawdling, mind, 'less you want a leathering."

Ten minutes later she was back, jug in one hand, steaming pudding in the other. She banged them on the table and clattered about to find crockery and a spoon. Harry gulped down the ale, then wiped the spoon on his shirtsleeve and heaped it high with a cascade of suet pastry, fat, gristly meat, and gravy. He crammed its dripping contents into his mouth, chewed, gulped, and drank several times more before his eye strayed from his dish to his daughter, who had resumed her position squatting by the fire. "Where's your dish, girl? Fetch it quick, or you'll go hungry."

Elsie scrambled to her feet and took a pewter saucer and a chipped stoneware mug down from the mantel shelf. She watched unblinking while he pared off a sliver of pudding and congealed gravy, spooned it onto her saucer, half filled her mug with ale, and thrust both toward her. He was sitting on the only chair in the place, so she perched on an upturned coal bucket to eat.

"So," said Harry Drake when there was no morsel left. "See anything today?"

Elsie shrugged. "Nothing different. I was there by six. Shop opened at seven-thirty by one of the apprentices. The two journeymen was there soon after. The gentleman from next door came round eight."

Harry Drake nodded, then knitted his brows. "When I happened by, I caught sight of you talking with someone, then running off. What was that about?"

"Nothing much."

"I'll be the judge of that."

Elsie thought of Agnes, of the pie she had bought with her

coins, and of the purse still hid in her pocket and the snatched orange she had eaten, rind, pips, and all. "Wasn't no lady. Only a servant going at me for sitting on her step."

"Not a servant of the Blanchards?"

"No, Pa. I ain't careless. Nor stupid neither."

Harry picked at his teeth with the point of his pocketknife. "My business there will be done this night. Tomorrow get back to the river. We are low on fuel. And see what else you can find."

Elsie nodded, holding the palms of her hands out to the fire. The flames were the same color as the orange.

Chapter Three

GENERATIONS of Blanchards had lived and worked in Foster Lane, and their grandly appointed shop had once been London's most fashionable silversmith. The street lay at the heart of the profession that had established the family's fortune. Here stood the great Goldsmiths' Hall, and craftsmen in gold and silver worked and prospered as they had throughout the centuries in the neighboring streets of Cheapside, Gutter Lane, Carey Lane, and Wood Street. The family house next door had been equally sumptuous, for the Blanchards had always considered themselves as being a cut above the craftsmen of other trades. At dinner, they ate off silver plate, with a dozen of the best beeswax candles burning in a pair of Corinthian-columned candelabra. This was no extravagance, argued Nicholas Blanchard: a well-appointed table was a canny business practice. When customers were invited to dine, nothing rivaled serving a perfectly roasted duck on a great oval platter, or a pyramid of syllabubs in trumpet vases, or pickles in scallop shells, to spur commissions.

Theodore Blanchard, Nicholas's only son, felt less certain of the need for ostentation. A year ago, after much prevarication, Nicholas had turned over the running of the business to him. But when Theodore had reviewed the accounts and order books, he had found that the seemingly thriving enterprise was far from profitable. Trade in small silver was dire. With one notable exception—a gargantuan wine cooler—no special commissions had been placed for months. Theodore had instigated economies: limited his entertaining; ordered his wife, Lydia, to reduce the household expenditures.

But when Nicholas got a whiff of these thrifty measures, he questioned his son's pessimistic view of the accounts. If the Blanchards were in financial difficulties it could be due only to Theodore's inexperience and inefficiency. Perhaps Theodore would prefer his father to resume control. Meanwhile, whether there were three or thirty at table, he would see his tureens and platters set out, and be reminded of what he had created.

On this particular late January evening, there were no guests at the dark mahogany dining table; the family were dining alone. Theodore took his seat between Nicholas and Lydia, while John, the footman, removed the domed lid of the tureen by its acorn finial, and ladled out the almond soup.

Theodore's appetite was always formidable, and now he slurped a spoonful, savoring the creamy sweetness, noting that Mrs. Meadowes had expertly prevented the soup from curdling and had seasoned it to perfection with a mélange of nutmeg, pepper, bay, and mace. Then he turned to his father. "I wonder, sir, whether you have given further thought to our conversation a week ago?"

Nicholas Blanchard's gaunt, heavily lined face regarded his son. "What was its subject?"

"Moving our business to a more fashionable part of the city. As I made clear to you before, one reason our custom has dwindled is that the city has spread westward. Other craftsmen have begun to decamp. There are now several highly prosperous workshops in Soho."

"And good luck to them," replied Nicholas. "But rest assured, *I* shall not follow. Since time immemorial the craft has been centered on this very spot. Why should I want to move?"

He continued in the same vein as he had last week and the week before that, and on every other occasion that Theodore had proposed alteration of any kind.

Theodore gulped, and discounted every word. "That is all very well, Father, but nothing stays the same indefinitely. Fashions change, cities alter. The name of Blanchard is not held so high as it once was. If we do not acknowledge as much, and search for a remedy, our business will founder and land us bankrupt in the Fleet. It is my solid belief that our trade would be greatly expanded if we moved west to one of the newer environs. Cavendish Square or St. Martin's Lane, perhaps."

Nicholas shook his head. "What would be the purpose of decamping? So that each day hours are wasted in traveling to and from the hall for pieces to be stamped? So that we lose sight of our rivals and they gain the advantage on us?"

"We have received few sizable commissions in the past months."

Nicholas fixed his steel gray eyes on his son. "What of Sir Bartholomew Grey's wine cooler? The most valuable object we have ever made!"

"Yes sir, but that is the exception—and at the present time, in my opinion, it is unlikely to be repeated."

Nicholas dropped his knife and fork on his fish plate with a clatter. "How many other silversmiths can boast such a commission? I have said all I wish to on this matter, Theodore. You know my opinion. It is founded on thirty years' experience. Ignore it at your peril and do not expect it to change."

Outside a steady rain had begun to fall. Theodore could hear windows sashes rattling in their frames. The footmen cleared away the dishes from the first course and replaced them with clean ones. Mr. Matthews replenished the glasses with burgundy. Theodore sat morosely, shoulders slumped. He tried to make conversation with his wife and picked over his dish of jugged hare (usually one of his favorites) with a spoonful of cauliflower pickle. But either the hare was too rich or his appetite had been soured by his father's intransigence. And Lydia was not in a communicative mood. After replying to his inquiries after their children, she fell silent.

Chapter Four

URING THE NIGHT, the gale turned so powerful that the lanterns in Foster Lane were all extinguished. A watchman was paid by various craftsmen to patrol the street and deter any villainy, but at two in the morning, reasoning that no villain would venture out in such inclement conditions, he decided to pass the rest of the night in his bed.

When the city bells chimed half past two, the moon was obscured by a cover of cloud. No one saw Harry Drake step out of Dolly's whorehouse in Cheapside, where he had spent half a sovereign most enjoyably, and creep toward the shadows of Foster Lane. Along the way he darted into a passage and collected a cart, borrowed for the evening from a rag-dealing acquaintance. The cart was empty and easy to push, although the wind hampered his pace. Some minutes later, Harry Drake reached the Blanchards' premises, where he had observed Elsie running off the day before. He left the cart nearby, and huddled in a doorway opposite, his eyes fixed on the Blanchards' shop and his heart thumping in his chest. The wind eddied down the street, moaning like a dying man. But Harry Drake was unperturbed, recalling the information he had gleaned from his daughter, which conveniently supplemented what he had learned elsewhere.

There were three apprentices who slept in the basement of the shop, each of whom had a four-hour watch. They started at eight, twelve, and four o'clock. The apprentice on duty was usually found in the first-floor showroom, keeping guard over the most highly prized pieces of silver, including the one for which Harry had come. He looked up at the three large windows that pierced the first-floor frontage. In one he discerned a yellowish dancing glow of candlelight and an indistinct form. This, Harry assumed, must be the apprentice keeping watch, seated in a chair. Harry had an hour and a half until the apprentice's colleague came to relieve him. What was he waiting for?

Harry took a strip of black cloth from his pocket and wrapped it like a bandage over his nose and mouth, tying it behind his head so that only the slits of his eyes were visible. From another pocket he extracted a length of rope, which he wrapped several times about his fist. Then he dipped into his trouser band and brought out a long-bladed knife. Clutching this tightly, he stepped out from his cover.

On one side of the Blanchards' doorway was the wide, bay-fronted shopwindow, but it was the narrower sash window at street level on the other side to which Harry Drake turned his attentions. He inserted the knife blade between the upper and lower sections of the frame. It was an easy matter to jiggle the blade and give it a swift twist so that the catch sprang back. Harry pushed up the sash, took out a file, and made quick work of a pair of iron bars. He flung his long legs over the sill and slid inside the downstairs showroom.

For a moment, Harry Drake sat on the floor in the pitch darkness to catch his breath and listen. Tension prickled in his spine. He began to unwind the rope from around his knuckles. If the apprentice upstairs had heard his entry, he would hear footsteps on creaking boards, and would be ready. But save for the complaining groans of the gale, he detected no sound.

He removed his hobnail boots and, holding them in one hand, inched forward silently. When he reached the corridor by the front door he put down his boots, then groped his way along the hall-way. He slowly mounted the stairs, setting his feet close to the wall so that not a squeak would betray his presence. At the top there were four doors leading off to the left and right of the landing, but he spied the telltale thread of candlelight beneath only one of them. He inched open the door. This was the most perilous moment. He must creep up on the apprentice and silence him before the boy had time to cry out.

The apprentice was seated before the dying embers of the fire. A burned-down candle stub flickered on a table beside him. His head had lolled forward limply; there could be no mistaking, he had fallen asleep on the watch. He could not have made the task any easier if he had tried.

Harry Drake did not dither for an instant. With the stealth of a pirate, in three strides he had gathered a turn of his rope about each fist and positioned himself directly behind the unsuspecting apprentice. He seized the crown of the boy's head and yanked it back so that his neck would be elongated for one swift twist of the rope.

He expected a quick gurgle and a struggle, not the sight that confronted him. But the apprentice's lips sagged open and his tongue protruded from the dark hole of his mouth, swollen and dark. His eyes were wide open and bulbous, as though something had surprised him. Something *had* surprised him. He was not sleeping. He was dead already, throat cut from ear to ear so deep that his windpipe was severed and his head hung on by no more than a few sinews.

Harry Drake released his grip on the apprentice's head, but the sudden movement caused a new torrent of blood to spurt over the floor, as dark and thick as gravy. He was reminded of the pudding he had eaten earlier that night, and his intestines writhed at the thought of it.

He moved away from the corpse, stepping over the pool of blood that was oozing wider as he watched. He picked up the candle stub from the table and held it aloft, anxiously surveying the silverware displayed about the room. His eyes flickered over all manner of chandeliers, dishes, tureens, and ewers and halted on a hefty sideboard by the door. There sat a massive oval vessel, over three feet long and two feet wide, as big as the copper basin his mother had used for boiling her washing. Only this was not a washing copper.

It was made of silver, adorned with mermaids, dolphins, tritons, and a pair of stampeding horses dragging a naked Neptune from the foamy waves. It was Sir Bartholomew's wine cooler—the most valuable item ever made in the Blanchard workshop; the largest piece of silver seen in the city of London for many a month; the prize that Harry Drake had come to steal.

He unbuttoned his coat and took out a length of sackcloth, which he laid over the wine cooler then tucked under each scalloped leg in turn, sighing pleasurably at the weight. It was as heavy, he reckoned, as Nelly the whore, who had clung about his waist earlier that night. Putting his hands under the cloth, he grasped the receptacle around Neptune's torso and a mermaid's breast, and careless of whether or not the staircase creaked, hurried downstairs. He recovered his boots and unbolted the door. Then, as brazenly as if he were Sir Bartholomew Grey himself, he went out into the stormy street.

Chapter Five

ROSE FRANCIS EMERGED surreptitiously from the kitchen door into the darkness of Foster Lane. The gale still blew, but for several minutes her mind was so taken up with thoughts of the step she had just taken and the rendezvous ahead that she paid little attention to the wind or her surroundings. But in the time she reached Cheapside her cloak billowed about, the lanterns on the shop frontages were all extinguished, signboards swayed eerily in the wind, and clouds gusting across the moon made the street grow disconcertingly dark. She heard the sound of footsteps a short distance behind her. Leather soles on cobbled streets, following the same route she had taken.

She hesitated, clutching her valise and lantern, uncertain whether to turn and look or pretend she had heard nothing and proceed. Perhaps by some misfortune it was the watchman, whom she had hoped to avoid. The bells of St. Paul's had recently chimed three. On this bitter night, at such an hour, she had expected to find the streets deserted. And she was quite alone, apart from the person behind her.

Rose peered over her shoulder, holding her lamp aloft. As if to help, just then the clouds cleared and silver moonlight fell across the street. Some twenty yards behind, near the great cathedral, she thought she glimpsed a shape. She was unsure whether it was a man or a woman, but the figure seemed to be of large to middling build, and dressed in a cloak that flapped about like hers. It was not the watchman—the figure carried no lamp or torch. Just at that moment, another cloud scudded over the moon and the figure melted into the dark.

Rose was, as a rule, immune from fears and fancy. She was headed to a rendezvous in Southwark, and, being conscious of the perils of London streets at night, she had armed herself before setting out. In her right pocket, tucked next to her purse, was a small pocket pistol with a silver-mounted handle.

When she stowed the weapon in her pocket, she was emboldened by her nerve, but now, she had a presentiment of danger that the pistol did nothing to dispel. Who was it? Please God let it not be one of the other servants from the house come chasing after her to bring her back. Surely that was not possible. When she had risen, the two other maids who shared her attic room had been sleeping peacefully. She had crept down the passage and back stairs, avoiding the basement corridor where the other servants slept. No one was up. No one could have observed her. No one knew her plan. Several hours would pass before any of them rose and began to question where she was.

What would happen then? Mrs. Tooley might be summoned from her bed, work herself into a state, and have to retire again. At the thought of the housekeeper sniffing her salts and flapping about, Rose couldn't help smiling. Then a vision of Agnes flitted into her mind. She imagined the cook stirring her sauce or mixing her fricassee, growing flushed with the heat from the fire. Agnes had always maintained her distance, requiring only that Rose perform her duties satisfactorily. But when Rose had been negligent, Agnes had hardly ever chastised her, and once or twice she had asked herself why this was, and grew remorseful. More often, she misbehaved expressly to provoke Agnes. When she never properly succeeded, it had spurred her to worse behavior. She had recounted her misdeeds afterward; Philip and John disapproved, while delighting in the accounts; Doris droned that one of these days she would lose her post. All of them were too dull-witted to see why she took such risks and was so careless of Agnes's and Mrs. Tooley's good opinion—she was leaving.

The footsteps distracted her. Was it her imagination, or were the steps getting closer? Rose increased her pace, gripping the handle of her bag and her lantern, so that the leather bit into her palm and the light wavered about. A few yards on, her anxiety mounting, an idea came to her. She could make a detour and head for the river. At any hour there were certain to be people about, and whatever her stalker's intentions, he could pose no further threat.

Invigorated with new purpose, she turned down Distaff Lane, a thoroughfare of overhanging clapboard houses, all the while gathering speed, and soon she was practically running. After several minutes, lungs aching, she stopped and listened. There was no sound. She believed, in that instant, that her scheme had worked, but then she heard the footsteps again, closer than ever.

Rose Francis transferred her bag to the same hand as the lantern and, with her free hand, took out the pistol. She flicked off the catch, then, turning abruptly right, slowed her pace. She felt cold perspiration gather on her face. She would confuse her pursuer into passing her. When he did so, she would reveal her weapon, and if necessary, she would use it.

But her pursuer failed to oblige. As if sensing a trap, he hung obstinately back in the overhang of a doorway. Rose edged forward, gripping the pistol in her quaking hand. She caught a glimpse of him lingering on the corner. Without pausing, she dashed in the opposite direction, into the first alley she saw. She zigzagged wildly through the labyrinthine passages and streets leading to the river. But whichever way she chose, her pursuer seemed to anticipate her every turn.

The cobbles gave way to mud. The wind was still fierce and the folds of her skirt and cloak tangled between her legs. Out of the corner of her eye she thought she saw a cloak and dark hat. Should she simply turn, aim, and fire her pistol? Reason told her she should, but the instinct for flight had overwhelmed her.

When she emerged breathlessly at Three Cranes Wharf, the clocks of St. Mary Magdalene and St. Austin's began to sound the hour with competing resonance. An oyster moon illuminated the river and the wharfs and warehouses lining its banks. It was low tide and she could see barges aground on the muddy foreshore, lying strangely angled, but gray and flat as if drawn on an engraving.

Rose searched for someone to assist her. There were fewer people than she expected, but at least she was no longer entirely alone. A bald-headed man was slumped comatose in a doorway clutching a gin bottle to his breast. Another man, wearing a greatcoat, was stooped outside a warehouse, tying a barrel to a winch. Beyond, two figures sat hunched over a brazier. None of them appeared to notice her as she emerged from the alley at breakneck speed.

In the hope that the figures by the brazier might be watchmen, Rose cried out to them, but they seemed not to hear. She glanced back at the man with the barrel, only to see him disappear into the warehouse. Directly in front of her were steps leading down to the foreshore. She sidestepped to the right, heading for the figures by the brazier.

Just then the winch with the barrel on it creaked and its chains rattled loudly. Rose jumped at the sound and let go of her lantern and bag, which dropped over the edge of the wharf. She heard them land with a heavy thud. Half crying, she hurried down the steps to recover them. As her boots sank into the mud, she lost her footing and felt herself tumble forward.

For a few seconds she lay sprawled there. Then, slowly, she stumbled to her feet. She stood in her sodden, ruined skirt, peering into the gloom in every direction. It seemed that the person following her had vanished.

Suppose he was still waiting in an alley? She thought for a moment. Her rendezvous was on the south side of the river, which meant crossing the bridge, a distance of half a mile. With the tide out, she could reach the bridge by keeping to the mudflats. This would be safer than returning to the streets, where her pursuer might be waiting for her.

Rose felt her courage return. She retrieved her belongings and picked her way toward the bridge. A dark-cloaked figure slipped out of an alley and, clinging to the shadows, followed.

Chapter Six

AT FOUR O'CLOCK, one of the Blanchards' three apprentices went to relieve the unfortunate Noah Prout of his watch. On discovering the corpse and the great pool of blood, and noting that Sir Bartholomew Grey's precious wine cooler was gone, he hurried to raise the alarm. He roused his fellow apprentice, then charged next door and banged repeatedly on the kitchen door until his fist was raw and bleeding.

It was a good ten minutes before Mr. Matthews arrived in his nightgown and nightcap. The butler's senses had been addled by sleep and several inches of port drained from the decanter, but the sudden blast of wind and debris that gusted in his face when he opened the door sobered him as effectively as a bucket of water to the head. It took him a minute or two to decipher the jumbled account of the nearly decapitated Noah and the missing wine cooler.

Leaving the apprentices ashen and shivering in his parlor, Mr. Matthews immediately went to Theodore's room. He knocked discreetly on the door and, hearing only raucous snoring, entered quietly so as not to disturb Lydia, who slept in the adjacent room.

Theodore was lying with his blankets tucked up round his chin and his nightcap over one nostril. The pointed tip of the hat puffed up and down with each great snore. Mr. Matthews had to give him several firm shakes before, with much incoherent groaning, he woke.

Pale and somber, he listened to the news, then sat in silence for some minutes. "A dreadful calamity, sir," said Mr. Matthews. Theodore twisted his nightcap in his hands, then scratched his stubbly head, but said nothing. "Should I send for the constable now, sir?" pressed Mr. Matthews, half wondering if his master had properly understood him. "The villain may still be in the vicinity."

At last Theodore spoke. "We are ruined. That wine cooler was the most valuable object ever made by this company. There can be no avoiding the fact—we are ruined." If he was taken aback by this admission, Mr. Matthews did not reveal it by so much as a twitch. "Surely not, sir," he said, in the tone of formal deference he found best in a crisis. "What would you have me do about the corpse?"

"Leave me in peace a minute, won't you? Don't expect me to think about that when such a catastrophe has taken place. Whatever am I to tell my father, and Sir Bartholomew? The wine cooler stolen the very night before it was due to be delivered."

When Theodore had recovered himself sufficiently to collect his thoughts, he instructed Matthews to call for the constable and magistrate and to send watchmen in search of the missing wine cooler. Theodore would break the news to his father himself in the morning, at breakfast. He expressly forbade Matthews to discuss the tragedy below stairs until that time. "And since you and I are the only ones who know, I rely upon your discretion, Matthews."

"You may rest assured upon it, sir," said Mr. Matthews with a small bow.

Then, with Mr. Matthews's help, Theodore dressed swiftly and went next door to view the scene of the crime with his own disbelieving eyes.

Chapter Seven

A S A RULE, Agnes Meadowes slept dreamlessly, or at least forgot her dreams by the time she awoke. But the storm had disturbed her, and next morning she was burdened by an unfamiliar sense of foreboding. Her bolster felt damp and her eyes were swollen. The dream that had disturbed her was indistinct, but she knew that it had caused her to weep.

Sitting up in bed, she suddenly understood. The previous evening she had finally retrieved her letter from the ailing Mrs. Tooley. Reading it before retiring had preyed on her mind and caused her nightmares. She plucked it from her night table and considered it again.

Twickenham, January 1750

Dear Mrs. Meadowes,

I should have written to you sooner, but since your last visit a terrible nervous fever brought on after I was caught out in a shower has afflicted me, and I have not left my bed. My sister Barbara has assisted me in caring for your boy, Peter, who has escaped the contagion and enjoys the best of health and spirits.

Now I am out of danger, but my head is still bad and I

must convalesce until I am properly well again. Peter needs more than I can give him at the present moment. I cannot wait till your next visit two weeks hence. For the time being Barbara tends him, but she must return to her own family next Saturday. After that you must find somewhere else.

Yours most sincerely and truly,
Maud Catchpole

Rereading the letter relieved and disturbed Agnes anew. She thanked God Peter was well, and yet where would she find another person to tend Peter at such short notice? She was permitted only one free Sunday a month and the next was not due for another fortnight. She would have to persuade Mrs. Tooley to allow her an extra day off, but the housekeeper was feeling frail and it would not be an easy task.

Agnes reminded herself that there was nothing to be gained from dwelling on her personal disturbances. Her duties awaited and should not be ignored. She would tackle Mrs. Tooley as soon as an opportune moment arose. After all, there were five days until Saturday.

It was now nearly seven. She splashed and scoured herself with a flannel soused in icy water, and donned her everyday garb: a pair of brown woolen stockings, a chemise, a petticoat, a worn gray skirt and bodice, a freshly laundered apron. With the exception of the apron, most of these items had belonged to Lydia Blanchard, who passed them on to her maid, Patsy. But Patsy, being rather larger than Lydia, was obliged to alter the clothes, and those she could not let out or down were passed to Agnes or one of the other servants.

Agnes was almost the same size as Lydia. The costume nicely outlined her narrow waist, but it had been several years since Agnes had taken more than the most cursory interest in her appearance. Today was no exception. She arranged her thick dark hair in a bun and topped it with a cap. A glance at her reflection revealed the effect of her worries over Peter. Her amber eyes were shadowed with purple, her cheeks were drawn. She looked away, and without further delay made her way along the narrow passage to the kitchen.

THE SIGHT that greeted her thrust all other worries from her thoughts. The range should have been burning steadily, yet smoke and yellow flames belched from the grate, a sure sign it had not been lit long. The black kettle that should have been boiling for early-morning tea was barely tepid. There was no sign of the trays of patted butter or the preserves and jellies that should have been set out in preparation for upstairs breakfast. And upon the hub of Agnes's realm—the kitchen table—stood a final outrage: a pair of muddy boots.

If the owner of the boots was unknown (though Agnes had her suspicions), there was no doubt who was responsible for the undone chores. Rose Francis should have been up over an hour ago, but was conspicuously absent. It was as if the girl were challenging her. Agnes determined that today, Rose would not shirk her responsibilities. Agnes would banish all thoughts of the larder and stand over Rose all day if necessary.

Agnes searched for her in the yard, the scullery, and, steeling herself, in the larder. Finding no sign of her, she headed toward the butler's pantry and was startled to see Philip emerge. He was the same height as John, but broader about the shoulder and stronger in the thigh. He had fine, chiseled features, a wide, full-lipped mouth, and a flash in his olive green eyes that showed he knew how handsome he was. But today those eyes were bleary and bloodshot, and his complexion was unusually pale. He was brandishing the hog's bristle brush he used for cleaning boots, and reeked of sweat and stale beer.

"Morning, Mrs. Meadowes," he mumbled with a barely disguised yawn. "Looking for something?"

"Have I *you* to thank for these?" Agnes inquired, waving over at the muddy boots in the middle of her table.

"Someone else must've left 'em. It weren't me," said Philip, without a glimmer of contrition. He yawned again, more loudly and unapologetically, and whisked the boots back to the pantry.

Agnes's brow puckered at the sight of several large flakes of mud left behind. She swept them into her hand, followed Philip back to the pantry, and brushed her palms together, depositing the mud on the bench beside him. "Who, then, pray?"

Philip was just moving aside a cloak and muffler that were lying on the butler's table. He winced and drew back. "Not so loud. I ain't deaf. How should I know? Ain't you got more to worry you'n that?"

"Such as?" she said no more quietly than before. "You mean Rose, I presume? Where's she got to?"

"Shh," said Philip, sliding a smooth wooden tree into each boot before beginning to scrub them. "Her whereabouts are naught to do with me." He jerked his head toward the kitchen. "Why don't you give me a rest and ask Patsy? There she is."

"Ask me what?" said Patsy, Lydia's maid, looking from one to the other as she burst in with a tea tray. She was dressed in a pale blue woolen robe of Lydia's and looked quite the lady. She put down the tray and smoothed a lace ruffle on her sleeve. "I suppose it's Rose. Everything's got behind on account of her. I'm not one to complain, but how am I supposed to do my work as well as hers? I oughtn't prepare Mrs. Blanchard's tray, only take it up."

"I'm sorry," said Agnes, feeling responsible for Rose's failings. She had been as remiss as Rose, in her way. "I can't think what's come over her."

Patsy shrugged petulantly. "Whatever her excuse, she's the cause of more trouble than anyone. I'd say she deserves a proper scolding. Anyway, I can't stop. I shall have to explain to Mrs. Blanchard why her tea is delayed." She shot a meaningful look at Agnes before scurrying off up the back staircase.

Agnes returned slowly to the butler's pantry, where Philip was still pretending to clean the boots. "So where is she?" Agnes pressed with uncharacteristic insistence.

Philip looked stubborn. "I told you before, I don't know."

"Are you certain you do not?" Her cheeks began to burn. A vision of Philip with his breeches round his ankles and his muscular buttocks flexed barged into her skull. She forced it away, looking over her shoulder to make sure they were alone. "Forgive me for asking," she said in a lower tone, "but was she with you last night?"

"No," said Philip, also speaking more softly. "Between you and me, I passed the evening at the Blue Cockerel in Lombard Street. But don't say nothing to Mr. Matthews about it or he'll cuff me. And hand on heart, after the night I passed there I wouldn't 'ave heard her if she'd been in bed beside me."

Agnes was tempted to say he knew as well as she did that nocturnal sorties were strictly forbidden during the week and she saw no reason to keep his outing from Mr. Matthews. But she said nothing. Embarrassment, coupled with respect for the hierarchy of the household, held her back. As cook, she was one of the upper servants, but as a male servant, Philip was beyond her jurisdiction. In any case, she was not surprised at his reluctance to speculate on Rose's whereabouts, nor did she believe his denial. Just because he had gone to the Blue Cockerel did not mean Rose had not accompanied him. Doubtless the pair of them had overindulged and he wanted to protect her from trouble.

Agnes stalked back to the kitchen, took a stick of cinnamon from a tin, and bit down on it. Her fingers were smutted black— polish from the boots, perhaps—which did nothing to improve her humor. She heard a clanking behind her. Doris, the flame-haired scullery maid, shuffled slowly in with a bucket in one hand, a mop trailing in the other.

"About time, Doris," Agnes greeted her sharply. "You are an hour late with that. What has happened to Rose? Is she indisposed? If so, you ought to have told me; if not, you must fetch her at once."

Doris's simple face flushed. "Sorry, Mrs. Meadowes. I never heard a squeak from her all night, but then I always sleep sound. And it being dark and all, I never noticed nothing when I got up. But Nancy says Rose were never in her bed this morning. And since she ain't here, it can only mean she's gone."

Agnes regarded her aghast. "Gone?"

"Aye. Her bed were empty. Nancy thought she'd come down ahead of her and left her deliberately to sleep on. The pair of them had a great falling-out yesterday, and it came to blows. But Rose ain't here, as you see. It was Philip what said she must 'ave gone off. Last night he saw Mr. Matthews lock up, and just now when he went to the coal store, the kitchen door was open."

Hearing this exchange, Philip added, "Lucky we wasn't all murdered in our beds."

Agnes remembered the bruise on Rose's cheek. Nancy and Rose often squabbled, but she had never paid much attention to them. Was this disruption her fault? "What was the fight about?" she inquired.

"Dunno, Mrs. Meadowes," said Doris. "But the screeching was something terrible."

"Both of them was sweet on me," said Philip. "*No* doubt I was what caused it."

Agnes shot him a reproachful look. "I thought you said you knew nothing of her whereabouts."

"She fought over me—that don't mean she told me where she was going."

Without troubling to reply to this, Agnes turned back to Doris. "You might have had the gumption to call me earlier."

Doris swallowed and blinked, looking down at her puffy hands. A limp strand of hair had emerged from her badly pinned cap and was stuck to her glistening forehead. She began picking at the hem of her apron with nails that were not as clean as they might have been. "I didn't know what to do, ma'am. Nancy said to leave you and Mrs. Tooley or we'd be in trouble. She said get on as best we could till you came."

"Nancy is only the housemaid," said Agnes darkly. "She's no right to give orders."

"Ain't that a bit harsh, Mrs. Meadowes?" called Philip from the pantry. Then to Doris, "Never mind her, beauty. I'll look out for you."

Doris's chin trembled and her cheeks flushed the same color as her hair. "Pardon me, Mrs. Meadowes. It was only after I'd scrubbed the floor and scoured the pots that John came down and told me he didn't know where anyone was, and if I didn't set to making the fire I'd catch it for knowing what had happened and doing nothing about it."

Agnes steadied herself and forced a smile. She knew Philip was right. "Yes, yes," she said. "I see you've done your best, though if you had let me know she had gone it would have been better. Even so, Nancy will have to help later on."

"You'll be lucky," muttered Philip, emerging with the boots between his forefinger and thumb and the cloak draped over his arm. He blew a kiss toward Doris.

"That's enough from you, Philip," snapped Agnes, forgetting hierarchy for once.

He responded with a good-humored wink, and went whistling up the back stairs. Doris, who sorely wished Philip had winked at her, and treasured his compliments like gold, curtsied and contrived to follow him. Agnes suppressed her annoyance and gently began to prod the fire. Philip was only trying to get his own way, an extra favor here, a perk there. But what right had he to butter any woman after what he'd got up to with Rose in the larder? It never failed to astonish Agnes that every other female in the household held him in awe.

Her thoughts turned back to Rose. The girl going off had come as a shock; nevertheless, in her heart of hearts, she was not entirely surprised. Rose had come to work for the Blanchards a year ago. Her previous position, so she claimed, had been in the London mansion of a lord, who had a staff of thirty, including half a dozen grooms, four carriages, a steward, and five servants just for the nursery. She had never mentioned what had made her exchange that grand establishment for the more modest one of Foster Lane, nor had Agnes asked. Nevertheless, Agnes had occasionally wondered whether a man had been the cause. And now that she had run off, Agnes believed it most likely that a man had lured Rose away with a promise of some kind.

Agnes's own experiences of men had left her with a pessimistic view of them. Her father had been a physician of substance, a stern widower who had been possessive of his only child and had hardly permitted her to mingle with other girls of her station, let alone respond to potential suitors. He had died leaving her with enough to live on independently, but Agnes had craved companionship and had hurried into marriage with one of her father's patients, a well-to-do draper. Not until after their nuptials did she discover that her husband suffered from ailments and misadventures caused mainly by his fondness for brandy, and that when he returned from a night in the tavern, his affable nature vanished and he grew careless with his fists.

On their sixth anniversary, by which time he had ruined his business and spent nearly all Agnes's inheritance, fate intervened. Her husband ate his supper, then left her to pass the evening in the Golden Magpie. At the stroke of midnight an overfriendly barmaid inadvertently shoved him in the ribs. He stumbled and tripped over a log basket and fell plumb into the hearth, where his heart was impaled on a cast-iron firedog. Agnes had been relieved to be rid of him, but had been left almost penniless, bruised, and with Peter to care for. She had risen to the challenge and supported herself and her child by pursuing her culinary inclinations. Cooking had always been a solace, never more so than now. Having achieved the elevated status of cook, she had formed the unusual opinion that relations with men were no substitute for an independent life. Provided she did her duty, she could be sure that she would have a roof over her head, a warm bed, and would never again be woken and punched senseless in the middle of the night.

Rose had yet to learn this lesson. But there was no doubt she would, and little doubt either that any promise a man had made to Rose would not be what it appeared. Perhaps, thought Agnes with mingled apprehension and hope, she would be back in a day or two.

Chapter Eight

A T EIGHT-THIRTY—half an hour late—Nancy, the housemaid, tapped on the door to Nicholas Blanchard's bedchamber and bade him good morning. He was blissfuly unaware of the previous night's drama and the morning's disruptions, and Nancy was eager that he should remain so. She deposited a scuttleful of coal and kindling on the hearth, and moved to the window, aware of Nicholas Blanchard watching her closely, like a cat observing a moth. Nancy drew back the curtains gingerly, for the heavy fabric had rotted in the sun and threatened to disintegrate in her hands. As she always did, Nancy rubbed a roundel in the mist on the windowpane to survey the sky. "Not bad today, sir. Frosty but bright."

Nicholas grunted a reply, whereupon Nancy began laying a new fire. When the flames burned at a steady crackle she glanced over her shoulder. Nicholas caught the look and, as he often did, threw back the bedcovers and called her over. Nancy unpinned her cap and went wordlessly toward him, feeling faint and a little queasy.

She removed her boots and loosened her bodice and lay stiffly beside him. He rolled on top of her and pinched her breasts with a bony hand. She tried not to wince, for they were much more tender than usual. He smelled different from Philip—of tobacco and pomade and claret, rather than sweat and ale. A minute later he had drawn himself in and was pumping up and down. Nancy lay silently, surveying the ceiling with its cupids and nymphs embracing one another, trying to breathe in shallow breaths to quell the nausea rising in her belly. Usually she felt grateful to Nicholas for singling her out as the recipient for his favors. She had saved most of the money he paid, and the sum now amounted to almost ten pounds. But her predicament had changed.

Should she confess to him that she was carrying his child? What would it be like to be swooped up by one of those nymphs and spend all day suspended in the air, with no chores and no child or Nicholas to please? She closed her eyes and imagined a world of white clouds and flowers and music. But suppose he denied responsibility and dismissed her? An instant later, Nicholas shuddered and finished.

He scrabbled under his pillow for his purse. He picked out a silver shilling and stuffed it in the top of her bodice. Then, unusually, he stuffed a further sixpence into her hand. "Leave me now. You are late—don't think I hadn't remarked it. Make up for the time lost or there'll be trouble with Mrs. Tooley. And you needn't expect me to take your part." He said this in a matter-of-fact tone, not unkindly. Then he patted her arm in an almost fatherly manner.

"Thank you, sir," she said, opening her palm and examining the extra coin. "'Course I won't dally." She straightened the bedclothes, then walked to the looking glass to quickly refasten her clothes. She looked thin and narrow, with neat, small features and hair that was glossy and smooth, the color of polished oak. She tidied her bun, then pinned her cap back on top of it. Her pale gray eyes were unnaturally bright, and the stubble on Nicholas's chin had given her cheeks a pink glow that improved her palid complexion. She turned her head sideways to examine a long red scratch on the side of her neck. She shivered, remembering the strident accusations of theft that Rose had made the previous after-

noon. Rose had accused her of stealing her letter and now, mirac-
ulously, Rose was gone. Nancy pushed the fracas from her
thoughts, then adjusted her collar, thankful that Nicholas had not
noticed the scratch.

The clock struck the quarter hour as Nancy opened the cupboard by Nicholas's bed and removed the half-filled chamber pot.
Despite the stench Nancy concealed any flicker of revulsion. She
placed a duster over the rim and, with a careful curtsy, left the
room.

AT NINE, Mr. Matthews swept in, bearing a tray of early-morning
tea, doing his utmost to conceal the fact that he had been up most
of the night with Theodore and the constable. He set Nicholas's
dressing gown of crimson brocade, matching hat, and embroidered slippers to warm before the fire, which thanks to Nancy's
ministrations was now giving out a steady heat. Then, reopening
the door to the back stairs, he descended as far as the first landing,
where he halted and bellowed down, "Oi there, Philip! What are
you waiting for? Hot water for the master. At the double, if you'd
be so kind."

He returned to Nicholas's room with a pair of polished shoes
in one hand and a well-brushed suit draped across his arm. While
he waited for the water to arrive, his mind was a torrent of
worry—how was he to break the news of last night's robbery and
murder to his master? Nicholas's reaction was sure to be explosive.
If the business was on the brink of ruin, what would happen to the
stipend Mr. Matthews had been promised to keep him in his old
age? Was he also to be ruined?

To calm himself he took out a leather razor strop and sharp-
ened the blade. He had shaved Nicholas almost every morning for
twenty years, and took considerable pride in the steadiness of his
hand and the fact that in all that time he had hardly caused a
scratch on his master's complexion.

He should also inform him of Rose Francis's disappearance, but he knew Nicholas would doubtless blame it on Agnes Meadowes. He had always regarded her as inferior to the French chef she had replaced. Mr. Matthews detested incurring Nicholas's wrath, but did not wish to cast Agnes in a bad light. In all his years he had known no cook more reliable than Agnes. It would be far better, he decided, to keep quiet on the subject of Rose. Lydia could raise it at breakfast, when Nicholas would be distracted by the news of the wine cooler's loss.

A good ten minutes passed before Philip arrived, carrying a steaming pail. Nicholas Blanchard had finished his second cup of tea and was growing restless.

Mr. Matthews glared at Philip. "Took your time, didn't you?" he hissed.

"Fire wasn't lit, was it, sir? It took twice as long," whispered Philip.

"I'll give you twice as long," muttered the butler, jerking his head toward the washstand. "That's what comes of having a trollop for a kitchen maid."

"You said anything to him about that?" said Philip, quiet but undaunted.

"No," whispered Mr. Matthews. "I'm waiting for the moment." Then in a louder, more formal voice that Nicholas Blanchard could hear if he chose to listen, "Pour it in the bowl, if you please, Philip. And mind you don't splash the floor. The master don't like his feet getting wet."

When Philip had gone, Nicholas stepped into his warmed slippers and allowed Matthews to ease him into the sleeves of his silk dressing gown. Lowering himself into a comfortable armchair before the fire, he stretched back his head so that Matthews might shave him and anoint him with powder and pomade, but not so far that he could not glimpse his reflection in the looking glass.

His face was large and angular, dominated by hollow cheeks and a long nose with hairy nostrils that flared when he was riled.

His head was a carpet of dark gray stubble, for almost a week had passed since Matthews last shaved it so that his wigs would sit comfortably. At the lower limit of his forehead, luxuriant brows formed an almost uninterrupted line. There was scarcely a trace of gray in them; when his wig was on, he often thought, he could pass for a man ten years younger.

Today, Mr. Matthews lacked his customary steadiness and the razor caught under Nicholas's nose. The nick was painless, thanks to the sharpness of the blade, but a pearl of blood beaded up on Nicholas's smooth skin. Nicholas saw rather than felt it, but that did not stop him from bellowing, calling Matthews a clumsy oaf. The butler murmured an apology, and with a trembling hand anointed the wound. Now was not the time to break the news of the robbery or murder.

Chapter Nine

ON THE STROKE OF TEN, still attired in dressing gown, cap, and slippers, Nicholas Blanchard descended to the morning room to take his breakfast. Philip was waiting to open the door for him; John was carrying a teakettle to the sideboard. When his master appeared he put the pot down and drew out a chair at the head of the table. Nicholas's paper—the *Morning Post*—and two letters were arranged in a neat pile beside his place.

Lydia was already seated, nibbling a piece of toast. She acknowledged Nicholas's entry by half rising and giving him a jerking curtsy, the expression in her gray eyes grave and distant. Nicholas nodded unsmilingly and muttered an inaudible reply.

Lydia rarely found her father-in-law easy. Today she could see from the brusque manner of his entry that his temper was up. Lydia had learned of Rose's disappearance from Patsy, and while her maid had dressed Lydia's hair and anointed her face with powder, positioning a beauty spot on her left cheek, they had pondered what reasons the girl might have had to leave. Patsy had reminded Lydia that Rose had been in the habit of wandering about upstairs, where as far as anyone knew she had no business to be.

"You recall the letter Nancy found?" Patsy had said.

Lydia had nodded uncomfortably. "Were there other occasions?" she'd sharply inquired.

Patsy's eyes had narrowed. "I believe so. Mr. Matthews caught her on the stairs leading to the best bedrooms only yesterday. And she caused a dispute with Nancy. The pair of them went for each other like dogs—John had to pull them apart."

"Dear God!" Lydia had said, eyes clouded with concern and concentration. "What was the reason for the altercation? Why ever did Mrs. Tooley not tell me?"

"It only took place in the afternoon, ma'am. No doubt she will tell you more when you see her this morning. Among the obscenities it was not easy to make out what they said. I believe it may have had something to do with the letter. Certainly the word 'thief' was used."

Lydia had shuddered. The dispute and the girl being upstairs when she had no business to be had an ominous ring. Nancy, she knew, already shared Nicholas's bed. Was Rose another of his amours? On more than one occasion his affairs had upset the smooth running of the house; several girls had fallen with child and had to be dismissed. Perhaps Rose—being a pretty bold girl, the kind that Nicholas preferred—found herself with child and had run off in distress. Or perhaps the argument had been some form of jealous spat and Nancy had bullied her into leaving. What else, wondered Lydia, might have caused Rose's forays upstairs, her argument with Nancy, and her sudden departure?

Lydia had intended to raise the subject of Rose with her father-in-law, but now, seeing his black look, she resolved to bide her time.

Nicholas broke the seal on his first letter and scanned it, while John poured him a cup of chocolate. "Damnation!" he declared, more to himself than Lydia. "The devil it was!" He tossed the letter in Lydia's direction. "Put this in Theodore's place, would you? It concerns a customer's grievance. There were never half so many complaints when I had charge of the business."

Lydia glanced at the letter. Finding it described nothing more dreadful than a broken handle, she nodded dismissively and murmured half to herself, "A trifling matter—one that will be easily remedied."

Nicholas affected not to hear. He took a sip of his chocolate and instantly spat it out. "God damn it, this is stone cold! Take it away, call for some hot milk—and let it be *properly* heated this time."

Helping himself to a couple of rolls from the basket, he was further distressed to find that the butter had not been impressed with the family crest, but lay on a serving dish entirely undecorated. "Dear God! Has Mrs. Meadowes taken leave of her senses? Lydia, you are too lax with her. I always said she was inadequate to the task. I never understood what possessed you to take her on as cook rather than engage a decent French chef."

"The fault doesn't lie with Mrs. Meadowes."

"Then where?"

Lydia gave him a sweet smile. There was no avoiding the subject now. "Perhaps you are unaware that Rose Francis, the kitchen maid, has run off. There was only Doris, the scullery maid, to assist Mrs. Meadowes at breakfast. No doubt that is why the butter was not molded as usual, and the milk is a little cooler than it ought to be."

"The maid has run off? Are you certain?"

"Patsy told me this morning," said Lydia. Nicholas frowned, seeming surprised and puzzled, but no more. If there had been something between him and Rose, he masked it admirably. "Have you knowledge of this, John?" Nicholas said, turning to the footman, who was hovering by the side table.

John exchanged a brief glance with Philip, who was disappearing with the milk jug. He was unaccustomed to being engaged in conversation while the family were at the table. "'Tis true enough, sir. The girl is gone."

"Can you add anything to Mrs. Blanchard's account?"

"No sir."

"Most likely she will have stolen something of value to take with her. Have you made checks, Lydia?"

"I regret not yet, sir. I am only just risen."

"Then please do so forthwith."

"As you wish." She hesitated. "I wondered if perhaps *you* might know why she went, sir?" she added.

Nicholas Blanchard raised his bushy brow and subjected his daughter-in-law to an indignant glare. "What on earth can you mean, madam? Do you imply I have some insight into the mental workings of a kitchen maid that you, as mistress of this household, lack?"

Lydia swallowed. It was on the tip of her tongue to reply that, yes, she did believe Nicholas might have an insight into the reasons for Rose Francis's departure. And for that matter, an intimate knowledge of Nancy, the housemaid. But then she saw that there was no reason to further rouse her father-in-law's temper when others might make discreet inquiries for her. So she replied demurely, "No sir, but I understand the girl was seen going on unauthorized excursions—I have reason to believe she ventured into the drawing room; and only yesterday Mr. Matthews caught her upstairs."

"Upstairs? What for? I have no knowledge of it. Matthews said nothing to me. You must get to the bottom of this."

"I intend to," said Lydia.

Suddenly, Theodore burst into the room. He wore no wig, his hair was uncombed, and his coat flapped open. His complexion was mottled and his eyes puffy. "Good morning, Father—and Lydia," he whispered in a strangely hushed yet agitated tone. He lowered himself into the chair John pulled out for him and, ignoring the astonished scrutiny of his wife, regarded Nicholas glumly. "Father," he declared, "I fear I have some news of the utmost gravity."

Chapter Ten

I T WAS AGNES'S HABIT, once breakfast had gone upstairs, to drink tea and peruse her book of recipes. This was how inspiration came before she arranged the next day's menu with Mrs. Tooley. She had just begun to contemplate ham and capon pie, pigeons the Italian way, and plates of beef ragout when Mr. Matthews entered her kitchen. He seemed not at all his usual commanding self. His mouth was unusually puckered, his forehead strangely taut; something had unstrung him. Perhaps, she thought, Rose Francis's departure has vexed him as much as me.

Agnes poured him a cup of tea and stirred in two large spoons of sugar. "Here you are, sir," she said, handing him an oatmeal biscuit to go with it. "It might not be as hot as you like, but I trust it's brewed to your liking."

Mr. Matthews thanked her and felt in his breast pocket for the silver flask he always kept there. He unstoppered the lid, and with trembling fingers added a hefty tot of brandy to his mug.

Shocked to see him needing a nip so early in the day, Agnes ventured, "Awkward, Rose leaving like that, isn't it?"

Mr. Matthews shrugged. "For you it must be."

Agnes tilted her head slightly in a confiding manner. "I believe your second footman, Philip, was sweet on her."

"That may have been so, but since Philip is here and Rose is not, we may assume he hasn't played a part in her leaving."

"I suppose not. Apparently there was an altercation between Nancy and Rose yesterday. Perhaps that had something to do with it."

"I have no knowledge of an argument, and what's more, I fail to see why, when you are one wayward maid short and there are so many graver matters to consider, you are wasting my time and yours on idle gossip."

The butler might bully his footmen where necessary, but he had no need to be abrupt with her. "The girl worked for me, Mr. Matthews. I am not gossiping, simply wondering what's become of her." Her unusual vehemence took them both by surprise. It was only a pinch short of rudeness, and Agnes was never rude.

The butler's narrow lips squeezed tighter still. "Your duties, Mrs. Meadowes, are not to wonder. They are what Mrs. Tooley and I tell you. Your maid may be missing, but that does not give you the right to abandon all decorum. Unless, that is, you wish to follow her pernicious model."

Agnes sat up straight and closed her book of recipes. "I don't comprehend your meaning, sir," she said softly, her eyes holding his.

"Come, come, Mrs. Meadowes, you know as well as I that your maid was hardly a model of propriety. *You* have already mentioned Philip."

She swallowed. "Were there others?"

"I believe she numbered the journeyman Benjamin Riley among her intimate acquaintances, and I hazard there was another gentleman, with whom Mrs. Tooley observed her in conversation last week. Only yesterday I caught her outside the master's room; furthermore, she made other unnecessary journeys upstairs. We may only surmise what took her there. On several occasions I scolded her, so too did Mrs. Tooley. But in my opinion she would have benefited from a more watchful eye than you gave her. Having allowed her too much freedom, you should not be surprised to find yourself inconvenienced now she has gone."

Agnes looked down at her book. Rose's intimacies with Philip were bad enough, and Agnes agreed that in her general manner Rose often lacked in modesty. But this was something else entirely. It bordered on depravity. "Thank you, Mr. Matthews," she said, as she got up. "I had no idea of these transgressions. Had I known, I should of course have spoken to her—taken a firmer hand. Nevertheless, I understand the reason for your disgruntlement. We should all be glad she has gone."

Mollified, Mr. Matthews grew contrite. "The reason for my agitation is not simply that wayward girl. Something far more dreadful than her running off happened last night; something that might threaten all our livelihoods. I intend to tell the rest of the staff at dinner. Until then you must keep it in confidence . . ."

Chapter Eleven

NANCY BLAMED HER lateness squarely on Rose Francis running off. If the bitch had got up when she ought, Nancy would not have overslept and be rushing now. It was her fault—it was always Rose's fault—and Nancy always bore the brunt of her failings.

In the drawing room, dropping her housemaid's box on a cloth by the hearth, Nancy kneeled down, feeling her belly press against her stays. She tried to ignore the discomfort, hurriedly raking out the ashes and sieving them so that the cinders could be used in the kitchen. She sneezed as the dust invaded her nostrils, and began oiling the metal bars of the grate and rubbing them with emery paper to make them shine. Then she laid the fire for later in the day. When she had finished, she stood up too quickly and felt faint, but there was no time for dizzy spells when the rest of the room waited. She rubbed her back briskly, then swept the floor and dusted the furniture, using an old silk handkerchief of Nicholas Blanchard's.

She repeated the procedure in the breakfast room, front hall, library, and dining room. When Doris came up with the message that Mrs. Meadowes wanted her help in the kitchen, Nancy's feet felt as if they might burst, like sausages fried too fast. There were still the three rooms upstairs to do. "Can't till I've done the bedrooms," she said curtly.

Doris put her plump hands on her bulging hips. "Ain't you finished yet?"

"Do it look like it?" retorted Nancy, irked by Doris's painful drawl. She noticed that Doris's apron was already stained. The girl was not only a numbskull but clumsy.

Doris looked at her in confusion—like a pig, thought Nancy unkindly, a dull-witted, fat sow. "Late, ain't you?"

" 'Late, ain't you?' " Nancy mimicked Doris's stumbling tone with uncanny accuracy. "You're a fine one to talk. Wasn't my doing. Rose was meant to wake me."

"I already said to Mrs. Meadowes why . . . I'll tell that to her now, shall I?"

Nancy tossed her head and flicked her hand disparagingly. "You poke off an' tell her what you want. What do I care?"

Doris's chin wobbled, but she could think of no answer, so she shuffled off down to the basement. A little revived by this exchange, Nancy climbed the stairs. Her routine was always the same. Theodore's bedchamber first, because he rose early for the workshop; Nicholas's next; Lydia's last, on account of Patsy, who liked to fiddle about, arranging Lydia's clothes—and trying them on if she got half a chance—after Lydia had gone down to breakfast.

In each room, Nancy took care to notice how everything was arranged, so she could replace things exactly as they were. "If a door is open when you enter a room, leave it so when you leave, unless you are told otherwise," Mrs. Tooley always said. "Likewise, if a dish is put beside a plate, do not put it back next to the candlestick."

Nancy reckoned she knew every inch of every room of the Blanchard house better than her own face. So when she entered Nicholas Blanchard's bedchamber for the second time that morning, she noticed something that seemed both curious and troubling. A mahogany box, lined with crimson silk and cushioned like a jewel box, always stood in the center of Nicholas's dressing chest. The lid was inset with a silver plaque, on which Nicholas's initials were engraved in script so curlicued they were nearly illegible. Inside, Nicholas stored his extensive collection of tie pins. There was one with a gold head shaped like a dog, one with a deep purple amethyst, another fashioned as a miniature sword.

The box also contained a pair of flintlock pocket pistols wrapped in a pair of silk handkerchiefs. Their butts were adorned with bone inlay and silver mounts, and there was also a flask of powder. Nicholas said the pistols were there in case any villain should dare burst into his bedchamber in the dead of night. They were always kept loaded, and every week Mr. Matthews brought them down to the pantry to clean and reload. Once, when Nicholas was out, Mr. Matthews had shown off to the rest of the servants by demonstrating how they worked. He had taken aim at a pigeon in the yard outside. Feathers and blood had sprayed all over the flagstones, and everyone had cheered. The bird flapped about refusing to die until John caught it and wrung its neck, and Mrs. Meadowes turned it into a tasty pie.

Nancy had no business opening the box, let alone touching pistols; she knew very well that they were dangerous. Dust and dirt were her business, not guns or jewels. Nevertheless, the temptation was too much to resist, and once or twice she had dared to unwrap the pistols and hold them in her hand. She liked to imagine herself pointing one at someone and squeezing the trigger and seeing him flap about like that wounded bird. Sometimes she imagined herself picking up the gun when Nicholas called her over. She pictured his great brow shooting up in fear as she got him in her sights.

Today, when she lifted the lid, she saw that one of the pistols was missing. She opened the top drawers of the dressing chest and poked about among an assortment of silken handkerchiefs. There was no sign of it. Mr. Matthews might have taken it away to clean, but usually he did this on a Saturday, and today was Tuesday. And why would he take one pistol and not the other? Nancy had no reason to suppose that Rose had taken the pistol; nevertheless, the possibility entered her mind unprompted.

Chapter Twelve

MRS. TOOLEY was so called out of respect rather than for her marital status. A slender, small-bosomed woman, erect of gait, with a floury complexion and wispy hair the color of dusty pewter, she had come to the Blanchards' as a scullery maid at the age of sixteen, and as far as anyone knew, she had never married or had any kind of romantic alliance. She occupied a cluttered suite of rather gloomy rooms, situated halfway along the back corridor in the basement. Her small bedroom was decorated with cheerfully embroidered samplers, which she had stitched herself, and a shelf containing an intricate shellwork tableau. In her parlor, the chimneypiece was crammed with pottery owls, sheep, and dogs, and dishes painted with blue and white Chinoiserie fruits and flowers. Along the picture rail of one wall was an array of brightly colored plates. Dotted about the other walls were half a dozen seascape engravings showing varying climactic conditions, from violent tempest to glassy calm. To the rear was an enormous closet that she used as a storeroom, packed with bottled delicacies such as greengage plums in syrup, quince marmalade, nasturtium pickles, and mushroom catsup, which infused all three rooms with the sharp but tantalizing aromas of vinegar, fruit, and spices.

Mrs. Tooley's temperament was as fragile as the objects on her chimneypiece. She was likely to grow flustered at the slightest disruption, if she observed a single mote of dust beneath a dressing chest, or if the ruffles on a pillowcase were not properly pressed. Her teacup would wobble, and she would be forced to rummage for her salts or a little of something stronger.

Agnes sometimes wondered whether Mrs. Tooley was quite as frail as she appeared, or if she exaggerated her weakness to elicit compliance, avoid argument, or relieve herself of tasks she had no wish to carry out. But there was no telling what the day's two calamities would do to Mrs. Tooley's nerves, or how long she might be indisposed. For this reason Agnes resolved she must broach the subject of her day's leave sooner rather than later. Her one free Sunday a month did not fall due until the week after next. But Mrs. Tooley was not in her bed. Agnes found her standing at a side table beneath a faded print of a brig in a stormy sea. She was counting plates and pickle dishes and jotting the results in a fat, leather-bound notebook. As usual, her clothes were immaculately clean, a skirt and bodice of charcoal gray, a collar of starched white linen, a pair of metal-rimmed spectacles attached to a black ribbon about her neck.

Agnes was not deceived. Counting china at this hour was an ominous sign.

Mrs. Tooley wagged her finger at the slate on the table, where they would write the following day's menu. "Make a start, Mrs. Meadowes. I'll be with you in a jot."

Agnes nodded dismally and sat down. Her thoughts drifted away from whether pea soup might be preferable to ox cheek, and speculation about the disappearance of Rose and the terrible events Mr. Matthews had related. How was she to collect Peter? Where would he stay? Her worries about her son pressed all other concerns from her mind.

"Well," said Mrs. Tooley, settling herself shakily in a chair, "I trust whatever it is you have planned can be made without your kitchen maid."

Agnes said as calmly as she was able, "I can't manage with only Doris. She is willing but slow. Nancy is much quicker. Could you spare her to help for an hour or two each day until we find a replacement?"

Mrs. Tooley's pale cheeks were suddenly suffused with pink and her eyes took on an injured expression. "Please, Mrs. Meadowes, spare me further upset. I am not myself. What of Nancy's other duties? Do you suppose we can leave the beds unmade, the fires unlit, the floors unswept?"

"Of course not, ma'am. But perhaps Philip could help with the fires, so Nancy wouldn't have so much to do upstairs."

Mrs. Tooley's upper lip quivered. "And rearrange the entire household while we're about it?"

Agnes regarded her slate. She willed herself not to succumb, but felt herself yielding to Mrs. Tooley's will, unable to raise the subject of her son. "I am only anxious not to let things slide."

"I'll speak to Mrs. Blanchard and place an advertisement directly," said Mrs. Tooley in a more measured tone.

"Thank you, ma'am," responded Agnes. "But what if she returns?"

"She will be shown the door," Mrs. Tooley whispered.

This was just what Agnes had expected to hear. She suppressed a flicker of sympathy for Rose, reminding herself that the girl's sins were greater than she had suspected, and that she had caused a great deal of inconvenience. One way or another, Rose was gone from her life. Yet the knowledge did not bring her relief. A niggling uncertainty remained, like a piece of gravel in her shoe.

"Mr. Matthews said you observed her last week in the company of a gentleman," said Agnes.

"That I did," affirmed Mrs. Tooley. "And he was not from this vicinity, either."

"Did you upbraid her?"

"Naturally. And naturally, being the brazen girl she was, she denied it. Told me that it was no more than a gentleman asking directions. I gave her the benefit of the doubt then. I see I should not have done so. I should have been firmer. But she could be so very forceful. And you know how arguments distress me."

"Indeed she could be forceful," replied Agnes, her sympathies with the housekeeper. "Perhaps 'tis a good thing she's gone."

Chapter Thirteen

ESPITE THE TERRIBLE EVENTS of the night, in the Blanchard workshop, the journeyman Benjamin Riley was preparing to take newly made items of silver for assay at Goldsmiths' Hall. He had placed a tea-caddy spoon with a pierced handle upside down on an anvil, fixing it with a vise so that the neck lay across the metal block, and took out the stamp (a small iron punch with the letters *NB* raised upon it) and a craftsman's hammer. Then, positioning the stamp above the neck of the spoon, he raised the hammer and brought it down with a whack. Sparks flew and the letters appeared in a small dent of dark metal. Thomas Williams, the second journeyman, looked up balefully. "Those spoons are delicate at the neck, mind you don't shatter them," he said quietly.

Riley bristled. "Oh, pardon me, sir," he muttered, bowing with mock humility. "I clean forgot my master was there."

"I don't have to be your master to see when you're taking care and when you're not." Williams was very distressed by the murder. He had been fond of Noah Prout and had taught the boy the rudiments of his profession. He was also the apprentice who had spent most time fabricating the wine cooler.

Benjamin Riley scowled, unclamped the spoon, and picked a caddy off the shelf. "What gives you the right to tell me what I ought and oughtn't to do? You ain't any better than me—despite your airs."

"God help me. Did I say I was any different? Don't you see we both want the same—work, business? And the way you're carrying on, you'll ruin it for both of us."

"I reckon the loss of the wine cooler will have more to do with that than a bloody spoon," said Riley with vigor. "Any case, I'm too busy for your nagging. Get off and mind your own affairs. Leave me be."

"Would that I could," said Williams, returning to his work.

ONE BY ONE, Benjamin Riley stamped the Blanchard initials upon four small silver boxes, three tea caddies, and half a dozen caddy spoons. Then he wrapped each object in a linen cloth to protect it from scratches, and loaded them into his basket. This done, he put on his coat and hat, smoothed his hair in its tail, and telling himself he looked handsome enough to pass for a patron rather than a purveyor of silver, he stepped out into the street. The Goldsmiths' Hall was halfway down Foster Lane. It was an imposing structure, built in the classical style, with large windows punctuating the front façade and an inner courtyard reached through a columned portico. Near the entrance Riley caught sight of half a dozen journeymen and apprentices standing in a cluster, all on their way to take their wares to be assayed. He was so bound up with looking to see which of his rivals were there that he failed to observe the comely figure of Agnes Meadowes drawing alongside him on her way to market. Thinking he had spotted a friend, he swiveled abruptly. Agnes caught no more than a glimpse of a dark brown hat, and beneath it a pockmarked, ferrety face and strands of lank brown hair, before his full basket collided forcefully with her empty one and she was sent sprawling into the gutter. Half a dozen pieces of silver from his basket tumbled alongside her.

"Oh my Lord!" exclaimed Benjamin Riley, as he scrabbled in the mud to retrieve a lid from here and a spoon from there. "Get away with you, thieving wretch!" he bellowed at a bedraggled girl. "Any closer and I'll call the watch and have you branded!"

"All right, mister, only tryin' to help," said the girl, shrinking away.

"My arse you was."

Excited by the rumpus, a cluster of onlookers gathered, laughing and pointing. Meanwhile, various street urchins calling out, "Sir—'e's taking it!" and "There, sir!"—making Riley spin round—added to the amusement. Squatting in the street to safely recover and stow the dropped silver, Riley finally turned toward Agnes, who now was back on her feet, brushing down her mud-spattered petticoats. He took the time to observe her slender ankles before he got up. "All right, miss?" he said as he took in every curve of her.

"No thanks to you," said Agnes, stepping back.

"Miss Meadowes, the Blanchards' cook, ain't it?" He stepped forward, squeezing her arm with what Agnes deemed to be over-familiarity.

"*Mrs.* Meadowes," she declared, jerking away from his grasp.

"*Mrs.* Meadowes. Forgive me. I see your dress is dirty—come back to the workshop with me, and I'll help you put yourself to rights." He winked.

Agnes bit her lip. She was tempted to tell him to go to the devil—that would take the smile off his greasy face—but she recalled Mr. Matthews telling her that Riley was friendly with Rose. Perhaps he knew where she had gone. She flashed Riley a half smile. "That won't be necessary, thank you, Mr. Riley. I haven't time to spare. I'm in a rush on account of my kitchen maid going off. I think you knew her. Rose Francis was her name."

Riley looked puzzled. "Gone? Run off?" he said.

"Do you know where she is?"

"Why should I?"

She flashed another appeasing smile. "I thought you and she were friendly."

Riley shrugged, but said nothing to confirm or deny this.

"When did you last see her?"

"I can't say for certain. Perhaps three or four weeks ago."

"She gave you no hint of her intentions?"

"None."

"What was the reason for her visit to you?"

"None, save that she was sweet on me," said Riley, grinning and exposing his uneven teeth.

Agnes shuddered. Whatever was it about Rose that made so many men believe she was fond of them? Whatever Riley said, whatever Mr. Matthews claimed, she could not conceive that this odious man had ever meant a fig to Rose. Philip was one thing— she could not deny he was well made, or that women generally found him charming. But Riley was quite the reverse: unsightly, with something palpably unpleasant in his manner. The very idea of Rose and him filled Agnes with revulsion. She thought of Rose and Philip in the larder. Surely Rose would not have stooped . . . would not have allowed him to take liberties . . . would she? But even if Riley knew more than he revealed, what did it matter? Rose had gone, and Mrs. Tooley would not take her back. Agnes had no obligation to her. Perhaps she should have taken more of an interest in Rose's whereabouts and paramours before, but they were nothing to her now.

Chapter Fourteen

GNES WALKED HOME from the market with a full basket. After she returned to the Blanchards', as she pulverized crayfish shells for her soup and dressed pheasants for roasting, and mixed stock, butter, flour, and lemon juice for fricassee sauce, she thought only of how she might find the time to make arrangements for Peter's care. She had yet to tackle the matter with Mrs. Tooley, knowing any request would be doomed. When Patsy asked her for a clove for a toothache, Agnes did not hear her until she bellowed the demand. But by the time the sauce had reached a smooth, thick consistency, a solution of sorts had presented itself to her.

Lydia Blanchard was a mother herself—her two children were both away at school at present—and she knew that Agnes had a son. When Agnes had replied to the advertisement in the *Morning Post* for an undercook and been called for interview, she had not concealed Peter's existence. Since then, Agnes had seldom conversed with Lydia; that was Mrs. Tooley's duty. Occasionally, after large parties, Lydia would come down to the kitchen to thank the staff; or when she wanted something particular for dinner and did not trust Mrs. Tooley to convey it properly, she would attend the morning meeting. Such appearances were rare, however. Agnes did not pretend any close rapport with the mistress of the house;

nevertheless, she reasoned that Mrs. Blanchard might understand her predicament. And if Lydia ruled that she should be granted a day off, there would be nothing Mrs. Tooley could do to stop her.

With a renewed sense of urgency, Agnes turned her attention to her immediate tasks. She made her pastry and set it to rest. Then, after instructing Doris to pick the flesh off a boiled chicken (washing her hands first), and set the brown meat in one bowl and the white in another, she ventured upstairs.

Agnes rarely visited the upper part of the house. The change in temperature between the steamy kitchen and the cool, oak-floored corridor struck her. She shivered, though whether this was caused by apprehension or a sudden chill she could not be certain.

The hall was modestly proportioned, but decorated to impress. The floor and doors were dark; grandiose Italian paintings in thick gilded frames were displayed against gray-blue walls. The only furniture was a pair of mahogany commodes, two hall chairs, and a long-case clock. Suspended from the center of the ceiling was a large silver chandelier. On the left were the dining room, drawing room, and Nicholas Blanchard's library. The breakfast room and front parlor, where it was Lydia Blanchard's habit to pass this hour of the day, lay on the right.

Agnes knocked gently, glancing nervously around. She had seen John out with Nicholas. At this time, Theodore should be at the workshop or busy on his morning's excursions. Philip was downstairs in Mr. Matthews's pantry polishing the silver; Nancy was still cleaning the upstairs rooms. What would she say if Mr. Matthews or, worse, Mrs. Tooley apprehended her? But her fears were unfounded. No one came or caught sight of her before she heard Lydia's muffled voice call, "Enter."

Lydia was embroidering a crimson rosebud on a shawl of pale blue silk, upon which she had worked an intricate pattern of flowers and trailing vines with great delicacy. On a chair beside her, a volume of poetry lay open.

No sooner had Agnes stepped over the threshold than she

sensed that her arrival was unwelcome. I should not have come, she thought. Lydia has never encouraged intimacy among her servants. Patsy is her chief ally and confidante; Mrs. Tooley's management of the household obliges Lydia to consult with her daily. But what need has she to confer with me?

Lydia furrowed her brow. "I thought you were Patsy come to read to me. What on earth do you want, Mrs. Meadowes?" She stabbed her needle in the design in front of her. "I have already approved tomorrow's menus with Mrs. Tooley."

"Thank you, ma'am. My business doesn't concern the menus."

Lydia shook her head. "I cannot conceive what it can be, in that case."

Agnes raised her chin and thought of her son. "It is a matter— of some delicacy."

"Then should not you discuss it with Mrs. Tooley?"

"If I broach the subject with her, I have no doubt she will refuse me out of hand. Being a spinster, she has no comprehension of maternal concerns."

"I'm not sure I follow your meaning," said Lydia slowly.

"It is my child, Mrs. Blanchard," said Agnes, speaking without pause, so that Lydia had not a moment to halt her. "I have had a letter from the woman who tends him. She is in poor health and says I must find somewhere else for him to stay directly. I have no choice but to ask for an extra day's leave to make the necessary arrangements."

Lydia frowned. "But if it is a day off you want, Mrs. Tooley will have to agree. I cannot upset her; you know that, Mrs. Meadowes. She is essential to the running of this house, and with the maid run off there is upset enough without courting more. Besides, even if I grant you an extra day off, where will you take your child? You cannot expect to bring him here."

"Of course not, ma'am, I wouldn't dream of proposing that. But I would find somewhere to take him. All I ask is for you to put a word in for me, so that Mrs. Tooley would be amenable."

Lydia's face took on an air of regret. "How would Mrs. Tooley cook for all three of us with Rose gone and only Doris to assist?"

"I can prepare everything so it's ready the night before. And with a little help from Nancy, Mrs. Tooley and Doris would manage."

Lydia appeared to consider the matter, but in the end said, "I see your dilemma; naturally, I am not unsympathetic. But under the present circumstances, it is impossible. You will have to find another means to resolve the problem."

Agnes wanted to plead, but she knew there was no purpose in losing her dignity and pursuing the matter. Lydia would not yield. "Very well, ma'am. Forgive me for interrupting you," she said, curtsying and making her way to the door.

But as she placed her hand upon the knob, Lydia summoned her back. "One moment, Mrs. Meadowes. There is another matter I would discuss with you."

"Yes, ma'am."

"Regarding your maid, Rose—have you any idea where she went off to?"

"No, ma'am, none at all."

Lydia frowned disappointedly. "Mrs. Tooley told me the same. And the other staff—I presume it has been the talk of the kitchen—has no one any notion?"

"Not so far as I've heard, ma'am."

"Do you think"—here Lydia lowered her voice confidentially—"she might have been—in trouble—you know what I mean?"

Agnes's blush showed she understood perfectly. "If so, I was not aware of it."

"You noticed nothing different about her—in recent days or weeks? No sickness, no swelling . . ."

"Nothing, ma'am."

Lydia seemed disappointed. Her mouth made a small moue. "Is there any talk about her and my father-in-law? You may speak frankly to me, Mrs. Meadowes. I am sure we are both cognizant of his tastes."

Agnes felt her cheeks flame. She did not discuss intimacies of this kind with anyone, let alone her mistress. "I don't know, ma'am," she said nervously. "I don't think so."

Lydia tilted her head, her gray eyes riveted by Agnes's discomfort. "Have you heard of the catastrophe that took place last night?"

"Yes, ma'am, although the other servants have not yet been informed."

"Do you think Rose might have had a hand in last night's robbery?"

Agnes was jolted out of her embarrassment. She answered after only the briefest consideration. "Whatever else she was, I do not believe Rose Francis was a thief or a murderess," she declared, startling herself as well as Lydia by her emphatic tone.

"That remains to be seen. Has anyone made a search of her possessions?"

"I don't believe so, ma'am."

"Then be so kind as to look. Perhaps something there might tell us what has happened to her. I ask you as the person for whom she worked, who must have known her best. Her departure on the same night as the robbery next door strikes me as a strange coincidence. Should you find anything, I would make it worth your while."

Lydia made no specific reference to the day off that Agnes had requested, but was that what she was implying? Agnes knew too little of her mistress to be certain; she could only pray.

AGNES WAS NOT generally prone to self-pity, yet she felt in danger of succumbing now. Lydia would not spare her time to find a new home for Peter, yet on some inexplicable whim was adding to her duties. Agnes had no inclination to involve herself in the private affairs of others. It went against her natural grain. With so much pressing upon her, how could she fail to feel sorry for herself? Nevertheless, Agnes could not forget Lydia's inference: please me in this and I might reconsider your request.

Why should Peter suffer because of Rose's misdemeanors? Surely the household could manage for a few hours without a cook and a maid. She wanted only to settle her son elsewhere, so that she might continue carrying out her duties as diligently as she had for the last five years. For a fleeting second, Agnes contemplated behaving like Rose—ignoring her duties, leaving the house, and traveling directly to Twickenham to whisk Peter away.

As she climbed the back stairs, to search Rose's belongings, Nancy came clattering down carrying a broom and her house-maid's box, and nearly collided with her. Her small, sharp features registered surprise at coming upon Agnes when she should have been busy making dinner. "I've only just finished tidying up there, Mrs. Meadowes. Sorry I couldn't come down and help before. Was there anything in particular you're wanting of me now?" she said, unable to keep the curiosity from her voice.

"Yes," Agnes replied crisply. "If you've a minute to spare, I should like you to point out Rose's bed and belongings to me."

Nancy's eyes grew round. "Whatever for?"

There was no reason, thought Agnes, to mention Lydia Blanchard's interest in Rose's whereabouts. If she breathed a word of it to Nancy, it would soon be common knowledge. "I think it only right that I should try to discover where she's gone," she replied cagily.

"You ain't wanting to get her back—not after all the trouble she's caused?"

"No, but suppose the poor girl's met with some misadventure."

"Didn't seem much of a poor girl to me," muttered Nancy.

"What was that?" Agnes quickly asked.

"Nothing," replied Nancy airily.

"I gather you and she had an argument yesterday."

"That were over nothing much—only my ticking her off for not tidying her bed. And I'd every right to do so. She was in a state over something—don't know what—and suddenly went for me. Good job John were there to pull her off." Unconsciously, the girl raised her hand to her neck, where Agnes caught sight of a livid red line.

"Did Rose do that?"

"Yes," snapped Nancy.

"Quite a temper over an unmade bed."

Nancy shook her head. "Like I said, she were in a state. Probably thinking of going off." Turning on her heels, she led the way up four flights of stairs to the garret. There were two attic rooms. "That there's where Patsy sleeps," said Nancy sourly, pointing to a door on the right. "This is ours." She led the way into a narrow, drafty garret with sloping ceilings and exposed rafters. Agnes shivered, thinking of her own snug quarters in the basement, which were warmed by the kitchen range. "Her bed is there by the window, and mine here, next to the door. Doris's is over there." She signaled to a third bed a short distance away by the washstand. "I made Rose's this morning—Doris and I took turns. Rose was never one for order, and if Mrs. Tooley comes up and sees the room in a state, all of us get a scolding."

Agnes looked down at the bed and its thin coverlet, imagining Rose half asleep first thing in the morning, her hair, the color and thickness of treacle, sprawled across the bolster. She walked to the casement window set into the eaves. The sky was fine and clear, with only the occasional strand of cloud marring the blue. She gazed out at the dome of St. Paul's, squatting above the patchwork rooftops of Foster Lane and Cheapside; at the spires rearing above the mottled roofs; at the warren of alleys leading down to the river. The water looked glassy and still. Somewhere in this panorama of shadow and light was Rose. But where? What had lured her away? She did not believe Rose capable of murder and the robbery. She turned back to Nancy. "Where did Rose keep her things?"

"In here, like the rest of us," said Nancy, throwing open the creaking doors of a small deal press cupboard painted a soft shade of green, and pointing to the uppermost shelf. "Those are hers."

Folded neatly was a meager assortment of clothes: a back-laced corset, a calico petticoat, a cotton slip, a patched underpetticoat, two pairs of yarn stockings, and two threadbare skirts and bodices, one of a dark blue woolen cloth, the other of yellow-and-green striped cotton. Agnes recognized these as Rose's usual workday clothes. There was nothing more.

Agnes pointed to the skirts and bodices. "As I recall, she had a Sunday gown of blue wool, did she not?"

Nancy nodded. "I hadn't looked afore now. And her cloak and bonnet and her best boots are gone. She must have been wearing them when she went out."

"Shouldn't there be more besides what is here? Underclothes and a nightgown? They aren't here."

"Perhaps. I hadn't thought."

"And had she no personal possessions—no letters, papers, keepsakes from her family?"

"If she had, I never saw 'em."

"She must have had some things," said Agnes carefully. "If nothing's here she must have taken them with her, which suggests she did not intend to return." She looked at the scant belongings on Rose's shelf, and then at the fuller shelves lower down—presumably Nancy's and Doris's possessions. All were neatly stowed in deference to Mrs. Tooley's inspections. She raised her eyes and caught a strange look on Nancy's face. "What is it? Has something else gone?"

"No, Mrs. Meadowes. Nothing from what I can see. It's only you asking me made me recall there was something in particular that was somewhere else. I haven't looked to see if that's gone. I pray you won't scold me for not mentioning it sooner."

"What do you mean?"

"A week ago, while I was changing the linen on her bed, I found it under her mattress—a purse stuffed with gold sovereigns. There were twenty of 'em."

Agnes's brow knotted. "Show me where you found it."

Nancy stepped over to Rose's bed and rolled the thin horsehair mattress forward to expose the wooden slats. She pointed to the top right-hand corner. "It was here."

"Did you speak to her about it?"

Nancy laughed and shook her head vehemently. "I wouldn't dare. No point in asking for trouble. She could be ferocious when she wanted."

How would a kitchen maid like Rose have come by such wealth? The accusations of Lydia and Mr. Matthews still rang in her ears. "Have you any notion how she got the money?"

"Must've been something underhand, mustn't it?"

"Did you mention the matter to anyone else?"

"No," said Nancy, her head down.

She was holding back something. "Why did you dislike her?" asked Agnes impulsively.

A sudden flush spread across Nancy's pale face. "I weren't like her, ma'am—she'd do anything for a man. Philip got taken in by her—more fool him. She were scarce better than a whore at times."

Agnes remembered now Philip's quip that he was the cause of Rose and Nancy's argument. "Was Philip the reason you fought yesterday?"

Nancy's gaze flashed toward the window, then she looked quickly back at Agnes. "I told you that was over nothing more than the mess she made. But there's something else, Mrs. Meadowes . . . although I don't know if it's aught to do with her running off."

"Yes?"

"There's a pair of pocket pistols that are always kept in a box in

Mr. Nicholas's room, with a small flask of powder. This morning when I looked, one was gone. I didn't say nothing before, on account of I shouldn't have been looking. Do you think she might 'ave took it?"

Agnes hesitated. "I don't know, Nancy."

What she meant was that she did not want to know, but she feared she would now be obliged to find out.

Chapter Fifteen

A T ONE O'CLOCK, the servants gathered for lunch. Doris had laid the table, knives and spoons haphazardly askew, and set out yesterday's leftovers—dropping a meat pudding, which burst all over the flags and turned them slippery as grease. Once everyone was seated, Mr. Matthews declared he had an important announcement, and a ripple of unease and excitement spread through the assembly.

The butler stood at one end of the table to say his speediest grace—"Lord, we give humble thanks for the fruits we are about to receive. Amen"—then without further pause, he cleared his throat. "Ladies and gentlemen," he said, with as much gravitas as a judge announcing a death sentence, "I have news of a tragedy." He looked at the assembled faces, waiting for hush to descend. "Last night as we slept in our beds, an interloper entered the premises next door and cruelly murdered the apprentice keeping watch. This same interloper then helped himself to a valuable wine cooler and made off with it."

As Mr. Matthews picked up his carving knife and fork and began expertly carving the bacon, he added further detail to his news. He had first heard the news from the apprentice who found Noah's body; the constable had visited the Blanchards' workshop soon after the crime was discovered. The justice had been left undisturbed until nine, by which time the undertakers had arrived and transported the corpse away on their wagon. The only obvious evidence of the crime was a large wine-colored stain on the ceiling of the downstairs showroom, where blood had dripped through the floor above. Despite the efforts of the other two apprentices, this had so far proved impossible to obliterate.

Greatly shaken, Mrs. Tooley had to forage in her pocket for her smelling salts and take several noisy sniffs before she was able to swallow a morsel. Agnes rubbed her forehead with the back of her hand, staring blankly at the crescent of bacon on her plate. Lydia Blanchard's suspicion that Rose was somehow involved in what had happened obliged her to take an interest in the conversation. Yet she did so unwillingly. That the young boy's death had been eclipsed by the theft of a valuable wine cooler seemed even more poignant, and everyone's vicarious delight in the drama seemed somehow indecent.

"John," Agnes said, in a tone inaudible to the rest, "do you think it possible that a woman could have had a hand in the murder and robbery?"

John put his knife down softly on his plate and turned to look at her. His face was narrower than Philip's, his features less regular—his nose long and aquiline, his eyes set at a slanting angle, his lips thin. Yet for all that, thought Agnes, it was a more appealing countenance. John was never presumptuous or unseemly. She could speak to him with an ease she never felt with Philip.

"I doubt any woman would have had the strength," he replied. "Butchering a man requires considerable force, don't it? And from what I hear the wine cooler was a sizable one—as big as a bathtub. Too heavy for a woman to carry."

Agnes nodded at this confirmation of her own suspicions. Whatever Lydia thought, Rose alone was unlikely to have been responsible. But had she had an accomplice?

"What do you know of Rose Francis's male acquaintances?" she asked.

John took a bite of bread and chewed it slowly before swallowing. "You think *she* was behind it, do you? Reckon it was more than a coincidence, her going off?"

Agnes shrugged noncommittally. "If it were so, who might have helped her?"

John smiled. "There was quite a collection of men friends, by all accounts. But the only ones I know came from this house, or the premises next door, and none of them have disappeared—so I somehow doubt it were any of them."

Agnes sensed that behind his shrewd gray eyes lay more. But John was never as keen to gossip as Philip. She wondered whether he held back from loyalty to Rose.

"I gather there was an argument yesterday between Rose and Nancy."

John's mouth tensed. "I witnessed it and cooled them down."

"What was it over—Philip?"

He shook his head. "Rose and he was no longer sweet on each other. Nancy could have him if she chose."

"What, then?"

"Something about a letter Nancy had taken that belonged to Rose."

"From whom? What did it say?"

John regarded her, then smiled again. "They never said, and I never asked. Just pulling 'em apart was enough to test me to the limit."

"Did you happen to hear anything about her and Benjamin Riley, the journeyman next door, or Mr. Blanchard, Senior?"

John tapped his nose as he had the previous day when informing her of Mrs. Catchpole's letter. "I don't suppose the rumors I've heard are any different from those that've reached you, Mrs. Meadowes. Seeing as how we all live in the same place and eat the same food and breathe the same air." He paused, wiping the rim of his plate with the last piece of bread. "And where's the use in picking over the same bone? 'Twould leave us all hungry." Then, before she could press him further, he swiveled himself pointedly toward Philip and broke into his conversation with the now giggling maids. "Now, what happened to all them candle stubs in the dining room? Was it you or Nancy that took 'em?"

AT THE UPPER SERVANTS' TEA in Mrs. Tooley's parlor an hour later, Agnes did not let the subject of Rose Francis rest. "Most of Rose's belongings are still in her closet. What do you intend to do with them?" she inquired, while Mrs. Tooley unlocked the tea caddy and spooned a mixture of green and black leaves carefully into the pot.

"Nothing, for the time being," returned Mrs. Tooley tartly, for in truth she was tired of the subject of Rose Francis, and now that she had overcome her initial shock, she was eager to press Mr. Matthews further on the terrible drama of the previous night. "But if Doris and Nancy are helpful till we find a replacement, I might offer them the pick of her things."

"Most of them are too worn to be much use to anybody," said Agnes. "She took the best with her."

"Didn't she ever," put in Mr. Matthews glumly.

"Dusters, then," said Mrs. Tooley decisively, locking the caddy and turning to the butler. "So, Mr. Matthews, you say the apprentice who found the body had no notion of what had taken place until he went in. He heard no sound at all, you say? And then the first thing he saw was Noah's head hanging on by a thread and blood flooding all over the floor?"

"That's according to him," said Mr. Matthews, nodding sagely.

"And the blood was quite prodigious—enough to soak through the ceiling, you said?" Mrs. Tooley shuddered, but seemed less distraught than Agnes had expected.

"There were footsteps all across the floor, leading to the exact place where the wine cooler was displayed. I saw them quite clearly when I accompanied Mr. Theodore last night."

Agnes found this gruesome exchange insupportable. She was eager to leave, but remembering her need to ascertain what had happened to Rose, attempted to steer the conversation her way. "Rose leaving those things in her closet shows she no longer needed them. That might mean she had money enough to buy new things."

As she spoke, she observed that Mr. Matthews's expression turned disdainful, as if this were a trivial matter of no interest to him. He picked up his tea and sipped it, gazing into the middle distance. Patsy, tall and elegant, paused with a teaspoon in her hand. She was a dark-haired, somewhat masculine woman with a longish nose. She patted the back of her neat coiffure with her large hands. "Rose Francis must have had a very rich friend indeed, to leave everything behind. Or perhaps she had more than one sponsor."

"She did not leave everything behind. Only her working clothes," insisted Agnes.

"Either way, we're all better off without her," said Mrs. Tooley, glancing toward Mr. Matthews for approval. But he was maintaining his air of disinterest and gazing at his tea, and thus did not notice her.

Agnes addressed the butler directly. "Nancy happened to mention there was a pistol missing from the dressing chest in Mr. Blanchard's room. Do you know anything of it?"

Matthews nodded self-importantly. "I have been apprised of the loss. Mr. Blanchard was as astonished and distressed to discover it as I. Naturally, we can only assume that Rose took it. I must make an inventory of the household silver at the earliest opportunity. We must hope nothing else is gone."

Agnes remembered that the day before, Mr. Matthews had found Rose upstairs, and wondered if stealing the pistol rather than intimacy with Nicholas was the cause. "Nothing," she said, "save a valuable wine cooler and a life."

"Upon my soul, Mrs. Meadowes!" exclaimed Mrs. Tooley. "You are surely not suggesting Rose—"

But before she could finish, there was a heavy thumping at the door. "'Scuse me for interrupting," said Philip, popping his powdered head around the door of the parlor. "I've an important message for Mrs. Meadowes. Mr. Theodore Blanchard asks that she attend him immediately. And by the by, he doesn't want to see you upstairs, ma'am, but in the showroom next door. Ain't you the lucky one? Don't forget to look up at the ceiling so you can tell us all what it's like."

Chapter Sixteen

AGNES COULD COUNT on the fingers of one hand the times she had entered the Blanchards' business premises. Usually she had been sent to borrow extra items of silverware prior to important dinners. Perhaps bowls for sweetmeats or leaf-shaped pickle dishes, or her particular favorite, salt cellars fashioned like muscular sea gods supporting open oyster shells—so realistically modeled that every stria of the shell was visible.

She knew that downstairs was the main shop, where smaller objects were displayed for customers, and leading off from the rear were the workshop and an office where accounts were prepared. Upstairs was a grander showroom, containing the magnificent silverware upon which Blanchards' reputation was founded. She had never entered this hallowed place, but according to Mr. Matthews, the pieces were of fabulous scale and intricacy, fashioned not simply for sale but to elicit commissions. Almost anything could be custom made: a set of serving dishes with a border design taken from a tea caddy, legs from a soup tureen, and handles like those on a teapot. There was almost nothing the ingenious Blanchard craftsmen could not fashion for a patron who ordered it. With a heavy heart, Agnes presented herself in the downstairs shop. Fortunately she was not left to linger. As soon as she mentioned that Mr. Theodore Blanchard awaited her (her eyes fixed firmly on her feet), one of the surviving apprentices scurried off to fetch a journeyman. Minutes later, someone clattered down the stairs at surprising speed. She raised her head, and discovered to her relief that it was not Benjamin Riley but Thomas Williams who had come to fetch her.

"Mr. Blanchard is almost ready, Mrs. Meadowes. He asked me to show you upstairs, and asks that you wait a moment there for him," said Williams in a somber tone, after bowing and bidding her good day. He was a stocky man, not much taller or older than she, with rusty-colored hair sprouting from his head in wild curls. His flat, wide face and rather solid jaw gave him a stubborn expression, which contrasted oddly with the somewhat melancholy glow in his green eyes.

Agnes greeted him with a brief curtsy. "Thank you, Mr. Williams," she returned as he held the door open for her. She was halfway up the stairs before she realized with relief that she had not once caught sight of the ceiling.

Williams ushered her into the showroom. "Please won't you sit down, Mrs. Meadowes," he said, walking to the far end of the room and arranging a chair near the fire. "Mr. Blanchard is finishing some business in the office. He bade me tell you he will join you shortly."

The room was long and thin, paneled in oak, with a carved chimneypiece in the center and a pair of large sash windows draped with elaborate swagged curtains at either end. It was furnished not as a conventional shop but rather as a dining room, with a dark red Turkey rug, a pair of consoles, a well-polished mahogany sideboard, and a matching circular dining table. Every surface was covered with silver: small candelabra and silver boxes fashioned in various forms. The dining table was set as if for the grandest of banquets, complete with candlesticks, covered dishes, silver wine coolers, goblets, salt cellars, condiments, plates, and cutlery. At each end of the sideboard stood a pair of massive twelve-branched candelabra. The only incongruous note was the large empty space in the middle. Agnes supposed that was where the wine cooler had stood.

As she took in the details of the room, Agnes was aware that Thomas Williams observed her. She felt anxious being scrutinized by a man she barely knew, but there were several matters with which Thomas Williams might assist her and she forced herself to make conversation with him. "I came upon your Mr. Riley yesterday. He was carrying a basket of silver and dropped it in the road."

Williams looked doleful. "Indeed? He never mentioned it. How unfortunate."

"It was," she said emphatically, then after a short hesitation pressed on. "I expect you knew that he was friendly with our kitchen maid, Rose Francis?"

Thomas Williams frowned. "I caught a glimpse of her from time to time."

"Where did you glimpse her, Mr. Williams?"

He scratched his head. "I don't exactly recall. In the street—or was it here perhaps? She visited occasionally." He hesitated again. "I hope I am not speaking out of turn—I would not wish to embroil her in any trouble."

Agnes shot him a piercing look. "Of course not. I only ask because Rose Francis has gone missing. Compared with recent events here this might seem a trivial matter, but I need most urgently to find her."

He looked up sharply. "Did you ask Riley?" he said in a more businesslike tone.

"Yes, but he refused to say much. Indeed, he offered no help at all."

Williams took a deep breath. The soft, mournful expression returned. "That doesn't surprise me." He fingered a candlestick. "I'm sorry to hear that she's gone," he said. "Riley has not mentioned the matter to me, and I have no knowledge of their dealings, or what they were to one another. I didn't pay much attention. Why are you after her? Is she in trouble?"

"No, though she caused me a deal of inconvenience. But Mrs. Blanchard would like to know what made her go off like that."

As she had hoped, this mention of Lydia's name seemed to sway Williams in her favor. "Then if it would assist you, I'll question Riley about it and see if he says any more."

Agnes congratulated herself. Perhaps she was better than she knew at the art of conversation. She smiled, feeling easier now. "Anything you discover would be welcome. Rose could be unpredictable. She was inclined to be overfriendly with her men friends. But to go off without a word—none of us expected that. Do you think Mr. Riley might have set her up in rooms somewhere close by?"

Williams gave a bitter laugh and shook his head. "On a journeyman's salary, I doubt it—besides, he has a landlady who's fiercer than a mad dog. He's forever arguing with her. But still, he might know where she is."

No sooner had Thomas Williams spoken than there was the sound of a door closing and the soft thud of footsteps on the boards outside. He moved speedily to open the door, and the earlier formality returned to his demeanor.

"This will be Mr. Blanchard for you. With your permission, Mrs. Meadowes, I will take my leave." His voice dropped to a half whisper. "Rest assured, I shan't forget my undertaking."

Theodore Blanchard strode in, followed by another man—an elderly gentleman, tall and well built, in an old-fashioned, full-bottomed wig and a dark brown coat. Agnes had never seen her master, usually the most easygoing and placid of men, so distracted as he looked today. His face was flushed to the color of port wine, his jacket half buttoned, his cravat undone. His forehead glistened as brightly as the silver in front of him.

Theodore strode across to the dining table and drew up a pair of chairs for himself and his companion, whom he introduced as Justice Cordingly. "You have heard, I take it, of the robbery last night, Mrs. Meadowes?" he asked without preamble.

"Yes sir. Mr. Matthews apprised us of what happened."

"Bad enough to lose the apprentice—he was a good one and becoming better by the day, and boys of such diligence aren't easily come by—but to lose the wine cooler, that is a veritable calamity."

"I am very sorry for the loss," returned Agnes. Inwardly, she was appalled at Theodore's callousness, but she reminded herself that he was in a state of agitation and not himself.

"At any rate, I daresay you want to know why I have summoned you like this."

Agnes glanced nervously at him, then toward the table, where six salt cellars in the form of miniature turreted castles caught her attention. "I did wonder, sir."

"It was my wife who first suggested it. She thought you might be amenable—"

"Perhaps *I* should explain," said Justice Cordingly, holding up an intervening hand in a lordly manner. "It is a measure of the high esteem in which you are held, Mrs. Meadowes, that you have been summoned here this afternoon. There is little chance of the forces of justice solving a complex tragedy such as this without additional cooperation. But we must pick our deputies with care. After my preliminary examination of the facts, it appears likely that someone inside this household has assisted in this crime. We therefore require someone inside the household to aid us, someone whose integrity is beyond reproach. Mr. Blanchard has consulted his wife and concluded that you should be the one to assist."

From somewhere nearby, the strident sound of hammering metal could be heard. It was piercing enough to make Agnes blink at every stroke, and she was not at all sure she had heard correctly. She was a cook, her place was in her kitchen—what assistance could she conceivably offer? She felt the men scrutinize her expectantly. She felt exposed, uneasy. "I'm sorry, gentlemen, I do not properly understand what you require of me."

Justice Cordingly scratched his long nose. "As I said before, we believe this was no casual crime. Only the wine cooler, the most valuable object in the building, was taken. That points to the fact that someone knew of the object and its value, and that the crime was carefully planned and undertaken with inside knowledge. We have elected *you*, Mrs. Meadowes, to be the servant of justice; to poke about, ask questions, encourage confidences, and report to one or the other of us anything—anything at all—you think significant."

As the metal was struck again and again, Agnes felt her temples flinch and her brain pound.

"And, most pressingly, you are to assist in the *recovery* of the wine cooler," chimed Theodore hastily.

Agnes was overwhelmed with misgivings similar to those she had felt after her conversation with Lydia. Once again, she was being forced to act against her natural inclinations. The truth was, she was not interested in others' private lives or dilemmas, any more than she wanted to share her own misfortunes. It was tragic that an apprentice had been murdered, she regretted the wine cooler's loss—but ultimately, neither of these calamities was anything to do with her. Nor, with all she had to worry over, did she wish them to be.

Dare she make this point to Theodore? Despite her usual docility, Agnes decided she would. She coughed tentatively and did her best to raise her voice above the noise. "I am honored by your offer, sirs. And I am gratified to learn that Mrs. Blanchard holds me in high esteem. But I am not at all certain I am suited to the responsibilities of the task."

"What?" said Justice Cordingly, his brow rumpling incredulously. "What did you say?"

Theodore snorted. The filigree of veins on his nose and cheeks darkened. "As we see it, you are the only choice. You are not so young as to be foolish, but more alert and able than either Mrs. Tooley or Mr. Matthews. Patsy is not below stairs enough to be useful. The others are too lowly to trust."

Just then the hammering stopped, leaving the room silent.

Agnes felt her stomach grow watery. She wished she were any-where but here. "Even so, sir, I am not certain I have the confi-dence of the other servants."

"In my experience," said Justice Cordingly in a coaxing tone, "those who wish to hear confidences have only to make themselves amenable. Most servants in your position would relish the oppor-tunity you are being offered."

Then perhaps in that respect I differ from most, thought Agnes as she gazed at him in unhappy silence.

Theodore mopped his brow with a crimson handkerchief. "Before you voice any further reservations, Mrs. Meadowes, I will mention one other point. As Justice Cordingly has said, the wine cooler was the most valuable object ever made by Blanchards'. Losing it could well pitch us into bankruptcy, in which case I and my family will land in the Fleet, and every member of staff in the household, you included, will lose their jobs. You have it in your power to prevent that happening."

There was a pause. Agnes felt as though someone was dragging her hand toward a hot oven and she was powerless to pull back. "But is it probable that something I hear below stairs will lead to the wine cooler's recovery?" she asked desperately.

"It isn't *only* listening I require of you. There is someone out-side the house who might find it," said Theodore, wiping his brow again. "I want you to act as my intermediary and pay him a visit."

Agnes gasped, incredulous. "Who is this person?"

"A man whose premises are close by here, in Southwark—a place called Melancholy Walk. He goes by the name of Marcus Pitt."

"Are you acquainted with the name?" said Cordingly.

"No sir. Should I be? Is he a servant, or a tradesman, or another silversmith, perhaps?"

"His profession is none of those. It is far more lucrative. He is what some consider a necessary evil, and others, myself included, a scourge of society—a thief taker."

Agnes had heard of men who used intelligence from tapsters, ostlers, and every variety of rogue to recover stolen property. Some appeared honorable and held respectable positions. But while they purported to offer a useful service to the unfortunate victims of robbery, they were rumored to be less innocent than they seemed, acting as fences, on occasion even engineering the theft of property they were later paid to recover.

She shifted uncomfortably in her chair. "I am very sensible of the kind of man to whom you refer, sirs. But I have no expertise in such matters. Why should you wish me to visit such a person for you?"

"Because, Mrs. Meadowes, as Justice Cordingly has said, there is no doubt that this murderous robbery has been most carefully orchestrated. Marcus Pitt is the most influential thief taker in this locality. Few crimes that take place hereabouts are unknown to him. It may well be that whoever inside our business or household betrayed us conspired to do so with his aid, using a thief under his control. Even if the culprit had no link to him, if anyone can find the wine cooler, it is he."

"If Mr. Pitt is so powerful and influential, is it wise to entrust me to speak to him? Would it not be more prudent for you to approach him directly?"

A shifty gleam appeared in Theodore's eye. "We would, but Pitt forbids it. He prefers to deal with an intermediary—says it only causes trouble if those that are robbed come too close to those that perpetrated the crime."

Agnes sensed that there was more to why she had been chosen than Theodore had revealed. "But am I a prudent choice for such an important role? There is Mr. Williams, can he not go?"

Theodore shook his head emphatically and flashed a knowing look at the justice. "Rest assured, Mrs. Meadowes. You are adequate for the task. Mr. Pitt is a consummate businessman. He conducts similar transactions every day. Besides, you may discover more than a man. I hear he has a taste for handsome women."

Agnes recoiled inwardly, trying not to dwell on this last remark, unable to see a way of averting the inevitable. Was she to be offered to this loathsome thief taker—a man who profited from others' misfortune—as bait to entice him to help? No, she told herself, Theodore would never misuse her in such a way. His earlier arguments—the age and fragility of the remaining upper servants, Mr. Pitt's preference for an intermediary—these were the reasons for her unwelcome appointment.

Theodore expected nothing but compliance, and interpreted her troubled silence as acquiescence. "You should not, of course, reveal that you are my cook—I do not wish him to take insult by my sending a domestic servant," he continued. "Rather say you are an engraver from my workshop, come on my behalf. I will notify him in advance. Do what you can to play on his sympathy—it can only help. Let him know you are recently arrived and fear you will lose your position if the business flounders, as it certainly will in the face of such a prodigious loss."

The hammering started up again. This time it was gentler than before, but Agnes shrank inwardly as she anticipated every stroke. "And how much do I offer to pay?" she murmured.

"To begin with he will merely require a fee to register the loss. Assuming he finds the wine cooler, the negotiations for its return will come later. At very least he will expect the melted value of the metal. I am prepared to offer that sum plus a modest additional payment. But I don't wish you to disclose that in the first instance. Nor do I want Sir Bartholomew Grey's name mentioned. Heaven forbid we attract Pitt's unsavory attention toward his household or I'll never see another commission from him." Theodore paused. "I should also say, if you acquit yourself well in this I shall reward you handsomely. Find the wine cooler and I will pay you twenty guineas."

Agnes's stomach tightened. Twenty guineas was six months' wages. She still felt a powerful presentiment of doom, but if she took on this role, she might not only save the Blanchard enterprise but benefit Peter. She nodded hesitantly. "Very well, sir," she said. "When shall I call on Mr. Pitt?"

Theodore smiled and mopped his brow again. His mood seemed less fraught. "Tomorrow at midday. I will tell my wife to inform Mrs. Tooley you are to be permitted extra freedom to assist me. Marcus Pitt will be expecting you. Philip will escort you to his premises."

"I could go on my own, if it is more convenient, sir," said Agnes, who did not in the least relish the prospect of a journey disturbed by the garrulous Philip.

Theodore shook his head. "Do not underestimate the dangers of this undertaking, Mrs. Meadowes. Pitt might pose as an arbiter of the law, but from all I hear he is as much a rogue as those with whom he deals. Heaven forbid the same fate should befall you as that poor fellow last night . . ."

Chapter Seventeen

S OME HOURS LATER, Agnes stood at the kitchen table with a newly boiled calf's head on a platter before her. She inserted the point of a sharp knife midway between the eyes and slowly raised the skin. Faced with the practicalities of preparing supper, she attempted to push all thoughts of Marcus Pitt from her mind. The only matter superseding the steaming head and its forcemeat stuffing was her pressing need to retrieve Peter from Mrs. Catchpole. Theodore's proposal offered money and, more immediately, a chance to escape her usual duties. She would thus be able to find somewhere for Peter to stay. She began to view the proposed mission with a measure of willingness—gratitude, even. And yet Theodore Blanchard's final thoughtless words of warning were not forgotten. The prospect of involving herself in matters outside her world frightened her. But if she could brazen out the perils for Peter's sake, she could return to her former existence.

Agnes's thoughts were then diverted along another path. Lydia had encouraged Theodore to choose her as his aid. Did Lydia's interest in Rose lie behind her recommendation? Or was she trying to help Agnes gain the freedom she had asked for without offending Mrs. Tooley? She had, after all, shown some sympathy to her plight. If Lydia had tried to assist her, it was only right that she should continue her efforts to discover what had happened to Rose. Besides, she could not deny that she too was curious to find out where the girl had gone.

Both Lydia and Mr. Matthews had suggested there might be an alliance between Rose and Nicholas Blanchard, and Mr. Matthews had seen Rose upstairs the day before she disappeared. But assuming Rose had stolen the pistol, thought Agnes, this was most likely when she had done so. It did not prove there was an improper alliance. Lydia had implied that Rose might have left because she was carrying Nicholas's child. What had caused her to form this opinion? There was only one person who had Lydia's wholehearted confidence, and she was currently standing fifteen feet away in the laundry room cleaning one of Lydia's hats with a velvet cloth.

Leaving the calf's head to cool, Agnes accosted Patsy. "Has Mrs. Blanchard said anything to you about her interest in Rose Francis?" she inquired with an ingenuous smile. Patsy looked askance, but a moment later weakly returned the smile. As lady's maid, she liked to pretend she had nothing in common with the other maidservants. She was older and more finely dressed, and to underline her importance she aped Lydia's manners—crooking her little finger when she drank tea, picking daintily at her food as if she had no appetite. Her placid expression and cool manner were also strangely reminiscent of Lydia. Agnes often wondered if this was a further affectation on Patsy's part or if she had unconsciously grown to resemble her mistress.

When it came to Agnes, however, Patsy was, as a rule, more convivial. Agnes suspected that this was because Patsy longed occasionally to exchange ideas with someone to whom she was not always expected to defer. Doubtless that was why, offered an opportunity to discuss the matter of Rose freely, Patsy seized it. "Yes, but I don't for the life of me see why. I should have thought she would be grateful the girl had gone," she said candidly, scratching a tiny blemish on the hat brim with her fingernail.

"Why do you say that—had Rose annoyed her?"

"Not exactly."

"What, then? Had it to do with Nicholas?"

"Mrs. Blanchard wondered why the wretched girl had been upstairs," said Patsy importantly.

"When was this—yesterday?"

Patsy gazed into the middle distance in the same unfocused way that Lydia had done in response to Agnes's request for time off. "No, not then. I don't recall exactly. A week or so back, perhaps. I think she mentioned it to Mrs. Tooley."

"Why did she not question Rose herself?"

Patsy paused, as though considering her reply. "She never caught her. It was something she discovered—a letter, I believe—that showed the girl had been there."

"A letter?" Agnes recalled John mentioning that a letter had been the cause of the fight between Rose and Nancy. "Was it Mrs. Blanchard who found it?" she pressed.

"No, I believe Nancy handed it to her."

"What did it say?"

Patsy shook her head ruefully. "It was written by Rose, and concerned a man. Mrs. Blanchard read it to me so quickly and I was tidying her things at the time, so I didn't hear exactly."

A man, Agnes thought; what else would a letter penned by Rose concern? "And what did Mrs. Blanchard say after Rose's disappearance?"

"She was troubled, though Lord knows why. If you want my opinion, Mrs. Blanchard hasn't enough to occupy her."

She would have liked to discover what else Patsy might reveal, but remembering the calf's head, Agnes returned to the kitchen table. As she assembled the stuffing with ingredients Doris had prepared—a pound of bacon fat scraped to beads, the crumbs of two penny loaves, a small nutmeg grated, a pinch of cayenne pepper, and a little grated lemon peel—she thought about the letter Nancy had found. Why had she lied earlier today when Agnes had asked her what the argument was about?

A few minutes later, Patsy emerged from the laundry room with the hat in her hand and the cord of an evening bag draped about her wrist, as if she were off to some grand assembly. She hovered by the table, as Agnes deftly mixed the stuffing.

"Lord knows why she went off," she proffered suddenly in a bitter tone, "or why there's such a fuss over her going. It seemed to me she gave us both the runaround on occasion . . . Mrs. Blanchard wanted me to ask you whether you found anything among the wretched girl's things to show where she has gone."

"You may tell her I have looked, but discerned nothing."

Agnes added the yolks of half a dozen eggs to her stuffing, cracking each one over a small bowl so the white ran into it, then dropping each golden orb into the crumbled mixture, where it gleamed like a small sun. Taking up a long metal spoon, she began to stir the ingredients together, cutting again and again through the mix until it had transformed to a rich yellow-tinged forcemeat. "Did Rose plague *you,* Patsy? If so, I never knew it."

"I wouldn't allow her to bother me, Mrs. Meadowes. But that didn't mean I was blind to what she was."

Agnes pressed a small quantity of forcemeat into each ear of the calf's head and the rest into the head cavity, molding the skin over so that it once again resembled a head. The sharp tone of Patsy's reply made her look up. "How d'you mean?"

"Rose lacked modesty. She was forever sticking her nose in matters that didn't concern her. You let her get away with it, but that didn't mean it was right."

Agnes knew she ought to have been more forthright, but Patsy's criticism galled her. Her feelings toward Rose were ambivalent—the girl had lacked modesty, but had she really been as black as everyone painted her? "She wasn't all bad, Patsy. She was quick enough around the kitchen, and no worse than you would find in any household."

Still riled, Agnes picked up the calf's head and plunged it into a pot with white wine, lemon pickle, walnut-and-mushroom catsup, an anchovy, a blade of mace, and a bundle of sweet herbs, then set the pot on the stove.

Patsy, meanwhile, seated herself at the table, still clutching Lydia's belongings as if they were a badge of office. She leaned forward toward Agnes. "Speaking confidentially, it wasn't what Rose did or said so much as what lay in her thoughts that made me take exception to her. She was forever trying to wheedle round me, wanting to know where I went with Mrs. Blanchard and who we met."

Agnes arched a brow. "You mean her attempts at conversation offended you? That was why you disliked her?"

Patsy frowned. "It was what inspired the conversation, more like."

"What, then?"

Patsy fiddled with the brim of Lydia's hat. "She wanted my position. She thought her duties as kitchen maid beneath her, and wanted to better herself. That's why she sneaked upstairs. She was scheming for my post and trying to engineer meetings with Lydia to get it. I can't pretend I'm sorry she's run off, and that's the reason why."

AFTER PATSY HAD GONE, Agnes wiped her finger around the inside of the bowl in which her forcemeat had been made and licked the savory mixture. There hardly seemed to be a soul in the house with whom Rose had enjoyed an uncomplicated relationship. She *should* have reprimanded Rose more. Why had she shied away from confrontation? Was it only her embarrassment at Rose's familiar manner with men? Agnes did not remember a time when she could speak to a man without self-consciousness and constraint. Her father had kept her apart from them; her unhappy marriage had shown her the dangers of them. And as for behaving as Rose had done in the larder—such wantonness was unimaginable. But then a worrying thought struck her: was a small part of her jealous of Rose?

Unsettled, Agnes posed a more straightforward question. What means could she employ to trace Rose? Was there a family to whom the girl might have written of her intentions? She mulled this over before it occurred to her, with a further stab of self-recrimination, that while she and Rose had worked together almost every day for the last year, their conversation had invariably been about food and its preparation. Agnes's reluctance to discuss her own history meant she rarely asked personal questions of those around her, and Rose had never volunteered any information. Not once had she mentioned her family, or where she had come from.

"FORGIVE ME for disturbing you, Mrs. Tooley. Might I trouble you for a bottle of preserved plums? I need them for my sauce."

"I suppose so, Mrs. Meadowes." Mrs. Tooley twirled her quill and peered over the rim of her spectacles as suspiciously as if Agnes were asking her for gold rather than a jar of fruit. Accounts from the grocer, fishmonger, butcher, and chandler were arranged in exact piles all over the table. She was checking them off against orders recorded in her household ledger; those she had verified had been impaled precisely in the center on a large iron spike.

Mrs. Tooley put down her quill on the pewter inkstand that had been a gift from Lydia Blanchard. She patted her linen cap and smoothed the lappets, as if reassuring herself of their pristine condition. Removing her spectacles, she bustled to her store cupboard and threw open the doors wide. The shelves were filled with a spectacular array of preserves and pickles as richly colored as jewels. She brushed a finger over the middle row, where bottled fruits were stored, giving a proprietorial glance to jars labeled quince, morello cherry, damson, peach, greengage, grape, and finally plum. She selected a jar of ruby-colored fruit and proudly handed it to Agnes. "I believe you'll find these as tasty and firm as any you've tried. Anything more you require, Mrs. Meadowes?"

Agnes hesitated. Realizing how little she knew of Rose's past had made her conscious that she was equally ignorant of Mrs. Tooley. Where did the housekeeper go on her days off? On a sudden whim she said, "I wonder, Mrs. Tooley, do you have any family to visit in your free time?"

Mrs. Tooley looked puzzled. "Family? I have a brother, but the last time I stayed with him I found the disorder in his house most disconcerting. It made me appreciate the tranquillity here. That was two years ago. I have not found the opportunity to go there since."

"I see," said Agnes, thinking that a little disorder was not necessarily a bad thing. She moved on to more pressing matters. "Has Mrs. Blanchard spoken to you on my account?"

"She has. I understand you are to make an excursion to a thief taker and might not be back in time to make dinner. I suppose I should be grateful that it is you being sent, not I. But do take care, won't you, Mrs. Meadowes? I cannot possibly manage without you." As she spoke, Mrs. Tooley raised a slender hand to her papery cheek, and her head began to tremble slightly.

Agnes felt touched and guilty that she had so quickly given up her attempt at friendly conversation. When she was less pressed she would try again. "Do not trouble yourself over my welfare," she said. "I shall return as swiftly as I can. But there is one other matter I should raise with you. I need to see Rose Francis's reference. Do you happen to know where it is?"

"What possible use can that be now?"

"Mrs. Blanchard believes there may be some connection between the murder and theft and Rose running off, and that she should be questioned on the matter—wherever she is. It occurred to me that her background might help ascertain her whereabouts."

"There was a written character," said Mrs. Tooley carefully. "I always insist upon it. As I recall, she stated at her interview that she had no family to speak of. Both her parents had died. She had gone into service for that reason, and came here from a large household in Bruton Street."

"The family name?"

"Lord and Lady Carew, as I recall."

"Carew?" echoed Agnes. The name meant nothing to her. "What reason did she give for her departure from their household?"

"She wanted to better herself and thought a position as kitchen maid might lead to her learning to cook."

"Who wrote her character reference? Was it Lady Carew, or a member of her staff?"

Mrs. Tooley colored. "I don't recall. I believe it may have been the housekeeper or steward. It was a hand of some education, finely formed and written on paper of quality. There was nothing out of the ordinary about it, if that is what you are implying."

"Oh, I did not mean to imply anything of the kind," assured Agnes quickly. "Do you have the letter still?"

Mrs. Tooley nodded. She opened a dresser drawer and took out a large card folder filled with a sheaf of some twenty or so papers. These she turned over slowly until at last she came to the one she was searching for. "Ah yes, as I thought, written by the housekeeper. Here it is."

"Thank you, ma'am," said Agnes.

To whom it may concern,

I hereby confirm that Miss Rose Francis has been employed as housemaid in this establishment for the past twelve months and is leaving of her own free will. Throughout this time she has shown herself to have an obliging, sober, and handy disposition. Her temper is by and large good, her character sociable. She appears sound of health.

Mrs. Moore, housekeeper to
Sir Henry Carew

She handed the letter back to Mrs. Tooley. "There is another letter that interests me," she said carefully. "I understand Mrs. Blanchard recently spoke to you about a communication she found upstairs belonging to Rose."

"That is an incident I should prefer to forget. My nerves were dreadfully frayed by it."

"I do not mean to upset you, ma'am. I simply wondered what was in the letter and whether you kept it?"

Mrs. Tooley shook her head. "I returned it to her after I had given her a talking-to. It was a note half a page long, unsigned, but written in her hand to someone addressed as 'Dearest.' The contents said little save that she was glad to learn he was well and would think over his proposal. She thanked him for his generous assistance, and hoped to see him on her next free afternoon to discuss the proposal further and give him her decision."

"Do you recall the address?"

Mrs. Tooley swallowed and fidgeted with her spectacles. "There was none—as I said, the letter was unfinished."

"And what excuse did she make for the letter being in the drawing room when you spoke to her about it?"

"She was aghast to learn where the letter had been found, and claimed that she had never been in there. She had left the note in her closet. She said that someone must have taken it and put it in the drawing room to cast her in a bad light."

"Did she say who she believed had done such a thing?"

"Either Nancy or Patsy, both of whom she declared were jealous of her. But since she had no proof of the assertion, I dismissed it."

"Did you ask for whom the letter was intended?"

Mrs. Tooley winced as if the question were painful to her. "When I asked whether she was writing to the man I had seen her with in the street, who she had claimed asked her for directions, and whether the proposal was one of marriage, she refused to disclose anything. I reminded her that maids were not permitted followers, and that if she did not behave properly, she would be denied her usual Sunday afternoon off. I had already heard rumors that she had been out without permission on several evenings with Philip." As she said this, Mrs. Tooley began to tremble again.

Agnes recalled her own difficulties with Rose and sympathized. "What did she say to your admonition?"

"She grew heated and said that Philip was neither here nor there. They were nothing to each other. And just because the note was written in an affectionate manner did not mean it was intended for a lover. I was viewing the matter unjustly. Even servants were surely permitted a life outside their place of work. And then she did something most untoward."

"What?"

"She stamped her foot like a petulant child, and said she had had enough of being put upon and tarnished just because the other maids were jealous of her. And she had had enough of drudgery too. I had made up her mind for her. She deserved a better life. And in front of my eyes, she tore the letter up. I said, 'I'll show you drudgery,' and set her washing pickling jars for her impudence. And before ten minutes were passed she had dropped a jar of apricots on the floor. It was spitefully done—I've no doubt of that whatsoever. I should have dismissed her then. I would have done if finding new girls was not such a trial . . ."

The effort of remembering and relating all this was manifest: Mrs. Tooley's color was heightened and her chin quivered with emotion.

"Of course," said Agnes, patting the housekeeper's hand. Such a dramatic and defiant gesture was typical of Rose. But if the letter did not refer to a marriage proposal, what proposal did it concern, and why be so secretive over it? She must have had something else to hide. An impending robbery, perhaps?

Chapter Eighteen

ONCE UPSTAIRS SUPPER had been served and all the other evening duties were completed, most of the servants retired to their quarters. Agnes, however, used an hour or two to tidy the kitchen, survey the pantry and larder, and determine what was needed for the next day. Often, too, she used these quiet hours to write letters to Peter. To be surrounded by the tools of her trade and the residual smells of cooking, and be warmed by the dying embers of the fire, brought Agnes comfort and a sense of belonging. The kitchen was where she felt most at peace.

But that evening, as she rearranged the boxes of spices on her dresser and stacked the stoneware dishes in a more orderly fashion than Doris had left them, she was unsettled by thoughts of the visit she had to make the next morning. Annoyed to see that a silver salver had been carelessly left out behind the pestle and mortar instead of being locked in the silver cupboard or taken upstairs, she moved it to a more conspicuous spot where John or Philip would be sure to notice it. When there was nothing more to tidy, she sat at the table with her recipes and papers, still feeling weighed down with dread. She wrote a brief line to Mrs. Catchpole, telling her that she regretted to learn of her ill health and explaining that she could not come immediately to take Peter away, but was making every attempt to do so soon and hoped for Mrs. Catchpole's forbearance. Next she penned an affectionate note to Peter, writing in large, clear script so that he would be able to read it himself. When this was done, to keep her thoughts from returning to Pitt, she began copying out a new recipe for orange tarts given to her by the local confectioner.

Agnes had scarcely put down her pen when she heard a gentle tapping at the kitchen door. She picked up the candlestick. "Who is there and what is your business?" she called out, checking hurriedly that the bolts were pushed to, for after last night's murder she had no intention of opening to just anyone.

"It is I, Thomas Williams, the journeyman."

Agnes opened the door an inch, then, seeing it was he, opened it until the gap was just wide enough to fit her head through. "Yes, Mr. Williams?" she said warily.

Williams removed his hat and gave a small bow. "Good evening, Mrs. Meadowes. I have come about the subject we spoke of this afternoon—Benjamin Riley."

"Oh yes, indeed. Please enter." She stepped back, cradling the flame of her candle against the sudden burst of air, feeling foolish for her caution and grateful for the interruption. It was something to keep her mind off tomorrow.

Thomas Williams put his hat upon the table, then prowled around, gazing at the vast range, the ranks of pots and coppers, and all the other equipment as if he had never before seen the like. "May I take a seat?" he said at length when his survey was complete. Agnes hesitated, and to her consternation felt a blush begin to spread across her cheeks. She was alone in her kitchen with a man who was not a servant in the household, a man she barely knew, and he wanted to sit down. She found herself wondering where Williams lived and if he was married, then a moment later scolded herself for being foolish enough to wonder such things. The admonition did not prevent her heart beating faster. She wondered how long would it take Mrs. Tooley or Mr. Matthews to come if she called. She reprimanded herself again. Williams had come at her invitation. There was no reason to suppose he was anything but a respectable craftsman who had helped a fellow employee.

"Please, Mr. Williams, do sit down," she said with an air of formality. She briskly closed her book of recipes and, to cover her awkwardness, offered him a mug of ale and a slice of cake. Thomas Williams pulled up the chair closest to her own, while Agnes prepared the refreshment. When she returned to her seat, she shifted it six inches in the opposite direction.

"Well," she said, sitting straight-backed, watching him drink, "what have you learned, Mr. Williams?"

He put down his mug and examined the backs of his surprisingly clean and long-fingered hands. "Nothing very much," he said bleakly.

"Nothing at all?"

"He said she was sweet on him, but that apart from a brief flirtation some months ago, there was nothing between them. But his opinion means nothing. He thinks every woman is a captive to his charms."

Agnes sat in silence for a moment. "Am I to take it you do not care for him much?"

Williams nodded, meeting her gaze in a piercing manner which disturbed her slightly. "Or trust him, either." He paused and looked away, his green eyes seeming to grow more wistful as he did so. "He and I work side by side, spend hours in each other's company, but neither of us has much time for the other."

Agnes nodded sympathetically. Feelings of estrangement from those with whom she worked were familiar to her too. She leaned a few inches toward him. "What gave you the impression he was not truthful?"

"I told you before—I saw Rose come to call on him recently, not months ago as he claimed."

"Did you tell him?"

"Yes. He said it was nothing—that she had been sent upon an errand by Theodore Blanchard."

Agnes frowned, instinctively rejecting this as most improbable. "What manner of errand?"

"Something concerning the pieces to be taken to Goldsmiths' Hall for marking."

"Marking?"

"Every piece that is fabricated in our workshop, or any other in London, is taken to Goldsmiths' Hall and tested for the purity of its metal. If the piece passes the test, it is marked with a lion."

Agnes furrowed her brow. Despite working for one of the most renowned silversmiths of London, she had no notion of such matters. She vaguely recollected seeing marks on pieces of silver, but had never paid them much attention or wondered what they signified. Recalling the salver carelessly left on her dresser, she went to fetch it. Four small symbols were impressed in the surface. Only one resembled a lion. She handed the salver to Thomas Williams. "But there is more than one mark on this."

He nodded. "And so there should be. See, here is the lion, walking to the left. A lion *passant,* it is termed. That is the mark that shows the piece contains at least nine hundred and twenty-five parts pure silver in a thousand and has been passed as sterling."

"And the other marks—what purpose do they serve?"

Williams laughed, but not unkindly, and leaned toward her, pointing one by one to the symbols. Distracted by the fact that his head was only inches away from her, she barely heard what he said. "There is the maker's mark—usually the initials of the silversmith. The *NB* you see shows the piece was made at Blanchards'. There is a date letter, which changes with each year—*P* shows the piece was marked this year. And the last mark shows where the piece was tested: a leopard's head in the case of Goldsmiths' Hall." As he spoke, he suddenly looked puzzled. He sat back with the salver and held it toward the light.

"And is every piece marked?"

Williams nodded. He was scrutinizing the salver with a strange intensity. "By statute it should be. And the purchaser is well advised to ensure it. The system is designed to prevent unscrupulous craftsmen using less-pure metal than they should."

"But why would Theodore Blanchard send a kitchen maid with a message concerning marking? If he had something of that nature to communicate, why did he not tell Riley himself—he is there every day, after all—or send one of the footmen?"

"I don't believe what he said any more than you do."

"What time of day did you see Rose come to the workshop?"

"I can't be certain, but from memory it was early afternoon. Around two or three."

Agnes half closed her eyes. Two or three o'clock—the hours she was busiest, serving lunch and up to her eyes with cooking dinner. At that time Rose might melt away and return without being noticed. Suppose there *was* a grain of truth in what Riley had said? Suppose Rose had called at the workshop on Theodore's business—it might give credence to Rose's involvement in the robbery. But why would Theodore use a kitchen maid rather than a manservant to convey a message?

"It would be helpful to know exactly what the errand entailed. Would Riley say nothing more on the subject?"

Thomas Williams looked up from the salver and swallowed. "No. Which is why I don't believe him."

"No more do I, but whatever he says may shed light on what happened."

"Then if you wish I will press him again." His attention strayed back to the salver. He examined the underside intently. He breathed on it, looked again, then buffed it with his sleeve. When finally he noticed her gaze on him, he put the salver down as if embarrassed.

"The marks seem to have captured your attention, Mr. Williams. Is there something out of the ordinary about them?"

Thomas Williams scratched his head, his brow ruffled in consternation. He opened his mouth, then closed it again without saying a word.

"What is it, Mr. Williams? I pray that you tell me, for I see plainly there is something."

Williams sighed, looking somber. "Very well. By statute, before any silver object may be sold, it is liable for duty—the sum of sixpence per ounce. The sum is usually paid immediately after the piece has been taken for assay. Unscrupulous silversmiths who wish to avoid duty have been known to cut out the marks from a small marked piece and set them into the metal of an untested piece. That way the heavier piece appears to be legally marked and duty is avoided. The practice is known as duty dodging."

"And you believe the salver has been tampered with—that this is an example of duty dodging?"

"There have been no salvers made to this pattern in the last two years. Two years ago, the date letter was *N,* yet the salver has a *P* impressed upon it—the letter for this year. The only possible reason for this discrepancy is if the original marks have been removed, a new piece of metal inserted, with marks from a recently assayed piece."

"Why did you breathe on the marks?"

"To verify my suspicion. You will see a slight ridge around the marks."

Agnes squinted closely at the marks. She breathed on them as he had done, and faintly detected a dark circle around them.

"I see it. But how does that prove the marks are not original?"

"If a new piece of metal is inserted into another, it can never be made as smooth as if it had been fashioned from a single metal sheet. That ridge indicates that the metal on which the marks are impressed has been set into the salver."

Agnes nodded slowly and looked up. "Did you know such deception took place at Blanchards'?"

Thomas Williams met her gaze. "No," he said. "I had no notion whatsoever."

With this he looked toward the fire with a distant, unfathomable gleam in his eye. Agnes too was lost in thought, wondering at the significance of what he had told her. Did duty dodging have any bearing on Noah's murder, the theft of the wine cooler, or Rose's disappearance? Was Rose somehow embroiled in the fraud?

But before she could draw any conclusions, Thomas Williams coughed loudly, and she looked up with a start. "Forgive me, Mrs. Meadowes, I was thinking of you going off to visit Pitt, and wondering what made you accept such a dangerous undertaking. Your husband cannot be happy with the situation—or perhaps you haven't told him?"

Agnes was caught unawares. She could not see how this abrupt remark was relevant to their conversation. Confused, and hoping she was not blushing, she said, "Danger? My husband? But I have none. He is dead."

As soon as these words were out, Agnes caught Williams darting a glance at the letters on the table. The one addressed in a large clear hand to "My darling child" and signed "Your loving mother" lay in front of him. Immediately she felt exposed, and she resented his queries. Peter's existence was a private matter, and she had no intention of discussing him with a stranger.

"Then if you alone are responsible for your son, is that not even more reason to be prudent?" said Thomas quietly.

Agnes gave him a short hard smile. "My reasons for going are my own, Mr. Williams. But I assure you my son's welfare is at the forefront of my mind. Now, since the hour is late, I believe it is time you left."

Chapter Nineteen

AT ELEVEN the next morning, Agnes dressed in a warm woolen coat and a fine velvet hat (which Patsy had lent her after much prevarication) and strode purposefully down Cheapside with Philip by her side. Unconscious of the tempting window displays of the haberdashers, goldsmiths, and linen drapers, she gazed briefly at a windowful of confectionary before turning right toward Thames Street and thence on to London Bridge and Marcus Pitt's office.

It was a fine, crisp morning. A heavy hoarfrost still glazed parts of the pavement untouched by the sunlight, and the open gutter that ran down the center of the street was semifrozen. A flock of sheep and one or two oxcarts had recently traveled the route, perhaps on their way to Smithfield, and here and there mounds of fresh dung sent up small steamy wisps like miniature bonfires. The earthy odor mingled with other familiar smells—smoke from countless chimneys, the ovens of Bread Street, malt and hops from the Barclay Perkins Brewery, burning chestnut skins, and above all the dank pervasive tang of the river, which wound its way behind the crowded wharves and warehouses.

"Did you and Rose like to promenade together?" Agnes asked casually, as Philip loitered at the window of a milliner's shop, pulling faces at a prettily dressed assistant.

He was too absorbed to hear her. He was posing affectedly, with his hand on the hilt of his sword. Agnes, annoyed, repeated her question more loudly, nudging his side discreetly, causing his sword to clash on the glass. He gave Agnes an amiable smile. "Beg your pardon, Mrs. Meadowes? Did you say something?"

"Yes," said Agnes. "How often did you and Rose walk out together?"

Philip shot a rueful glance back at the window. "To begin with it were once or twice a month. Whenever we was both off together on a Sunday. She liked somewhere lively: the pit at the Newgate Theatre, an excursion to Vauxhall."

Agnes watched as a sedan chair drew to a halt on the pavement and a gentleman dressed with foppish elegance descended directly in front of them, forcing them into the doorway of an under-taker's. Without so much as a word of excuse the gentleman darted into a coffeehouse. Philip yelled an insult and stepped after him. Agnes yanked Philip back and told him to mind his manners in her company.

"Did she ever mention family or friends?" she continued.

"Never," said Philip, after thinking for a moment. "It wasn't a subject either of us raised. I wouldn't want her thinking I had intentions when I hadn't. I enjoyed her company right enough, but I enjoy the company of others too. And I can't marry or I'll lose my position, won't I? I reckon that was why she cooled toward me."

A sudden disturbing vision sprang to Agnes's mind of the pair of them in the larder, Philip with his breeches open and muscular buttocks on display, Rose's pale thighs spread wide. She could not conceive of Rose disporting herself in such a manner if she did not at least hope it would lead somewhere permanent. But the subject of physical love was one in which she was ill equipped to judge others. Nevertheless, she unwillingly recognized that she needed to know more. "Then when you went out on your excursions, was it just as companions—no more?"

Philip winked. "Depends what you mean by companions, I s'pose. I kissed her, and did more than that if she was agreeable and we could get somewhere out of the way. Mind you, it wasn't only me—she relished a good tumbling as much as I. At the beginning, that was."

Agnes remembered that John had said their affair was over. "Did she change, then?"

"In the past few weeks she did. She went out the afternoons she was allowed, but it was never with me. And she wouldn't let me near her."

Agnes recalled Lydia's suspicions. "You don't think she might have been carrying your child?"

Philip grinned as though the thought amused him. "No—not that. I reckon she found someone new."

"Did you not ask who it was?"

"Of course. But she was devilish secretive on occasion—she wouldn't say."

"Perhaps it was Riley she was set on?"

Philip regarded Agnes from the corner of his eye. "Like I said, she never let on anything to me. But as far as Riley goes, I should doubt it. She said she'd tired of him, or he of her—I forget which—before we became friends. I saw them talking once or twice, a while since, but that was all. And from the look of things there was nothing between them."

"And what about Nicholas Blanchard? Did she ever mention him?"

"The old goat? It wasn't Rose that interested him, it was Nancy—though he won't be happy with her for much longer, I'd say."

Agnes remembered Nancy's jealousy at being spurned when Rose arrived. "Why? Are you and she friendly again?"

"A bit, maybe, but that don't mean she'll pull the wool over my eyes. You asked me if Rose was with child. Ain't you remarked how Nancy's filled out? And you a mother too?"

Doubtless Philip did not intend this remark to be as hurtful as it was. But whatever his intention, Agnes was disconcerted. How was it that he had a better understanding of what drove both Rose and Nancy than she did? But as they continued on at a brisker pace, Agnes thought that if Nancy was with child, she must be in a state of turmoil. She remembered Nancy's resentment toward Rose. But even if Nancy did feel bitter about Rose coming between Philip and herself, she surely could not blame the girl for forcing her into Nicholas's bed or her present predicament.

Soon the Monument and the church of St. Magnus the Martyr came into view. They veered sharply to the right toward London Bridge. She gazed between the gaps in the decaying wooden houses that lined the bridge, out across the sparkling sweep of the river, and tried to think freely. She thought again of the money Nancy had reported seeing under Rose's mattress, and wondered how Rose had come by the hoard. The disturbing notion occurred to her that if Rose was as fond of intimacy as Philip implied, perhaps she had come by her fortune by selling *herself*. Perhaps another life as a whore had taken her away.

"By Nancy's account, Rose had a large sum of money in her possession—about twenty gold sovereigns. Did you ever see it? Did she mention how it came into her possession?"

Philip blanched. "Twenty sovereigns? God's teeth—the bloody jade! And her grumbling on about how little she had and how she was born to better things."

"To what better things was she born?"

Philip shrugged. "I don't rightly recall. She'd had a maid of her own. Her father had died, and she had been forced to seek employ." He shook his head and laughed. "I shouldn't give it much credence if I were you. She was always one to give herself airs if she thought it would get her out of a chore." Suddenly, his eyes glistened with tears as he spoke.

"Then could not the money have been an inheritance?"

"No," said Philip unhesitatingly. "That was one thing I never doubted about her story. There was no inheritance. She had to work and she detested it."

Once across London Bridge, they headed toward the Borough. In the distance were St. George's Fields, a black latticework of leafless trees in front of the wintery slopes upon which a scattering of cows and sheep grazed. Philip's eye, meanwhile, settled on a cluster of pretty girls outside the George Tavern, one of whom winked at him and raised her skirt high enough to expose a well-turned ankle. Agnes caught Philip blowing her a kiss. She strode briskly to the tavern courtyard to ask for directions to Melancholy Walk.

Agnes narrowly avoided collision with all manner of men and conveyances, all jostling and barging in their efforts to load or unload, water, feed, harness, or unharness their horses. She found a groom who was able to direct her, but when he tried to engage her in further conversation she cut him short. "Philip," she cried out brusquely, waving her arm to summon him hastily to her side, "this gentleman informs me the place we are looking for is this way. Let us leave now. There is no time to waste."

Melancholy Walk was a narrow alley nestling in the shadow of the Southwark Glass House and the Clink prison. The houses here were newly built—tall, narrow structures, four stories high, with a single window on each floor. According to the directions that Theodore had provided, Marcus Pitt's office was the fourth house along.

IN ANSWER TO Agnes's knock, the door edged open and a puffy, pockmarked, unshaven face peered out. Taking a deep breath, Agnes announced stoutly, "I have an appointment on behalf of Mr. Theodore Blanchard. My name is Agnes Meadowes."

"That so?" replied the man. His smile revealed a gash of blackened teeth. "And mine's Grant. If you're expected, I s'pose you'd better come in."

Grant's physique, Agnes now saw, was as unwholesome as his face. His body was vast and round; the coat and shirt he wore were incapable of covering his girth; and slivers of hairy flesh protruded where buttons were missing and fastenings undone. Agnes averted her eyes and stepped into the hallway. Philip made to follow her, but Grant stepped forward, blocking his path. "Not you. He wants her alone. You wait here," he said, shoving him in the chest.

Poised on Marcus Pitt's threshold, and separated from Philip, Agnes felt her pulse quicken, and darts of apprehension prick her spine. However, she had no choice but to face the ordeal. She peered around Grant's bulky mass. "It's all right, Philip," she said. "Do as he says. I'll call if I need you."

She found herself in a long narrow corridor, sparsely furnished with two seats set against the wall close to the front door and nothing else save at the far end, where a pair of benches were occupied by three boisterous boys playing a game of dice. They were all dirty and raggedly dressed, aged about twelve or thirteen, she guessed. Had she seen them in the street she would have assumed they were pickpockets and kept clear. Presumably, thought Agnes with an apprehensive shudder, it was by keeping lads such as these in his pay that Pitt derived his insight into London's murky goings-on.

"If you would care to wait a moment," said Grant, signaling to the chairs by the door, "I will inform Mr. Pitt you are here." Then, turning toward the lads, he bellowed, "You lot, mind your manners—there's company here."

Agnes sat down gingerly as Grant sidled through an entrance leading off the corridor and swiftly yanked the door shut. The boys paid no attention to her presence, but continued their unruly brawling.

From behind the closed door, Agnes could hear the low sonorous sound of conversation, although the subject was impossible to discern above the racket. Then there was the crash of a door and the sound of heavy footsteps on wooden boards.

"He's ready for you now," said Grant, poking his head out of the doorway. "This way, if you please."

It was not at all what she had expected. The shutters in Marcus Pitt's office were half drawn across the window. Nevertheless, there was enough light for her to see that the room was orderly and the furnishings were of quality. There was a mahogany desk; two or three carved chairs; a cabinet, upon which stood a row of cut-glass decanters and half a dozen wineglasses, two of which were half full; and a coat stand, upon which was suspended a long black cloak, a tricorn hat, and a silver-topped walking cane.

The air was stuffy and sweetly scented, thanks to a blazing fire and a pastille burner that gave off a strong, sweet perfume—sandalwood or musk, Agnes guessed. The walls were lined with bookshelves, upon which stood row upon row of identical dark blue volumes. Agnes noticed that the spine of each was marked with two dates and that the books were ranged chronologically. The significance of the dates was not clear, but the care with which they were ordered brought a certain sense of formality to the room that she found reassuring.

Marcus Pitt was seated at his desk writing in a volume identical to the ones on the shelves. Agnes recalled the voices she had just heard. Judging from the wineglasses, Pitt had been entertaining company before her arrival. She could see a small door set into the paneling. Presumably his previous visitor had left through it.

Pitt put down his pen, rose to his feet, bowed, and held out his hand to greet her. He was tall, long-faced, and clean-shaven, with a thin nose, well-defined mouth, deep-set dark gray eyes, his hair impeccably dressed in tidy rolls over his ears and caught back in a shiny black ribbon. "Mrs. Meadowes, good morning to you. I received word of your visit from Mr. Blanchard. Allow Mr. Grant to take your cloak and hat." His voice was surprisingly genteel, and the hand that shook hers well manicured, its grip authoritative and cool. His dress befitted a well-to-do gentleman: a fine blue velvet coat, silk waistcoat, buckskin breeches.

"That is quite all right, thank you, sir," she said. "I prefer to keep them."

Pitt smiled indulgently. "You have traveled some distance," he continued with a look of solicitude. "Perhaps I can offer you some refreshment. A glass of wine?"

"Thank you, no," said Agnes, blushing at the offer. "I am pressed for time. Mr. Blanchard is most anxious I return as speedily as I am able."

"Naturally." Marcus Pitt bowed slightly. "How could he fail to be eager for so charming a lady's swift return?"

Remembering the delicacy of her commission, and that Theodore had expressly ordered her to capitalize on her charms, Agnes suppressed her instinct to make a cutting remark. "You are mistaken, sir. I come on business. I speak in a professional capacity."

A slight twitch now played at the corners of Marcus Pitt's mouth, as though her formality amused him. "Your propriety is commendable; it must come as a great relief to your husband. I take it you are both in the same profession?"

"My husband is dead," replied Agnes diffidently, all too aware that this was the second time that she had been obliged to mention him in twenty-four hours. She hurried on, feeling herself blush as she spoke. "I have recently joined the Blanchard workshop as an engraver. This robbery threatens their business and thus I am fearful it might also jeopardize my position. As a widow, with a child to support . . . you will appreciate my concern."

"Indeed, and I admire your fortitude, Mrs. Meadowes. You are most courageous. Now tell me properly about the business that brings you."

"I have come, sir, to enlist your assistance in retrieving a valuable silver wine cooler that has been stolen from the Blanchards' business premises in Foster Lane."

Pitt nodded. "Blanchard referred to the matter in his letter. He knows, I presume, there is a fee for my services? One guinea, payable in advance."

"I have it in my purse." She felt in her pocket, deriving a moment's comfort from the cool disc of gold that Theodore had given her for this purpose. She placed the coin on the desk in front of her.

Marcus Pitt took a brass key from a bunch attached to his belt, unlocked a drawer, and took out a metal-bound strongbox. Selecting another key from his collection, he unlocked the strongbox, placed the coin inside, then secured the box again. "Now tell me more precisely what happened; describe the stolen property in as much detail as you recall. Not too fast, mind, I must write it all down."

So Agnes explained the events as they had been told to her, recounting how the shop had been broken into, how the apprentice who had been guarding the shop at that hour had had his throat cruelly cut from ear to ear, and how nothing but the wine cooler had been taken. Mr. Pitt recorded the details in his book with swift fluency in a small, spidery script. At the end of his report, he looked up. "And now tell me about the appearance of the wine cooler, if you please."

Agnes had never set eyes on the object, but Theodore had shown her a detailed drawing and Agnes described it as best she could. "It was most expertly wrought, measuring three and a half feet long and nearly two feet wide, adorned with mermaids, dolphins, tritons, horses, and a figure of Neptune bearing a shield with the patron's armorials."

There was a short pause while Pitt wrote rapidly in his ledger. Then, leaning back in his chair, he steepled his forefingers under his chin and regarded her with a directness she found unsettling. "You haven't told me yet the most crucial detail of all."

"And what, pray, is that, Mr. Pitt?"

"The weight."

Agnes flushed awkwardly but did not avert her gaze. "Twelve hundred ounces."

Pitt blinked, his eyes wide in mock astonishment. *"Twelve hundred ounces,"* he repeated slowly. "No wonder, then, that Theodore

Blanchard is in a lather. What will Sir Bartholomew Grey say when he knows it has gone missing, I wonder. I take it the wine cooler was assayed and the duty properly paid?"

"I beg your pardon, sir?" Agnes said, remembering in a flash her conversation with Thomas Williams the previous night. Was Pitt suggesting that the duty might have been avoided? Why should *he* care? Then, not wishing to alert Pitt to her thoughts, she swiftly replied, "I assume so, Mr. Pitt, though I don't see why that should be significant. The wine cooler is unique. You have certainly enough to identify it, with or without marks."

"I expect you are right," conceded Marcus Pitt, the suspicion of a smile still playing about his mouth. "Now, Mrs. Meadowes, if you would allow me to explain how my system works."

"Very well, sir."

"I will ask around among my numerous contacts and perhaps place an advertisement in a publication or two. When I've found something, I shall send one of my young assistants to fetch you."

He said all this with an air of solemnity better suited to a man of law or a physician than a man who held sway over the city's underworld and employed a retinue of rogues to assist him.

"How long is this process likely to take?" Agnes inquired deferentially.

"No more than three or four days. I wager we'll be enjoying each other's company again before the end of the week."

"Mr. Blanchard will be delighted to hear it."

"Of course he will," responded Marcus Pitt with alacrity. "He's twelve hundred ounces at stake. By anyone's standards that is a considerable sum, not to be taken lightly."

"Will the villain responsible be apprehended at the same time?" asked Agnes.

Pitt's expression turned suddenly grave. "That question, Mrs. Meadowes, is much trickier. Sometimes it is best to be content with the property and not look further. My business, you see, depends upon the trust of rogues. Mr. Blanchard will understand."

Agnes nodded in silence. So the murderer of Noah Prout would go free in order for Pitt's business to prosper. And Theodore would raise no objection, provided he recovered his wine cooler.

Pitt rose and bowed to her. "I will be counting the days—unless, that is, you would consent to put me out of my anguish before."

Agnes regarded him uncertainly. "I don't think I follow you, Mr. Pitt."

"Then the fault is mine for not making myself clear. What I want to do is offer you an invitation. Would you care to accompany me to the New Theatre on Friday? I will send a couple of assistants on ahead to keep our places in the pit, and we can dine first. I guarantee I'll entertain you royally and give you a night you won't forget."

Agnes could not remember the last time a gentleman had invited her on an excursion. A flush of flattered astonishment spread across her cheeks. But she reminded herself sternly that for all his posturing, Pitt was not a gentleman but a villain, and she too was masquerading as something she was not. No doubt Pitt was as much drawn by her supposed profession as by her charms. "That is a most generous offer, Mr. Pitt, and please don't think I am ignorant of the honor you pay me. Nevertheless, I regret I am not at liberty to accompany you. I have commitments that proscribe evening excursions."

Even as she spoke, Agnes knew there was too much regret and not enough distance in her tone. She sensed that Marcus Pitt was well versed in feminine wiles and would notice this. He nodded, shrugged his shoulders, and sighed with mock chagrin. "The ripest fruits are always the first to be picked. 'Twas ever thus." Striding round his desk, he helped her from her chair. Then, before she knew it, he had taken her bare hand in his and kissed it. "Until Saturday, then, God willing. Good day to you, Mrs. Meadowes."

"Good day, Mr. Pitt." The sensation of his soft lips and scratchy chin touching her hand was not unpleasant, but she drew back her hand as if she had burned it. An unmistakable thrill had rushed through her veins, as though she had gulped a mouthful of brandy. This was the allure of dissipation, she told herself sternly. Why had she not put her gloves on sooner? She had a sudden vision of herself with a blackened eye and split lip. Being beaten was no less painful if the man who struck the blows was handsome and on occasion charming.

Chapter Twenty

TAKING HER LEAVE, Agnes felt new fear, and new puzzlement too. Quite apart from Pitt's question concerning duty, she could not explain his comment: "What will Sir Bartholomew Grey say when he knows it has gone missing, I wonder?" On Theodore's emphatic instruction, she had never mentioned that the wine cooler had been made for Grey. So Pitt's knowledge was most obviously explained by an illicit involvement with a member of the Blanchard staff; Pitt had unwittingly confirmed Justice Cordingly's and Theodore's suspicions that the robbery was no casual crime. Duty dodging was neither here nor there. Pitt must have been commissioned to orchestrate the robbery of the wine cooler, which he had now been employed to recover. The question was, by whom?

In the hallway, the towering bulk of the manservant Grant stood sentinel. Agnes opened her mouth to tell him she was leaving. Just at that moment, her eyes flickered past him to the three boys who were still rough-and-tumbling at the end of the corridor. But now, she observed, they had been joined by a fourth person, a young, dark-haired girl. She had a long, thin face, straggly, unkempt hair, and catlike eyes. Her mouth was small and round, her feet bare, her clothes ragged and nondescript, but her crimson shawl wrapped about her shoulders. The splash of glowing color amid the monochrome gloom caught Agnes's attention.

She was the girl Agnes had seen waiting outside the day before the robbery. The girl to whom she had offered three farthings, and who had stolen her purse and an orange. Her humiliation and outrage came flooding back; she half wanted to take hold of the girl and shake her. But remembering where she was, and anxious not to draw attention by staring, Agnes briskly turned away, pulled on her gloves with trembling fingers, and adjusted her hat in the looking glass. She noted how darkly her eyes gleamed against her pale complexion and how fast she was breathing. "I am ready," she said quietly to Grant, who opened the front door for her.

Philip was slouched against the railings outside. Catching sight of Agnes, he leaped up. "All go well, Mrs. Meadowes?"

She nodded curtly. "I believe so, thank you, Philip. But I don't wish to waste a moment more. Let us go."

As they headed back toward the Borough, Agnes's mind was racing. Thank God, she thought, I had the presence of mind to say nothing! Had I revealed that I knew the girl while I was still on Pitt's premises, heaven knows what might have happened. Pitt would surely not have let me return in safety. The girl must have been set to observe the comings and goings at the Blanchards' premises to decide the most opportune moment for the robbery. Agnes recalled the girl mentioning she was waiting for her pa, and the shadowy, long-coated figure glimpsed just before she had run off. Had he been the perpetrator of the dreadful crime? She resolved to mention the matter to Justice Cordingly at the earliest opportunity. There might not be proof, but at the very least, she thought, the girl's father should be identified and questioned over the matter.

Within ten minutes they had arrived at London Bridge. They were a quarter of the way across when a man wheeling a barrow piled high with old rags trundled past with a couple of dogs growling at his heels. From the opposite direction, a sedan chair careered up at considerable speed, just as a large wagon, drawn by a couple of oxen, creaked to a standstill behind the man with the barrow. To avoid the obstruction, Philip and Agnes crossed to the other side of the road, skirting several shops and stalls selling quack remedies, gloves, and ribbons. The air reverberated to a melee of shouts. *Make way!... Move over!... Make haste!... Watch behind you!* As the barrow drew alongside her, Agnes heard a thin, high voice yelling out to her, "Wait, missus! For Gawd's sake, stop! A word, if you please."

Agnes peered round the swaying wagon and the oxen's bony haunches and saw a flash of crimson cloth—it was the girl again. She had no desire for Philip to see her in discussion with the child. Doubtless he already knew that an urchin had robbed her; John and he had few secrets. Given half a chance, they might well ridicule her about a second encounter. "Continue on, Philip," she said as the traffic passed and the way ahead cleared. "There is an order I want to place at the chandler for Mrs. Tooley. I'll catch you in a minute." Without further explanation, she darted into one of the shops lining the bridge.

The girl came charging up, but when she saw Agnes inside the shop she did not enter. Agnes waited until Philip was out of view before she emerged. "So, miss," she said warily, "what is it you wish to say?"

The girl had evidently run all the way from Melancholy Walk, for she was panting and her cheeks were flushed. "You know who I am," she said between gasps, meeting Agnes's scrutiny boldly.

"I saw you outside the Blanchards' shop two days ago. You were waiting for your father and stole an orange and my purse, even though I gave you three farthings."

The girl did not bother to deny the charge. "I want to know what you're intending to do about it. Did you tell the man you're with?" She jerked her head in the direction Philip had taken.

"No."

"Then who will you tell?"

Agnes pondered. The girl's presence at Pitt's could not be ignored. Agnes had already resolved to tell Justice Cordingly; Theodore Blanchard should also be informed. What steps were then taken to discover who had helped Pitt—perhaps this girl's father, if he was the figure she had seen—was for them to decide.

Then it occurred to Agnes that if she played along, the girl might inadvertently confirm her father to be the murderer and tell her who at Blanchards' had assisted him. But she was unsure how to extract information from a wretch who would no doubt rob her again, given half a chance. "Tell me first, what's your name?" she said cautiously.

"Elsie."

"Elsie what?"

"Elsie Drake."

"So, Elsie Drake, whom do you advise me to tell?"

"I suppose you think you should tell your master, so's he might try and nab my pa, but I've come to warn you not to. Not yet, at any rate. It won't help your chances."

This was the last thing Agnes expected to hear. "Why not?"

"If Mr. Pitt gets wind of it, he'll have the wine cooler melted down and sold for bullion, and then Mr. Blanchard'll never get it back."

The girl's logic surprised Agnes, not to mention her nerve, which was quite beyond expectation. "What does the wine cooler matter to you?"

"It don't, but my pa do, and he's all I got. If Mr. Pitt finds out the justice is after my pa, he'd most likely give him up to be hanged just to get the forty guineas reward, rather than let the justice take him and get nothing. And if that happens, he'll melt the wine cooler down just to keep himself on the safe side, so we'll all be the loser."

Agnes grasped the girl's reasoning. As a thief taker, Pitt received payment from the authorities for any criminal he apprehended. This was how he disposed of villains who rebelled against his control, or any he suspected might be apprehended and incriminate him.

"Your father—what's he called?"

"Harry."

"Harry Drake? Does he work for Mr. Pitt?"

Elsie nodded, looking at her feet.

"And what does he do for him?"

She shrugged sulkily. "I don't know much. He don't talk about it."

Agnes had no doubt this was a lie, but then, she thought, what else could the girl say? Her father, despite most likely being a murderous thief, was all she had. "Did someone else help your father? Someone inside Mr. Blanchard's shop?"

"How should I know? I just watched outside an' told 'im what I saw."

"Told who?"

"My pa." Elsie looked at her, unblinking, hostile.

Sensing she would get no further, Agnes changed tack. "What time did you start watching?"

"He wanted me sitting there most of the night—said the night was what interested him most."

"And the night of the robbery, were you there outside?"

"No."

Agnes's disappointment must have shown.

"Why d'you ask?" said Elsie craftily. "Feeling guilty? Worried I saw you do summat you shouldn't?"

"Did your father mention seeing a woman leave the house? She was young and handsome, dressed in a cloak and a dark blue dress," persisted Agnes firmly, ignoring the taunt.

Elsie's eye flickered for a second, but she held Agnes's gaze. "No, he never said nothing," she said. "I said before, never does."

Agnes looked at the miserable face, the ragged costume, the bare feet blackened with grime. Elsie's willingness to risk approaching Agnes and answering her questions showed her anxiety on her father's behalf. Agnes had little doubt that Harry Drake was the murderous thief who stole the wine cooler. Bitter experience had shown her that his daughter was inherently untrustworthy and far from innocent. But given Elsie's circumstances, the loyalty and affection she felt toward her father was remarkable— touching, even. Regardless of rights and wrongs, Noah Prout was dead, the wine cooler was gone, and the Blanchards were prepared to pay for its recovery. If Harry Drake swung for the murder, Elsie would be fatherless, but Pitt would still profit.

"So, missus," pressed Elsie. "You won't say nothing, will you?"

"No," said Agnes wearily, "I won't."

AGNES SOON CAUGHT UP with Philip, and when they arrived at Foster Lane, she sent him on to the house while she went next door. Theodore had instructed her to report to him the minute she returned.

When she entered the shop, Thomas Williams was the first person she saw. Judging by the neatness of his dress—hair tied back in a queue, blue coat, black cravat, black breeches—he had been attending to customers rather than working. "Good day, Mrs. Meadowes," he said, bowing decorously. Then in a whispered undertone he added, "I am relieved to see you safely returned."

"Good day to you, Mr. Williams. I have come to speak to Mr. Blanchard."

He bowed again, more stiffly this time. "I shall tell Mr. Blanchard you are here."

She thought suddenly how solid he looked, with his broad shoulders, silver-buttoned coat, and stocky calves clad in white stockings. How different he was from the languid, elegant, dangerous Pitt. As he turned in she said, "Before you announce my arrival, Mr. Williams, there is something else I should like to ask."

"Very well. What is it?"

Agnes scrutinized a row of snuffboxes in the window, as she tried to calm her conflicting feelings. Williams seemed to be an honest, kindly fellow—but so had her husband when she'd first set eyes on him. She steadied herself and met his gaze. "'Twas nothing of significance," she said casually. "Only today, when I called on Mr. Pitt, he mentioned the subject of marking and duty. Bearing in mind our conversation on that subject last night, can you hazard why?"

William drew his brows together. "Well, as I said, the duty must be paid according to the weight. The rate is sixpence an ounce. On a wine cooler weighing twelve hundred ounces, that would be a considerable sum—thirty pounds. Perhaps Pitt was curious to know whether Theodore had already paid the duty so he could calculate what to ask for its return. Duty would add to the total loss if the wine cooler were not recovered."

"Was it you or Riley who made the wine cooler?" asked Agnes suddenly.

"Mostly it was me, though he helped with some of the first castings."

"And you took it to assay?"

"No. Riley usually goes. He says he likes the change, and I've no inclination to stand in line for an hour if I don't have to."

"Then perhaps Rose Francis's business with Riley had something to do with duty dodging; it might explain her visits to him and why he is reluctant to speak of them. And perhaps it also explains the gold in her possession."

"What gold?"

"One of the maids recalled seeing twenty sovereigns in a purse hidden under her mattress."

This did not seem to surprise him in the least. "Come, come," he said, shaking his head and folding his arms across his chest. "It is surely far-fetched to believe a kitchen maid would be caught up in a matter such as this. If you do not understand the marking system, why should she?"

"Riley could have taught her; if he somehow enticed her to

bring him articles from the Blanchards' house for the marks to be removed and placed on more valuable items, that would explain their discussions. Why else would she have called on him?"

"Hmm," said Thomas Williams uneasily. "It is possible, I suppose. But I confess I do not give it much credence. Blanchards' sells few items more sizable than a salver. The wine cooler is an exception. Besides, even if they did operate such a scheme, how would they profit from it? All the objects made and sold here are listed in the accounts, which Mr. Theodore Blanchard keeps."

"Then perhaps he was involved too." Agnes walked away from the window and gazed at an arrangement of silver candlesticks on a mantel shelf. Even to her, the theory seemed far-fetched. And there was no proof, apart from the visits to Riley and a single salver. Surely, she thought, Rose could not have been embroiled in such an intrigue.

Footsteps sounded on the landing upstairs, a stiff cough wafted down, and Theodore's voice called out, "Mrs. Meadowes? Is that you I hear? What are you doing down there? Williams, bring her to the upstairs showroom forthwith."

THEODORE SLUMPED in a leather armchair by the fire. The same place, thought Agnes, where Noah Prout had been sitting two days earlier when Harry Drake had slit his throat. "Well," he said, waving her in impatiently the minute the door closed behind her. "Come, come, Mrs. Meadowes. Sit down. Tell me, what did Pitt have to say for himself?"

Agnes perched on the edge of a seat. "He gave the impression he was confident of recovering the wine cooler," she said cautiously. "He expects to have news within the next few days. Most significantly, however, he knew without my telling him that the wine cooler was intended for Sir Bartholomew Grey."

"Did he, by Jove? So our suspicions were correct, there is a traitor here."

Agnes nodded. "A traitor is here or *was* here. Mrs. Blanchard suggested Rose Francis's disappearance might have some bearing on the theft, and requested that I should try to find her. I wondered whether tomorrow morning would be an opportune moment to—"

"No, no, no, Mrs. Meadowes," broke in Theodore, thumping his fist on the armrest and shaking his head so violently that his chins wobbled like blancmange. "Let us get one thing clear. I do not wish you to waste time or deliberately divert your attention from what is paramount: namely acting as an intermediary with Mr. Pitt. Moreover, my wife was most concerned that Mrs. Tooley should not be unnecessarily upset. She says I should make only sparing use of your services. Therefore, let us wait to see whether Pitt recovers the wine cooler, then if the traitor is in the vicinity and chasing after him is necessary, Justice Cordingly will decide how best to do it."

"But if Rose Francis was involved in the robbery, she might lead us to the wine cooler without you having to pay to recover it, and Pitt would not profit from his crime," she protested.

Theodore snorted. "Have I not told you clear enough, Mrs. Meadowes? Whether or not the girl was involved is irrelevant. She is gone. She cannot help us. Looking for her will waste time and cause disruption in the household. More importantly, if word reached Pitt he might be inclined to melt down the wine cooler and sell the silver for bullion. I cannot afford to take the risk. If you wish to keep your post you would be wise to remember it."

Agnes turned her head sharply, as if slapped on the cheek. Out the window, a gray fog had descended that half obscured the façades opposite. Elsie's suggestion that the wine cooler might have been melted down rang in her head.

Theodore cleared his throat. "Did Pitt pass any other remark of interest?" he asked.

"He wondered if the wine cooler was marked and the duty paid."

Theodore's eyes bulged. "Duty? *He* mentioned duty? I can scarce credit it! And what did you say?"

"That I assumed it was."

Was Theodore aghast at the implication that such a nefarious practice as duty dodging might have been perpetrated on his premises out of concern for his reputation? Or was he worried that his own involvement in such a scheme might be exposed? "What do you suppose he meant, sir?" Agnes probed warily, curiosity overcoming her trepidation.

"Meant? How in heaven's name should I comprehend the workings of a mind such as Pitt's? Naturally the wine cooler had been properly marked. But that is by the by. So long as he recovers it, that's all that need concern any of us. You included, Mrs. Meadowes."

Chapter Twenty-one

DURING THE MORNING Mrs. Tooley had stood in for Agnes as she had stood in for Mrs. Tooley on so many previous occasions when contagions had struck. A simple dinner had been prepared. The first course comprised soup *à la reine,* chicken stew with celery, fried tripe, and boiled cauliflower; the second course, a wholesome ragout of pig ears, macaroni pie, roast mutton, mushrooms, and cabbage in butter sauce; for dessert there would be jam tartlets and apple pie. Mrs. Tooley had enlisted the help of both Doris and Nancy and they had made a good start. The desserts were prepared, the stew set to simmer, the mutton already darkening on the spit.

With an hour left to complete the rest, Agnes rose to the challenge, which she felt better equipped to handle than consorting with thief takers and street rogues. Turning first to the soup, she picked up a pot containing lean beef and a knuckle of veal, onions, carrots, celery, parsnips, leeks, and a little thyme, which had been simmering for most of the morning. She strained it through a muslin cloth, then thickened it with bread crumbs soaked in boiled cream, half a pound of ground almonds, and the yolks of six hard eggs. She licked her little finger thoughtfully and adjusted the seasoning, while issuing a barrage of further instructions to Doris.

"Water on for the vegetables, then slice up the ears in strips; then baste the joint—careful, mind—so the fat don't catch on the fire."

Cheeks glowing from steam and heat, Agnes wiped a damp hand across her brow, then began on the gravy, adding a pinch of mace and a glassful of claret as the French chef had taught her. She poured the gravy over the sliced ears. "Into the hot cupboard with this, Doris. And then get me the cabbage and cauliflower, please." She basted the mutton with a long-handled spoon, and fried the tripe in a deep pan of lard until it was brown and crisp. She set a pan of mushrooms alongside, and tossed the cabbage leaves in a pan of boiling water and the cauliflower in another. "More cream, Doris. Are the plates warmed?" she called, shaking the mushrooms while tasting the macaroni. "Vegetables need draining. Where are John and Philip?" Without waiting for a reply, she garnished the tripe with parsley and poured the soup into a large tureen. "It's nearly time, Doris."

As if he had heard her, Philip burst in through the door. He had just finished setting the table under the eagle eye of Mr. Matthews, who had chastised him roundly for his carelessness in not keeping the dessert spoons at perfect right angles to the knives and exactly one inch distant from the forks. Philip threw himself into a chair, sighing exaggeratedly, his large muscled legs apart.

"At last, Philip! Sharpen the carving knife, if you please, so Mr. Matthews can carve the mutton," said Agnes, irked by his lack of decorum. "Dear God, the stew must be ready by now. Take it off the heat please, Doris."

Her dress was now sodden with steam, and yet in the midst of all this activity, she found an unlikely sort of peace. The demands of dinner brought solace of a kind. For the time being she could not fret—she had to get on.

COMPARED WITH the clutter of Mrs. Tooley's parlor, the butler's pantry was an altogether more spartan, less homely place. There were no colorful samplers or seascapes, no saucers or teacups, or ornaments on the mantelpiece, apart from a single uncolored engraving of George II in his coronation robes. There was a silver cupboard, which was always kept locked; a table upon which Theodore's and Nicholas's clothes and the menservants' liveries were pressed; a lead-lined sink where the footmen washed the glasses; a wooden horse, where sundry articles were dried; and three wooden chairs.

But Mr. Matthews's surroundings were not devoid of decoration. Unrolled and laid out on the table beside him, weighted down with two dessert knives and a lump of beeswax, was a gaudily colored print of the king displayed half unclad, clutching a string of German sausages and engaged in the clumsy seduction of Lady Yarmouth.

Mrs. Blanchard had instructed him to make a tally of the silver to ensure nothing was missing. He saw no reason not to lighten the task with occasional glances at something a little more entertaining. He subscribed to a nearby print shop which provided a loan of these salacious images for a modest tuppence a week. Mr. Matthews had counted the knives (sixty-eight) and forks (fifty-four) without incident. He had just reached the twenty-second spoon when John barged in wanting candles to replenish the sconces in the hallway. The sudden gust of wind that came with him blew the print onto the floor. Mr. Matthews started guiltily, recovered the print, and had begun to roll it up before he realized it was only John. "You!" he exclaimed. "See what you made me do!"

But once the door was firmly closed behind him, he said in a more convivial manner, "Take a look at this, dear boy, and tell me if you ever set eyes on anything half so droll before."

The two of them shared guffaws and exclamations at the parted thighs, the unbuttoned breeches, the dog running off with the king's garter. The butler sneezed and wiped his nose, shaking his venerable head. The distraction had caused him to forget his count of the spoons. He replaced them hurriedly in their box, locked it, and returned it to the silver cabinet. He poured a bottle of port through a silver funnel into a cut-glass decanter, resolved to allay Mrs. Blanchard's fears and tell her the silver was untouched. She would be none the wiser.

Just then the curvaceous figure of Agnes Meadowes appeared on his threshold. She was surprised to find the atmosphere so jovial. The butler's face fell; he slapped the print upside down on the table.

"Excuse me, sir," she ventured with an apologetic smile, "may I have a word alone?"

"I am engaged, as you can see."

"It is a matter Mrs. Blanchard has asked me to discuss with you," said Agnes, not entirely truthfully.

Mr. Matthews heaved a sigh and turned to John. "Best be off with those candles then, eh." John grabbed a handful from the box and left.

"Well, Mrs. Meadowes, what can I do for you?"

"Mrs. Blanchard believes Rose might have had some involvement with the murder and robbery. She has asked me to discover what I can of her whereabouts."

Mr. Matthews hesitated, sucking in his haggard cheeks. "And you suppose *I* know the answer to that, do you?"

"Of course not, only you may unwittingly know something that will shed light on it."

Mr. Matthews tutted with disapproval and returned to his decanting. "Well, I grant you it would provide a reason for her running off. But it seems implausible to me. A woman could not have carried off something so heavy."

"She might have called upon an assistant."

For a minute or two he said nothing, and Agnes noticed how deftly his long, slender fingers cradled the bottle and delicately supported the funnel. Plainly, she thought, he has yet to sample the contents, or his hand would not be so steady. When the last sediment-free drop was safely poured, he turned to her. "Whom have you in mind?"

"Mr. Riley—the journeyman next door."

Mr. Matthews looked unconvinced. "I doubt Rose had anything to do with the robbery. There is a far simpler reason for her departure, in my opinion."

"What, then?"

"Guilt," said the butler flatly. "Have you forgotten that she stole the pistol from Mr. Blanchard's room?"

"I have not forgotten its loss. But can we be certain it was she who took it? And if so, what was her motive for the theft?"

"I told you, I saw her upstairs on Monday morning while you were out at market. She had a furtive manner; she must have taken it then."

"You implied before that her sorties upstairs were because she engaged in intimacies with Nicholas Blanchard."

"I was not aware then that the gun was missing," replied Mr. Matthews smoothly. "Besides, one misdemeanor does not preclude the other."

No, thought Agnes, but it stretches credibility, and Philip—an undoubted expert in such matters—had said there was nothing between the pair. "Perhaps not." She nodded. "Although I would hazard Rose did not run away because she took the pistol. Rather the reverse—she took the pistol *because* she was running away."

"Come, come, Mrs. Meadowes, surely you are splitting hairs. Whatever way you turn it, the girl was guilty as sin."

Agnes bit her lip, an obstinate gleam in her eyes. "Apart from Monday, did you see Rose upstairs on other occasions?"

"No, but Nancy did—and gave proof of it, too."

Agnes presumed he was referring to the letter. "Might not something quite innocent have taken her upstairs? Perhaps she wanted to speak to the master or mistress on some matter."

"What concerns might a kitchen maid have had that she could not discuss with me or Mrs. Tooley—or you even?"

Heaven knows, thought Agnes. But suppose Rose had had a personal matter that bothered her? Would she have discussed it with an ailing spinster housekeeper, or an elderly butler, or an introverted cook who shut herself off and knew so little of the ways of love? Perhaps Rose *had* tried to seek out Mrs. Blanchard, as she herself had done, hoping that her mistress might view her predicament more sympathetically. That might explain why she had questioned Patsy about Mrs. Blanchard's comings and goings—she did not want Patsy's position, only a moment or two alone with her mistress.

Mr. Matthews was pondering too. "Now I think on it, I recall that one time Nancy caught her upstairs, Rose was carrying away a small silver salver. It was the one from the hallway upon which visiting cards are presented. She wouldn't have done that if she was so innocent, would she?"

"When was this?"

"A week or so ago."

"Did you confront her?"

"Naturally. She said she was not taking it away but putting it back. Riley had repaired it and had given it to her to return. She said that Nancy was a liar and was only trying to get her into trouble because Philip preferred her. And I need not think she was sweet on Philip, for she wasn't; they were friends and no more than that. The impudence of her manner, I'm sorry to say, was not unusual. When I checked the story with Riley, he backed her up. And that made me suspect there was something between them. I contemplated telling her there and then that there was no place for such insolence, but Mrs. Tooley begged me not to, saying you and she would never manage without her."

How likely was it that Nancy had really found the letter in the drawing room, *and* seen Rose with the salver, *and* discovered the cache of money under her mattress? The menservants came and went upstairs, yet had seen nothing. Doris, who shared a bedroom with Nancy and Rose, had not seen the purse. Plainly Rose was capable of untruths—she had lied brazenly over her friendship with Philip. But was Nancy lying too, in the hope of discrediting Rose, whom she hated, in the eyes of Mrs. Tooley? She probed Mr. Matthews further. "Was it the same salver that was left out on the dresser last night?"

"Yes," said Mr. Matthews. "Philip is prone to almost as many lapses as your Rose. He brought it down yesterday to polish and carelessly forgot to put it back. I have already reprimanded him most sternly." He paused. "It was a pity you did not take a similarly strong line with Rose."

"I did not need to," said Agnes. "She went anyway." Then, embarrassed by her boldness, she curtsied hurriedly and returned to her kitchen.

Chapter Twenty-two

WHEN THE TIDE WAS LOW, one could often find things of value a few yards out from the steps at Three Cranes Wharf. A bucket of coal, a handful of nails (copper ones were best), a piece of rag, a foot of rope, or a few bones washed down from the abattoir—such riches awaited anyone willing to scratch about the rubbish-strewn mudflats of the River Thames. The most fruitful place was the most precarious: between the moorings, beyond the shoals, where the retreating tide etched small channels that intersected like the frayed fibers of old rope. Those who ventured here trod with care, for there were quicksands and channels that could pull a person down and drown him before he had time to call out. One day it might be safe to scrabble in a certain spot; the next, the river's course would shift with the wind and tide. This was where Elsie Drake had come.

She walked toward the receding water that was whipped by the stiff wind into angry peaks and troughs. Wading barefoot through the noxious slime, she avoided the bricks and sharp stones, her head hunched forward, thin shoulders bent double, hair streaming in the wind. She carried a willow basket on her back and a stick in her hand. Being accustomed to the dangers, she advanced slowly, poking the stick in the mud ahead, testing the firmness and feeling for anything hidden beneath it.

This time, however, Elsie's search was not for the usual flotsam. Mrs. Meadowes's question regarding the woman in a blue dress had triggered her recollection of an event she had witnessed and then forgotten. On Monday night, the night of the robbery, Elsie had come down to the river at low tide before dawn in search of coal. A woman had cried out, then stumbled and fallen down the steps. Elsie had seen her pick herself up, gather her possessions, and run off over the mud. It had been too dark to see the color of her dress, but not too dark to observe the figure pursuing her—a tall man. Assuming that they were lovers having a tiff, or that the woman was a whore who had tried to fleece him, Elsie had thought little of the episode at the time. But Agnes had reminded her.

Elsie had worked herself into an almighty stew over Agnes Meadowes. The minute their discussion on London Bridge was over, she kicked herself for initiating it. Agnes's promise meant nothing. Why would she keep quiet about seeing Elsie outside Blanchards' and again at Marcus Pitt's? Why had Elsie foolishly run after her and begged (so far as she was capable of begging) for her silence? Why had she confirmed her father's involvement? It was all down to the charity Agnes had shown her. Few servants deigned to give Elsie a kindly look, let alone three farthings. But Elsie now saw that she had given Agnes the opportunity to trick and betray her!

Nothing prevented Agnes from handing her and her father over to the justice. So one way or another, her pa would hang, and she would most likely be transported. After dwelling on this for several hours, a means of altering her fate came to her. What if the woman she had seen running over the mud was the same one Agnes was asking after? It was the same night, after all, and very few people were out at that hour. What exactly the woman meant to Agnes, Elsie was uncertain, but cunning told her that she was important. And that being so, if Elsie could find some evidence of her, she might use it to keep Agnes quiet.

When Elsie had last seen the woman, she had been running over the mud near the grounded barges, and had dropped her bag. Elsie was not certain whether or not she had recovered it. It had been too gloomy to see. But if the bag *was* still there, its contents might serve her very well.

Ignoring the freezing water and oozing mud, and the salty spume whipped in her face by the north wind, she stepped toward the dark hulks where she had lost sight of the woman. Three boats were moored side by side, ropes dangling over their hulls like garlands on a door. She saw no watchman, but for once, Elsie made no attempt to filch the ropes. Instead she began prodding the riverbed with her stick. The water in most places was still six inches deep, although here and there sandbars protruded like smooth gray islands. She walked slowly, stooping down, when the stick met resistance, to grope in the muddy slush. Then she poked again.

Half an hour later, her basket was a quarter full with sodden wood and coal, but she had found no trace of the bag. Knowing that she did not have long before others came, Elsie walked back toward a spit of mud beyond the barges. There her stick struck something soft. Elsie took a board from her basket and used it to scoop away the mud. At first she saw nothing, but as she dug deeper she could see a patch of silt-encrusted black cloth. She began to scoop out a wider circle, revealing a larger expanse of the cloth. But then came a disturbing flash of something mottled and purplish-gray.

Elsie squinted down, uncertain, fearful, yet hopeful, then wiped at the mud with her numb fingers. She excavated around the object, examined it closely, then nodded and knelt back on her heels. Her pulse was pounding. It was not the bag, but a body.

She had uncovered the tip of a finger. After ten more minutes of careful excavation, Elsie had revealed most of the corpse. It was clad as Agnes had described, in a blue dress and black cloak of middling quality. Her hair was chestnut brown but tangled with mud and grit. Her lips were puffed and purplish black; her mouth, nostrils, and eyes filled with mud.

Not far away from her claw of a left hand lay the bag. It was made from brown canvas with letters stenciled in black upon the side, but Elsie could not read them. She had seen plenty of bodies before in the dingy parts of the city she inhabited. Without pausing to consider how the woman had died, Elsie deftly unbuckled the bag and found inside several items of clothing. Then turning back to the corpse, she unlaced its boots and tugged them off, then briskly unfastened the bindings of the cloak and, grasping one edge, yanked on it. As the body rolled onto its side and then tipped back again, Elsie saw that it had been slashed across the neck. The wound was so ingrained with silt that she had not seen it at first, but moving the body had made the head loll back, revealing a long incision so deep the head seemed to be hanging on by the merest thread. There was no sign of blood—presumably it had all been washed away. Instead the flesh had a strange, inhuman, spongy appearance.

Elsie had seen several bodies hauled out of the river before, but never one so brutally damaged. She was surprised how much the sight disturbed her. Presumably the man she had seen chasing the woman that night had done this. She considered reporting her discovery to Agnes. Perhaps the murderer would be caught and punished for his wickedness. But Agnes might force her to give up the clothes and boots. Elsie glanced down at her feet, bluer than the lips of the corpse. She would keep the boots and reckoned that if she dried the other clothes, the ragman might give her enough for them to save her from having to scavenge here for most of the winter.

Elsie then turned her attention to the laces of the bodice. Once the skirt was off, she felt in the pockets and found them empty save for a small black heart-shaped object. A brisk rubbing revealed it to be a small silver box decorated with leaves and flowers. Elsie opened the lid, which was engraved inside with some writing—the woman's name, she guessed. Here was all she needed to weave a tale for Agnes.

She glanced back to the riverbank and against an angry yellowish sky could see a straggling line of five or six people standing on the mudflats, peering in her direction. From their present position they would not be able to make out the body, but once they approached and saw what it was, they would want to know what she had found on it. If they discovered her haul, they would force her to share it; or, worse, they might try and steal it from her.

She stuffed the silver box down inside her clothes until it rested safely on the waistband of her skirt. She tipped the coal and wood chips out of her basket and packed in the clothes and boots, pressing them down as far as she could, then covering them with a layer of coal and wood. The task took no more than a minute or two. Using her board, Elsie hastily began covering the corpse and bag with mud and she smoothed it over until she was satisfied her excavations were no longer visible. For good measure, she scattered the surface with a few bricks and stones.

She slung her basket on her back and forced herself to walk slowly and miserably back toward the bank as if she had found only coal and bones and wood chips.

None of the other river finders said a word, save Marge, the oldest and most garrulous, who was picking over some empty crates close to the steps. A mud-stained lantern with a broken glass was tied around her waist with a piece of string. "Get anything?" she inquired as Elsie trudged past.

"Nought special."

"You're back up quickly, then." Marge's eye darted over Elsie's basket. "You wouldn't be back 'less you'd got summat."

"Hush, I ain't got nothing. Hand on heart I ain't."

"Yes you 'ave. Show old Marge now. Ain't I been good to you, letting you share my fire? What is it you got?"

Elsie shivered as a gust of wind stabbed through her thin bodice. She looked glumly at her feet. "Went out an hour ago, found a load of wood wedged under one of them boats," she mumbled. "Won't all go in the basket. Thought I'd go back once I'd got rid of this."

"Where?" whispered Marge, taking hold of Elsie's elbow.

"Don't say nothing to the others."

"Not a word."

Elsie pointed wordlessly toward the barge farthest away from the spit where the corpse was buried. Several others nearby must have heard snippets of their conversation; two or three trudged off in the direction she had indicated. She shuffled up the steps; she suddenly did not feel the chill wind or her damp clothes or her icy feet. It would be a long time, she thought, before she would have to poke about in the mud again. She had boots to wear, clothes to sell, and the means to keep Agnes Meadowes quiet.

Chapter Twenty-three

I T WAS SOON AFTER eleven o'clock when Agnes set out to market next morning. Elsie Drake was lingering on the corner of Foster Lane and Cheapside. "You still after the woman with the blue dress?" she queried, popping out of a dark doorway and giving Agnes such a fright she nearly dropped her basket.

"Yes," said Agnes breathlessly, surreptitiously checking her purse was still in her pocket. "Have you remembered something about her? Did you see her, after all?"

"Better'n that," said Elsie proudly, "I've got summat to show you." She turned her back on Agnes, and rummaging among the grimy folds of her skirt, extracted an object wrapped in a square of hessian. She unfolded the cloth, and with hand outstretched, she spun round for Agnes to see.

A small blackened heart-shaped box engraved with leaves and flowers lay upon Elsie's hand. "What's this? Where did you find it?" asked Agnes.

"I didn't find it. She gave it me to show you."

"*Who* gave it to you?"

This was not the reaction Elsie had expected. "That woman in the blue dress, the one you asked after. Take it an' 'ave a look—it's got some writing on it. Her name, I'll be bound."

Agnes took the box. She saw that it was made from silver and contained a perforated grill. It was a vinaigrette, in which a lady might keep her smelling salts. Engraved upon the inside of the lid were the words *Forever Yours*. Nothing that linked the box to Rose. "Where is she?" said Agnes distractedly. She did not give the girl's tale much credence—if her father was a thief, she could easily get her hands on some valuable trinket like this and pretend it was Rose's.

"That I can't say."

"What d'you mean, you can't say? You must know, if she gave this to you. If it *is* hers."

Elsie regarded her feet. "She told me not to let on," she mumbled. "Made me give my word."

"So you have spoken to her?" said Agnes sharply. "What exactly did she say?"

Elsie kept her head bowed. "Just that I was to show you this—a sign she's well. She knows you're looking for her, and says she wants you to stop. She says she don't want no one from Blanchards' bothering her now, however fond they may be of her. But if you've a message from time to time, you might pass it to me to convey."

Agnes looked again at the box. The outside was filthy, but she was struck by the beauty and delicacy of the decoration. She could see it was valuable, not the sort of thing a kitchen maid might own. And even if something so precious did belong to Rose, why would she entrust it to such a disreputable urchin as Elsie?

Looking down, Agnes was startled to see that where before the girl had always been barefoot, now she was wearing a pair of stout brown leather boots that seemed a little large. "I don't believe Rose told you any such thing," she said sternly. "She and I were not friends. She would not send me messages, or expect to receive them from me. She worked as a kitchen maid. How would she have something like this in her possession? And why would she send it to me?"

Elsie looked surprised and disappointed. "You deaf or summat? That's what I said. I said she's had enough with you. She don't want nothing more to do with you . . . And you ain't keeping that box—she only wanted me to show it to you." She made a sudden lunge, but by some miracle Agnes anticipated her.

Agnes clenched her fist and raised it over her head. "I'll keep hold of this, if you don't mind. You can tell Rose it's safe with me. And tell me, by the by, where did you come by those boots?" She clasped Elsie by her bony shoulder, forcing her to meet her gaze. "You stole this, and those boots too I wager. They *are* Rose's, even if this isn't. You stole from me once before." She brought her face close to the girl's. "And just now you tried to do the same. Now unless you want me to call the constable, tell me where Rose is and when you robbed her."

The girl could not hide a flicker of shock. "I never robbed her."

"Then let us call a constable to ask the same question. He might well take you to the Round House. And while he's at it have your father arrested."

"But you promised you'd keep him out of it." Elsie tried to squirm from her grasp.

Agnes tightened her grip. "What makes you think I am any more trustworthy than you? Tell me where you came by those boots and this box, or I'll send for the constable directly."

"I never robbed her. What makes you say I robbed her?"

Agnes called out to an errand boy a few yards away. "Boy! Here's tuppence if you run now and fetch the constable. This creature just tried to rob me of my silver box. I'll see to it she's taken before the justice and branded."

"I never! She's tricked me up! I give her the box and she's gone mad."

"'Course you did," said the lad, winking at Agnes. "An' I'm Dick Turpin back from the dead, and I just gave her a sovereign to boot."

With this, the weakness of her situation seemed to dawn on

Elsie. She stopped struggling. "I'll give you the lot if it's what you want. But you're a bitch an' a half to take it off me."

Agnes ignored the insult. "So you robbed her of more, did you? I want nothing except for you to tell me what you know. Where is Rose?"

"I never robbed her, and you won't never speak to her," said Elsie, half spitting the words.

"Why not?"

"She's dead. I found her."

There was silence for a minute, after which the lad began tugging at Agnes's basket. "So, ma'am, am I going for the constable or not?"

Agnes handed him a penny. "No. Now be off with you." She turned back to Elsie and tried to steady her voice. "Where is she?"

"Down on the mudflats. Near the barge mooring at Three Cranes Wharf. I found her yesterday at low tide. She was buried. I uncovered her."

"Dear God! She must have fallen into the river and drowned."

"No. Her throat was slit from ear to ear."

Agnes felt faint and a bitter taste rose into her throat. But she knew that Elsie was a slippery customer who would run off if she gave her an inch, so she focused on getting more information out of her. "I suppose you also found her twenty sovereigns. I take it that was the reason for your reluctance to reveal this discovery?"

"No, there was not a penny on her. I swear."

Agnes was unconvinced. "I do not want the money, Elsie—so far as I am concerned, even if it was a hundred guineas you might keep it. Just tell me frankly how much there was. Remember the constable, Elsie. Remember your father."

"I told you. I still got the clothes, if you want to see. But there was no money."

Agnes could see she would get no further. "What else did you find—a pistol and a bag, perchance?"

"The bag was there," said Elsie, "but no pistol. Although I think I saw her drop it and pick it up. It's my guess the man chasing after her nabbed it. And the money, too."

Agnes was taken aback. "You saw her? When? What man?"

"I never saw much, but he were tallish and dressed in a cloak, with long dark hair tied back in a queue, and he ran like the blazes . . ."

Chapter Twenty-four

AGNES WAS THROWN INTO a state of unusual indecision. A murder had been committed. She could hardly leave the poor girl's body to rot in the mud. But if she observed convention and told the justice, he would demand to know how she had made the discovery and she would have to declare Elsie's involvement. The girl's pathetic attempts at deception had infuriated Agnes, but she had no real desire to see her apprehended.

In the market, Agnes drifted blindly. She was scarcely aware of whether the pears she purchased were worm-eaten or the cardoons stringy; she neglected to squeeze the mutton for tenderness, nor did she ascertain whether the eels were as lively as she required.

Returning to Foster Lane, Agnes was so engrossed that the faces she passed were invisible to her. It was only when a firm hand clutched her elbow that she realized that someone was addressing her.

"Mrs. Meadowes, might I have a word? Mrs. Meadowes, did you hear me? Are you quite well? Has something distressed you?"

"What? Oh, Mr. Williams," said Agnes, blinking vaguely. "Forgive me, but I didn't hear you. My mind was in another place entirely."

"So I see," said Thomas Williams with a forlorn half smile.

Agnes spoke without her usual caution. "My apologies, sir. I meant no insult. To tell the truth, I have just had a great shock."

"What on earth was it?"

Agnes gave him a full account—her encounter with Elsie, and how the girl had spotted Rose running over the mudflats on the night of the robbery, and had just found her body buried there in the mud. She confessed uncertainty as to what to do, now having promised to keep Elsie out of trouble. Then she showed him the silver heart-shaped box.

"Elsie says she discovered this upon Rose's person. Lord knows how she came by it. Do you think Riley might have given it to her?"

"Good God!" said Thomas. He gave the box a cursory look and ran the flat of his thumb over the engraving. "I should doubt it. Riley doesn't strike me as the kind to give her such a thing. Perhaps it was a gift from a past paramour." Then, he colored and altered tack. "If Drake was responsible for the death of the apprentice, where is the wrong in having him apprehended?"

"If I do so, I will punish Elsie as well. She has no other family; so she would be an orphan and have to choose between the workhouse and the street. Surely it is better to have a parent, however deficient, than none at all?"

"Perhaps," said Thomas Williams uncertainly. "But that doesn't alter the fact that her father is a murderer and she is his assistant."

Agnes did not doubt Drake was the thief, but something in Elsie's description had shaken her conviction that he was the killer. Rather than voice this uncertainty, she concentrated on an argument that she knew held weight. "If Marcus Pitt hears we know the culprit is one of his men, there is every chance he will melt down the wine cooler, in which case Mr. Blanchard will be ruined and we will all suffer. But I cannot, in all conscience, leave Rose's body in the mud to rot without a decent burial."

"Rest assured, Mrs. Meadowes," said Thomas Williams. "But I hold that if Drake slit Noah Prout's throat, you cannot describe him merely as deficient—he is evil, and should be punished. I pity anyone with such a man for a father. Do you think he killed Rose too?"

She would have to confess her thoughts. "Prout and Rose met identical deaths—their throats were slit, which suggests the same hand murdered them. But I don't believe Drake murdered Rose. Elsie said she saw a man chasing Rose, but if it had been her father, she surely would have recognized him and said nothing. It follows then that Drake did not kill the apprentice either. Which means that the murderer must be someone else—most likely the person in the Blanchards' employ who involved Pitt and Drake in the first place."

"Do you trust the girl?"

Agnes shook her head. "Truth is not a commodity Elsie holds in high regard."

"Then do not allow her to deflect you into forming unsound theories."

"My instinct tells me she isn't lying in this instance, and I don't believe my theories *are* unsound."

Williams scratched his corkscrew curls. "But murder is a matter for the law to resolve."

"Quite," said Agnes. "How do I inform the justice of Rose's murder without letting Elsie's identity be known, thus causing the wine cooler to be lost forever?"

After a lengthy silence, Thomas Williams's jerked his head up. "I believe I have the resolution."

"What, then?"

"*I* will tell the constable that I saw the body. I will say I was walking past the river at low tide and caught sight of something that appeared to be the body of a woman lying on the mud, surrounded by river scavengers. The reason for my particular anxiety is that I have heard a kitchen maid is missing from this household."

Agnes had not known what to do; now Williams had provided her with a workable solution. But should she trust him? He was, after all, a man. "You are most charitable, Mr. Williams, but I hesitate to accept. Your intervention might result in you enduring unexpected inconveniences. I should manage the matter myself."

"What is life if we don't occasionally engage ourselves in the lives of others and offer our assistance?" he said stoutly. "Besides, I have an hour to spare, and don't want to be cast out without a job any more than you do. Perhaps you should keep this. I am quite certain Rose would have wanted you to have it."

He thrust the box back into Agnes's hand and before she had time to object, he raised his hat, bowed, and strode off in search of the constable. Just before he disappeared from view around the corner, he called over his shoulder, "Listen for the door this evening. I will come to tell you what passes."

THE SERVANTS ATE their last meal of the day at around eight, two hours or so before the upstairs supper was served. Upper and lower servants ate at the kitchen table in strict order: Mr. Matthews at the head, Mrs. Tooley on his right, Patsy on his left, Agnes beside Mrs. Tooley, and then the others strung out in descending order like pearls on a necklace, with Doris at the farthest end. Usually the downstairs meal was a simple affair of ale, cold meats, bread, and reheated leftovers. Tonight there were two quarts of ale, cold brawn in jelly, cold mutton, a piece of cheese, a loaf of bread, and a dish of warm cauliflower.

It was Mr. Matthews's or Mrs. Tooley's habit to lead the conversation, to prevent an unholy row ensuing. There were times when one of the lower servants spoke out of turn, but provided the butler had not sampled too much wine, it was more likely than not they would be sternly rebuked for it.

But this evening, no sooner had Mrs. Tooley asked Mr.

Matthews why a constable had called than the news of Rose's death was out and the table was in uproar.

"Oh, my heavens!" said Mrs. Tooley, crossing herself. "Who ever would have thought it?"

"Her throat was slit from ear to ear and hanging by a thread?" echoed Doris, looking pale.

"And was there nothing about her person?" asked Nancy. "No letters, nor nothing to show where she was headed off to?"

"It seems," said Mr. Matthews portentously, "she was stripped of all her possessions save her chemise and petticoat."

"'Tis a crying shame, that's what it is," said Philip in a tone entirely devoid of his usual flirtatious sparkle.

"Hear, hear," echoed John.

Mr. Matthews passed no disparaging remark, but Agnes thought that he, too, seemed uncommonly upset.

"What a horror!" said Patsy, resting her long thin fingers against her cheek. "Though one cannot say it is entirely unexpected. To go off in the middle of the night, unprotected, is to invite calamity."

"Most likely she wasn't unprotected," said Nancy flatly. "She had the pistol. Ain't that nor her bag been found, Mr. M.?"

"I haven't heard. No doubt some guttersnipe has sold it for a few shillings when at the very least it should have fetched five guineas."

"All this talk has quite unraveled me. I feel a headache coming on," whispered Mrs. Tooley. "Perhaps you would kindly all excuse me."

DESPITE THE DRAMATIC REVELATIONS, the servants attacked the day's final duties with military precision. Having departed earlier, Mrs. Tooley was unable to help Agnes and Doris get the dishes ready for upstairs. Patsy went off to tidy Lydia's dressing table and put out her nightdress. John and Philip, loaded with buckets of coal, replenished the fires in the drawing room, library, and dining room, then changed into their evening regalia for serving supper. Nancy took three copper warming pans filled with hot coals and three new candles to the Blanchards' bedrooms. She drew the velvet curtains, turned down the beds, folding a precise triangle of linen sheet over each eiderdown, stoked the bedroom fires (lit by Philip earlier in the afternoon), and ensured the chamber pots were all in the night tables.

Mr. Matthews, meanwhile, put Nicholas's nightshirt and cap to warm, and set out the things for his toilette next morning. He folded the towels neatly and laid out the razor, soap, and badger-bristle shaving brush. He ran a finger round the washbowl to make sure there was no trace of scum, then conveyed several items of clothing to his pantry for John to brush and press.

This done, he turned to the more pleasurable duties of the dining room. Proudly, with all the pomp and majesty of a royal attendant, he placed a decanter of claret on a silver salver and bore it upstairs. Setting it gently on the side table, he trimmed the wicks of the lighted wall sconces, and lit the candles of the candelabra. He then bellowed down the back stairs to John and Philip to get a move on and took up his position by the door, ready to summon the family.

During these preparations, a steady downpour began to thrash the windows. Agnes looked up from the supper trays at the fat drops streaking the glass and shivered. Just then there was a hesitant tapping at the kitchen door. "Shall I see who it is?" asked Doris.

"No," said Agnes, stepping in front and blushing furiously, for she was certain it must be Thomas Williams and was anxious to avoid arousing gossip and speculation. "I'll see to it. Leave the butter and go quickly to the scullery now and make a start on those pots. I shall manage quite well here."

Agnes opened the door. Thomas Williams was not alone. Her jaw dropped, yet no words came.

"Well, Mrs. Meadowes," he said, "that's a strange welcome on a very nasty night. If you can think of nothing to say, perhaps we could come in and sit down until you do. I found my companion on your doorstep. He's quite drenched through—and in urgent need of warmth and food, I'd hazard."

Feeling the blood receding from her cheeks as she spoke, Agnes murmured, "You had best both come in."

Chapter Twenty-five

"PETER!" Agnes scooped her bedraggled son to her bosom. "What on earth has happened? How did you arrive here?" The round-cheeked, raisin-eyed ten-year-old was bleached with cold. His dark curly hair (which closely resembled his mother's) was plastered to his head, and rain dripped from his sodden clothing in puddles on the floor.

Between spasms of coughing and shivering, he explained. "Mrs. Catchpole's condition got worse. Her sister was too busy with looking after her to have the bother of me, and said I'd have to go to you. So she put me on the coach and paid the driver's lad to bring me to Foster Lane. But when we arrived at the Strand he was taken over by thirst and said I could make my own way, I only had to follow my nose, a simpleton could manage it."

"The scoundrel! The rogue!" said Agnes, pink with outrage. "To abandon a defenseless child beggars belief. What wouldn't I like to do to such a man . . ."

"You're not angry with me, Ma? I was afraid I might get you into trouble, so I waited outside the door until this man arrived and forced me in with him."

Agnes stroked his damp head and dropped a quick kiss on his crown. "Angry with you? Not a bit of it, child. Only furious with those that should know better," she said, marching to the butler's pantry to fetch a large brown blanket. She kissed the top of his head again, then stripped his wet clothing, wrapped him up so that only his thin neck and head and spindly ankles were visible, and told him to sit in a large high-backed chair. "When did you last eat?"

"I'd a cup of milk this morning."

"Poor child, you must be famished. I've some strong broth I'll warm, and you must have some toast."

"Thank you, Ma," said Peter, sitting up tall to watch his mother's bustle.

Agnes was in the midst of buttering a thick slice of toast when Mrs. Tooley entered the kitchen in search of a spoon for her elixir. The housekeeper was dressed in her nightgown and her hair dangled down over one shoulder in a stringy plait of pewter gray. She rammed her pince-nez in position and shot an incredulous look at Thomas Williams and the child wrapped in a horsehair blanket seated close to the fire. Bewildered eyes moved to Agnes, whose face seemed to radiate greater warmth than she had ever seen before. In contrast, Mrs. Tooley's pale complexion turned as gray as her plait. "Mrs. Meadowes," she said in a faltering voice, "I should not need to remind you of all people that servants in this house are strictly prohibited visitors of any kind! This man does not belong here. Neither does this child. I trust you can provide some proper explanation for their presence and that they will be on their way forthwith. You know I am unwell. How could you commit such a transgression? I really had thought—"

"May I introduce Mr. Thomas Williams," said Agnes, breaking in. "He is one of Mr. Blanchard's journeymen. He brings information pertaining to Rose and the missing wine cooler. You know I am helping to recover it."

Mrs. Tooley seemed only slightly appeased. Her head oscillated on her neck like a wind-shivered leaf. "And the child? Is it his?"

Agnes ladled a little warm soup into a cup. "No. Mr. Williams rescued him from the doorstep and brought him here because he had nowhere else to go," she said. She handed the bowl to Peter, but upset by Mrs. Tooley, he shook his head and hung his hands by his sides, and refused to take it.

"He rescued him from the doorstep? Then may I ask, Mr. Williams, what gave you the impression this kitchen doubles as an orphanage or hospital for foundlings?"

Crimson now, Agnes took up the spoon and tried to coax a little of the hot liquor into her son's mouth.

"Of course I never thought that for a moment, madam," replied Thomas Williams, avoiding Agnes's eye. "I was only trying to help. The child is well cared for, but has somehow contrived to lose himself. I thought we might provide him with a little shelter and then ascertain where he belongs."

"Your philanthropy is most commendable, sir," said Mrs. Tooley, drawing herself up and contracting her lips as though she were sipping vinegar. "But what gives you the right to pursue it in my kitchen? No doubt he's brought lice and all manner of vermin in with him. Doris will have to scrub the whole place with caustic tomorrow."

She turned to Peter. "If you know what's good for you, boy, you'll take your clothes and leave. Otherwise I shall be forced to send one of the footmen out for the watch."

"No! I won't allow it," said Agnes. "If he goes, so will I."

"I beg your pardon? Mrs. Meadowes, have you taken leave of your senses? What concern of yours is this urchin?"

"He is my son. The woman who has charge of him is ill and, being unable to care for him, has returned him to me. I will not have him sent out into the rain. I repeat, if he goes, so too will I."

Mrs. Tooley gave a gasp and seemed to sway on her feet. She put out one hand to steady herself, and raised the other to her brow. When she spoke again, her voice had dropped an octave. "Of course, the hair, those eyes—I should have known. How could I not have guessed!"

While she now comprehended the predicament, Mrs. Tooley

was too entrenched in her habits to see how she might allow an inch of leeway; yet unaccountably, she felt uncomfortable imposing what she knew to be right. "The fact that he is yours does not mean he can stay here," she said, fumbling for her salts.

"But what would you have me do, Mrs. Tooley? Send him to the workhouse or out into the street?"

Mrs. Tooley sniffed her salts loudly. "That is for you to decide, Mrs. Meadowes," she murmured feebly. "But whatever you choose, you will have to do something this night or I shall be taken ill, and then the matter will reach upstairs and we shall all have the devil to pay. And now, if you'll excuse me I think I must lie down. I feel an attack coming on."

Agnes lowered herself stiffly into a chair just as Peter began to cry. Thin whimpering sobs racked his little body and turned his smooth complexion an angry red.

"There, there," said Thomas Williams, patting the child on the back with gauche kindness. "It ain't so bad. Your ma won't leave you at the workhouse or out in the cold. 'Course she won't. Anyway, I believe I have the answer to the problem."

"What's that?" said Agnes, rubbing Peter's wet curls with a dishcloth.

"My landlady, Mrs. Sharp, lives two streets away, on Bread Street. Her husband is a sea captain who is away for months at a stretch. She has a child of her own, who is seven years of age, and I warrant she would be quite willing for a short while to look after Peter. I will make the introductions if you wish."

Agnes could have wept for joy. But she had noticed that this was the second dilemma Thomas Williams had solved for her that day. Why would he take such trouble over someone he barely knew? To ingratiate himself into her favor for some improper purpose of his own? Her wariness remained, but for all this, she could not refuse his proposal. "Thank you, Mr. Williams. If your landlady is truly willing to take Peter, I would be most grateful," she said stiffly. Then, to cover her embarrassment, she rubbed

Peter's head so vigorously with the cloth that he protested and wriggled away. Agnes let him go. The chance to see her son more regularly brought her a surge of pleasure. She flashed a smile over Peter's head at Thomas Williams. "I can pay ten shillings a week, will that suffice?"

He smiled back hesitatingly. "Come and discuss it with her now."

Chapter Twenty-six

A GNES WALKED OUT with Peter to one side of her and Thomas Williams to the other. The rain had eased, but the light from houses and shops streaked the wet streets. A keen northeast wind had begun to blow.

"I gather the constable found Rose's corpse," said Agnes quietly to Thomas as they strode the short distance to his lodgings. "He paid the Blanchards a visit this afternoon."

"Yes," returned Thomas in a subdued tone. "I accompanied him and showed him the place you described. He ordered the ground to be dug up and we found her without difficulty. I was able to identify the body."

"What condition was she in?"

Williams shook his head as if the memory were one he would sooner forget. "You would not have liked to see her," he said quietly. "She was badly disfigured by mud and water, stripped by scavengers of all her clothing save her undergarments."

Agnes clutched Peter's frail hand tighter in hers. "Unless we understand why she left Foster Lane that night, I cannot see how we will unravel her death. I did think before that a man must lie behind it, and that her going off was quite separate from the robbery. But the fact that the apprentice and Rose were both killed in the same way suggests a link between them."

"It is possible, I suppose, that she somehow assisted in the robbery and was killed after serving her purpose," said Williams.

"Duty dodging may have played a part," returned Agnes. "Mr. Matthews told me Rose was caught handling a salver without any convincing excuse—the same one that you examined."

"Hmm. I should say an affair of the heart was more likely behind it."

Agnes said nothing for a moment and gazed instead at the great dome of St. Paul's, which loomed above the diminutive rooftops. Viewed from such close proximity, it seemed to belong to another city, a place built on a different scale entirely. Was it Sir Christopher Wren's intention, she wondered, to cow spectators with architectural puissance and majesty, and thereby ensure their submission?

"I did presume, like you, that a man lay behind it," she said. "But now I have changed my view. Perhaps love is not involved here. Rose lacked modesty and had an appetite for the opposite sex, but little need for romantic affection. Put together with the salver and the money in her possession, she may have run off as a result of her involvement with duty dodging and Riley."

"You believe that having dabbled in a minor duty fraud, Riley suddenly grew more ambitious and organized the theft of the wine cooler, killing both Rose and the apprentice?"

"Don't you think him capable?"

"Perhaps," conceded Thomas. "But in my experience a craving for physical affection does not preclude a desire for romance. Rather the reverse."

Agnes was uncertain how to respond. She had steered herself onto unsteady ground, where her naivete must be plainly apparent. Was this a preamble to his own improper intentions? she wondered. Thanking God for the dark night, which obscured her flaming cheeks, she avoided this argument.

"Let us ignore Rose's physical desires for one moment, Mr. Williams. I told you of Nancy's account that Rose had twenty sovereigns hidden under her mattress. Elsie says she never found the money, but I do not give her denial much credence. I still believe it possible Rose accumulated that sum from her duty-dodging scheme with Riley. That would give her enough money to live independently of men, for a few months at least. I hazard, therefore, that she was fleeing a threat of some kind. Perhaps she found out Riley's plan regarding the burglary and decided it was too much for her. Maybe she feared if she refused to help Riley he might turn against her, so she ran off, but he caught up with her."

"It is a possibility, I grant you," said Thomas Williams as they stopped outside a scuffed door halfway along Bread Street. "But to tell the truth, I do not believe she and Riley could have accumulated such a sum from duty dodging."

"But you told me yourself the duty on the wine cooler would have been thirty pounds."

"Yes, but as I said before, that was an unusually large commission. Nothing close to its size has been made for months, and the wine cooler itself was far too conspicuous for Riley to risk avoiding duty. And Mr. Theodore Blanchard has charge of the accounts."

Frustrated by his disbelief and her own lack of expertise in the subject of silver as well as love, she averted her eyes. "God willing, we shall discover the truth when the wine cooler is recovered, Mr. Williams." Then she brushed away a strand of hair that the wind had blown across her lips, turned to her son, and giving his small hand a squeeze, said, "Here we are, Peter."

Ten minutes later, Agnes was sitting in a comfortable parlor before a blazing fire with Peter on her knee. The room was simply furnished with two armchairs, a settle, and a circular wooden table. On the mantel shelf stood a jug in the form of a cow, a figurine of a shepherd and shepherdess, and a pair of plain brass candlesticks. Mrs. Tooley would approve, she thought. The homely surroundings were all she could hope for.

Thomas was in the kitchen, helping Mrs. Sharp, a placable,

buxom, middle-aged woman with sandy hair and shrewd gray eyes, prepare refreshments. Above the rattling of the windows, Agnes could hear the gentle murmur of their voices drifting through the door. A few minutes later they returned to the parlor, Thomas carrying a tray full of wine and glasses.

"Here, Peter, this will warm up those chilly bones of yours. There's milk and honey and nutmeg and a little ale in it," Mrs. Sharp said, handing him a cup of hot posset.

"Say thank you to Mrs. Sharp," said Agnes fondly.

"Thank you, ma'am."

"Should you like to stay here?" Agnes asked.

"Yes, Ma, if Mrs. Sharp let's me, I think I should be most content."

"And you'll be good and do Mrs. Sharp's bidding."

"Yes, Ma."

"Of course he will," interjected Mrs. Sharp. "I know a well-behaved lad when I see one. And Edward will be glad of a playmate."

"So, Mrs. Meadowes, didn't I tell you we'd find an answer?" said Thomas with a smile. "Mrs. Sharp says ten shillings a week for Peter's keep is most satisfactory."

"I hardly know how to thank you, madam," said Agnes, rising and beaming with relief.

"Never mind that, Mrs. Meadowes. Sit down, please do. I'm only glad to be of assistance. Mr. Williams has told me the circumstances. 'Tis a crying shame to hear of any respectable mother separated from her child as you are forced to be."

"The lady who had care of Peter was kind enough. There was never a day's problem till now."

Mrs. Sharp folded her arms over her capacious bosom. "Twickenham is some distance. At least here he will be closer. Tell me, why do you not leave service and start an ordinary chophouse or something of the kind? I cannot conceive how I could endure any position that necessitated my being separated from my Edward."

Agnes had never contemplated what else she might do if she did not cook for the Blanchards. "Are we not all servants in one way or another, Mrs. Sharp? Do not all of us endure restrictions? I daresay on occasion Captain Sharp makes requirements of you that, given a choice, you might prefer to avoid."

"I heartily wish Captain Sharp would make *more* requirements of me," responded the landlady mischievously. "But he is away at sea for months at a time and I am mostly left to my own devices. That is why poor Edward has yet to get himself a brother or a sister."

At this, Thomas's mouth began to twitch with the suspicion of a smile, and Agnes turned scarlet and looked at her wine, wondering if this were quite the place for Peter, after all. She sensed that beneath Mrs. Sharp's warmth lay a measure of disapproval, that she deemed Agnes somehow wanting as a mother. This was not a view Agnes had ever held, and she found herself unsettled by it.

"Let's drink a toast to the resolution of your worries and your son's happy stay here," said Thomas, breaking the silence and handing round the glasses. "Here's to your very good health, Mrs. Meadowes—and to Peter's."

Agnes rarely touched wine or spirits, but she swirled it in her mouth, enjoying its soothing sensation.

Later, when the bottle was empty and Agnes's cheeks had colored, Peter began to yawn and rub his eyes. He would sleep that night in a truckle bed in Thomas's room and move in with Edward Sharp in the morning.

Thomas went up to light the fire and make up the bed. When Agnes arrived with Peter a few minutes later, Thomas ushered them into his room. The room was not yet warm, and had a masculine smoky smell that Agnes did not find unpleasant. The wine had made her rather dizzy and eased her embarrassment. All the same, she averted her eyes from Thomas's bed.

Agnes undressed Peter, tucked him beneath the coverlet, and kissed his forehead. She snuffed out the candle so that the only light came from the orange flames in the hearth. "Sleep well, Peter. Be good and do as Mrs. Sharp bids you. I'll visit tomorrow evening, if I can."

As soon as she got up to leave, Peter grew fretful. His eyes, which a minute earlier had been heavy with sleep, opened wide, and he begged her to stay.

Agnes sat down on the bed, stroking Peter's hand gently. She was aware of Thomas standing by the fire, watching her. When Peter fell asleep, Thomas moved forward and took her by the arm. She presumed he was about to help her find her way in the darkness, but he drew her close, pressing his lips to hers. Part of her knew she should resist, but part of her welcomed the embrace. She had not experienced such sensations for many years. What was the purpose, Agnes thought suddenly, in pretending she had not missed them? It was as futile as her pretense that she did not mind her separation from Peter. She could smell the earthy scent of his clothes; warmth emanated from his body. After the first moment of shock, Agnes abandoned all thoughts of pulling away and kissed him in return.

Chapter Twenty-seven

AGNES WAS MAKING liver pudding when Nancy stepped out of the scullery bearing her housemaid's box. She was wearing Rose's better working dress, a yellow-and-green striped cambric. It fitted her surprisingly well. Agnes noticed that there was no perceptible swelling about Nancy's waist beneath the folds of her skirt, but she seemed broader in the hips. This confirmation of Philip's assertion strengthened Agnes's resolve, and she assailed Nancy with unusual forthrightness. "Did you think I would not suspect you were lying?"

"Pardon me?" said Nancy, swiveling round.

"I said I believe you to be a liar."

"What do you mean, Mrs. Meadowes?" Nancy looked at her in astonishment. "It is most unjust of you to accuse me of any such thing."

"Some things you have told me concerning Rose may have been true, but others were wide of the mark—deliberately so— weren't they? You said them to cast a slur on Rose because you were jealous of her, and, I presume, to deflect attention from your own predicament."

Nancy slapped a defiant hand on her hip. "What predicament?"

Agnes eyed Nancy's belly. "I think you know what I mean."

"You've got no proof. Nor any right to speak to me like that."

"On the contrary, you have given me all the proof I need. Rose Francis was never in the slightest way tidy. You were forever saying how sluttish she was and complaining of the mayhem she created. But when we looked through her things they were all as neat as a sixpence. The only possible reason for that was that you'd been through them already. Perhaps that, rather than oversleeping, was the reason you were late down for your duties that morning. And as for my right to accuse you—Mrs. Blanchard herself has asked me to look into what happened to Rose."

"We all know what happened to her—she got her neck slit."

"But we do not know who slit it or why. Perhaps it was your hatred that drove her away, Nancy. Perhaps she could take no more of you meddling with her possessions, stealing her correspondence, quarreling with her."

Nancy looked perplexed. "No, ma'am, you malign me, I done nothing like that. She irked me now and then, but I liked her well enough, I swear. I wouldn't do nothing to—"

"Don't feign ignorance, Nancy. Or would you prefer that I suggest that Mrs. Tooley search through your possessions? She already has her suspicions regarding you. Rose told her you were jealous, and that you took a letter and left it in the drawing room to cast her in a bad light. And John says a stolen letter was the cause of your fight. But I think you took something else of hers as well. Her purse, perhaps? No wonder she wanted to leave."

"'Course I never took the purse. Would I have mentioned it if I had?"

"Then was it another fabrication?"

Nancy scowled. "No, it was not. There was money right enough."

"Why then did you quarrel?"

"I told you before, it were nothing."

Agnes would not be fobbed off. "I don't believe Mrs. Tooley has yet noticed your secret, although I hazard if she did she would not view it kindly." She disliked threatening the girl, given her predicament, but Nancy was not the type of girl to succumb to an appeal to her finer feelings.

"No, ma'am, don't do that—you know what she's like," said Nancy, round-eyed with fear.

"Then I repeat, what else did you take?"

"It were a letter, like you said." Nancy gave a sullen shrug. "It were nothing but a bit of fun. Patsy told me Rose had been laughing at me with Philip behind my back. And he and I was friendly, till she came."

"But that incident took place a week ago. Why did Rose wait till Monday to confront you?" As soon as she asked the question, Agnes realized that Rose would not have waited. "That was the second letter you took, wasn't it? Not the one you left in the drawing room, but another. That was what the fuss was about. What was in the letter, Nancy? Where is it now?"

Nancy raised her chin defiantly. "It ain't as if it was anything much. I only found it 'cos the room were in such a mess, with all her things falling out of the cupboard, and Mrs. Tooley got mad at me on account of it. She set me to tidy it 'cos she were afraid of Rose's tongue. And I found it lying under her bed."

"Do you have it still?"

"It's nothing what'll tell you who slit her throat."

"Go and fetch it."

By the time Nancy was back, Agnes had lined the pudding basin with dough. Nancy handed her a sheet of paper. "Here you are."

Agnes wiped her fingers on her apron and took it. The letter was dated the day before the robbery and Rose's disappearance.

Dearest Rose

I am much pleased to learn of your change of heart. I will wait for you at the Red Lion at five-thirty tomorrow morning. Our tickets are bought and our passage from Dover arranged. God willing we will be in Calais that night. I need not say how greatly I look forward to that moment.

Yours in affectionate expectation,

The letter was written in a clear strong hand, but the signature was an illegible squiggle, and there was no mention of an address. After Agnes read it several times, Agnes stood for a moment lost in thought.

How deluded she had been in ignoring her first instinct that it was an affair of the heart that had caused Rose to run away! But why would Nancy have taken the trouble to steal a letter belonging to Rose, once she had read it? She must have had another purpose.

"Did you wait up that night for Rose to leave and follow her?"

"No, 'course not. I was glad to see the back of her. Why would I go after her?"

"Did you see her go?"

"Yes, but there ain't no crime in that."

Agnes slowly began packing her basin with chopped liver. "You believed this note was written by Philip, did you not?"

"'Course not." Nancy blushed scarlet. "That thought never came into it."

Agnes could see she was lying. Nancy was aggrieved that Rose had come between her and Philip, and was further distressed to find herself with child. What effect would the letter have had on her if she believed he had written it to arrange an elopement? Had she hoped to entice Philip into marrying her? This seemed unlikely. Philip had a lowly post, which he would lose if he wed. But perhaps in her distress she had believed she could persuade him to seek other employment where marriage was not prohibited. Agnes placed a circle of dough on top of the meat filling, carefully sealing the edge with her fingertips. "If you believed this letter was from Philip, and that Rose was about to run off with him, you might have felt impelled to follow and stop her."

"That's not only daft, it's downright impossible."

Agnes cut a hole in the top of the crust to allow the steam to escape. "Philip had gone out earlier that night to the Blue Cockerel, but you were not to know that. If Rose left before he returned, you might have followed her, assuming she was on her way to meet him. You might have killed her in order to prevent her taking Philip away from this household and you."

Nancy shot her a sly look. "I told you it couldn't be. I never thought he wrote that letter."

Agnes's hands grew hot. She pressed too hard on the dough, making it sticky. "Oh, and why is that, pray?"

"Answer me. How did you know this wasn't Philip's hand?"

There was a long silence, then Nancy began to giggle.

"'Cos Philip don't have no hand save a cross. He don't know how to write, do he?" Nancy went off, humming with satisfaction.

Agnes, infuriated and shamed in equal measure, deliberately scraped the dough off her fingers and summoned Doris to help her. And when she put the pudding in the steamer and scalded her arm, her temper only worsened. It wasn't only Nancy's cutting tone that disturbed her, or the letter that she had just stowed in her drawer. She would never have accused Nancy if she had not kissed Thomas Williams last night. He had stirred up sentiments long forgotten. Now she thought of the scent of Thomas Williams's room, the wiry feel of his hair, his warmth, the carvings on his headboard, her hair and laces undone. Doubt overwhelmed her. Nothing appeared uncomplicated, and suddenly she was uncertain of which path she should take.

PHILIP MARCHED INTO the kitchen from the yard, dressed in his leather apron. "Letter's come from Mr. Pitt this morning, Mrs. M. It was addressed to you. You heard what it says yet? Don't suppose you know where my gloves have got to? Mr. Matthews is after me for losing 'em." He helped himself to a sliver of pheasant from Agnes's bowl.

Agnes moved the bowl away from him. "Get away. How do you know the letter was from Mr. Pitt?"

"It came while I was clearing the dining room fireplace. A special messenger brought it, Mr. Matthews was there and dealth with it, but I heard your name and Marcus Pitt's mentioned. Suppose that means you and I'll be going back to see Pitt soon."

"Perhaps," said Agnes, feeling a prickle of apprehension. I haven't seen the letter. But I daresay we shall discover its contents soon."

"Go on, Mrs. Meadowes. Can't I 'ave summat to eat? I'm half starved. What about that drumstick—there's only pickings on it."

Agnes opened her drawer and took out the letter she had extricated from Nancy. "In a minute. Look at this first. Tell me, did you write it?"

Philip regarded the letter, then glanced at Doris and grew awkward. "Not that thing again."

"What do you mean?"

"Nancy showed it to me."

"When was this?"

"A few days since, as I recall."

"Monday—the day before the robbery?"

"Reckon so."

"What does it say?"

A sudden flush spread across Philip's countenance. He shrugged nonchalantly. "Like I told her, never learned my letters, did I?"

Agnes nodded. "Surely you must have asked her what it said?"

Philip seemed to forget his consternation. He smiled and ruffled his dark hair, as if trying to beguile her with his charms.

Agnes was unmelting. "Well?"

"'Course I did. There's no pulling wool over your eyes, is there? Nancy said Rose was planning to go off."

"So did you follow Rose when she left for her rendezvous?"

He shook his head vehemently. "No. 'Course not. I told you where I was that night—at the Blue Cockerel in Lombard Street. There's plenty there to feast the eye and more besides . . . Ask the landlord, if you like."

"Then why did Nancy show you the letter? And why did you say nothing before?"

He tensed his mouth thoughtfully. "Perhaps she wants to incriminate me as the father of her child. To do so she reckons she has to turn me against Rose. But why would I fall for it? I told you before, things between Rose and me cooled some weeks ago. I didn't say nothing before because even if our affair was over, I was still fond of her. I wouldn't have wanted her to get into trouble with the Blanchards."

Without waiting for further invitation, Philip fell upon the drumstick with a victorious smile and began to gnaw it hungrily. "By the way, how's Mr. Williams keeping? Coming to visit again today, is he?"

Agnes saw Doris's eyes pop open. "None of your business, Philip. Any more cheek like that and I'll feed you crusts for a week."

"Beg pardon. Didn't mean to give no offense."

"P'raps that's why Mr. Matthews kept your letter—he wants to tear a strip off you, ma'am," piped in Doris.

"Why on earth should he want to do that?" said Agnes.

"'Cos of what Mrs. Tooley told him. You being with Mr. Williams and your boy in the kitchen."

Agnes colored, and told Doris to stop being foolish and fetch the oysters from the larder. If Doris knew, and Mrs. Tooley had told Mr. Matthews, then by now the entire household must be aware of Thomas Williams's presence in her life. Grim-faced, she scattered bay leaves and juniper berries on the top of a shin of beef.

She moistened it with pig's trotter jelly, then covered it with a lid and carried it to the fire. What did Philip and Doris know of her predicament? Or her desire? Was this what Rose had felt— misunderstood in her desire? Besides, what more could she expect? All households thrived upon gossip; it was human nature. She wiped her hands on her apron and went in search of Mr. Matthews and Marcus Pitt's letter.

Chapter Twenty-eight

THERE WAS NO SIGN of Mr. Matthews in the butler's pantry, nor in his office. As Agnes returned to the servants' corridor, she walked past the small paneled door which concealed a narrow staircase to the cellar. The door was usually kept locked to keep out pilfering servants, but Agnes noticed that it stood an inch or two ajar. She pushed it open and peered down the first flight of dingy stairs. It was dark as soot and she felt a sudden draft of cold damp air. Was that a muffled voice drifting up from below? She called out, "Mr. Matthews, is that you?" When she heard nothing, she called again, more loudly, "Mr. Matthews, are you there?" Still there was no reply.

There were no windows in the cellar. Whenever she had ventured down here before on Mr. Matthews's instruction she had always taken a candle with her. She used her folded handkerchief as a wedge to prop open the door and turned down the stairs.

The air became danker. An unwholesome smell of mold and dust caught the back of her nose and made her want to sneeze. She was three quarters of the way down when the handkerchief slipped out and the door creaked closed. Enveloped in chilly darkness, she groped her way forward, feeling along the wall with her hand, her nails catching on the peeling distemper. When she arrived at the bottom she peered into the musty gloom.

A dim light emanated from a wall sconce in front of her, which had been lit to one side of a half-opened door. The door led to a long narrow chamber, much of which was obliterated by shadows, but halfway along, on an upturned barrel, a tallow candle flickered. By its smoky halo of light Agnes could see the curved ceiling vault, a long wall lined with racks of wine, and, facing it, another crammed with wooden kegs of varying sizes. From above she could hear the servants' clock striking, Doris clattering pots in the scullery, the sharp rap of someone at the door, the faint cry of a knife grinder in the street. But in the cellar itself there was no sound at all except her own breathing and the soft rustle of her skirts.

It was only after several minutes, when her eyes had grown accustomed to the dark, that she noticed a niche in the wall at about waist height, just a yard from where she stood. She saw that there was something indistinct, an object about the size of her fist, resting upon it. Agnes reached forward and picked it up. It was wrapped in a cloth and was surprisingly heavy. Leaning toward the light from the wall sconce she began to unwrap it. It was a pistol. Small enough to fit in a pocket, the hilt was inlaid with silver decoration that was filthy with mud and grit. Was this one missing from Nicholas Blanchard's room? As the thought struck her, she heard the chinking sound of glasses or crockery from somewhere nearby. There was no mistaking the voices now: Mr. Matthews was in conversation with John. Before she had time to call out, another door creaked open and the pair emerged from the darkness.

The butler held a lantern in one hand. In his other he clutched a pair of glasses and a bottle. John carried a wooden crate.

Agnes knew that she should announce her presence. She was holding a pistol that everyone believed had been lost. If Rose did take the gun to protect herself, it was most likely left here by the person Elsie had seen chasing her on the mud. The murderer.

Mr. Matthews was now no more than a few yards away. Agnes

hastily rewrapped the gun in the cloth and place it back on the ledge. Suddenly, Mr. Matthews halted. Putting down the bottle, the glasses, and his lantern on the upturned keg, he placed an arm around the footman's shoulder.

"Dear boy," he said, slurring his words, "leave those bottles now. As soon as you've finished your other duties come back and take a couple of 'em off to Berry's chophouse. I'll leave the door unlocked for you. Tell him I said it's to be kept aside for us—ready for our celebration next week."

John put down his crate. "As you wish, sir. But are you not fearful the loss might be remarked?"

Matthews shook his head vehemently. "Never mind that. Who's there to notice? After all my years of service I'm entitled to a little reward. And if I choose to share it with you, that's my affair." Matthews's face was no more than an inch from John's. "You richly deserve it."

John was several inches taller than the elderly butler. He stared down, then he smiled uneasily, licked his lips, and shook his head. The gesture made Agnes shudder. She could see the moisture glisten on his lower lip. "Thank you, sir," he said softly. "I am most grateful." He held up the butler's hand and pressed his palm against his cheek before planting a kiss upon it. "Where'd I be without your kindness?" he whispered. "Still scrubbing pots in some hellhole kitchen."

The gesture so astonished Agnes that for a moment she half wondered if it was a trick of the shadows. She had not even been conscious of a special rapport between the two, let alone suspected anything like this. She had witnessed something intimate, untoward, something both Mr. Matthews and John would desire to keep hidden. She had heard of such alliances, but never had she encountered them firsthand: men in love with each other—mollies, they called them. She was uncannily reminded of the unsettling kiss that Pitt had placed upon her hand, and involuntarily brushed her palm against her skirt.

She backed slowly toward the staircase, but she had climbed no more than four or five steps when the heel of her shoe caught in her petticoat and she stumbled forward. Instinctively she put out her hand to break her fall, but not before her ankle twisted painfully beneath her. She let out an involuntary cry.

"Who's there?" called Mr. Matthews, grabbing his lantern. "Who is it?" He walked briskly toward her. "Answer me, damn you! What do you want?"

Blanking out the agony in her ankle, Agnes hobbled up the steps, and when she had almost reached the top, turned and made as if she was descending. "Mr. Matthews?" she called out. "Where are you, sir? Is that you? I hear there's been a message from Mr. Pitt."

Mr. Matthews halted at the foot of the stairs. "Mrs. Meadowes! What on earth are *you* doing here?"

"I beg your pardon, sir. I didn't mean to trespass. It was only that I've just now seen Philip, and he says there's been a message from Mr. Pitt," she said, hoping she sounded calm.

"What if there has?"

"Nothing, sir. I only mean, that's the reason I came looking for you. I went to your pantry and office and then, seeing as the cellar door was open, I thought I'd see if I might find you down here. I only wondered if you knew anything about the message, and whether Mr. Blanchard will need me to visit Mr. Pitt again."

Mr. Matthews started up the staircase toward Agnes. The breach in his defenses was apparently of greater concern to him than Pitt. "The door was open? How curious when I distinctly recall that I closed it."

"Perhaps the wind blew it. At any rate, if it's inconvenient just now I won't trouble you any longer. I haven't much time myself— I must check that pie doesn't burn."

"Not so fast." Mr. Matthews grabbed her wrist. Agnes winced. "What's this? Hurt, are you?" He drew her palm close to the lantern. "You have a nasty scratch. How did you come by it?"

"It's nothing, sir," said Agnes. She pulled her hand away and stepped back.

The butler moved next to her and placed an arm behind her so she could withdraw no further. He drew his face close—so close Agnes could smell brandy on his breath, and his pale eyes seemed full of menace; he reminded Agnes of a snake. "It might be nothing, Mrs. Meadowes, but I wish to know," Mr. Matthews whispered urgently. She looked desperately to John for help, but his face seemed empty, neutral.

Agnes summoned her resources. She spoke firmly but softly, in a voice she had mastered long ago to mask her inner fright. "I stumbled just now, sir, when I began to descend without a light. And then you came out with your lantern."

"You weren't spying on John and me, I don't suppose?"

"Spying on you? Whatever for, Mr. Matthews? I assure you I have no desire to cause trouble. I only wanted to speak to you. If you don't believe me, ask Doris or Philip. They will tell you I was in the kitchen with them not two minutes ago."

Mr. Matthews finally seemed to take her at her word and withdrew a little. "Very well," he said, "in that case I shall give you the benefit of the doubt and let it pass. But you are not to come back down here without my permission. No matter how urgent the matter seems to you, it's more than likely it'll be a trifle to me. Do I make myself clear?"

"As daylight, Mr. Matthews." Then, emboldened by her narrow escape, she coughed. "And if I may be so bold, the letter from Pitt, sir?"

"Ah yes, it was nothing urgent or I should have said. Mr. Theodore has it. He wants you to go to him directly after dinner on account of it. He did not tell me why. Becoming quite the favorite, aren't you?"

"I think not, sir."

"Now, just so there are no more accidents, let me light your way." He edged past Agnes and pushed open the door. "Careful now. Dear me, this door seems tighter than usual. Is something caught?" Before Agnes could intercept him, he had bent down and pulled out the handkerchief she had folded and wedged there. "What's this?" He shook it out, then glared at her. "Has it anything to do with you, Mrs. Meadowes? Can you hazard how it came to be so strangely positioned?"

Agnes looked at the white square that now wafted between his finger and thumb. Thankfully she had never been much of a needlewoman, and had never embroidered her initial on any of her belongings. "I suppose Mrs. Tooley or one of the other servants must have dropped it, sir. But unless there's a name or initial sewn on it, there's no way of telling. It might belong to almost anyone."

Chapter Twenty-nine

AT SIX THAT SAME EVENING, Agnes went upstairs to learn what message Pitt had sent. Snow had settled over the rutted street and obliterated the city's dirt and danger. Theodore had retired to the library to enjoy a decanter of port. Agnes found the room in semidarkness, the book-lined walls and velvet curtains lost in shadow. A fire burned fiercely in the grate, framed by a pair of squat brass andirons with lion's paw feet. Light from a silver candelabrum illuminated a drum-shaped table in the center of the room, on which an opened folio of engravings and other papers was scattered. The engravings were designs for antique urns and sarcophagi, which Theodore was scrutinizing through an ornate silver-handled magnifying glass, making notes on a sheet of paper. At the sound of Agnes's tread, he looked up, with eyes that seemed unfocused and dull.

"I've come, sir, because Mr. Matthews said a letter was delivered, and you wished to see me on account of it."

"A letter," echoed Theodore. He set down his glass, belched gently, and began rummaging through the papers on the table. "Yes, yes, indeed. Mr. Pitt's communication, delivered by one of his assistants earlier on."

"It was good news, I hope?"

He nodded morosely. "Promising enough—and all I had hoped for, given the circumstances. Mr. Pitt claims he has located the villains that stole the wine cooler. It is still intact, and will be returned forthwith, provided we pay the sum required."

"Is the sum reasonable?"

Theodore's lips puckered as though there were a bitter taste in his mouth. He lowered his eyes to the engraving in front of him and, with his forefinger, slowly traced the curvaceous outline of a funerary urn, whose handles were shaped like elephant ears. "Two hundred guineas," he declared miserably.

Agnes gasped. "Will you pay it?"

Theodore's eyes shone as though tears welled in them. He turned to another engraving, of a candelabrum in the form of a Corinthian column. "If I do not pay, the wine cooler will be melted down, and the metal untraceable. Pitt isn't prone to making idle threats, he knows precisely what he's doing. I think I told you before, our business is not as strong as it once was. A loss like this might land me in the debtors' prison."

The engraving turned Agnes's thoughts to the salver that Williams had examined. If Theodore was operating a duty-dodging scheme, the loss would not be as great as he claimed. The sum he would have charged Grey for making the wine cooler would have included duty—an extra thirty pounds. Assuming the wine cooler had never been taken to Goldsmiths' Hall, that sum would go straight into Theodore's pocket.

Agnes thought of Rose's unexplained forays upstairs and to the workshop, and her association with Riley. Much pointed to her involvement in the scheme. Perhaps Theodore had used Rose as a go-between, and she had grown greedy, and knowing she was about to leave to join her lover, wanted more for her assistance than Theodore was willing to pay. Had her greed led to her death? But given that the robbery was most likely orchestrated by the same person who had killed Noah and Rose, this theory fell apart. It was ludicrous to suppose that Theodore would engineer the robbery of his own premises, murder his own apprentice, and pay for his own property to be recovered.

Having dismissed Theodore as a possible suspect, Agnes was on the verge of mentioning to him her discovery of the gun. But he had told her unequivocally that his only concern was the wine cooler and there was nothing to be gained by bringing up a subject certain to rile him. She was overcome by a sense of gloom as she considered her predicament. The room began to feel stifling, the rich smell of port overpowering. Theodore was not ready to dismiss her yet.

Eventually Theodore found the letter among his papers and put on a great show of perusing it. "Ah yes, here we are, Mrs. Meadowes. Yes, Pitt has addressed himself to you although the communication concerns me. What he says is this!

"If I am in agreement with his terms, you are to send word to him this evening. The messenger who delivered this will be waiting outside to take the reply. Tomorrow morning, first thing, you are to deliver the payment to him and he will then set in motion the return of the wine cooler. Since it is a sizable sum, and he has no wish for you to be robbed, he will send his own driver and carriage to fetch you. You may bring a single escort of your own to assist you in recovering the wine cooler."

Agnes felt a sudden burning in her chest and tried to breathe deeply. "Has Justice Cordingly been apprised?"

"Not until the transaction is complete. He might insist upon intervening, and if Pitt got word that the law was involved, there would be no chance of a satisfactory conclusion to this business."

"With respect, sir, two murders have taken place that are almost certainly connected with the wine cooler. Surely they merit his intervention? Should not Pitt at least be apprehended and questioned on the matter?"

"You know very well that Justice Cordingly has both matters in hand. And why ever would I insist upon Pitt's arrest when there is no evidence to connect him to either crime and he is poised to engineer the return of my wine cooler? I should be a dolt to do so, Mrs. Meadowes."

Agnes remembered Pitt's kiss, the touch of his lips upon her fingers, his insinuating glance. Her agitation grew. She did not want to believe the murderer could be someone with whom she lived and worked. She did not want Theodore or John or Philip or Nancy or Mr. Matthews to be guilty. Could Pitt have accompanied Drake on his nocturnal adventure, killed Noah Prout, and then murdered Rose only because she happened to pass him on her way to her rendezvous? Improbable though this hypothesis was, Agnes wanted to believe it in order to negate the other more disturbing possibilities. But there was one obstacle she could not reason away: if Pitt were the murderer, how did the gun get in the cellar?

She had only to mention Elsie's name, and the link between Pitt and the robbery would be established. But she had given her word, and the repercussions would be terrible for Elsie if she broke it. Instead, she attempted further deferential argument. "With respect, sir, does not Pitt's proposal strike you as suspicious? He has countless henchmen at his disposal. If he knows I'm carrying two hundred guineas, even if I have a man as protection, what is to stop him organizing another assault?"

Theodore fixed her with his bloodshot eyes and shook his head. "I need hardly say that I too have my concerns. Yet I know enough of Pitt's modus operandi to comprehend that that is not the way he does business. After all, he has a reputation to nurture just as we all do. Besides, I didn't say so before, but his letter implies he is quite taken with you." Her pulse began to pound in her neck. "Then you will let Philip go with me, just as a precaution, won't you, sir?"

Theodore frowned. "Not Philip. This time I think it would be better if you take one of the journeymen—Williams, I think—he is sharp-witted and more diligent than Riley, and knows the wine cooler well. I would not want Pitt trying to fob you off with a replica."

Agnes desisted from asking why, if such a swindle were possible, being held up with two hundred guineas in her possession was not. Besides, the news that Thomas Williams was to be her escort bolstered her spirits; she bowed to the inevitable.

Theodore waved her to a chair on the opposite side of the table. "Read his letter. Since it is addressed to you, the reply must come from you. Take this quill and paper. Say that you have discussed the matter with me and I have agreed. He may send his carriage at nine tomorrow. You will see where he invites you to step out with him. I commend you on the way you've charmed him. It can only work to our advantage if you give him some hope that he might be accepted. But rather than accepting outright you should remain a little vague—it will help sustain his eagerness."

Agnes perused the letter. The first paragraph concerned the details as Theodore had described them. The last part caused her cheeks to burn.

The nature of my profession ensures I encounter a great many people from all walks of life. At our first meeting you impressed me greatly, not only by your radiance and composure but also by your wit. When I asked you before to do me the honor of accompanying me to the theater, you declared "present commitments precluded it." May I query your exact meaning? Does that mean no invitation of mine will ever be favorably received, or was my overture inconvenient in that instance only?

Agnes had a sense of foreboding as real and dark as the liquor in Theodore's glass. Nevertheless, duty overcame her better judgment, and instead of demanding that someone else go in her stead, she wrote precisely as Theodore dictated. She wrote concisely in her usual elegant hand, accepting the terms Pitt had stated and concluding with the following:

I am honored you have taken the trouble to offer a further invitation to me. I cannot promise acceptance. Let us conclude the present business before pursuing our private pleasures.

When she had finished, she sanded the page and read it through. The last words seemed to her larger and less flowing than the rest, as though someone else had written them. She handed the sheet to Theodore, who smiled grimly. "Very good, Mrs. Meadowes. Admirable indeed. The final sentence will have him tossing all night, I wager." He glanced up and caught her blush. "Don't look coy when I compliment your skill." He folded the page into three, tucked the ends over, and sealed it with scarlet wax. "Take it out into the street. There will be someone waiting for it."

Agnes curtsied and retreated. John was waiting in the hall directly outside. From the strange look he gave her, she wondered if he had heard their exchange and knew thus of her perilous mission the next day, or if he was remembering their encounter in the cellar. She had many questions she wanted to ask him. Who put the gun there? Did you see Rose leave early that morning and follow her? Did either you or Mr. Matthews have a hand in her death? But she knew that if either of them were guilty, to press them in such a way would only place her own life in jeopardy, and then Rose's killer would never be found. So she drew a breath and looked coolly at him. "Mr. Blanchard says there is a messenger waiting outside for this letter."

John smiled faintly. "Follow me." At the front entrance he pulled open the hall door. A blast of whirling snow and wind rushed in, and with it a small body that had been hunched up against the door. John took a step back. The body jolted into life and sat up with a start. Agnes recognized the pinched triangular face, the red shawl, and the overlarge boots.

Elsie had apparently been waiting since midday, when she had delivered Pitt's letter. Having paced an hour or two to keep warm, she had grown tired and taken refuge on the doorstep. From time to time John or Philip or Mr. Matthews had caught sight of her through the hall window and shooed her away. Only when they became engaged with other duties had she at last been left in peace. Now John was infuriated to see her here.

"Move off! How many times did I tell you already not to park yourself here?" He gave her scrawny haunches a prod with the pointed toe of his shoe. "What d'you think the master would have to say if he saw you here?"

Elsie scrambled hastily to her feet as if she expected another, harder blow to follow. She shot him an indignant look. "I told you before, I ain't what you think. I've orders from Mr. Pitt to await a reply." Her face was white with cold, her lips were gray. Her crimson shawl was coated with snow, like flour on raw meat.

John clearly gave her remark little credence. He jerked his chin toward the street to indicate she would be wise to clear off now. But Elsie caught sight of Agnes standing behind John, staring worriedly in her direction and returning her gaze with an equal measure of anxiety. Agnes comprehended the underlying reason—her father. "Tell him, missus," Elsie said with a show of bravado. "It's the least you could do after the age you've kept me waiting."

"I didn't know you were here, Elsie," said Agnes, maneuvering her way past John.

"Never mind that. 'Ave you penned the answer yet?"

Agnes held out the paper. "I have it here for you."

No sooner had Agnes uttered these words than Elsie plucked the letter from her grasp and stuffed it in her pocket. Agnes recalled the orange and the purse, stolen with similar swiftness, and the silver box. But the sight of the pathetic retreating figure aroused no anger; the image of Peter as he had appeared in her kitchen last night, bedraggled from the rain, came into her mind. She couldn't scold the girl for snatching the letter; nor, in all conscience, could she watch her trudge off in such a miserable condition.

"Wait a moment, Elsie. Have you eaten today?"

"How could I, waiting so long for you?" said Elsie, shooting her an accusing look as if to say, "You told them, didn't you?"

"Then won't you let me make amends by giving you something warm to eat before you set off back to Mr. Pitt's?"

Elsie stamped her boots and looked anxiously toward the river. "It'd be more'n my life's worth. Pa'll be wanting his supper, and Mr. Grant said I wasn't to do nothing but go straight here and come straight back with an answer."

"Mr. Grant?"

"The man what tells us Mr. Pitt's orders and keeps an eye on us." She wiped a drip from her nose with the back of her hand, then whispered, "You didn't say nothing about me or no one else, did you?"

Agnes was conscious of John hovering inquisitively. And behind him she now sensed the shadowy presence of Mr. Matthews. How much did they know of these matters? She would be wise not to reveal her familiarity with Elsie's background, or keep her longer in their presence than necessary. Suppose John remembered Elsie from the morning before the robbery and saw that she was a link between Pitt and the theft. Ignoring her question, Agnes said, "You'll be dead from cold before you reach the bridge if you don't get something warm inside you first. Come down to the kitchen. I'll give you something to eat on the way."

Elsie shrugged her bony shoulders. "I don't mind, then," she said ungraciously, mounting the steps.

"Don't think of coming this way," said John, blocking her path. "Pardon me, Mrs. Meadowes, I cannot but wonder at you inviting creatures such as this in here, and with so many valuables about."

"Quite right, John," concurred Mr. Matthews loudly from the shadowy hall.

Elsie flinched as though John had hit her. There was a gleam of fear in her eyes. "I didn't ask—you heard her offer."

"Wait, just a moment!" cried Agnes, skidding down the steps and grabbing Elsie's arm.

"Let me alone! What are you doing?" Elsie wrenched her elbow free. "Leave me be and save yourself some bother."

"No." She leaned down and whispered in Elsie's wind-reddened ear. "Go down those steps by the railings, they'll bring you to the kitchen door. Wait there a minute and I'll bring you some food."

Elsie regarded Agnes with doubtful eyes. Agnes patted her on the back and went inside with the others.

"The recklessness of some people never ceases to amaze me," said John as he fastened the bolt and watched Agnes stamp her snow-clogged shoes on the doormat. "You're asking to be done over a second time with that one, Mrs. M., you mark my words."

"Quite probably, John," said Agnes darkly. There was every possibility he was right. Yet somehow, when she was faced with Elsie's misery, his scorn seemed unimportant.

In the kitchen Agnes reasoned that one less pasty would not be missed from the servants' supper—and that if anyone went short she would ensure it was John or Mr. Matthews. She grabbed one from the warming tray and she opened the door.

For a minute she stood there, with the cold wind howling in, listening for the sound of a clumping boot or a glimpse of Elsie's shawl. But there was nothing. She gingerly mounted the icy steps leading to the street. At the top were some narrow footprints, descending three steps and no further, as though Elsie had started to step down and had then changed her mind. Where the stairs reached the street, the footprints were indiscernible among other trampled imprints. Had John frightened the girl away as soon as Agnes had gone? A man hovered in a nearby doorway, sheltering from the blizzard or waiting to be admitted. In the snowy distance she could vaguely make out a couple of muffled figures walking briskly away.

Agnes took a frustrated bite from the hot pasty, feeling the meat and potatoes warm her as she had wished them to warm Elsie, then went back inside. The girl was nothing to her, she reminded herself.

Chapter Thirty

AGNES HAD PROMISED PETER she would see how he was settling in at Mrs. Sharp's. Nothing on earth would make her disappoint him—but neither had she any desire to beg Mrs. Tooley's permission and have her request refused. She claimed a headache and told Doris to see to the servants' supper. She was going to her room to lie down until it was time to put out the upstairs meal.

She was reluctant to confess it even to herself, but there was more than Peter to draw her out on that snowy night. She had seen and heard nothing from Thomas Williams all day. Several times she had found herself looking up at the windows, but she could only make out the lower portion of passersby, the tailcoats and calves of gentlemen, the hems of ladies' cloaks. Whenever she glimpsed a pair of well-muscled legs marching past, she blushed and wondered if they were his and whether he might be on his way to call on her, or if he might contrive to send a message on some pretext or other. He did not call or make any attempt at communication.

That morning she had not blamed him for taking what she had freely offered him, nor had she regretted her actions. But now that hours had passed and no word had come, shadows of her old self returned. His failure to communicate led her to only one conclusion. He must think she was in the habit of comporting herself thus and deemed her favors of so little worth they did not require acknowledgment.

She decided that henceforth, whenever she met him, she would be a model of decorum. Last night's aberration would never be repeated. He would not inveigle his way into further intimacy. The bolts would be redrawn.

SARAH SHARP'S HOUSE was only two streets from Foster Lane, but Agnes, being prudent in matters of dress, as in every other portion of her life, put pattens on her feet and a woolen shawl over her head. She fastened her cloak tightly and picked up a muff, in which she inserted a small paper parcel that she had wrapped up earlier. As protection against footpads, she concealed a small kitchen knife in the pocket of her cloak. Then she slipped out.

The snow had ceased falling but lay several inches deep; moonlight mottled its surface with silver, filling the rutted streets with ghostly streams of light, broken only by occasional mounds of horse dung and detritus in the gutter. Against an inky sky, familiar landmarks were transformed. The dome of St. Paul's had become a luminous orb, pediments resembled white brows, signboards were wiped clean. Agnes turned left at the bottom of Foster Lane into Cheapside, then, passing Gutter Lane and Wood Street on her left, turned right into Bread Street. She walked with her head down, crunching over snow as crystalline as salt, wondering if the river would freeze, and if so whether Sarah Sharp would take Peter and Edward to see the boats and barges frozen at their moorings.

"Mrs. Meadowes! What a night to come out on," said Sarah Sharp two minutes later, when a pink-cheeked Agnes knocked upon her door.

"Mrs. Sharp. My apologies for coming so late. Duties delayed me."

"Don't trouble yourself over that. You took me by surprise, that's all. Come in out of the cold."

The smell of chicken broth and bread filled the narrow hall-way, soothing Agnes with its homeliness. The thought flashed through her mind that if her feckless husband had not perished, she might be living in such a house as this. Agnes found herself feeling less stoical than usual. She was disturbed at the hand fate had dealt her and the choices she had made. Is it possible, she won-dered, I have taken the wrong path?

Pushing this worrisome thought away, Agnes removed her cloak and asked after Peter.

"Come and see for yourself. My boy, Edward, has taken to him very well. They have entertained one another all day."

The kitchen was lit by tallow candles whose light reflected off an array of shiny copper pots. The fire was low but smoldered comfortingly. The furniture was plain and sparse, but well pol-ished and spotlessly clean.

"Ma!" Peter cried, leaping up as Agnes appeared at the thresh-old, "I thought you'd forgot. This is Edward. I taught him how to play checkers." Peter was sitting at the table beside a fair-haired little fellow, with the same round face and pale blue-gray eyes as his mother. Both boys were sipping bowls of broth and were dressed in nightshirts and nightcaps. Peter's cheeks were scarlet, his eyes bright, the hair on his forehead ruffled and damp as though his face had been recently washed.

Agnes embraced her son. "However could you think I'd forget you?" He seemed a different child from the woebegone wretch of last night. An image of Elsie floated across her thoughts. "Pleased to make your acquaintance, Edward," she said, forcing it away. "And what have the pair of you done today?"

"We went out in the snow, and threw snowballs. And we ate chestnuts. Then Mrs. Sharp said we should come back inside lest we catch our deaths."

"And Peter fashioned a horse from a piece of wood. And I

made a model of my father's ship," added Edward, pointing to two roughly hewn models on the windowsill.

"And Mrs. Sharp said I should give you mine when it was done," interrupted Peter.

Agnes smiled at the boys' excitement.

She took from her muff the small parcel she had brought, and handed it to Peter. "Here's something for you both—when the broth is finished."

Thomas Williams was nowhere to be seen. Should she be relieved, or disappointed? Neither, she told herself firmly. She was unmoved, and would remain so.

Peter gulped down the last of his soup and tore away the paper. Inside were two gingerbread figures with currant eyes and buttons down their fronts, and almond mouths and hair. The boys grinned and began a mock fight with them. As biscuit limbs snapped and currant eyes came loose, they munched swiftly until there was nothing left but the heads.

Mrs. Sharp drew up a chair by the fire and indicated that Agnes should settle herself in it. Just then there came the sound of heavy stamping by the back door. A moment later Thomas Williams marched in. He was carrying a bucket of coal. His hair was in its customary disorder, a mass of chestnut spirals; he wore a shirt and mustard-colored waistcoat, but no coat, and was shivering from the cold. As he caught sight of Agnes, a new light seemed to enter his eyes. "Mrs. Meadowes, good evening," he said with a courteous bow as he deposited his load by the hearth. He sprinkled a shovelful on the embers, causing them to crackle and spit. "I wasn't aware you were intending to visit. Had I known, I'd have come to fetch you. It isn't safe to travel alone—you ought to know that."

"'Tis a distance of only two streets, and I'm well acquainted with this district," said Agnes nonchalantly, responding to his bow with a tiny inclination.

Thomas's expression was somber. "Even so, a woman alone,

unarmed—and after what happened to your kitchen maid. It is folly to tempt fate in such a manner."

Agnes thought of Rose and of the kitchen knife in her cloak pocket, and the gun in the cellar. With a murderer at large, she was probably no safer in her kitchen than in the street, but she saw no reason to argue the matter. Let Thomas fret a little. Hadn't she passed more time than she cared to acknowledge watching for him?

She regarded him levelly. "In my son's case it was a risk worth taking. I could not rest easy unless I knew he was well. And now I see him very well, for which I thank Mrs. Sharp heartily."

Mrs. Sharp must have guessed from this stilted exchange that there was some misunderstanding between them. She turned the conversation to lighter subjects: the latest entertainment at the theater, a production by Garrick, which she had heard from an acquaintance was most diverting; the price of herrings at the market; and the likelihood of the river freezing and the boys being able to go skating. When they had consumed the last crumb of gingerbread, the boys traipsed upstairs to bed and Mrs. Sharp bustled after them, ordering Agnes to sit a while longer with Thomas until she called.

Anxious to steer matters away from the events of the previous night, Agnes told him matter-of-factly about her discovery of the gun in the cellar, and the letter that Pitt had sent—and that Theodore had decided he should accompany her to deliver the money and collect the wine cooler.

"Has Justice Cordingly been informed of any of this?"

"No," said Agnes. "Theodore can think of nothing but the wine cooler. He is adamant that Justice Cordingly should be kept in the dark until it is recovered. I never told him about the gun—I feared if I did he would have seen it as an effort to undermine this determination and it would only have annoyed him."

The explanation sounded lame as she said it, but Thomas Williams was gracious enough not to criticize her. "He is willing to stake our safety against Pitt's integrity in order to safeguard the business—a dubious bargain, in my opinion," he said. "And even if Pitt is not the murderer, he surely knows the murderer's identity. It cannot be right just to allow the fellow to evade apprehension."

"I agree wholeheartedly," said Agnes, thinking of Rose lying dead with her throat cut. "Moreover, the gun suggests the murderer is someone in the household. But I dare not contradict Theodore's order. And since we cannot doubt that the business depends upon the recovery of the wine cooler, your position is as much at risk as mine. But on the subject of the murderer, there is one more thing I would like to ascertain, but I cannot easily do so by virtue of my sex."

"What is it?" said Thomas.

"There is an alehouse in Lombard Street called the Blue Cockerel. Philip was out on the night of the robbery, but he claims he spent the evening there in the company of various ladies. He says the landlord will remember him. Would you be so kind as to call on him to verify it?"

Thomas muttered inaudibly, poured himself a tankard of ale from a jug on the dresser and silently gulped it, gazing at the fire as he did so. The clock struck the half hour and Mrs. Sharp summoned Agnes upstairs. After bidding Peter good night, Agnes wasted no time in taking her leave. "I should return directly," she said to Mrs. Sharp, avoiding Thomas's eyes. "There is still upstairs supper to put out."

Thomas helped her into her cloak and then strapped on his sword and donned his overcoat and hat. Agnes feigned nonchalance. "If you are coming out just on my account, I assure you, Mr. Williams, there's no need. I shall be as safe on my return as I was coming here."

His green eyes settled on hers intently. "I insist. It is foolhardy to travel alone at this time of night."

Agnes ignored his look. "I am quite able to protect myself."

"Then humor me and allow me the pleasure of your company," he said, holding open the door for her. As she passed, he lowered his voice so that Mrs. Sharp did not hear. "Besides, there's something more I wish to say to you—in privacy."

Few people were abroad now, and Thomas walked close to Agnes's side, holding a lantern in one hand and extending his other arm so that she could rest hers upon it to steady herself on the street. She felt uncomfortable taking his support and they walked for some moments in silence, their feet crunching over the snow, clouds of white breath mingling in the dark night. Agnes was acutely aware of his stocky presence close to her; from time to time she sensed his eyes slide toward her and then away. She wondered what it was he wished to say, but offered him no assistance, waiting for him to speak.

When they reached the corner of Bread Street and Cheapside, Thomas cleared his throat. "I wanted to tell you to be careful, Mrs. Meadowes. I spoke to Riley today regarding the box you showed me. There was something dark in his manner. I don't pretend to comprehend what it was, but it worried me all the same. When I told him Rose's body had been found, he seemed little surprised or sorry to hear it. Soon after that he inquired after you. I don't know how he discovered it, but I had the impression he knew there was something between us."

Finding herself a subject for rumor was what she had feared almost as much as Thomas Williams's poor opinion of her. She shook her head and managed to cover her dismay. "Never mind Riley's interest in me—I don't suppose he offered any theory on Rose's death?"

Thomas looked at the ground. "Nothing. His words, as I recall, were that she was a meddlesome, flirtatious girl who doubtless was killed as a result of one of her intrigues."

"He made no further suggestion that might help?"

"None. His chief concern was to probe my friendship with you."

Agnes swallowed uncomfortably. "He must have heard some idle rumor. Philip, our footman, is friendly with him and one of the apprentices. In any case, Riley is the least of our worries. The assignation with Mr. Pitt tomorrow is a far more perilous undertaking."

"But that at least is an easily recognizable danger."

They were now halfway down Foster Lane, passing Goldsmiths' Hall. In a minute they would reach the steps leading down to her kitchen. A few yards from the railings, Thomas Williams paused and drew a deep breath. "It wasn't only Riley I wished to discuss, Mrs. Meadowes." He hesitated, his arm still supporting hers, looking down at his snow-caked boots. "It is a delicate matter. But it needs to be said, and I beg you won't think me presumptuous for voicing it."

Agnes raised an arched brow, but said nothing. After a minute Thomas hesitantly continued. "Last night I fear I may have imposed upon you. I never meant to do so. Today the thought occurred to me that perhaps you did not reciprocate willingly, but acted rather from some misguided sense of obligation on account of your son."

Agnes felt the blood drain from her cheeks. Her lips felt brittle and dry in the frosty night. "What do you mean, 'misguided obligation'?" she asked hoarsely.

"When I embraced you I thought your response spontaneous; but afterward I wondered if all was as it seemed. I have little experience in such matters, but once before I mistook a lady's purpose. It has made me nervous in affairs of the heart. In short, I wanted to assure you that whatever your feelings may be toward me, I should rather you expressed them honestly. I detest subterfuge in such matters. Your son won't be affected. I would rather know where I stand."

"Do I understand your meaning, Mr. Williams?" said Agnes sharply. "You believe I behaved improperly on my son's account, and that such liberties as I allowed you were not necessary?"

"Impropriety and liberties have nothing to do with it," said Thomas, reddening under her harsh scrutiny. "I only meant that I hold you in high esteem, whatever your feelings toward me. I don't wish our friendship to be distorted by other matters. I beg you to be straight with me."

"Nevertheless, you suspect I reciprocated your advances for reasons other than straightforward affection."

"I said nothing of the kind. You are putting words into my mouth. Don't look for insult where none was intended. I can't say any clearer what I meant."

But the subject he had raised was one to which Agnes was acutely sensitive. She stood in the snowy street, unable to move or find the words to respond. Thomas seemed to be confirming her earlier conviction that he believed her accustomed to behaving improperly. Her face burned with humiliation. She swiftly reminded herself of her resolution: she would maintain her indifference. Her mind felt clearer. She raised her chin. "How can I fail to feel insulted by the opinion you have formed of me? You have said you thought I might be bought by showing kindness to my son."

"Far from it," said Thomas, his tone growing louder as his patience wore thin. "I never had an ungentlemanly thought regarding you, either before or after last night. Whatever caused what happened between us, we cannot alter it—nor do I wish to. And since I see you are determined to think the worst of me, I have as much right as you to feel insulted. Good evening, Mrs. Meadowes. I think I shall go now to the Blue Cockerel."

Without a word, Agnes curtsied and descended at perilous speed down the icy stairs to her kitchen.

Chapter Thirty-one

AGNES SLEPT FITFULLY, going over every word of her exchange with Thomas, wishing she had thought to say this, that, or the other, to slight him as much as she felt his words had slighted her. When she awoke next morning, it was to a dismal overcast sky and snow that was rapidly thawing to unprepossessing slush.

At ten minutes to nine precisely, Agnes presented herself at the shop next door. Thomas Williams let her in. She noticed that once again he wore his sword for protection. Was this on Theodore's order? she wondered. He greeted her as if they were barely acquainted. "I went to the Blue Cockerel," he declared coldly. "The landlord recalled that Philip was there the night of the robbery with one or two other fellows. He did not remember who they were, save that one of them was Riley. Nor did he know what time any of them left." His eyes seemed cold as flint, and the face that had seemed friendly and reassuring before now seemed utterly impassive, as if it were hewn from marble. "And now, Mrs. Meadowes, Mr. Blanchard awaits you," he said, as he bowed and led her into the small back office.

She wondered if she had been too hasty with him. Had she misconstrued his fumbling apology for having made love to her? But no sooner had such a possibility arisen than she coldly dismissed it.

Their falling-out would not have happened were it not for his crass reference to such a delicate matter. And bearing this in mind, her earlier resolve to behave with detachment and the utmost propriety seemed the only dignified course open to her.

Theodore was in the back office. His wig was hanging on a hook by the wall, his bristly head was bowed over a bench. He looked up briefly as Agnes went in. There was an air of glum preoccupation about his tense mouth and unseeing gaze. The surface before him was crowded with dozens of small candlesticks; in the middle a space had been cleared. In this void Theodore had piled up twelve small towers of gold, ten coins in each. He now placed the gold, column by column, in an oak strongbox. The chink of metal made a knot in Agnes's stomach. She was conscious of Thomas standing on the other side of the bench, but dared not look in his direction, instead keeping her eyes fixed on the glittering heap in the box.

When all the coins were in, Theodore closed the lid, fastened iron bands over a hasp, and inserted a padlock through it the size of Agnes's fist. He locked it with a shiny key and threaded the key onto a length of cord. This he handed to her. "Put it about your neck, Mrs. Meadowes, and conceal it in your bodice." He spoke in a monotone, as if numb from the enormity of what he was about to do. "You are not to give the key to anyone but Pitt himself. And only once you have the wine cooler in your sight. Do I make myself clear?"

"Perfectly, sir."

Thomas Williams coughed. "Wouldn't it be more prudent if I were to have the key, sir?"

Theodore turned stiffly. "Why, Williams?"

"Only on account of her—Mrs. Meadowes, I mean—being a woman. It might be safer if a man had it."

Theodore blinked, astonished that his judgment should be questioned. "On the contrary, Mr. Williams, that Mrs. Meadowes is female makes her well suited to this task. Pitt is much stricken with her; I hazard he will be eager to keep to his undertaking partly to ingratiate himself further into her favors."

Thomas's pale cheeks darkened. "Forgive me, sir—I was unaware there was something between them."

"There is nothing between us," said Agnes hotly, then wished she had kept quiet. She slid the cold metal key beneath her bodice. Thomas avoided her eye and said nothing. Soon after this, a shadow fell over the shopwindow and the snorting of horses and clink of harnesses was audible. A deep red equipage, drawn by a pair of lively black horses with steaming nostrils, juddered to a halt in the slushy road. The carriage's velvet curtains—of the same hue as the paintwork—were tightly drawn, but there was a coach-man sitting up front, and to the rear, a pair of shabbily liveried footmen. Beneath their unbuttoned red greatcoats, both were armed with pistols.

No sooner had the carriage creaked to a halt than the footmen jumped down. One positioned himself close to the carriage door; the other, a portly man with lank hair drawn back in a bow, barged in without troubling to knock or remove his hat. Agnes recognized him as Grant, Pitt's corpulent attendant. "Mr. Pitt's carriage," he announced.

"She will be with you directly. Kindly wait outside," said Theodore. He instructed Thomas Williams to put the strongbox inside the carriage, sit beside it, and keep his feet on it at all times. Then he turned to Agnes. "Well, Mrs. Meadowes, are you ready? After the letter you sent, I hazard Pitt will be in a lather of expec-tation for you."

Agnes dared not look in Thomas's direction.

"It won't be necessary for your man to carry that," said Grant, suddenly barging back into the shop. "Mr. Pitt gave orders we should take it. And he'll only have Mrs. Meadowes inside the car-riage. Her man is to sit up front. This way, madam, when you're ready. Follow me."

As Agnes was ushered outside, Pitt's second attendant held out his hands for the box. Theodore stood at the doorway of the shop, legs braced, hands on hips, watching as a small fortune in gold was carried off to be delivered into the clutches of London's most infamous thief taker. Despite the winter chill, sweat beaded his brow. He opened his mouth as if to proffer another word of advice to Agnes, but then closed it again and waved her off with his hand.

Agnes's apprehensive gaze swung like a pendulum between the glittering façade of the shopwindow, resplendent with its silver display, and the ominous carriage, a gash of vermilion set against a bleak winter prospect. She wished she were anywhere but here; a powerful presentiment of misfortune caused a burning sensation in her throat. We are all in turmoil, she consoled herself, all of us groping in the dark, Theodore and Thomas as much as I.

Grant let down the carriage steps and bundled Agnes unceremoniously into the shadowy, curtained interior. Scarcely had she pulled her feet in than Grant cried out. "Quick now, stand away, ma'am," and the door crashed closed and was fastened behind her.

Agnes groped around the strongbox to her seat. As the door was closed, she had the impression of a shadowy form in the far corner of the carriage. And now she peered toward the corner. But the gloom was so dense after the daylight, she could see nothing. She reached forward to draw back the curtain on her side. As she did so, a hand grasped hers. A voice whispered directly into her ear. "I prefer you to leave that for the time being, if you please, Mrs. Meadowes."

Agnes flinched and drew back. The voice was soft but recognizable. "As you wish, sir." She added hesitantly, "You are Mr. Pitt, are you not?"

The voice was deeper and stronger now. "How astute you are to recognize me, madam. I take that as a compliment."

"I cannot conceive why. It was nothing but a question, Mr. Pitt," retorted Agnes, forgetting her fear and that she was supposed to beguile him with her charms.

Pitt laughed but said nothing more. As her eyes grew accustomed to the dark she began to distinguish his outline. He was tall and angular, as she remembered; a broad-brimmed hat obscured his upper profile, and he appeared to be wearing a long dark coat. The air in the carriage had the same pungent, sweet, spicy smell as his room. He was holding a cane topped with a silver orb, which Agnes could see gleaming like a diminutive moon, with the knobbly shape of his fingers clenched round it. Once again, she was conscious of Pitt's allure. What am I thinking? I am in the presence of evil. I ought to be repelled. She turned her head away.

Abruptly, Pitt thumped the orb hard on the window frame. "Grant—tell the driver to depart directly."

"Very well, sir." After that came a muffled shout to Thomas Williams, who was ordered to climb up in front, and to the footmen, who resumed their positions behind. The vehicle sagged and lurched at their weight, then Grant called out, "All in place, let's go!" The coachman cracked his whip and the carriage jolted drunkenly, metal-bound wheels slewing through the snow.

Agnes was thrown back against the velvet upholstery. The strongbox knocked against the door as the carriage veered into Cheapside. Then it lurched again as it picked up speed. Once they were bowling along, the pace steadied; Pitt pulled the strongbox over toward him, stretched out his legs, and rested his crossed feet on it as if it were a footstool. "Forgive me for startling you just now, Mrs. Meadowes."

"Were not the curtains and the dark intended expressly for that purpose, Mr. Pitt?" said Agnes, determined not to reveal any sign of the trepidation pulsing in her veins.

"I meant you no harm by them. Only it suited my purpose that Mr. Blanchard should remain ignorant of my presence."

"Oh, and why is that?" said Agnes, recalling that Theodore was equally eager to avoid a meeting with the thief taker, whom he claimed might derive some profit by their association.

"I find it safer to avoid unnecessary contact with my clients. I prefer to deal with intermediaries. Matters run more evenly and are concluded quicker as a consequence."

"I confess I still cannot see why such complications were necessary. Would it not have been simpler for Mr. Blanchard to hand you the money in person?"

"And deprive myself of the pleasure of your company?"

Agnes tossed her head. "Whatever your reason for this arrangement, I don't delude myself *I* had anything to do with it."

Pitt laughed. "Then if you want the honest truth I shall give it you. Once the money is handed over I make a habit of ensuring all transactions are properly concluded. I won't be with you when you recover the wine cooler. Should a constable stray into the vicinity, it would not do for me to be found with a large sum of money on my person and stolen property in my presence. Nevertheless, I shall observe proceedings from a distance—and if anything goes amiss you may be assured steps will be taken to rectify it."

Agnes shuddered, recalling poor Elsie's fears that Pitt would sacrifice her father if he deemed it expedient to do so. What Pitt meant was that he lived and prospered by the terror he engendered in those around him. "Whatever the reasons for your presence, I assure you I have no intention of duping you, Mr. Pitt. My only desire is the same as yours—to recover the wine cooler and trouble you no longer."

Pitt laughed mockingly again. "But therein your desires differ dramatically from mine, madam. Your pretty face and charming ways made an impression upon me. I had hoped from the tone of your letter that our acquaintance would continue. Or was that merely a contrivance to make me more eager to assist you?"

Knowing that she was now on perilous terrain, and that it would be prudent to affect at least some modicum of interest in him, Agnes answered with care. "It was no contrivance to say our future depends entirely upon how the business is concluded. For as I told you, I am a widow reliant upon my trade. Any person who helps secure my position, I will naturally regard with warm sentiments."

"Then I shall hold you to your promise, Mrs. Meadowes."

Some minutes later, the carriage slowed and Agnes judged they were in the vicinity of the bridge.

"Now we are a safe distance from Foster Lane, you are at liberty to open the curtain if you find the darkness distressing," said Pitt.

Agnes pulled back the velvet awning. They were in a narrow alley, lined on either side with tall, decrepit, windowless buildings, with a maze of small courts leading off. The pedestrians were shabbily dressed and gawped with unseemly interest at their elegant carriage. The buildings might be abandoned warehouses, she thought. If only she could get a glimpse of St. Paul's, or a church spire or some other landmark with which she was familiar, she might form a more exact impression of her whereabouts, but the low carriage roof and the narrow way obscured the skyline.

Agnes turned to Pitt. Half of his face remained in shadow. His expression was distant, unreadable; he sat erect and alert in his seat, his long slender fingers curled over the knob of his cane, as if he were prepared to act at a moment's notice. "Where are we?" she said, sitting forward and gripping the edge of her seat. "Why have you brought me here?"

"Have patience. You'll discover where you are in good time. Each of us knows the other's requirements. Provided you have brought what I asked, you will be safe and your master's wine cooler will be returned within the hour."

Agnes might have remonstrated further, but just then the carriage lurched to a halt. They were in a deserted alley scarcely wide enough for a single carriage. All she could see was decrepit wooden walls, a broken window, a shadowy doorway with a pile of dung mounded to one side. She tried to push down the glass so that she could gain a better view, but Pitt put a restraining hand on her arm. "Best not do that, my dear. In time you may admire the surroundings at your leisure. But not just now, eh?"

He tapped his stick sharply on the window. Grant descended, and a minute later his greasy, pockmarked face peered in on Pitt's side. Pitt leaned forward. "Is he still hooded up top?"

"All the way since Cheapside."

"Any sign of our friend yet?"

"No sir—but it may be he's there before us."

Pitt regarded his pocketwatch.

"One of you go and look." He gave the strongbox a nudge with the toe of his boot. "Meanwhile, I'll need help with this." Pitt turned to Agnes. "The key, if you please, Mrs. Meadowes."

"I was ordered to hand it to you only when I saw the wine cooler," she returned stoutly.

Pitt smiled, lowering his eyelids. "And so you shall, so you shall, madam," he said soothingly. "But as I said, I make a point of never being in the same place as stolen property. You have nothing to fear, provided you do as I ask. Now hand over the key that I may count the contents."

"But that is not what Mr. Blanchard ordered me to do. He said I must see the wine cooler first," countered Agnes bravely.

"Don't be rash, Mrs. Meadowes. Blanchard doesn't know how my business works. And he didn't want you to vex me, did he? Hand me the key and your worries will cease. The wine cooler awaits you, even now." When Agnes still resisted, he drew closer and whispered, "Then perhaps I should look for it myself. There are only a certain number of places a lady may secrete a key upon her person."

"How dare you!" cried Agnes. But instead of yielding, her fingers unthinkingly reached into the pocket of her cloak to find the knife she had put there last night.

"Then surrender the key. I repeat, there's not much I don't know about a lady's secrets. I wager I'll find it in an instant."

Agnes's fingers closed about the handle of the knife. As Pitt's face loomed over her, she thought of her husband drunkenly assailing her, and steeled herself. "Get away from me or I won't—"

"Won't what, my dear?" Pitt laughed joylessly as he slipped a hand inside her cloak, splayed his fingers over her breast, and squeezed as though testing the ripeness of a peach.

She held the knife blade against his invading hand. "I won't be responsible for my actions. I dislike being imposed upon, Mr. Pitt. Draw back now, or the knife might slip."

Pitt gasped at the sight of the cold metal blade and Agnes's sudden resolve and snatched his hand away. His lips drew tight and his eyes gleamed unnaturally bright, the pupils tiny peppercorns of black. "All right, Mrs. Meadowes. A very clever game. But pretty though you are, don't think I have brought you here just for conversation. Perhaps you'd like it if Grant assisted in persuading you to be more obliging."

Agnes, trembling, did not answer. Tears welled at the back of her eyes. She was enraged with herself for allowing this to happen. Why had she not just given him the key? He could easily break open the strongbox if he was so inclined. The battle she had fought with him, she realized, was needless. Nevertheless, she consoled herself. It was a victory of sorts to have caused him consternation. She fumbled for the ribbon at her neck. "Very well," she said, slicing the ribbon with the knife and flinging the key to the floor of the carriage, "if this is what you want, then take the wretched thing."

Glowering, Marcus Pitt unlocked the giant padlock, removed the hasp, and threw back the lid. Agnes watched as he ran his fingers through the sea of gold, then emptied the coins onto the floor of the carriage and counted them back into the box. His muttered counting and the way he deliberately ignored her seemed infinitely more frightening than his threats and advances.

When he had satisfied himself that the box contained the required sum, Pitt snapped the lid shut, locked it again, and put

the key in his pocket. Then he opened the carriage door and summoned Grant with a tap of his cane. "Well?" he said.

"A word if you please, sir."

Pitt stepped out. Snatches of their conversation drifted in to
Agnes.

"He was there . . . ," said Grant.

"Then you must . . ."

"But I never . . . And how . . ."

"I repeat . . ."

From their tone, Agnes judged that something unexpected had
taken place. The conversation lasted for so long that Agnes's
curiosity overcame her fear. She slid across to Pitt's side of the carriage to try to make out more. From behind the curtain she could
see Grant in full flow, facing Pitt. His face was flushed with agitation and he was gesticulating wildly. She could see only the back of
Pitt's long cloak and his silver-topped cane, which he was twirling
thoughtfully. When eventually Grant stopped, Pitt made some
staccato remark that sounded like "You must get it, then," and
jerked his head in the direction of the carriage. Grant nodded and
stepped round the other side. Agnes guessed that he was coming
for her, but from the vibrations behind her she judged that he was
delving about in the basket at the rear of the carriage. When she
summoned the courage to look out the window again, there was
no sign of him. All she could see was Pitt pacing about, still rotat-
ing the silver-topped cane in his hand.

A good ten minutes passed, during which Agnes watched from
her window, listening intently for any sign of what was to come.
But nothing happened and no one outside the carriage spoke a
word. Eventually, she heard the heavy crunch of Grant's footsteps
returning. Her door was thrown abruptly open and the steps were
let down. "We are ready for you now. Descend, if you please,
madam," said Grant.

Agnes did as he bade, and Thomas Williams was summoned

to join her. While she waited for him to clamber down from his platform next to the driver, she noticed that Grant's greatcoat sleeves were filthy—the dark red cloth was almost black and there were damp patches on it. His hands and face were smeared with dirt. He looked as though he had been digging in a coal pit.

Williams had traveled with a hood over his head. The driver had removed it just before letting him descend, and he was still blinking and looking dazed from the sudden daylight when Pitt addressed them. He signaled to a dark narrow passage leading off to the left between two buildings.

"A short distance down there is a terrace of three houses by the river's edge. The door of the last building is unlocked; enter it and you will find the wine cooler waiting for you."

Pitt spoke coldly, avoiding Agnes's gaze. In trying to obey Theodore's order she had slighted him. She wished now that she had not acted with such foolish haste. But the words were spoken, the knife had been brandished; and she was sure that somehow or other he would demonstrate his displeasure.

Chapter Thirty-two

AGNES PLUNGED DOWN the nameless passage, closely followed by Thomas Williams. She sensed that even if he had not heard their exchange, he must have noticed her unspoken strain with Pitt. She knew that in their precarious circumstances, it would be wise to improve matters between them. But she still burned when she remembered his clumsy remarks, and with the shock of Pitt's assault she was not in the mood to soften her manner one jot.

There was not a living soul to be seen. How was it possible, she wondered, to find such a deserted spot in the largest city in the world? With each step, Agnes half expected Pitt or Grant to jump out at them. She tried to tell herself that if Pitt wanted to exact revenge, he was unlikely to do so while his business might be jeopardized, and while she was protected. Any attack would surely come once her role in this business had played out and she was alone. Nevertheless, she remembered Pitt's words—that he always stayed in the vicinity to make sure the stolen property was returned, but kept himself concealed. She peered apprehensively into every shadowy gap. Was he watching even now? she wondered.

For his part, Thomas appeared untroubled by their predicament and impervious to her coolness. He spoke no word until they had passed a large decaying warehouse and the passage widened. "Have you any idea where we are?" he said eventually, gazing around for a familiar landmark or a street sign.

She started at the sound of his voice, then recovered herself. "Did you not glean any detail of interest during the journey?"

"Not a thing. The hood was placed over my head before we left Foster Lane, and the coachman never spoke a word to me, apart from telling me to sit tight. But it doesn't surprise me in the least."

"What do you mean?"

"It was Pitt's intention to confuse us and make us fearful. It gives him the advantage, helps him conclude his business with a minimum of fuss."

In that case, Agnes thought, he has certainly achieved his aim.

The passage suddenly opened onto an expanse of marshy wasteland beside the river. Traversed by a stinking sewer, the ground was littered with discarded rubbish: weeds, broken bricks, old bones, rotten wood, a mound of rubble, the mangled carcass of a cat. Rats scurried boldly about in the murky water. A row of dilapidated houses with boarded-up windows overhung the water's edge. The buildings had been shored up by wooden pilings, and in between these supports, the structure sagged like a necklace. In the sky wheeled a dozen or more gulls, their cries carried off like clouds of smoke in the gusting wind.

Agnes walked down toward the water and Thomas followed. The tide was high. Far off to the left, they could see a fleet of fishing smacks beating their way upriver into the wind. To the right several coal barges were moored; the men who lowered their brown sails resembled industrious ants. Faintly visible beyond the curve of the river were the great pillars of London Bridge and the jagged outline of its shops and buildings.

Agnes turned toward Thomas. "We have traveled east when I thought we had gone south. I warrant from the smell and the gulls we are not far from Billingsgate market," she said.

Thomas nodded inscrutably and looked back toward the row of decrepit houses. "The place he means us to go must be there," he said, striding ahead to the last door in the terrace. "Let us see if the entrance is unlocked as he promised." He drew his sword, turned the handle, and pushed. The door creaked on its rusty hinges and juddered open.

It led into a dingy narrow passage, with broken stairs rising off to the left and two doors leading off to the right. Thomas pushed open the door of the first room with the point of his sword and glanced in from the threshold, holding his sword aloft. Agnes was forced to wait behind, where she could not see a thing. Then he swiftly closed the door and progressed several steps along the corridor toward the second doorway.

Doubtless, Agnes thought, he expected her to follow. But Pitt's assault had left her angry and distrustful of everyone. She wanted to survey the place independently and make certain she was not being duped. Reopening the door to the first room, she peered in. The boards on the windows made the interior cavernous and shadowy, but there were enough chinks of light to see that the room was small and unfurnished, and that there was a large damp patch on the floor. The room reeked of soot, which emanated from a mound of black debris in the empty fireplace. There were also sooty smears leading from the fireplace across to the damp patch on the floor and thence to the door.

For several minutes Agnes could hear Thomas's footsteps pacing about next door. The pungent smell of soot suggested that it had recently fallen down the chimney. From the marks leading across the floor, it appeared that someone had recently entered this room. Both these details might be explained if that person had concealed something up the chimney—a valuable item, perhaps, something that could not be left on open view in an unlocked house. Agnes remembered the sooty marks on Grant's coat when he had returned to the carriage. And she had felt him rummage about in the basket behind before he left. Had the wine cooler been in the carriage all along? And had Grant deposited it here for them to recover? But if so, thought Agnes, that meant Pitt had risked being caught with money and stolen property on his person—a situation he claimed he avoided at all costs.

And why would he hide the wine cooler in such an inaccessible place? After all, once the money was paid, he wanted it to be found. Perhaps something else of value had been concealed here, that Pitt wanted to remain hidden.

Agnes went over to the fireplace and peered up the flue. It was wide enough, she judged, to hide something sizable. She groped into the chimney, dislodging soot and rubble so that she was forced to turn away her face and press her cheek to the chimney breast. Still she could feel nothing untoward, nothing to explain the mound of soot or the smudge marks.

At the farthest limits of her reach, the chimney seemed to broaden out sharply, forming a ledge inside. Suddenly her fingers brushed against an unexpected obstruction, a substance that was neither stone nor soot but wood—two planks wedged across the ledge. Further fumbling exploration revealed that they were supporting something. Whatever it was was wrapped in some variety of coarse hairy fabric—sacking, she concluded. Agnes prodded and felt something hard inside.

With renewed determination, Agnes tried to dislodge the planks and then haul the sack and its contents free, but the wood was securely wedged After some minutes she was forced to abandon her efforts.

Just as she had stepped away, Thomas's head poked round the door; the expression on his face was less stern than before—relief mingled with bemusement. "What on earth are you doing, Mrs. Meadowes?"

"There's something hidden in the chimney," she said, tasting granules of soot as she spoke. "Grant had soot on his clothes when he returned to the carriage. Perhaps it is something of value."

Williams shook his head. "Whatever it is, it cannot be the wine cooler; that was what I came to tell you—I have found it hidden in a closet in the room next door."

"Nevertheless, there is something here. There are planks supporting it. I tried to remove them, but I can't reach them. I think we should discover what it is."

Thomas heaved a sigh. "Very well. Let me try."

Agnes watched him gingerly push his sword up the chimney. He wrinkled his nose in distaste. "How far up is it?"

"As far as you can reach."

Thomas's face reflected his disbelief, and his regret at having to dirty his jacket. But then his weapon hit an obstruction and his eyes lit up. He retracted his sword and felt with his hand. "It feels like a sack, and whatever it contains, it is a sizable object."

Thomas bent his knees and gave a sharp upward thrust with his arm. A cascade of rubble and soot tumbled to the hearth, along with two wooden boards, and a section of brown sacking. Half the sack was now wedged in the chimney, bound by a cord.

"Allow me," said Agnes. She felt for the knife in her pocket and with a single swipe, cut the string. The sack's contents rolled at their feet, and Agnes and Thomas gasped in horrified unison.

A human head. The tongue half protruded from the mouth and had been nearly bitten through; a stump of spine and a few ragged sinews several inches long were still attached. What was most striking was the surfeit of blood. The hair was matted with it; blood had run into every imaginable cavity—the ears and nostrils and eye sockets—and clogged in the lids and lashes and brows; a trail of thick viscous red seeped from both corners of the lips.

Agnes glanced up at Thomas Williams. He was gray as a ghoul and had clamped his hand over his mouth. She too felt an acrid taste rise in her throat, but she swallowed several times and summoned all her resources of detachment. The murderer will escape, she told herself bitterly, if I cede to emotion. And she was determined to convey her invulnerability to him. He might waver and feel ill; she would not.

As it turned out, her aim was easily achieved. Thomas bolted from the room and she heard him retching outside. Agnes was quaking and her heart pulsed wildly, but she forced herself to reach into the chimney. With trembling hands, she gave the sack and its remaining ghastly contents a firm, hard pull.

Chapter Thirty-three

AGNES TOSSED THE SACK from the chimney onto the floor. Biting hard on her lip, she examined the headless corpse. Every now and again she turned to compare it with the head. At the sound of Thomas's entry, she looked up. "Are you quite recovered, Mr. Williams?"

"Of course," he said, then seeing the headless corpse, he stepped back. "What are you doing?" he mumbled.

Agnes breathed deeply to quell the heaving in her own stomach. "Trying to ascertain what has happened."

Thomas coughed uncomfortably. "Is it not perfectly transparent what has happened? His head has been cut off."

"Quite so, Mr. Williams, but by whose hand? And why?" Her insides felt molten with the shock of handling the body, and there was a burning sensation in her throat. But she forced herself to remain composed. "Does anything in particular strike you about this killing?"

"Not especially," said Thomas, keeping his eyes glued to the boarded window. "What do you make of it?"

"His throat had been cut just as Noah and Rose's were, which suggests it was committed by the same hand. I don't suppose you recognize him, do you?"

"No," replied Thomas uneasily.

Noticing his returning pallor, Agnes said more kindly, "You say you recovered the wine cooler."

"Yes," he said, looking at his feet.

"Then while I finish here, may I suggest you go in search of some means of conveying it back to Foster Lane? I shall stay and guard it."

"Are you not afraid to wait alone?"

"What relevance have my fears? The wine cooler is too heavy for us to carry any distance."

It was unlike him to give in to her with so little protest, but either he recognized the truth of what she said or his stomach was heaving once more. In any case, he needed no more persuasion to nod and disappear. Agnes wondered if she had been wise to send him away. What would she do if he didn't return?

The head was sunken-eyed, hook-nosed, and unshaven, and—to judge from the smell of tobacco and stale sweat—unwashed for heaven knows how long. She attempted to draw an accurate impression of the man's means from his costume. It was saturated with blood, but she could see that, while it was undeniably shabby, it had curious touches of eccentricity. His coat was worn and ingrained with filth, but his lapels were lined with velvet and the cravat was silk. She rummaged through his pockets and found a silken handkerchief, a couple of pennies, a small pocketknife, a length of rope, a pair of knitted gloves, and a silver wine label engraved *Shrub*. Nothing that shed any light on who he was. It was only when she turned over the wine label that she discovered anything of note. The marks were those of Blanchards'.

She was still clutching the label when she heard the sound of a soft footfall close behind her. Swiveling round, her eye caught a pair of flawlessly polished black boots standing by the door. She looked up slowly, taking in a pair of black breeches, a black under-coat surmounted by a long black cloak that nearly brushed the ground, a gloved hand holding a cane with a silver knob.

"Mrs. Meadowes," said a suave but chilling voice. "How very unexpected to find you still here. What on earth are you doing with that corpse?"

It was the voice she most dreaded, the man she most feared. She rose swiftly to her feet and faced Marcus Pitt. "As you see, I am examining it. Do you know him?"

"May I ask why you think I should?"

"Because you sent us to this house, and the wine cooler was hidden in the next room. It seems probable to me that he is therefore a member of your confederation of rogues." She was still clutching the wine label and suddenly a realization dawned. "Is he Harry Drake?"

Pitt snorted but did not deny it. "And you think I killed him, do you?"

"No," said Agnes, still maintaining her bravado, "I do not."

Marcus Pitt nodded. "Why is that?"

"Why would you have him decapitated when you might have got a reward for handing him over to the justice?"

"Very good, Mrs. Meadowes. *Very* good. Who would suspect that beneath that feminine exterior there beats such a steely heart?"

Agnes held her head high. Her eyes narrowed. "It has always been my experience that exteriors are deceiving, sir. Most of us, when called upon, can convincingly conceal the person we really are. But that is by the by. May I inquire what has prompted you to return here? I thought you never risked entering a building where stolen property was present."

Pitt flashed a dangerous smile. "On rare occasions I find it behooves me to take a risk. After all, what would this humdrum existence of mine be without a little danger—a dull thing, a very dull thing indeed. Where one as winsome as you is concerned, is it strange that I abandon my usual precautions?"

"So you expected to find me here," said Agnes. Her pulse was beating wildly again and fear spread like a stain.

Pitt grinned; the malice in his eye was unmistakable. "So you know what has brought me here, do you?"

"You wished to see Drake's corpse with your own eyes."

"Why should I want to do that?"

"Because you are as surprised as I by his death. No doubt you wished to do the same as I—try and ascertain who did kill him. I believe Grant must have discovered the body this morning lying on the floor, where there is a large dark stain. I hazard it was he who hid it up the chimney, so that Mr. Williams and I would not find it and become distracted from our task. That was the reason you held me so long in the carriage, and why Grant's hands and suit were so noticeably sullied when he returned."

Pitt gave a noncommittal smile. "I congratulate you, Mrs. Meadowes. Your answer contains an element of the truth. Drake's murder has surprised me, and I dislike surprises. But I also dislike being refused something upon which I have set my heart."

"Who do you suppose killed Drake?" said Agnes quickly.

"I have my suspicions, but let us save them for later. You know very well I am taken with you. I think you were teasing me in the carriage." He pulled back his lips in a leering grin and advanced toward her.

"My apologies, Mr. Pitt, if I misled or offended you," said Agnes, backing away from him. "I meant no harm; it was only that you took me by surprise when you asked for the key."

But Pitt seemed not to hear these remonstrations. "Do you think I don't see the heat in your cheeks, or the desire in your eyes? Come here—let me hold you. But first, let's throw away that knife in your pocket, shall we?"

With this, he grasped Agnes firmly by the wrist and twisted her arm behind her back. He began to rummage in her cloak, and after much unnecessary probing of her person, withdrew the knife. "A very nasty weapon," he said. He examined its blade with his thumb, then flung it away. He drew Agnes toward him and pressed his mouth into her neck. "Ah, this is what I've waited for!"

he said, as he held his other hand against her chin and pressed his moist lips to her cheek.

Once again, Agnes noticed the pungent sweet scent of him. But whereas before in his office he had thrilled her, now she was sickened by his proximity. "Release me, Mr. Pitt! Let me go at once!"

"Such effort is futile, Mrs. Meadowes. There's no one to hear and it will only excite me further. Or is a bruising what you want?" he whispered in her ear.

Agnes kicked out viciously at his shins. Pitt clamped his hand across her mouth and pushed her toward the corner of the room. Seeing that she would soon be trapped, she gave his fingers a hefty bite.

"Bitch! What the devil do you mean? Now I'll give *you* something you don't like."

"Get away! Leave me be!" she screamed as he shoved her against the wall and rammed a leg between her thighs, then extracted a pocket pistol.

"Is this what you want?" Pitt cocked the weapon and brandished it in front of her, before pressing the muzzle to her forehead and wedging her into the corner, arms pinioned by her sides. "Now spare me any more theatricals and I'll finish with you more quickly—isn't that what you want?"

He fumbled with his breeches then pressed against her, his free hand probing among her skirts. Mustering all her remaining strength, Agnes brought her heel down hard on the top of Pitt's foot. Pitt withdrew an inch or two, and she wrenched her arms free and gave his shoulders an almighty shove. He lurched backward and sprawled on top of Drake's prostrate corpse . The pistol went flying into the sooty fireplace. Agnes did not bother to recover it—she dodged past Pitt and bolted for the door. She was nearly through, but he clambered after her on his hands and knees and grabbed hold of her skirt. "Now, my lovely, before you run off, think of this. If you leave, the wine cooler will be unguarded and any rogue might come and steal it. Then it might be melted down, and what would Blanchard have? No wine cooler—no money, either."

"That isn't your way," said Agnes, hesitating.

"As I told you before, on occasion my ways alter."

In the distance Agnes heard a dog bark and the sound of a barge man shouting. If only she were outside, on the river. Without the wine cooler, Blanchards' would be ruined. And what of Peter—how would she care for him? There was no longer any doubt in her mind what she should do. Her face was as pale as milk as she drew back her leg as he clutched her skirt. Then with all her might she planted a firm kick on the side of his head. There was a thump, then a howl as he released her. Agnes, feeling a swell of pride, scrambled for the door.

She careered headlong into a figure coming in the opposite direction.

"Mrs. Meadowes, what is it? Where are you going? Didn't we agree you would await my return?"

"Thomas," cried Agnes wildly, "do not go in there under any circumstance. Forget the wine cooler. It is of no consequence. Pitt is there, armed with a pistol."

"Calm yourself, please," he said, holding her shoulders. She felt his gaze lingering on her face; she could feel a bruise burning on her neck and an impressed circle pulsing in the center of her forehead, where Pitt had thrust the pistol at her. "Wait there," he said.

"Didn't you hear what I said? He has a pistol, he put it to my brow."

Thomas nodded. "I have not come unaccompanied, Mrs. Meadowes. This morning, prior to our departure, I thought it prudent to notify the authorities. They followed us and were waiting a safe distance away all along. A constable and his two deputies should be more than a match for Mr. Pitt, no matter how violent his temper."

Agnes glanced over his shoulder. Standing in line behind him were two stout fellows holding wooden staves and another leaner man with a pistol. She recalled Theodore expressly ordering that the authorities should not be apprised of this transaction. Yet Thomas Williams had not been afraid to defy him. She had never been so glad of insurrection in her life.

"Gentlemen," called Thomas, "this way if you please."

Pitt was on his way out the back door when the constable and his deputies apprehended him. Realizing there was no escape, he held up his palms in a gesture of mock submission as Agnes and Thomas reentered the house. "Very well," he declared. "But don't think I am beaten entirely. A certain judge of the King's Bench— a most influential man within the judiciary—happens to be an old acquaintance of mine. I recovered a pocketbook of his not long ago; it made most interesting reading. He was so delighted to have it returned, he promised to assist me if I ever fell foul of the law. There's no proof of my involvement in the robbery."

"There is proof you tried to force yourself upon me," said Agnes hotly. "And I shall testify against you." She paused and shot him a crafty look. "Unless, that is, you tell me where your carriage has gone."

"Why do you wish to know that?"

"Because now the thief is dead, you do not need to pay his reward. Your claim to be an innocent intermediary can thus only be credible if you return the gold Mr. Blanchard paid."

Realizing that Agnes had outmaneuvered him, Marcus Pitt scowled.

"You bitch. You're no better than a common whore and a thief."

"That's no way to address Mrs. Meadowes. Answer her politely. Where is your carriage and Mr. Blanchard's gold?" Thomas Williams grabbed the neck of Pitt's shirt and screwed it tight so Pitt had difficulty in breathing. Pitt's deep-set eyes watered with the discomfort of Thomas's grip, but he refused to speak.

"So, Mr. Pitt, you prefer me to make a statement to the justice, do you?" said Agnes.

Still Pitt said nothing.

Thomas Williams tightened his grip until Pitt's face turned puce. When Pitt began flapping his hand up and down, making strange gurgling sounds, Thomas lightened his grip. "Well?"

"The carriage is in the court at the end of the road," he stuttered. "But don't think I'll forget this, Mrs. Meadowes."

Agnes regarded him coolly. "It strikes me, sir, that unless you tread with care, freedom of memory will be one of the few liberties you have left."

Chapter Thirty-four

THOMAS AND AGNES traveled back to Foster Lane with the wine cooler squatting on the floor of the carriage like a splendid footbath, the strongbox of gold recovered from Pitt's carriage, and one of the constable's deputies as escort. The constable and the other deputy traveled in a separate vehicle to convey Pitt to the roundhouse and Drake's body to a certain barber surgeon, who paid good rates to dissect the corpses of criminals.

For much of the way Agnes was silent, preoccupied by the disturbing sequence of events. Elsie was now an orphan. Did she know her father had been brutally murdered? Who would mind her now? Agnes wondered how she could ever have considered Pitt anything but repellent. What would have happened to her had Thomas Williams not arrived when he did?

She saw that her resentment over the crass comments Thomas had made last night was trivial. She wanted to tell him so, and thank him for what he had done and for the great change he had effected in her. But she could not bring herself to raise a subject so personal in front of the deputy constable.

She studied the wine cooler at her feet. She had seen drawings, but she was awestruck by its sheer scale and opulence. Every inch of its surface was rippled with lively ornament—mermaids reaching out to smooth their hair; dolphins exploding from the waves, shell-wielding tritons astride them; and a great seminaked figure of Neptune, drawn by a pair of large-eyed, nostril-flaring horses. Agnes pictured the wine cooler filled with wine and ice at a grand banquet, resplendent on Sir Bartholomew Grey's sideboard. And unlike the magnificent tables of food I create, she thought ruefully, this will not be demolished in a matter of hours. Thieves permitting, it will endure for generations.

She wondered briefly whether or not the marks on it had been transposed from another piece to avoid duty. She wanted to ask Thomas where they were, and if he would examine them to determine whether or not they had been tampered with. But making such a request in front of a deputy constable might imply that Blanchards' had been involved in illegal practices. So for most of the journey Agnes lost herself in silent pondering.

WHEN THEY WERE nearly back in Cheapside, Agnes cleared her throat and asked Thomas to halt the carriage and set her down. There was a new softness to her voice as she explained that she had an urgent commission she wanted to perform before returning to the kitchen. "What is it? Where are you going?" he replied, astonished.

"I intend to call in at Bruton Street, the home of Lord Carew. Mrs. Tooley told me that Rose Francis used to work there before she came to Blanchards'."

"But why worry now the wine cooler is recovered? Whatever Rose's involvement was, it is irrelevant now."

Agnes was disappointed to hear Thomas echo sentiments that Theodore had expressed. She expected more of him. "The wine cooler is recovered, but three people have been murdered. And we are no closer to knowing by whose hand. I, for one, won't rest until I know who the murderer was."

Thomas regarded her sternly. "But that is a matter for Justice Cordingly."

Agnes turned to the deputy constable, who was plainly agog at the dispute unfolding before him. "Sir," she said, "do you suppose it likely the justice will ever discover who brought about the deaths of an apprentice, a kitchen maid, and a thief?"

The deputy, a portly fellow with a broad florid face, shook his head. "In my experience, most murderers who are apprehended are caught by someone connected to the victim who makes an effort to trace them. The justice has too many other matters to occupy him. Rich corpses tend to make more racket than poor 'uns, if you take my meaning."

Agnes turned back to Thomas. "I recall you once saying we should all occasionally involve ourselves in matters outside our immediate concerns, Mr. Williams. I have never done so till now, always believing I was better equipped to manage my own affairs than anyone else. But today, without your assistance, goodness knows what might have happened to me. I thank you heartily for your aid, and for revealing my earlier deficiency. Be in no doubt that from here on I intend to rectify it. And I shall start by trying to bring the murderer to justice."

Agnes expected Thomas to be mollified by this but he appeared quite unmoved.

"But what makes you believe Lord Carew has anything to do with all of this?"

"I don't know precisely. Intuition, perhaps. But it strikes me that none of us in the household knows much about Rose's background. I should have asked her more about herself, but I never did."

"Even so, after all that has happened this morning, now is hardly the time to pay a gentleman such as him a visit."

"It is my only chance. Now the wine cooler is recovered, I will have no excuse to escape the kitchen."

"Then let me go in your stead."

"No," said Agnes. "This is something I should do myself. You were barely acquainted with her; it will be easier for me to uncover her past."

"Forgive me for mentioning it, Mrs. Meadowes, but what I meant was you are scarcely in a condition to make social calls."

Agnes realized that she was, as usual, entirely oblivious of her appearance. She peered down at her distorted reflection in the curved bowl of the wine cooler. Her clothes were disheveled, her face was smeared with soot. She wet her fingers with her tongue and attempted to clean it off. Then she rearranged her hair, pushing a few stray tendrils back into her bonnet, and brushed at the sooty stains on her sleeves. She was far from pristine, but under the circumstances, it was better than nothing.

"Have you money?"

"Enough for a hackney there and back."

"Then if there's no way I can persuade you otherwise, I suppose I'll have to let you go."

Chapter Thirty-five

ALF AN HOUR LATER, Agnes arrived at Bruton Street, a fashionable thoroughfare of wide houses a world apart from the dismal landscape she had recently been in. Lord Carew resided in in a gracious mansion, five stories tall, with draped and valanced sash windows on either side of a grand columned entrance. Agnes's hackney drew up at the front of the house, and she spent some moments gazing at it in awe. Remembering Thomas's criticism of her appearance, she decided against presenting herself at the front door and instructed her driver to go round to the mews at the rear, promising him a shilling if he waited while she made her way to the servants' entrance.

A plump curly-haired scullery maid was emptying a bucket of slops into the gutter. "Looking for summat?"

"The house of Lord Carew."

She jerked her head at an open door set back through a yard. "Then look no further. You have found the place."

"Are you employed here?"

"I am," answered the girl curtly. She looked Agnes over. "But I can tell you straight, we don't give out food to those that come begging."

"I'm not a beggar," said Agnes, bristling. "If I look a little disheveled, it's only because I've come straight from the Newark coach." She was surprised at how glibly this lie slipped out.

"Have you, indeed? Then what brings you here, may I ask?"

"I seek news of a cousin of mine, who I have reason to believe works here," Agnes continued untruthfully.

"And who might that be?"

"Rose Francis."

The maid's face relaxed a smidgeon. "Forgive me, ma'am, if I appeared unfriendly. I meant no harm. 'Twas only my manner. 'Tis true those coaches can turn the best laundered dress into a rag in a few hours."

"So do you know my cousin?"

"No, but her name is familiar. She quit this house some while ago. I took her place after she'd gone. If it's recent news of her you want, you'll find none here."

"But perhaps someone who knew her might know where she has gone."

The maidservant shrugged. "You'd best speak to one of the upper servants. They might know. Come in and I'll see if they've a moment to spare."

Agnes followed the girl into a kitchen that was four times the size of her own in Foster Lane. An entire wall was given over to the vast fire and ovens, another to dressers, cupboards, and shelves. A parade of copper pans and molds and baskets of every shape and form was suspended from a line of meat hooks strung out upon a wooden beam. Arranged on a table twelve feet long were a bowl of dried fruit, a basket of eggs, a pat of butter, a basin of flour, and a half chopped cone of sugar. At one end, a woman stirred a vast basin of ingredients.

She was around fifty years of age, stoutly built. Her complexion was pink, and smooth as a sugared almond, her features small and fleshy. She wore her dark hair caught in a plump bun. Two stains the size of apples beneath her armpits bore testimony to the heat of the kitchen and her present exertions.

"Mrs. Lugg," said the scullery maid, raising her voice above the hubbub of half a dozen maids and pot boys, "I found this lady outside; she wants a word."

"Does she think I've nowt better to do than prattle to whomsoever comes calling?" replied the woman, sniffing bad-temperedly as she jiggled the spoon vigorously in the bowl.

"I'll tell her to go then, shall I?"

"Should have done so in the first place," snapped Mrs. Lugg. "Those what have time to waste nattering in the street generally find they're up betimes to catch up on the work they ain't finished."

"That will be a sizable cake when you've done," said Agnes, stepping hastily forward and peering in the basin.

"Reckon you know something about cooking, do you?" said Mrs. Lugg, regarding Agnes whilst wiping a drip from her nose with the back of her hand.

"In a manner of speaking, yes," said Agnes. "Only I reckon from the proportions of your basin the household I'm used to is not half as sizable as yours. We've only three upstairs and fewer than ten below."

"There's more than twice that in this establishment," said Mrs. Lugg. "So you'll comprehend why I've no time for chitchat. What brings you here? Ain't no good searching for employ without a character, I'll tell you that straight off. And I'd advise you to pay a visit to the bathhouse before you come presenting yourself to a respectable place like this."

"It ain't employ she's after," broke in the scullery maid. "It's news of one what used to work here—her cousin, she says. She's all messed up from the coach."

"A cousin? And who might that be?"

"Her name is Rose Francis."

Mrs. Lugg set down her spoon, made fists and placed them knuckle-down upon her hips. "Rose Francis!" She nodded as though she should have guessed. "Sharp so-and-so, wasn't she?"

Agnes nodded. "On occasion, though she was not all bad, I think."

"'Tis a while since I heard her name mentioned. After the way she behaved, 'tis a wonder she's the nerve to own to having anything to do with us here."

"Who in heaven's name is this person?" said a clear, somewhat shrill voice.

Everyone from the pot boy to the cook fell silent.

"Mrs. Moore!" said Mrs. Lugg, looking as if she'd been caught with a finger in the treacle. "I was just about to send a maid in search of you, ma'am. There's a visitor come. She wants a word."

The newcomer was a woman considerably younger than Mrs. Lugg, slender as a lily and infinitely more regal in bearing. Her dress was of fine-quality wool, dyed an attractive shade of pale blue and buttoned high about her neck. Her cap and collar were of fine lawn, pristine and ironed. Her features were strong and striking, a straight nose, well-chiseled lips, gray eyes. A large bunch of keys tied about her waist dangled in the folds of her skirts. This, Agnes supposed, must be Lord Carew's housekeeper.

"Oh, and why's that?" said Mrs. Moore, looking Agnes briefly up and down. "The kitchen is not a place for visitors—especially not those of disreputable appearance. Go away, please, this instant. There's no takings to be had here."

"'Tis news of Rose Francis she's after. Says she's her cousin."

Ridges of surprise erupted suddenly on Mrs. Moore's smooth brow.

"It's Rose you're interested in, is it?"

Agnes nodded.

"And your name is?"

"Mrs. Agnes Meadowes."

"In that case, Mrs. Meadowes, you'd best come with me."

Mrs. Moore led Agnes down a labyrinth of back corridors to her parlor. No sooner had she crossed the threshold and closed the door behind her than she rounded on Agnes with a look of ominous determination. "And now, Mrs. Meadowes, may I inquire as to your real reason for coming to Bruton Street?"

"I believe my cousin once worked in this household," answered Agnes guardedly.

Mrs. Moore compressed her lips and shot Agnes a withering glare. "You are correct in that respect. But why should it concern you? I may say your assertion that she's your cousin cuts no ice with me."

"What makes you say that?"

"Because Rose has no family—that was how we were persuaded to take her in. But that is by the by. I ask again, what is your interest in her?"

Agnes wavered, and glanced about the room. The only adornment on the walls was a series of five silhouettes in oval frames hung on either side of the chimney—two were of men, two of ladies, one of a child. Was this Mrs. Moore's family? Agnes wondered. Or was Mrs. Moore as alone in the world as Mrs. Tooley? Will I become someone hard and intractable like this, or fragile and fussy like Mrs. Tooley, with nothing to show for my life save a few ornaments and years of service? No, I have Peter. Then, seeing suddenly that unless she spoke firmly she would get nowhere, Agnes said, "To tell the truth, Rose worked under me when she left you. I am the cook at a house in Foster Lane where she took up her position. She disappeared a week ago without explanation. We subsequently found a letter that showed she had an assignation with a lover with whom she intended to run off. I hoped perhaps someone here might have had news of her that mentioned his name and would help trace her."

Mrs. Moore regarded Agnes unblinkingly. "Rose Francis left this house a year ago. We've heard nothing since. That is all I can tell you."

Agnes had avoided mentioning the full catalog of events to

avoid causing unnecessary distraction and upset. But with Mrs. Moore being so unforthcoming, she found it hard to fathom how else she could avoid mentioning them.

Suddenly the events of the day took their toll. All the determined vigor that had brought her here seemed to seep away. She wished for a moment that she had heeded Thomas Williams and not come, or that she had considered more carefully how to approach the household. If she had sent word beforehand advising of her interest and the reason for it, Mrs. Moore might have greeted her more openly.

But just as she was poised to take her leave, Agnes reminded herself why she had acted so precipitously. The wine cooler had been recovered. She would be expected to resume her usual duties; it might be days before she had the chance to come again. She had to discover all she could now, even if it meant revealing more than she would have liked.

Mustering all her flagging energy, Agnes drew a deep breath. "Let me explain more plainly what I meant to convey. The same day Rose left, a valuable wine cooler was stolen and an apprentice was murdered. A few days later, Rose herself was discovered dead. My employer, Mr. Blanchard, will not rest until he knows the exact circumstances of the robbery and the deaths. He believes that someone inside the house may have been involved, and that perhaps Rose was somehow embroiled. Were there any signs of dishonesty when she was with you?"

Agnes saw Mrs. Moore start at the mention of murder, but no sooner had she finished speaking than the housekeeper's stony manner returned. "Do you ask these questions with your employer's authority?"

Agnes nodded. "Both Mr. Blanchard and Justice Cordingly have sought my assistance."

"I see. Then I suppose that does alter things."

There followed a long, long silence while Mrs. Moore, paler but no more friendly, indicated that Agnes should sit down. She toyed with a narrow silver band on her finger, but did not reply to Agnes's question. Finally, she said slowly, "I suppose I ought not to be surprised at her demise."

"Why is that, Mrs. Moore?"

The housekeeper seemed lost in her own train of thought. "Rose Francis worked here for less than a year," she declared at length. "I expended considerable energies on teaching her how to carry out her duties. When she left without so much as a day's notice I felt let down—deceived, even. But then, judging by your account, she made a habit of mysterious departures."

Agnes let this pass, though the bitterness in Mrs. Moore's tone did not escape her. "Under what circumstances did she come to you?"

"She applied for a post in writing. As I recall, the letter declared she had been raised in the north of England, but sought a position in a London establishment, there being no permanent vacancies in the vicinity and all her family having recently perished in an outbreak of cholera. Her mother had taught her the rudiments of domestic economy. She had been to school until the age of thirteen, could sew neatly and read and write fluently. Her letter was well penned—her hand was one of the neatest of any servant I've ever known; it could have passed for that of a lady. As I later had reason to believe it did. You asked me if she was dishonest. That was her first transgression."

"What makes you say so?"

"Her letter enclosed a character, purportedly to be written by the housekeeper of a north-country mansion. She claimed Rose had worked there during the summer months when the house was in use. I made attempts to contact this person but received no response. After some weeks I contacted the local rector. From him I learned that not only had the housekeeper never written the character, but such a mansion never existed. But he did reveal that there was a girl by the name of Rose Francis in the vicinity. She was the daughter of the local schoolmaster. Both parents had died from cholera while her brother was abroad. Thus she was forced to leave her home and seek employ elsewhere. As far as the rector knew, she cut herself off entirely from all previous acquaintances. Nobody had heard where she had gone. But since work was hard to come by in that part of the country, it was assumed she had gone to London."

Agnes was struck by a strange thought. She had never dreamed she and Rose had anything in common, yet now she saw similarities in their sad pasts. Rose had been forced, as she had, to leave the genteel life into which she was born and enter service. But where Agnes had resigned herself to her fate, Rose had not.

Agnes studied Mrs. Moore thoughtfully, and detected a gleam of wistfulness in her face. Perhaps beneath her implacable exterior lay someone as torn as Agnes herself. "What impressions did you form of Rose when she first began working here?" said Agnes.

Mrs. Moore gave a brief smile. "She was clever, quick, winsome when she desired to be, but as I soon discovered, lacking in constancy."

"In what way?"

Mrs. Moore sniffed. "No sooner did she grow accustomed to the duties expected of her than she began to behave as if she deserved something better. She turned into a troublemaker, resentful of being ordered about, ignoring household rules, and inciting others to act as willfully as she did. And whenever I reprimanded her or punished her, she was without remorse or contrition."

"What kinds of rules did she transgress?"

"She went out at nighttime without permission. She was bold, and caused ructions among the male staff. She often neglected her duties, and was ill tempered with her superiors when reprimanded. Need I continue?"

"No," said Agnes. "But can you fathom why, if she wished to improve herself, Rose took another post as a kitchen maid in a smaller establishment than this? Surely that was a backward step."

Mrs. Moore shrugged her shoulders. "That is why I am astonished to learn where she went. She left here without giving any notice or a word of where she was going. Nor did she ask for a written character. To tell the truth, I would not have written a kind one. I was on the brink of dismissing her anyway. I always assumed she had gone to get married or take up a more lucrative position. The first news I've heard of her since she left is from you."

Agnes sighed. But something must have caused her to leave Lord Carew's household so precipitously. "You mentioned you thought she might have run off to get married. Had she a sweetheart that you knew of?"

Mrs. Moore sat up stiffly. "Servants are forbidden alliances in this household, as in most other respectable establishments of my acquaintance."

"I did not wish to cast aspersions upon the propriety of this household, but those determined to pursue affairs of the heart invariably find ways to avoid apprehension. Servants *do* marry; and as you have already stated, Rose was flirtatious of disposition."

Mrs. Moore regarded her hands, stony-faced. "I did not press her on the matter, but there may have been someone."

"Did she mention a name?"

"No, but when she arrived she wore a silver band on her engagement finger. I asked about it when I first saw her. Naturally, I wouldn't have taken her if I knew she was engaged. But she said the ring had been left to her by her mother." She paused. "A day or two before she left, one of the maids found her sobbing on her bed. And when she asked what the matter was, Rose threw something at her and stormed from the room. The other maid retrieved the missile—it was a silver ring—from under the bed. She left it for Rose on the night table by her bed. After Rose had gone, the ring was found hidden under the mattress."

"Are you certain it was hidden? Might it have been mislaid inadvertently?"

"I suppose so. But in any case, she never asked for it to be sent to her."

"Where is the ring now?"

"I have it here." She slipped the silver band off her finger. "I looked, but there is no inscription on it."

"Peculiar that she should leave it," said Agnes, examining the inside of the ring. There were five marks instead of the four she expected, and she recognized only two—the leopard's head and lion *passant*.

"Would you consent to lend me this for a day or two?"

"By all means, if you think it will help you. I only wore it to keep it safe. I always expected that one day she would send some communication and then I would return it."

Agnes held the ring carefully in her palm, then threaded it onto her ring finger. As she tried to push it on, it bit painfully into her flesh; she pressed harder and eased it over her knuckle.

"Now I think on it, she had another unusual possession, a small silver box—a vinaigrette, I believe it was—heart-shaped, prettily engraved with flowers and leaves," said Mrs. Moore.

Agnes immediately recalled the box Elsie had found in Rose's pocket. "Did she ever say where it came from?"

"I did ask her where she got it. She said it was a parting gift from the mansion where she had worked before coming here, but I suspected that wasn't the truth. I had yet to learn that the character she had written was a fabrication, or anything of her probable history, but since the box was not the sort of thing most servants possess, I felt it my duty to take it to Lord Carew and ask if it belonged to him or one of his guests." Two crimson stains had appeared suddenly in Mrs. Moore's pale cheeks. Agnes was reminded of Mrs. Tooley's discomfiture when she had interviewed Rose over the letter.

Agnes shifted in her seat. "And what did he say when he saw it?"

"He looked long and hard at it, and declared that though the work was extremely fine, he didn't believe he had seen it before, nor to his knowledge had any of his friends lost it. He surmised that far from being a gift from her previous employer, the box might be a love token and that I should give the girl a talking-to over consorting with the opposite sex."

"I see, and how long after this did you discover the matter of the forged character?"

"A month or two—it was partly seeing the box and sensing there was something unusual about it that made me pursue the matter."

"And having found that Rose's character was forged, did you raise the matter again with Lord Carew?"

"I would have done so, naturally, but by then he was visiting his country seat in the north, as I recall. By the time he had returned, she had gone."

Chapter Thirty-six

ON RETURNING TO Foster Lane, Agnes scarcely had time to change her dress and wash her face before she was thrown into the thick of it. Mr. Matthews was complaining loudly about a wine label missing from the dining room, while instructing John on how to clean two claret jugs by mixing a confetti of brown paper with soap, warm water, and a little pearl ash. "Mr. Blanchard will expect you at one in the library," he called out when he caught sight of her passing his pantry door.

"What wine label has been lost?" said Agnes, recalling the one she found in Drake's pocket, which was now lying in her own.

"Shrub wine," replied John. "Missing since yesterday. You seen it on your travels?"

"I'll keep a look out." Trying not to blush, she hurried to the kitchen.

AGNES SUPPOSED THAT Theodore wanted to thank her for recovering the wine cooler and his money. Retrieving both was a better result than he could possibly have hoped for. Undoubtedly, the future of Blanchards' would now be secure. But an appointment in half an hour scarcely allowed her time to peruse the dinner menu and ascertain what still needed to be done, let alone make a start on it. "Very well, Mr. Matthews," she said, as she read what Mrs. Tooley had written on the slate:

First course: leek potage, broiled eels, small salad, Scotch scallops
Second course: mutton with haricots, calf's liver stew, cardoons, dish of jelly
Dessert: flummery, brandied apricots, Spanish biscuits

Agnes surveyed the table, the range, and the larder. She felt none of her usual enthusiasm for her work. Her limbs were leaden; her feet heavy in her boots; there was a sharp pain in her neck. Mrs. Tooley appeared to have done nothing save put the haricots to soak and make the jelly. According to Philip, she was currently occupied with checking the linen with the laundry maid who came once a week. Doris was in the scullery, scouring a tray. The dresser and kitchen table had been scrubbed and the floor mopped, but she had yet to make a start on the vegetables.

Wearily, Agnes instructed her to wash the leeks, peel the potatoes, and string the cardoons. Turning her attentions to the mutton, she unlocked the meat safe, unwrapped the joint from its bloody muslin, and set it in her copper stew pot, adding onion, carrot, celery, bay and thyme, half a dozen peppercorns, and the soaked beans. Then she filled the pot with water and put it on a low hook over the hottest part of the fire so it would come swiftly to the simmer.

She was vague and restless, scarcely conscious of what she said to Doris. She cut her thumb while she was slicing onion, and it bled so profusely she was forced to wrap it in a bandage, which only added to her clumsiness and made her drop a basin of eggs on the floor. Normally, Agnes might have chastised herself for such a waste. But as she mopped up the slimy pool, she told herself that half a dozen eggs was a trifling matter.

Philip stood in the hall trimming the lamps when Agnes presented herself for her appointment with Mr. Blanchard. "I see you are returned from your morning's adventures. And I gather the wine cooler was recovered," he said amiably.

"Indeed it was. And the money, too. I presume that is why the master has asked me to see him in the library."

"Has he? Then you'll have to wait. He ain't come yet."

Agnes went in. The windowpanes were fogged with moisture, but she could dimly discern icicles along the top of the window frame, thawing and dripping noisily onto the outer sill. Beyond was the usual traffic of the street: an urchin wheeling a barrow of cabbages; an oxcart laden with barrels of water; a cart full of cackling poultry; a coach and four, the coachman so swaddled by scarf, hat, and coat that only the tip of his nose and brows were visible.

Agnes surveyed the brown wheel tracks in the muddy snow; then, shivering, moved toward the fire. She wondered whether Theodore would keep his word and pay her the twenty-pound reward he had promised. She would set the money aside for Peter's schooling and ask Mrs. Sharp if she would keep Peter on even after Mrs. Catchpole recovered. Having Peter where she might see him three or four times a week seemed preferable to sending him back to Twickenham.

She put her hand in her pocket and rubbed her thumb over the label recovered from Harry Drake's pocket—apparently the same one lost from this house yesterday. Either Drake had somehow entered the house before meeting his death, or someone had given it to him. But why? Was this the reason he had died? Should she give it to Mr. Matthews, or mention it first to Mr. Blanchard?

Still shivering, she regarded the ornaments upon the mantelpiece. A pair of silver candlesticks embellished with shells reminded her of the wine cooler. She wished she had found the means to ask Thomas to examine the marks, and confirm whether or not they had been transposed. If they had been, then Theodore must be behind the fraud; but what would have been his motive? She had heard talk of friction between Theodore and his father,

that Theodore wanted to move the premises west. Was this suffi-
cient reason for Theodore to devise a scheme to cheat his own
father? She remembered Thomas expressing doubts that such
fraud could be perpetrated on so sizable an object. Now that she
had seen the wine cooler, and appreciated its magnificence, she
agreed. In their present straitened circumstances, the Blanchards
would want to advertise the commission, not keep it secret. In
which case it would be impossible not to pay the duty owed.

But Agnes could not dismiss the matter entirely. Thomas had
no doubt that the marks on the salver *had* been transposed; therefore, someone had been profiting. And since Theodore had control of the books and all marked items were listed, it seemed
probable that he was the guilty party. But if he was culpable of
such petty crime, was he also capable of something graver? Suppose Theodore, tired of the small sums gained from duty dodging,
had engineered the theft to take a share of the reward behind his
father's back and thus gain the wherewithal to move the business
without his father's approval. If so, the theory she had previously
dismissed as implausible might be correct, and Theodore had
committed all three murders.

Agnes did not want to believe it. Her livelihood and that of all
the other servants in the household depended on Theodore; she
owed him her loyalty. But then she recalled how Thomas had defiantly summoned the constable and deputies. Loyalty was all very
fine, she reminded herself, but not if it defied reason.

At last, the door swung open and Theodore, Lydia, and
Nicholas Blanchard entered, accompanied by Justice Cordingly.
Agnes expected smiles and congratulations, but Nicholas's face
was ominously set, Lydia glowered, Theodore looked uncomfortably at the carpet. Only Justice Cordingly had arranged his features in an expression of neutrality.

Her stomach drawing itself into a knot of apprehension, Agnes
bobbed a curtsy, bade them good afternoon, and waited. Nicholas
addressed her first.

"Justice Cordingly desires a word with you. But it wasn't he that sent for you, Meadowes. I have a grievance which I wish to convey to you in person."

"A *grievance*, sir?" She had just saved Nicholas Blanchard's family from ruin.

"I have just received word from Lord Carew that this very morning you went uninvited to his house and subjected his house-keeper to a rigorous interrogation. The poor woman was so disturbed by your visit she mentioned the matter to him—and he, being curious and concerned as to your purpose, apprised me of the fact. It seems you deliberately duped her into believing you were authorized by Justice Cordingly and my son. Do you disagree with my account in any way so far?"

Agnes looked helplessly at Justice Cordingly and Theodore, but their attention was fixed upon Nicholas. "I did not dupe her, sir. Mr. Blanchard and the justice did ask me to assist, by reporting what I knew and helping with Mr. Pitt."

"One moment," said Theodore, interrupting. "You twist the truth, Mrs. Meadowes. I gave you no such authority to pursue the matter as you please. Indeed, I recently ordered you to leave the subject of Rose Francis alone. I certainly never would have sanctioned such a visit had I been forewarned of it."

Agnes looked at Lydia. "Mrs. Blanchard also requested that I should find out what became of Rose."

"Is this true, Lydia?" said Nicholas sharply. "What was your reason for that?"

"I asked her to search the girl's room. But I certainly never gave her authority to chase across London calling upon whomsoever she chose."

Nicholas nodded at this further affirmation of his suspicions. "I have striven to discover a reason for your duplicitous actions, Mrs. Meadowes. Lord Carew is a man of considerable influence; if we irk him, he has it within his power to ruin our reputation."

Agnes could not believe her ears. The morning's dramas had

worn away at her usual circumspection. After all she had endured on this family's behalf, what right had any of them to speak to her in such a tone? "I would not have called on Lord Carew's house-keeper unless I thought it useful. After all, unless the murderer is captured, what is to prevent such a thing happening again?"

Justice Cordingly regarded Agnes with renewed interest, but Nicholas paced up and down, pretending to examine papers and objects. Then he stopped, his thumbs hooked into the armholes of his waistcoat, lowering over her like a malevolent colossus. "I do not comprehend your meaning, Mrs. Meadowes. Cordingly tells me the dead man in the chimney was Drake, a notorious house-breaker. Undoubtedly it was he that committed the theft, killed the apprentice boy, and perhaps also killed Rose Francis, who I gather was on her way to some romantic assignation. And Drake was killed no doubt by Mr. Pitt or one of his henchmen. In what way could such an unauthorized visit conceivably have proved useful?"

"Harry Drake committed the robbery, but I do not believe he killed Noah Prout or Rose. Nor do I think it creditable that Mr. Pitt murdered Harry Drake."

"Have you evidence for this assertion?" said Justice Cordingly.

"Yes sir. I went down to the cellar yesterday and saw the pistol that was taken from Mr. Blanchard's room. Assuming Rose Fran-cis took it, who returned it here? The only explanation I can fathom is that whoever killed her has been in this house since the robbery. Moreover, the apprentice, Rose, and Harry Drake were killed in an identical manner. This surely points to the same hand. Therefore it is my belief that Drake was merely a servant in the scheme, not the murderer; the murderer lives among us."

"I always thought something of the kind was the case," said Theodore with a look of satisfaction.

"Be quiet, Theodore," said Nicholas, glaring brusquely at his son. He swiveled his gaze back to Agnes, thumping his fist on the table. "You discovered my gun!" he exclaimed, balls of spittle spraying from his agitated mouth. "Then why on earth did you not say so sooner? Why was *I* not informed of it?"

Agnes quivered with indignation, but outwardly she remained cool. "I assumed, sir, that Mr. Matthews knew it was there and that he would return it to you. It was encrusted with dirt when I saw it. Perhaps even now he is cleaning it for you."

"Your silence was foolish, Mrs. Meadowes," blustered Nicholas. "Common sense seems to have abandoned you. You saw a valuable gun that you knew was missing and said nothing of it. I find that quite incomprehensible. I want no repetition of such misdemeanors, and no more harrying of important personages. Especially not Lord Carew. If you value your position, you will remember that."

Anger now began to cloud Agnes's mind like a fog. And in its midst came the image of Pitt's leering face as he pressed himself against her, kissed her neck, and held his pistol at her head. Was she not due even a word of thanks for what she had endured? Were her opinions worthless? She opened her mouth to say as much, just as Theodore rose. "Enough, Father! We should be grateful to Mrs. Meadowes for recovering the money as well as the wine cooler. Undoubtedly she has saved us from ruin."

"Ruin of your making."

Theodore turned to her. "I regret our having to speak to you like this, Mrs. Meadowes. Your actions were certainly misjudged. But now we must all let this matter rest. I will endeavor to smooth things with Lord Carew—perhaps I might invite him to visit our showroom and he will offer us a further commission and this business will have a happy conclusion." With this, he gave a brief laugh. He extracted a sheaf of folded banknotes from his pocket and peeled one from the pile. "Here is the reward I promised, Mrs. Meadowes. And as a further sign of our gratitude you may have tomorrow off. I understand you requested it of my wife. All things considered, apart from your last error, you have acquitted yourself satisfactorily."

Agnes took the money with murmured thanks, but saw that he had given her a mere five pounds instead of the promised twenty guineas. She briefly considered reminding him of his promise, but then dismissed the notion. Such impertinence would only result in further reprimands or even dismissal. Instead, she wondered, did the face of a swindler or a cruel murderer lie behind Theodore's placatory smile?

Nicholas glared at his son and wordlessly stepped to the other side of the fire and tugged at the bell pull. John entered immediately, which made Agnes suspect he had been listening at the door. In a curt tone, Nicholas ordered him to fetch his cloak and hat and call a carriage, then he shot his son another venomous look. "Good day, Theodore. I'll leave you in conference with Mrs. Meadowes, who appears to have taken over at the helm of our family's business."

Theodore's cheeks colored and the veins in his neck pulsated visibly. "Come, Father, can you deny she has acquitted herself well and deserves our hearty thanks and reward?"

"I cannot say Williams or Riley, alone or even acting together, wouldn't have done as well—and made fewer blunders."

"I told you before, I suspected that they or one of the servants might have been involved. Someone inside the workshop or this house must have told Pitt the wine cooler was ready. Mrs. Meadowes is only reiterating what I believed all along," he said in a low, tremulous voice.

"Then why in God's name did you not send a man from the household—Matthews, for instance?"

"But Father, Matthews is not what he once was. He is too old to be capable of such an onerous duty. It is all he can do to mount three flights of stairs. Besides, thanks to Mrs. Meadowes and Thomas Williams, this situation has been resolved more successfully than any of us could have hoped."

"That it ended thus owes more to luck than good judgment— or Mrs. Meadowes's doubtful skill." Then he shook his head as though he could not be bothered to argue anymore. "I am going to

White's—I trust I shall find someone there with whom to talk sense." And with this Nicholas stalked out.

THE MOMENT THE door closed, Justice Cordingly finally spoke. "Returning to your earlier conversation, Mrs. Meadowes, if the gun Rose Francis supposedly stole is in the cellar of this house, where is the proof *she* took it? Might not one of the other servants be guilty?" Agnes thought of her promise to Elsie and wondered how she would parry this question. But with Harry Drake dead, there was no longer any reason to keep Elsie out of it; with judicious promotion she might gain a position in the household. "There was a witness to Rose running off," she replied. "A most obliging young girl I happened to meet. She saw Rose down by the river close to where her body was found. She said Rose was chased by a man and dropped a gun, which she believed the man pursuing her later recovered. The pistol I saw in the cellar was ingrained with mud. It seems probable, therefore, that the same man who pursued and killed Rose put it there."

"And since the same person, we believe, killed the others, it follows that the murderer resides in this house, or has frequent access to it," said Cordingly, drawing the same inevitable conclusion as Agnes. "Is the pistol still there?"

"I have not returned to the cellar since."

"Then let us send someone to retrieve it."

Theodore tugged the bell pull. John appeared again almost immediately. "It seems the weapon that went missing from my father's room is secreted in the basement. Mrs. Meadowes saw it there. She will go with you and show you where it is. Be so kind as to bring it here immediately."

"Very well, sir." John shot a look in Agnes's direction.

Agnes felt cornered. John would report all this to Mr. Matthews, and more questions would inevitably follow. She nodded to the others and, forgetting to make a curtsy, left the room.

Chapter Thirty-seven

AGNES HURRIED ACROSS the empty hall toward the back stairs with John trailing close behind. Neither Philip nor Mr. Matthews was anywhere to be seen, though to judge by the clatter coming from the dining room, one or both were engaged in laying the table.

Glancing through the dimpled panes of the hall window, Agnes observed two men across the street. Mr. Matthews was deep in conversation with Thomas Williams. Mr. Matthews was turned slightly away; he appeared to be listening intently and was nodding his head, while Thomas spoke with adamant gestures.

Most probably, she thought, they were discussing the recovery of the wine cooler. Mr. Matthews always liked to be well informed of events concerning the household. Or perhaps Thomas was asking him to convey a message to her.

"When you're ready," said John impatiently.

"Isn't that Mr. Matthews outside, with Mr. Williams?"

John peered suspiciously through the glass. "What? Where?"

Just then a wagon drawn by a pair of oxen and laden with sacks of coal plodded by, temporarily obstructing her view. The driver whipped them along, but his cracking leather and discordant shout wrought little change in pace. By the time the vehicle had passed, the two figures had gone.

"I see nothing," said John firmly. "Now, shall we get on?"

They found no sign of Mr. Matthews in the pantry, but he came in a minute later.

"There you are, sir," said John.

"Why, where else might I have been?" replied Mr. Matthews sharply.

"Mrs. Meadowes fancied she saw you in the road with Mr. Williams."

"Nonsense," said Mr. Matthews crossly.

Agnes noticed that the back of his white stockings were splashed with mud.

John nodded. "I told her the very same. And now, sir, may I trouble you for the key to the cellar."

Mr. Matthews set his lips firm. "Oh, and what for?"

"Mrs. Meadowes believes she saw Mr. Blanchard's pistol hidden there. She has said as much to Mr. Blanchard and Justice Cordingly, and now they both wish to see it," said John, exchanging a meaningful look with his master.

"Saw the pistol down there, did you? When was that?"

"The other day, sir. When I came to find you—I chanced to see it."

"Then why did you not say so at the time?"

"I thought you must already know it was there." Agnes forced her expression into one of chagrin and deference.

"'Course you did," muttered John.

"I hope that was all you saw," said Mr. Matthews darkly.

"Yes sir. I would never pry."

"Good. You're a fine cook, but that don't mean I want ructions below stairs. Now *where* exactly did you see this gun?"

"There is a niche at the foot of the stairs. It was lying there wrapped in a cloth."

"Very well, John, I shall accompany her myself."

And so the butler lit a lantern and led the way slowly down the stairs. Agnes tried to peer over his shoulder at the ledge where she had last spied the pistol. When they reached the bottom, he turned round to face her, his light held aloft. "Now where did you see this weapon?" he demanded with undisguised disbelief.

"It was here, sir." Agnes pointed to the deep ledge. "Wrapped in a cloth. I only caught sight of the handle."

Mr. Matthews stretched his lantern toward the recess, illuminating the cobwebs and the flaking whitewash and render. A lumpy bundle appeared in the flickering glow. "There!" said Agnes.

Mr. Matthews reached for the parcel and unwrapped it, letting the cloth fall to the floor. Encrusted with mud and the barrel rusted, it was indeed Nicholas Blanchard's missing pistol. "Terrible," he muttered, "the damage that water can do. Even with oil and spirit and pumice I doubt I shall ever get this right again."

Agnes murmured something noncommittal, but only half heard him. She noticed with a jolt of surprise that the cloth the weapon had been wrapped in was a square of checkered muslin, of the variety Mrs. Tooley preferred for dusters.

Back upstairs, Agnes was preoccupied by questions of who had wrapped the pistol in one of the household dusters, Thomas's conversation with Mr. Matthews, and the butler's coyness on account of it. The haricots and mutton were simmering faster than they should. It was only at the sound of spluttering and hissing that she realized. They had nearly cooked dry. Absentmindedly she added more stock and prodded the meat with a wooden skewer. Doris was dawdling in the scullery, pretending to wipe an iron pot with oil when she might have been doing any one of a dozen more useful tasks. The reason for her tardiness was obvious. Philip, wearing a leather apron, his shirtsleeves rolled up on his muscular arms, was standing at the adjacent table, mixing scrapings of beeswax with turpentine, resin, and Indian red to make furniture polish. The pungent smell wafting through the kitchen irritated Agnes as much as the sight of Doris moon-eyed beside him.

"Doris," she called out impatiently, "would you leave that and come out here this instant. I asked you to wash the leeks, peel the potatoes, and string those cardoons, and they're all still as dirty as they were when they left market. As for you, Philip—why do you choose to do that in my scullery when the proper place is the butler's pantry? I can hardly breathe for the stench of it."

Doris started guiltily. "I was just about to do 'em now, Mrs. Meadowes. Won't take more'n a couple of minutes."

"If you do them properly it will."

"Apologies, ma'am," said Philip good-humoredly. "No offense intended—I was only keeping this peach company." He winked at Doris, who turned as red as a rump of beef.

Agnes sighed with exasperation. Philip's appeal was beyond her comprehension. She went to the barrel of eels in the larder, caught one writhing body firmly just behind the neck, and carried it to the kitchen, where she gave its head a sharp knock on the edge of the table. Usually she performed this operation without feeling squeamish. But today, although she knew that the eel was dead the moment its head struck the table, its spasmodic twitching disturbed her. She breathed in uncomfortably as she swiftly cut round the skin of the neck, pulled away the skin, and removed the innards, the long fins, and bristles running up the back. The dark muscular flesh reminded her of Drake's decapitated body. Had he twitched in such a manner? Had Rose done so too before her body was encased in its muddy grave? Banish such fancies, she told herself crossly. They help no one and will not let you think clearly. She coiled the cleaned eel round in a shallow fish plate, poured just enough water to cover it, and set it on a hook over the edge of the fire to come slowly to the boil.

"Put the cardoons in a dish with a little red wine, if you will, Doris, and fetch me the livers." As Agnes looked up she saw Philip with his arm round Doris, gazing down at her upturned face and the swell of her bosom. He was whispering something, then blowing softly downward, much to Doris's delight. Agnes opened her mouth to scold them, but just then Nancy burst in and caught sight of them. "Gawd sake, Philip," she screeched. "Don't you stop at nothing, not even that dog?"

Philip's head jolted up. "Don't be jealous just 'cos I ain't with you," he said evenly. "We had our fun, and it was you what called it a day."

"That's a lie," yelled Nancy as Doris, scarlet and, to judge from her swaying, apparently dizzy with passion, glared angrily and tottered off to the larder. "It was you going off with Rose that done for us."

"Well, Rose ain't here now, is she? An' I'm sure I could find a moment for you." He advanced toward Nancy and tried to put his arm around her.

"Not bloody likely," she said, recoiling. "Now I see what type o' man you is I wouldn't go with you, not even if you begged me."

"Is that so?" Philip released her and rubbed his belly. "Then I reckon that's 'cos you've more'n me to worry over now."

"My worries ain't none of your affair," retorted Nancy, her voice shrill.

"And ain't I glad to know that."

Just then a shadow appeared in the doorway. "What on earth is this racket?" Mrs. Tooley came in with a couple of neatly starched pillow slips folded over her arm. "Enough, Nancy. Go to your work. And Philip—another word out of you and I shall call Mr. Matthews." Then, turning to Agnes, "I've no notion what started all this, but one thing I do know—my poor head cannot stand it. I feel quite wretched." Then after a further pause she added, "Is all in order for dinner?"

"Yes, Mrs. Tooley, perfectly so," Agnes quietly replied, as Doris plonked down the bowl of gleaming livers and the dark reek of blood filled her nostrils.

At a quarter past three, the kitchen was taken up with the final preparations for dinner service. John and Philip disappeared into the butler's pantry to put on Valencia waistcoats, change into clean white gloves, and brush their coats until the velvet pile stood up like moleskin. Mr. Matthews had decanted a magnum of claret into a pair of crystal jugs. These vessels were only three-quarters full—he had carefully sampled the rest to ascertain its condition, and his cheeks had a matching garnet glow. With studied care, he transported the jugs to the dining room, stood them on the sideboard, then lit the candles with a taper, paying attention not to spill wax onto the damask cloth. "First course up in five minutes, Mrs. Meadowes, if you will," he ordered on his return.

Agnes added cream and nutmeg and a little lemon juice to the leek potage, but distracted, she let the soup boil and curdle. She added half a pint more cream to it, and ladled the mixture into the tureen. "Scrape me some cheese to finish the cardoons, please, Doris," she said, while she thrust the salamander into the flames.

Usually she would have warmed the Scotch scallops gently, but today the sauce got too hot and before she knew it, they turned gray and curled at the edges. "Ready here," she declared, nonchalantly scooping the now overdone scallops into a serving dish and covering it over before Mrs. Tooley came in.

"Salad, Mrs. Meadowes? I don't see it here."

With her spoon Agnes pointed to a dish on the dresser. "There, ma'am. I'll leave Mr. Matthews to dress it at the table, the cruets have already gone up," she said as she sprinkled Cheshire cheese over the cardoons, took the salamander out of the fire, and pressed it down on the cheese to brown it. Nothing was quite as it should have been, but she finally declared, "First course ready, Mr. Matthews."

In stately process, John took up the tureen of soup, Philip the eels, Mrs. Tooley the Scotch scallops and salad. Agnes heard Mr. Matthews knock upon the door of the drawing room and distantly announce, "Dinner is served." Suddenly, she remembered she had left the salamander on the cardoons too long; sure enough, when she lifted it the cheese was charred and hard.

"Just the jelly we're waiting on now, Mrs. Tooley," said Agnes several minutes later when the housekeeper returned to ensure the second course was as it should be; she had covered her mistake with chopped parsley.

"Scallops looked a little overdone," Mrs. Tooley remarked, adjusting her spectacles. She lifted the lid of the cardoons and scrutinized the burned cheese. "That's not like you, Mrs. Meadowes."

Agnes flushed. She dipped the copper mold into a basin of water and inverted it onto a plate. The jelly should have emerged shimmering and tremulous, like a miniature castle. But she failed to warm the mold evenly and part of one side broke as it slid away from the mold.

She surveyed the four dishes set ready for serving upstairs, their domed covers gleaming almost as resplendently as Sir Bartholomew Grey's wine cooler. "Second course ready to go up, Mr. Matthews," she yelled up the back stairs.

AGNES WIPED HER FOREHEAD against her sleeve and opened the drawer in the kitchen table where she had put the silver box that Elsie had found in Rose Francis's pocket. She tugged Rose's ring off her finger (using a smear of lard to ease it) and compared its marks with those on the box. They were almost the same: lion, leopard's head, the three tiny crosses in a shield, the initials *AW* in an oval stamped along the inner edge. Only one was different— the letter mark. The box was stamped with a *K,* while the ring had the letter *M.* Agnes tried to recall what Thomas had told her. The pair of initials denoted the maker, the lion represented the silver standard, and the leopard's head showed the piece was made in London. Thus, she deduced, the objects were made by the same maker, but in different years.

But, confusingly, there was a fifth mark on both pieces—a shield impressed with three tiny crosses. She frowned; was there another mark Thomas had explained that she had forgotten? She racked her brains, but remained certain he had mentioned only four. She pulled the label she had retrieved from Harry Drake's body out of her pocket and turned it over. They were as she remembered—four in a row—a lion, a leopard's head, a date letter, and the initials NB. What then did the fifth mark on Rose's silver signify? Agnes knew that she would have to ask Thomas to explain, but if the label were discovered in her possession, it would land her in trouble. She ought to give it to Mr. Matthews or Mrs. Tooley and tell them truthfully where she had found it, but neither alternative seemed safe. If she gave it to Matthews and he or John were somehow embroiled in the murders, he might see her gesture as a threat. If she gave it to Mrs. Tooley she would fly into a state and doubtless tell Mr. Matthews. It would be better all round, she decided, to return the label quietly, so that no one knew where it had come from.

At this hour, with both footmen on duty, it was impossible to venture upstairs and not risk being seen. She resolved to return it to Mr. Matthews's pantry, where silver was often brought for polishing while the butler was supervising the the men upstairs. Agnes knocked on the pantry door, and when there was no reply, peered cautiously in. Mr. Matthews was sprawled in a chair with his stockinged feet up on the table, snoring loudly; his mouth had lolled open and a trickle of wine had dribbled down his chin. The decanter from dinner stood empty on the table next to him, and beside it an empty glass and a couple of letters. "Mr. Matthews," said Agnes softly, "may I come in?"

Mindful that Mr. Matthews was a light sleeper and had been known on occasion to start awake and, finding a footman in the midst of some transgression, box his ears, Agnes tiptoed in. She glanced around for somewhere to put the label where it would not be conspicuous. The silver cupboard was the most obvious place, but Mr. Matthews was fastidious about keeping it locked. Agnes saw that the drawers beneath the cupboard had no locks. She slowly pulled open the top one very slowly, one hand on the underside, one on the knob, so as to make as little sound as possible.

Despite these precautions, the drawer's contents rattled as they moved. Mr. Matthews stirred, making a throaty groaning noise, and shifted his hand from his armrest to his groin. Agnes froze. But Mr. Matthews seemed to settle down deeper in sleep, and his breath came more evenly. The drawer was crammed with assorted bric-a-brac: several horn buttons, a tangle of twine, a lump of beeswax, dried pieces of soap wrapped in wax paper, morsels of chalk, a phial of camphor, a coiled and cracked razor strop, and a razor with a broken handle. It was a perfect place to leave the label.

She buried it beneath the other contents, then pushed the drawer closed, wincing with every creak and rattle. But Mr. Matthews snored soundly. As she skirted the table, her eyes lingered on the post. The top letter was addressed to Mr. Theodore Blanchard. On a sudden whim, she pushed it to one side to regard the one beneath. The hand was vaguely familiar, large and clearly formed and black. "Miss Rose Francis." It came to her in a flash— the hand was the same as on the letter Nancy had stolen, the person with whom Rose had her assignation on the night of her death.

Without considering the consequences, Agnes snatched the letter and hurried out of the pantry. Returning to her kitchen table, she prised the wax away from the paper with her sharpest knife.

14 January 1750

My dearest sister,

I was never more surprised than when you did not arrive to meet me. I do not comprehend why you did not at least send me a note to explain your change of heart or circumstance. I can only think that perhaps your engagement is mended, though after all the shilly-shallying I confess I have my doubts it will last. I waited for you all day in Southwark, and next morning, since the passage was booked, was obliged to leave. I write this from Dover, where I await a packet to France. A storm has brewed that makes the crossing impossible. If you change your mind and wish to join me, you may write and tell me so at the address written at the bottom of this letter. I must take up my duties as schoolmaster immediately. Do not fear that you will find it hard to adapt to our new life. Any life must be preferable to the one of servitude that you have been forced to adopt since our father died. Your talents will certainly be better employed in teaching than drudgery.

I am your faithful brother, as ever.

Agnes sat in front of the fire and considered how she had misjudged Rose. She had been escaping romantic entanglement, when Agnes believed that was what propelled her. But to whom had Rose been engaged? Philip? Riley? Some other person of whom she knew nothing?

Agnes took out a clean paper from her drawer and addressed a note to the name at the bottom of the letter—M. Paul Francis, Vieille Pension, Rue Marte, Calais. She outlined for him the sad fate of his sister. When she had finished she pressed her fingers on her eyelids, sealed the letter, and put it in her pocket. She penned a second brief note to Mrs. Sharp, telling her that she would come the next day at ten to take Peter out. Then she put on her coat and stepped out in search of the post boy, and to call on Thomas Williams to give him the letter for Mrs. Sharp.

Chapter Thirty-eight

BENJAMIN RILEY WAS ALONE in the workshop, seated at his workbench, hunched over a coffeepot, a flickering lantern suspended on a hook above his head. He looked up at the sound of the door opening. "Mrs. Meadowes, returned safely from your adventures this morning, I see."

"Thank you, yes, Mr. Riley. Forgive me for troubling you. Is Mr. Williams about?"

"As you see, he is not."

She was uneasy being alone with Riley. Her earlier suspicions toward him resurfaced. Whether or not he had been engaged to Rose, he was almost certainly involved in a duty-dodging fraud. "Where is he?" she asked casually, her gaze fluttering over what she presumed must be his table. It was strewn with an assortment of small articles: pillboxes, vinaigrettes, snuffboxes, patch boxes, bonbonnières.

Riley sat up and folded his arms. "Why do you ask?"

"No particular reason, only I had something to tell him." She knew she should say more, or he would grow suspicious—but what? "I saw Mr. Williams earlier today in conversation with Mr. Matthews. I thought perhaps he gave him a message for me, concerning our excursion this morning. Only Mr. Matthews fell asleep and has told me nothing. But if he is not here, then I will leave you in peace."

Riley shot her a curious look. "I doubt Williams gave Matthews a message for you. It was your butler that had business with *him*."

"Oh. How can you be sure?" She remembered the furtive look on Mr. Matthews's face, and his denials. Any hint of subterfuge made her anxious. Perish the thought that Thomas was somehow embroiled.

"He mentioned it on his return. It seems Matthews has a nephew who is due to come of age in a few days' time. He was inquiring what manner of gift he might give him."

"A nephew?" said Agnes, temporarily disconcerted. But an instant later she recalled the conversation in the cellar, and Mr. Matthews's denial at being observed in the street. The gift must be for John—the celebration they planned was to mark his coming of age. Doubtless the gift was a surprise. That was why Matthews was perturbed that Agnes had seen him talking to Thomas, and why he'd denied it.

Riley got up. "Don't let me delay you, Mrs. Meadowes. I'll let Williams know you called for him." With this, he stalked to the door.

Realizing that Riley wanted to be rid of her as much as she wanted to get away from him gave Agnes courage. Since Thomas was not there and she had braved Riley thus far, why not broach the subject of duty dodging? "One more thing before I leave, Mr. Riley," she said with affected nonchalance.

"Yes?"

"There is a salver in the hall of the Blanchards' house."

"What of it?"

"Did you give it to Rose not long ago, after some repair?"

Riley's cheeks paled. "What if I did?"

"What repair did you carry out?"

"That is none of your affair."

"I only ask because Rose was observed not long ago with the

salver in her hand. Mr. Williams happened to see the same item and was perplexed at some discrepancy with the marks. He explained a certain fraud to me—duty dodging, he termed it. He also said it was you who takes pieces to assay. Were you and Rose operating such a scheme?"

"Williams!" muttered Riley, running his hand over his chin. "Naturally he planted the seed in your thoughts." He paused, then spoke in a lighter tone. "Have you mentioned these suspicions to anyone else?"

"Not yet."

Riley nodded. "It is well you did not. Has it occurred to you that Williams might have misled you? In our profession, duty dodging is a widespread and trivial offense—hardly the heinous crime he makes it out to be."

"Then you would not mind if I mentioned such a 'trivial offense' to Mr. Blanchard?"

"Do so and I warrant he would tell you to mind your own affairs. And mention it to Mr. Nicholas and you will cause a violent ruction between him and his son which will hardly benefit the business, which is already in a dire predicament. Either way, you risk losing your position. It may be me that alters the marks, but I do so at Theodore's instigation. He is prepared to go to almost any lengths to salvage his business. Even the few pounds saved from duty are worth it in his eyes. I cannot refuse him any more than you could when he sent you unwillingly to the thief taker."

"And what was Rose's role in all this?"

Riley gave her a bitter half smile. "You are very quick to think the worst of her, but let me assure you she had nothing to do with it, save transporting pieces here and returning them on one or two occasions."

Agnes raised a skeptical brow. "Why would a kitchen maid be chosen for such a task? Why not one of the menservants? Or Theodore himself, since he comes here every day?"

"As I said, it was only on occasion—mostly Theodore did bring pieces, or we used those from the workshop. It was I who asked Rose to return something to the house the first time, when we were still friends. I asked her to put back a box without being seen. She was forever bemoaning the drudgery of her work and saying it wasn't what she was used to, and that she relished a challenge. I never told her why it was important she was not observed, but she must have known there was subterfuge of some kind. Not that it bothered her in the least. After that, Theodore employed her too if it suited him."

"I see," said Agnes. "And when you say you were 'friends,' is what you really mean that you were engaged?"

Riley shot her a calculating look, then smiled more openly. "No, it wasn't me that was engaged to her. You ask your Mr. Williams who it was."

"What do you mean?" said Agnes, with as much composure as she could muster. "What does he know?"

Riley smiled maliciously. "Rose and he were engaged before either came to London," he said flatly. He glanced at Thomas's desk, and the array of silver items spread upon it, then turned back to face her. Agnes could feel the blood flood her cheeks, though she tried to maintain an air of calm. "Williams did not serve his apprenticeship at Blanchards'. He learned the trade in Newcastle under his father, Andrew Williams, a master silversmith. He came here as journeyman two years ago. Sir Bartholomew Grey was somehow involved. I do not know in what manner exactly, but he has an estate in those parts."

"Go on," said Agnes. She remembered the strange marks on Rose's ring and box. The maker's initials were *AW*.

"Before he came to London, Williams was friends with Rose's brother; I think he told me they had met in the classroom. Rose's father was a schoolmaster, I gather. Rose was well educated, and Thomas and she became sweethearts while he was still apprenticed in his father's silversmith shop. They became engaged when he became a journeyman and found a post in London. Soon after,

Rose arrived in London. She had found employ as a maid. I do not recall where."

He paused and gazed at Agnes. The gleam of malice had disappeared. Agnes fancied there was a look of pity in his eye, which irked her even more.

"At Lord Carew's," she said.

Riley nodded. "She was not used to domestic drudgery. She hated being a maid. I am not entirely certain what happened between her and Williams, except that there must have been a falling-out. All I know is that one day a year ago she appeared next door, and set to buttering me." He paused and frowned. "What is it, Mrs. Meadowes? Surprised to learn your Mr. Williams isn't all you thought him?"

Agnes shrugged. "Why didn't you tell me this before?"

"You never asked."

"I spoke to you on the morning of Rose's disappearance."

Riley snorted. "All you asked was if there was something between me and her. I don't know how that notion was planted in your head, but I told you the truth. She and I were friendly at one time, but not for long. That was when Williams took against me. She would flaunt her affection for me in front of him. It was deliberate, what she did, as though she wanted him to see. I enjoyed her for a while, but then I met a pretty milliner in Fleet Street who wasn't half so demanding. After that I think she took up with Philip. She was no more discreet with him, let me tell you—but I daresay you already know that. There may have been others, I cannot say. In any case, if anyone deceived you it was Williams for concealing his engagement. But even if he has, there's no cause to blame me on account of it."

Agnes was speechless. Rose and Thomas—the very thought of them together was insupportable. Her throat burned, her fingernails bit into the skin of her palm. Rose's ring felt branded into her flesh. She wanted to fling it to the ground and trample on it, but would not give Riley the satisfaction of seeing her distress. But if

Thomas were here now, she thought, I should fly at him. She battled to compose herself. Why had she blindly assumed that it was *Riley* Rose was after? The answer was plain. She had been lured along the wrong path by Thomas himself. By hinting that Riley was dishonest and was involved in some secret affair with Rose, he had deliberately deceived her.

Agnes abruptly took her leave and strode briskly to Sarah Sharp's house and pushed the letter through her door. On her return to Foster Lane, she stood for several minutes at the top of the steps, mastering her self-control before descending.

Her self-possession remained shaken by what Riley had told her, but she had not entirely lost her powers of reason or forgotten her morning's adventures. Was it possible that what Riley said was true? If so, how did this fit with the theft of the wine cooler and the murders? Thomas's assistance remained an indubitable fact. And Riley was someone she had never trusted—but nevertheless his account seemed too particular to be a fabrication. So much deceit, so much lying, so much unfamiliar ground. Agnes fumbled for the truth. She told herself she owed Thomas a chance to redeem himself. But then, if he had deliberately lied and deceived her—as it seemed he had—would he tell her the truth now?

She would be wise to arm herself with further evidence before confronting him, she concluded. Who else might shed light on this perplexing matter? In the end, just one name presented itself: Sir Bartholomew Grey, who Riley claimed had brought Thomas to London, and for whom the wine cooler had been made. Nicholas had warned Agnes against further unauthorized forays, but given the present urgent circumstances, this was an instruction she chose to ignore.

Somber but resolute, Agnes was unable to taste a morsel of her supper, nor did she feel inclined to start the evening meal preparations. She was quite prepared to leave most of them to Doris and slip out at the earliest opportunity. But as fate would have it, Mr. Matthews roused himself from his slumbers when he was sum-

moned upstairs by a bell. He returned to the kitchen some minutes later with particular instructions from Lydia Blanchard.
Nicholas had not returned from his earlier excursion and was presumed to be staying at his club. Theodore had gone after him and
Lydia had accepted an invitation to play cards and would sup elsewhere. There would be no upstairs supper, and thus, Agnes had
no further duties that night.

Chapter Thirty-nine

BEFORE LEAVING FOR Sir Bartholomew Grey's residence, Agnes considered her appearance for once. She donned her finest garb: a bodice and skirt of gold-colored wool that deepened the amber of her eyes, a clean lawn collar that nicely emphasized the curve of her breast. She regarded herself in the looking glass on her dressing chest and saw that her eyes had a fierce gleam in them. No matter what anger I rouse in the Blanchards, I shall get to the root of this, she thought. Even servants are entitled to justice and to know the truth.

She dressed her hair in a tight knot and dipped a forefinger in egg white and vinegar to coil a single fat ringlet over one shoulder. She bit her lips and pinched her cheeks, things she had not troubled herself to do for many years. Then, so that no one should remark on her finery and question her destination, she swathed herself in her cloak before she slipped into the night.

It was raining softly and she avoided the puddles. There were no stars, but by the moonlight filtering through the wafting clouds she could see there was still some traffic about. Agnes took shelter in a doorway and waited. A carriage and four trotted past, spraying muddy water, then came a hackney with a pair of passengers, then several more equipages. Before long, Agnes's boots and the hem of her cloak were drenched and there was still no sign of an empty carriage. Suppressing her frustration, she waited a short time longer, until at last a free hackney came by. She hailed the driver and settled back on the cold seat.

The carriage reeked of tobacco smoke and damp. As it jolted its way toward Cavendish Street, Agnes clutched the door frame and stared through the rain-speckled window. Pedestrians muffled against the weather hurried into doorways. She saw barefoot beggars cowering in corners and drunkards sprawled in the gutter. She listened to the distant curses of watermen, and the occasional cries of the watch, and tried not to think of the risk she was running and why Thomas had deceived her.

Presently the carriage lurched past the elegant façades of Cavendish Street. Lanterns burned on each side of the entrance to Sir Bartholomew Grey's house, and through the fanlight blazed a large chandelier, heavily swagged with droplets of crystal. The windows on either side of the hall were dark—was this because the curtains were drawn or because there was no one within?

Telling the driver to wait, Agnes stepped out and knocked at the door. A liveried footman wearing a powdered wig answered, bowing and clicking his heels as he bade her a lofty good evening. Agnes saw that his uniform—deep crimson velvet with gold epaulets and shining silver buttons, and without a single bald spot anywhere to be seen—was ten times more splendid than the Blanchard livery. Despite her best gown, she felt drab by comparison.

"Good evening. I have come to visit Sir Bartholomew Grey," she said with as much hauteur as she could muster.

The footman puffed his chest and stared. "Are you expected, ma'am?"

"A matter of urgency has arisen. There was no time to forewarn him."

He folded his arms and raised his chin. "Then I doubt he will see you. He is currently occupied at the card table."

Agnes had come too far to be cowed by a spotless velvet suit. "My good man," she said, drawing up to her full height, "the fact that I have no appointment is neither here nor there. Go to your master, and inform him a Mrs. Agnes Meadowes desires a moment of his time. She has been sent by Mr. Blanchard and Justice Cordingly, on a matter of grave importance concerning his wine cooler."

The footman dropped his arms to his sides. He opened his mouth as if to say something, but then, thinking better of it, closed it wordlessly. Bowing again, briskly and more deeply than before, he ushered her in and departed through a double door, without allowing her a glimpse of what lay within.

Agnes strode about the hall, anxiously waiting. The fire was unlit, the stone floor shiny with polish yet inhospitable. How many housemaids had spent hours scrubbing and buffing here until their arms ached? she wondered. A bracket clock on the mantelpiece ticked with agonizing slowness. She regarded a row of marble busts of Roman emperors ranged on columns. She began to pace the corridor, unsettled by the curious sensation that the ranks of blank alabaster eyes saw through her ladylike posturing and disapproved. Then she caught sight of the wine cooler. It stood resplendent on a marble-topped commode, flanked by a pair of blazing candelabra.

So Thomas had been here. Perhaps he was here still. She ran her hands over the sides of the great object, her fingers brushing over dolphins and mermaids' tresses, and the smooth musculature of Neptune's arms and the prickle of his trident. She was uncertain whether she hoped or feared that Thomas had gone. She was not ready to confront him.

Just then, her eye alighted upon the marks set in a line on the flat rim. There was the leopard, the lion, the letters *NB* for Nicholas Blanchard, and *P* for the year. Had these letters been transposed? She recalled the way Thomas had ascertained the tampering on the salver. She breathed on the shining surface around the marks. It remained perfectly smooth; there was no ridge to indicate that the marks had been tampered with. No doubt Thomas had introduced the whole business of duty dodging simply to divert her from the truth.

The footman reemerged. "Sir Bartholomew will spare you a moment of his time in the saloon." He rang a bell, and a short while later a second footman arrived and carried off her cloak and gloves. Nervously she flattened her collar and smoothed her skirt. When she was ready, she nodded. The first footman threw open the double doors and stood to one side, bowing slightly, arm outstretched. "This way, ma'am." Heart pumping, Agnes entered.

The room was lit by a chandelier twice as large as the one in the hall, and furnished with carved gilt-wood sofas upholstered in vivid green silk, and mahogany commodes with marble tops. One wall was punctuated with two long windows draped in gold damask. Opposite was a grand marble fireplace, and suspended above was a large dark painting of naked women drinking wine and cavorting with swarthy muscular men, some of whom appeared to have goats' legs, and horns on their heads.

She was no more than a foot across the carpet when the footman cleared his throat. "Mrs. Agnes Meadowes, sir," he announced in a ringing tone, before retreating backward and closing the doors behind him. Agnes was overwhelmed by a flood of panic. She saw the folly of this visit and longed to retreat.

But Sir Bartholomew was seated at a card table in the center of the room. Seeing Agnes standing stock still on the carpet, he rose and held out his hand. "Mrs. Meadowes," he said slowly, with an air of perplexity. "I have heard something of you from Mr. Williams, who left here only an hour since. He never said you would come calling on me in person. You are the family cook, I understand. What brings you out at this time of night?"

He was stout and florid of complexion, with a bulbous nose, small blue eyes, and a slightly receding chin. He was formally attired in a silk jacket of dark purple damask, black velvet breeches, and an old-fashioned full-bottomed wig. Cards and ivory tokens were strewn across the table. A black lace fan with silver sequins lay at the empty place facing him. On a sofa nearby a book lay open.

"I have come, sir, to ask a favor of you."

Sir Bartholomew's ruddy countenance flickered with unease. "Blanchard said nothing of any favors. Do not expect to take advantage of me, just because you recovered something of mine that should never have been lost in the first place. And if it's a position you are after, I have to tell you I already have a French chef."

"I do not seek to take advantage," said Agnes, as her pulse sturdied. "Or a post. Only answers to certain questions."

Grey rested his hand on the table, as though bracing himself against an unfavorable onslaught. "Questions on what subject?"

"Three murders took place around the time your wine cooler went missing. But unlike it, those lives can never be recovered. All I ask is your assistance in finding the killer and bringing him to justice."

Sir Bartholomew Grey got up and began to pace around the room. "I suppose your aim is worthy. But it strikes me that a woman of your position should not be meddling in such matters. Why has Blanchard never mentioned this? I assumed he would inform the justice, who would pursue the villainous thief. Tell me his name and I'll have him apprehended directly."

"The thief's name is Harry Drake," said Agnes, "a professional housebreaker, who operated with the connivance of the thief taker Marcus Pitt. But as for apprehending the pair—you need not concern yourself over that."

"Why?"

"Drake is dead, and Pitt is in the roundhouse awaiting committal."

"Then I confess myself baffled, Mrs. Meadowes. What more do you want?"

Agnes smiled sweetly. "As I said, the murders are all connected to the theft of your wine cooler. But I don't believe either Drake or Pitt was responsible for them; I think it was someone inside Blanchards'. The break-in was not fortuitous. Drake was instructed on what to steal—he entered knowing that the wine cooler was the most valuable item Blanchards' had ever made and that Mr. Blanchard would pay a sizable sum for its return. That sum was doubtless to be shared between the three conspirators."

"You mean Drake, Pitt, and the anonymous traitor would all have shared in the reward?"

"Precisely."

"But the money was recovered, I understand. So the plot was foiled."

"Only in a material sense," Agnes countered levelly. "There are still three murders that Justice Cordingly has little inclination to pursue. The murders of a servant girl, an apprentice, and a housebreaker do not apparently merit the same justice as the robbery of someone of means."

Uneasily, Sir Bartholomew nodded. "But did not Pitt commit the murders?"

"I do not believe so; he tends to keep himself distant from his crimes—though he must know who did."

Grey pulled up another chair and offered it to Agnes before sitting heavily in his own. "Then leave the matter in my hands. Justice Cordingly is an acquaintance of mine. If Pitt has been apprehended, it will be no hard task for one of his constables to wheedle out the identity of the traitor inside Blanchards'."

"I'm not certain Cordingly will do so when he learns the range of Pitt's influence. I think the chances of Pitt remaining in custody and revealing who employed him are remarkably slim."

Grey began to pile the counters into perfect columns. "Do I take it you have another scheme?"

"Perhaps," said Agnes, sitting erect, head held high. "But first I should like to ask you about another matter, which I believe may somehow have a bearing on these events."

Sir Bartholomew nodded and waved his hand, signaling her to proceed. Agnes drew a deep breath. "What I should like to know, sir, is what you can tell me of the background of the craftsman who made your wine cooler, Thomas Williams."

"Surely you do not suspect that Williams, one of the most talented silversmiths of my acquaintance, could be a cold-blooded murderer?

"I think there is more to him than we know."

"I very much doubt it. His father is a craftsman of the highest skill. He supplied me with much of the plate for my house in Newcastle. Thomas is his second son; he served his apprenticeship under his father, but wanted to better himself and thought London was the place to do it. He asked me for assistance in finding a suitable master who might offer him a place as a journeyman. I was happy to assist and mentioned him to Theodore Blanchard, who was in need of additional help following the retirement of his father. And so he was taken on."

"Are you familiar with the family mark?"

"Naturally. As I said, I have been a patron of the father's for many years."

Agnes pulled the heart-shaped box from her pocket and handed it to him. "Is the mark on this his father's?"

Sir Bartholomew took up a magnifying glass from a nearby side table. He plucked the box off Agnes's palm and held it between forefinger and thumb close to the candelabra, turning it and raising and lowering the glass to gain the best view of the marks.

After a while he nodded, then put the glass and box down on the table. "Yes, as far as I can tell the initials are his father's mark. And the extra mark, the one that resembles three small turrets, shows the box was made in Newcastle."

Hearing Riley's account thus partially confirmed, Agnes's spirits plunged. Thomas had deceived her. Her dismay made her reckless. "Were you aware of the engagement between Thomas Williams and Rose Francis, who was kitchen maid for Lord Carew and then moved to the Blanchards'?"

"A kitchen maid?" Sir Bartholomew looked at her as if she were mad. "You cannot suppose I involve myself with maidservants. My housekeeper takes care of such matters."

"Do you know Lord Carew?"

"He is a casual acquaintance of mine."

"But you never set eyes on the girl?"

Sir Bartholomew adjusted his cravat, and blew his nose noisily in a lace-edged handkerchief. Then he began to pace again. "As I've told you, no. I assume you are not suggesting they conspired to aid Pitt to steal my wine cooler, or that Williams committed the murders. What motive would he have?"

"Money, perhaps." She sensed his patience was at an end, but there was yet more she wanted to discover. "And what did you think on learning she was in the employ of the Blanchards?"

"Nothing!" he exclaimed, twirling round with an air of majesty. "How many times must I say this? You cannot suppose a man of my standing pays attention to the servants of every household he happens to visit. So long as the meat and gravy are on the table, I do not bother myself over who puts them there."

Agnes recoiled as if he had hit her. At that moment there was an unexpected creak from the far end of the room. A door hidden in the wainscoting was abruptly thrown open and an elegantly dressed young woman stepped through. She was clad in a silk dress of inky blue with a deep ruff of creamy lace around the décolletage; her neck was slender and white, her hair elaborately dressed with black silk flowers. She looked young enough to be Sir Bartholomew's daughter. Seeing Agnes, she pursed her lips in a moue of displeasure, walked to the table, and began to fan herself slowly. "Who is this, my dearest?" she said softly.

"'Tis no one but the cook of a tradesman of my acquaintance."

"Then are we not to finish our game?"

"Certainly we shall finish it," said Sir Bartholomew, ushering her to her seat, then hurrying to ring the servants' bell. A knot rose in Agnes's throat. Seeing them together made Agnes think of

Thomas and Rose; the woman had something of Rose's noncha-
lant bearing. The footman appeared an instant later. "This visitor
has concluded her business, and is leaving," said Grey. "Miss
Katherine and I will finish our game without disturbance—no
matter who calls." Then, turning to Agnes, "I do not comprehend
your purpose in coming here or what you have learned. But whatever it was, I trust you are satisfied for I have no more to tell you.
Good evening to you, madam."

"Good evening, sir." She curtsied, then remembered
Theodore's injunction. "Before I leave, if I may make one last
request."

"What then?"

"I would ask that you keep this conversation to yourself."

Sir Bartholomew regarded her carefully. "It is my belief that
when servants exceed their duties, only mayhem ensues. Your visit
has done little to change my view. Therefore I cannot give you any
such assurance. Good night to you."

Chapter Forty

THEODORE HAD GRANTED Agnes the next day off, so she sent up a larger breakfast than usual—a cold knuckle of gammon, coddled eggs kept warm over a dish of hot water, and deviled kidneys. After writing down suggestions for the next day's menu on the slate, she headed over to Bread Street to see Peter.

The morning was fine and bright, and she decided to take him for an excursion on the river. But she could not get out of her mind her visit to Sir Bartholomew. Thomas had lied; he and Rose had been engaged and he had concealed their engagement. But *why*? A few minutes later, she presented herself at Mrs. Sharp's door. But Mrs. Sharp seemed puzzled to see her. "Forgive me for disturbing you, Madam Sharp. I won't delay you. I trust you got my message. Is Peter ready?"

Mrs. Sharp now looked truly baffled. "What? But he is already with you—I thought you had returned for something he had forgotten."

"What do you mean? I wrote to tell you I would collect him this morning."

"I got the note. But an hour ago a young girl came, saying you had sent *her* to fetch Peter. You were going out for a drive, you had a carriage arranged, she was the driver's girl. She showed me the carriage—it was waiting at the corner of Cheapside. I saw a woman's face and a gloved hand wave. I assumed the woman must be you."

Agnes was speechless. Her heart filled her chest and her head pounded unbearably. Somewhere close by she heard a cat mewing for food. "Tell me," she said faintly, "what did the girl look like?"

"Like an urchin—ill-kempt, scrawny, hair unwashed, wearing dirty clothes, infested with vermin of all kind, I daresay. She had a red shawl wrapped round her head, as I recall."

Agnes sank against the doorjamb. Why would Elsie commit such an act of betrayal? But no sooner had Agnes framed the question in her mind than the answer presented itself. Elsie knew that her father was dead, and must believe that Agnes had had a hand in his murder.

"Do you know who these people were?" asked Mrs. Sharp, now looking anxious herself.

"I fear I know who the child was, which leads me to suspect who was behind the deed—Marcus Pitt the thief taker, who warned me of his influence."

"Pitt! Would *he* take your child?"

"I wager he would enlist the aid of someone who would do worse besides take him."

Mrs. Sharp shook her head in disbelief. "What do you mean?"

"The murderer who employed him is concerned that, even though the wine cooler has been recovered, I intend to pursue him."

"Shall I send for the constable?"

"No, that would only waste precious time. I will have to go after them and get Peter back."

"But where will you start?"

"Pitt's premises in Melancholy Walk are as good a place as any."

As she spoke, a shadow emerged from the stairwell. The disheveled figure of Thomas Williams, dressed only in breeches and a half-buttoned shirt. "And what will you do when you get there?" he said. "Employ your feminine charms to persuade the murderer to give Peter back?"

She stared at him mutely for an instant. "I will fathom some means when I get there. And now I must take my leave. Good day to you both."

She picked up her skirts and hurried off in the direction of the river. A hackney carriage rumbled past, and she darted out into the road, waving feverishly. The driver drew swiftly to a halt. "Melancholy Walk—quick as you can!" she cried. Grabbing hold of the door, she clambered in. "A shilling extra if you get me there within the quarter hour." Just as the driver cracked his whip and began to move off, Thomas Williams came careering up and grasped the door handle. Agnes shook her head. Thomas leaped round to the rear as the vehicle gathered speed. Agnes saw him stumble and fall back, but then he ran faster and leaped success-fully onto the step. Through the rear window, she could see his face pressing against the mud-spattered glass as if he were clinging on for dear life.

The vehicle, with Thomas clinging to the back like a barnacle, jostled through Watling Street and down toward the bridge. Agnes watched as the dilapidated Nonesuch House passed her window, and the great stone gateway came into view. The air was filled with the stench of urine from the tanneries, bones from the glue makers, boiling fat from the makers of soap. Agnes tried to think of how she was going to trace Elsie. It was better than imag-ining what might be happening to Peter.

At the south side of the bridge, the carriage drew up at the gateway while a wagon came thorough in the opposite direction. Agnes peered over the parapet and glimpsed a grayish brown expanse. At the top of some decrepit stairs leading down from the quayside she saw a carriage.

Today being Sunday, there was little activity or traffic, making the sight of a carriage all the more noticeable. Close by stood a man, and two figures of short stature, one of whom wore something red. As she watched, the figure in red began running along the wharf and disappeared.

Agnes pushed down the window and shouted to the driver, "Take the road leading to St. Olave's, then turn left toward the quayside. I'm looking for a dark carriage."

The driver turned the horses but he had traveled no more than twenty yards before the road narrowed to an alley, with another, wider road leading off to the right. He pulled up the horses, jumped down from his platform, and opened the carriage door. "Can't go further, never turn round if I do."

Agnes got out. The river—a flash of silvery brown light—was just visible through the black frame of buildings. A few indistinct figures were shuffling down the alley; a stray dog sniffed the detritus in the gutter. There was no sign of the carriage. Agnes reasoned that if the hackney driver could not pass this way, the carriage she had seen must have taken another way down to the wharf. The distance was not great, and it would be easier to find the carriage and its occupants on foot.

Thomas Williams was standing some distance away, watching a woman hang laundry from an upstairs window.

"I never asked you to come," called Agnes ungraciously to him.

"I would have been a fool to let you go alone on such a mission."

"Peter and I are not your concern."

"Perhaps not. Nevertheless I should not wish harm to befall either one of you."

"That's a shilling and sixpence if you please," interrupted the driver.

Agnes fumbled in her pocket and thrust a handful of coins, far more than the sum requested, into the driver's hand. Her cheeks aflame, she mumbled, "I cannot prevent you from following me, Mr. Williams, but I implore you to keep your distance." Then she charged down the passage.

At the quayside, the warehouses and factories loomed over the river behind her, their chimneys spewing foul-smelling smoke. The wharf on the opposite bank was bathed in winter sun, but this side was shrouded in purplish shadow. She saw no sign of the carriage, or Peter.

Moments later, Thomas emerged from a passage farther up the river toward Pickle Herring Stairs. He pointed downriver, beckoning her wildly. She hurried along, and when she was no more than ten yards distant called out, "What is it? Did you see something?"

"No, but that laundress did—a carriage. She had an excellent view from her garret, and one had passed beneath her not ten minutes earlier. She saw a girl, a boy, and a man descend and head in this direction."

"And do you see anything now?"

"Nothing. But perhaps we should proceed farther down."

A keen wind made her shiver. She walked down to the foreshore. The tide was low, and when she reached the bottom of the stairs, she could see the sagging underside of the wharf on her right. The massive wooden pillars were encrusted to the waterline with barnacles and olive green slime and ribbons of weed. To her left, the mud banked steeply down to the water's edge, its surface scarred with flotsam—wood, stones, rusting chains, lumps of coal, patches of slime, and yellowish sludge. In some places the mud was no more than a yard or two wide; in others it extended like probing fingers into the choppy brown water. Here and there, the surface was traversed by foul-smelling rivulets, where the sewers and gutters of the city disgorged raw sewage into the Thames.

Fishing smacks, barges, wherries, hay boats, and schooners were moored offshore; others were stranded by the tide, aground on the mud. There was no sign of life on any of them, but a stream of raggedly dressed people were combing the mud for whatever they could find.

Agnes searched among the darker shadows for Peter. Some moments later there was a flash of unexpected movement and something seemed to emerge from the dark shadows, then disappear.

Thomas saw her stop and called down to her from the sagging wharf. "Did you see something?" She shook her head. Thirty paces on, she saw it again—a spidery, hunched form, picking its way beneath the wharf. She ran toward it.

"What is it?" shouted Thomas.

"There!" she cried.

Thomas dropped to his knees, but could not see directly beneath the wharf. Finding no steps nearby, he launched himself onto the mud. As he landed, a shower of black water sprayed his stockings and breeches. He ran to catch up with Agnes.

"What is it? What did you see?"

"Under the wharf . . . fifty yards ahead . . . see them now, rounding that pier," she gasped, pointing. "Two figures, one of them Peter."

She ran closer to the wharf, skirting areas of soft mud which were impossible to cross, her eyes fixed upon the figures ahead.

But when they were still more than thirty yards apart, the shadowy form turned and caught sight of her. It was Peter. He froze for an instant, then looked up at his captor and back again at Agnes, and silently held out his hands in her direction. The captor then turned and, seeing Agnes and Thomas, stepped out from under the wharf.

Legs braced on the mudflats, the man stood, gripping Peter by the wrist. The front brim of his tricorn was pulled low over his brow. A muffler covered the lower part of his jaw.

Agnes waited for him to speak. I will know him then, she thought. But the man remained silent, staring at them as though willing them to move. Thus challenged, she began slowly to advance, but she had progressed no more than a dozen paces when Peter began to pull in her direction and cried out. "Help me, Mama, please help me. He won't let me go."

Agnes knew whatever she said would only make matters

worse. "Don't worry, Peter, do as he says and he'll treat you kindly. Be good." Then she watched, horrified, as the man yanked Peter out across the mud, toward the deeper water.

The tide crept toward them. Peter called out, again and again, shrill, indecipherable pleas. Finally the man must have issued some threat, for after that Peter stopped.

"Do as he says, Peter!" cried Agnes. Furious at her own impotence, she plunged after them, oblivious to the piercing cold and to the stares of the river finders, who had withdrawn with the incoming tide and were now watching this spectacle from the wharfside. Several times she stumbled on some submerged obstacle or stepped in a patch of quicksand, but each time she recovered her balance and continued. Thomas Williams kept pace, but said nothing and never attempted to divert her from her course.

Some ten yards distant she saw a wooden rowboat moored to a post. The water was now up to Peter's chest and he began to wail as muddy waves splashed in his face. The man hoisted Peter onto his shoulders, and minutes later, they reached the boat. He lifted Peter and clabbered over the gunwale after him.

"Wait! Wait! Don't take him alone—take me, too. Whoever you are, whatever it is you want from me, you shall have it," she called out wildly.

The man glared in her direction, but made no reply. He proceeded to retrieve the oars from the hull and slot them into their leather bindings.

"Wait! Please wait!" she implored again. But this time he did not even look up.

Suddenly, Thomas surged past her, waving his sword in the air. He reached the boat just as the man cast off the mooring rope. Thomas grasped the stern and made lunges with his sword. The man remained out of range, so he wrapped his legs round the rudder and began rocking the vessel as though he meant to capsize it. "Give back the boy or I'm not letting go," he shouted between gritted teeth.

"Ain't you now?" the man mumbled, and swiveled the right-hand oar out of the oarlock and dropped it down flat on the crown of Thomas's head.

Thomas fell back into the water as blood gushed from a wound on his temple. He attempted to clamber onto the boat, but the man hit him again and steered the boat clumsily away toward deeper water, where it caught the current downstream.

Soon Peter was nothing more than a pale gray shadow, his features lost, his shape almost indistinguishable from the dull sweep of the river.

Chapter Forty-one

"I'LL FIND ANOTHER BOAT and pursue them." Blood and muddy water ran down Thomas's cheek, his lips were gray with cold.

"No," Agnes said. "He cannot row fast, it will be easier to follow them on land." She could not bring herself to look at him, but asked, "Who was it? Did you see who it was when you were close?"

"I caught no more than a glimpse of him before he clouted me."

Agnes began to wade downstream toward shallower water. Was he someone she knew? She considered the tall, lean outline, the flapping coat, the hat and muffler. None of it was distinctive or outwardly remarkable.

And what did he want? He had had ample opportunity to kill Peter before now, if that was his intention. Perhaps he had arranged a hiding place for Peter somewhere close to the river. Agnes guessed that the boat had not been part of the original scheme. She had precipitated their flight by pursuing him. But why snatch Peter in the first place? Agnes had known the answer to this all along. Peter was a lure. She was the real target. Pitt might adopt such a tactic, but he was in the roundhouse awaiting committal.

But that being so, why hadn't he taken her when she had chased him? She concluded that the presence of Thomas Williams or the audience of river finders had deterred him.

Agnes watched the man rowing inexpertly, splashing water and spinning the boat. He veered back toward the shoreline, which made it easy to keep track of him.

"Where are they going?" asked Thomas.

"I am not certain. Perhaps to Marcus Pitt's premises."

Thomas took out his handkerchief and wiped away the blood from his eyes. "What makes you say so? Pitt has been apprehended."

"Have you a better place to start?"

"I should begin by calling on Justice Cordingly."

"Then go, if you wish. But what will he care for the missing son of a cook? He has done precious little about the murders thus far. Besides, whether or not he wielded the knife, Pitt lies at the heart of the murders and the robbery. The murderer knows him and knows his house. He might regard it as a refuge." She regarded the expanse of bleak brown water ahead. "In any case, why should I justify my reasons to you, Mr. Williams? After the lies you have spun, you are hardly above suspicion yourself."

"What? That's nonsensical. If I had been involved, would I be here offering you my assistance? Would I have saved you from Pitt yesterday?"

Agnes knew he spoke the truth, and she did not seriously believe him capable of murder, but she remained furious at his deception. "Then if you are so innocent, as you claim, why conceal the fact that you were enamored by Rose for years, and that you were engaged to marry her? Perhaps you killed her out of jealousy when she took up with Riley and Philip."

"I kept the engagement from you because I knew it was irrelevant to recent events and would only mislead you—as indeed it has. Rose broke our engagement, and caused me much heartache. Perhaps I was wrong not to have been more open. But my deception was mainly caused by my fondness for you. And I have never made that secret."

Then, without further prompting, he confirmed the story Riley had told her. Rose and he had been engaged. She had followed him to London following the death of her father, and so detested her work at Lord Carew's she had wanted to marry him sooner than previously arranged. "I would have agreed were it not for my situation with Blanchards'. The company's dwindling fortunes worried me; I did not want to wed and find myself unable to provide for her. So I asked her to be patient and wait a while longer at Lord Carew's. But Rose broke our engagement in a fit of pique, saying she believed plenty of other eligible men would happily provide for her if I would not. A month later, she changed her mind and tried to mend things between us. When I hesitated, she came to the Blanchards'. Soon after, rumors reached me of her flirtations with Riley and Philip; I believe she took up with them to spur me to take her back. But her antics worried me. I saw I should never be able to trust her and I told her I could not. Had I acted differently, she might be alive today."

Thomas halted and seemed to wait for her reaction. But Agnes walked on, the wind whipping her soaking wet skirts and boots. The boat with her son and his unknown kidnapper was now no larger than a walnut shell, a blurred shape against a swath of oily water. It disappeared through one of the cavernous openings between the piers of London Bridge, as if Peter were being consumed by some river monster. Thomas marched ahead toward the wharf steps. She shouted after him to make herself heard above the wind. "I have no appetite to argue the matter further now."

With this, Thomas swiveled round, looking down at her from halfway up the steps. "You talk of me deceiving you, when it is *you* who deceive yourself."

Agnes climbed up the steps until she was nearly level with him. "What do you mean by that?"

"If you really believed *I* was involved in Rose's murder, why would you have spoken yesterday of your errors of judgment, or permitted my assistance as you just did? You have fabricated doubts in order to barricade yourself from the truth."

"On the contrary, I am perfectly open to the truth. Yesterday, thanks to your deception, I did not know it. And as for your assistance just now, much good that proved!" Then, infuriated as much by her own ingratitude as her weakness, she raised her hands and added more softly, "For pity's sake, Mr. Williams, leave me be."

But he gripped her by the elbow. "And now you intend to go off alone?"

Agnes wrenched her arm from his and turned toward the towpath. A thin gray mist was falling over the water. Squinting into the gloom, Agnes fancied she could see the rowboat draw in to the quayside. Some yards ahead the path forked, the left-hand branch turning inland in a southerly direction; and she reckoned it must lead toward Melancholy Walk. Even as she watched, Peter's kidnapper moored the boat to a large metal ring on the quayside below.

Agnes instinctively pressed herself into an adjacent doorway and pulled Thomas with her. The two figures stepped from the boat and made their way to the street above. They then plunged into an alley out of view. "Not a word, he must not see us," Agnes whispered. "And when we arrive at the house, please stay back. Do not follow until I beckon you to come. It will be better all round if I approach alone."

"As a woman, you are hardly equipped to attempt such a rescue."

"Peter is my son. After all I have recently endured, I believe I am well able to manage my own affairs."

"Very well, then, if that is your choice. Do you prefer me to leave?"

"Not now, or someone might see you."

"Indeed, then would it not be in Peter's interest for us to formulate a plan on which we both agree?"

Agnes had to concede his logic. For some minutes, they argued in whispers and eventually agreed that Agnes (who was unyielding on the point) would proceed ahead and find a means of entry without being observed. After ascertaining the abductor's whereabouts and identity, she would make herself known, thus allowing him to believe she had fallen for his trap. On her signal, Thomas would arrive and apprehend the villain and she would rescue her son.

Thomas protested that the plan was too sketchy and it would be better if they went in together. But she argued that two of them would be more likely to be noticed, and that once the element of surprise was lost, the abductor would have the advantage over them and might easily slip away. "Once we are certain who he is, at least if he escapes we may inform the justice and have him apprehended. Without proof, we can do nothing."

With Thomas still muttering objections, they proceeded, taking the left-hand fork. A narrow alley was lined on both sides with a high wooden palisade. On the right reared the backs of a row of tall buildings. "Which house is it?" said Thomas.

"One of those over there," whispered Agnes, waving at the houses. "But the road is on the other side and from this vantage point I cannot tell exactly which it is."

They edged their way up an alley leading to Melancholy Walk. Presumably Peter and his captor must have traveled this way, but there was no sign of them. As she reached the corner, Agnes peered gingerly round into the street. Then through the mist, she glimpsed a pair of silhouettes, one tall, one short, hurrying away. "I see them," she said. "I will go alone from here."

Thomas nodded. She sensed his misgivings, but he made no attempt to follow her. Clinging to the wall, Agnes proceeded as far as she dared. A few yards on, the pair halted in front of a house, then mounted the stairs and knocked. She recognized the house as Pitt's. She could see Peter peer about, the dark-cloaked figure looming over him like a colossus. After a while the door creaked open. An occasional word drifted to her—"boat . . . pursued . . . wait here . . ." A minute later they stepped inside and the door crashed closed.

Agnes crept up to the house. The sash windows were dark, the shutters closed. She climbed the four steps and tried the front door. But as she expected, it was locked fast. She looked up at the façade, searching for a means to enter without being noticed. To one side of the main entrance, a narrow stone staircase led down to the basement, the wall punctuated by a casement window. The window might have been large enough to squeeze through, but it was locked and barred. Impossible. But then she saw that to one side of the basement, hidden beneath the stairs leading to the front door, was another, smaller entrance.

Filled with trepidation, she went down and tried the door handle, praying it would open. But the handle did not budge. She put her shoulder against the door and gave a sharp shove with all her weight, but the door was stout and there was no give in it at all. She would have to alter the plan and knock on Pitt's door to gain entry after all, she decided. And then rely upon her wits to save Peter. There was no other way.

But as she turned, her boot caught upon something. Beneath the stairs leading down from the street, a wooden cover with a thick rope handle was set into the flagged basement floor. Hope rising once more, she yanked on the rope, but the wood was sodden and swollen shut. Taking a firmer grip, she yanked harder. The rope bit into her palms, the cover creaked, she fancied she felt it give a little. She heaved again with all her might. This time she nearly fell backward as the lid pulled off.

Panting, Agnes squatted down and peered into the black opening. She could see nothing but a glistening black mound some four feet beneath her: the coal cellar. She swung her legs into the opening, then let herself fall.

The drop was greater than she had calculated and she wrenched her ankle as she landed and cried out involuntarily. Coal dust filled her eyes and nostrils but she stiffled her cough. As her eyes began to adjust to the darkness, she could make out the walls, the beams supporting the ceiling, and a small arched doorway set into one wall.

Chapter Forty-two

GNES LIMPED ACROSS the cellar and tried the handle; the door opened easily. She pushed it out a few inches and looked gingerly through the gap. There was a corridor leading, she supposed, to the kitchen. But all was silent, chill, deserted.

She stepped into the corridor. Doors opened to the left—disused sculleries and pantries and a larder filled with nothing but cobwebs. The corridor opened into a kitchen with a staircase in one corner. Agnes glanced disapprovingly at the rusted, unlit range, and a heap of pots encrusted with scraps of foul-smelling food. A rat scuttled beneath the skirting. Shuddering with cold and apprehension, she mounted the stairs.

Agnes found herself in the upper hallway. To the left was the front door and the room facing the street, where she had first met Pitt.

At first the place seemed deserted, but then she thought she heard a faint sound coming from the back—the muffled sound of footsteps, someone coughing. She moved toward it, barely able to keep from calling out Peter's name. Her scalp prickling with anticipation, her breathing shallow, she inched open the door and squinted in.

The room was sparsely furnished—a couple of deal chairs, an

old splintered table, and a desultory fire burned in the grate. Standing in the center of the room was Elsie. The girl looked strained and worn, as if she hadn't slept for days, and she was coughing quietly into a grimy handkerchief. Rose's boots were still on her feet.

Boots, Agnes thought—that is what was troubling me. That is what I recognized. She recalled then the boots she had found on her kitchen table the morning of Rose's disappearance and the lean, dark form she had seen at the river, and nodded slowly. But a moment later, she was overcome by a surge of bitterness. Elsie had assisted in Peter's abduction. Elsie, with whom she had sympathized, whom she had tried to help.

"So, Elsie, I have found you at last," she said.

She swept into the room and grabbed her arm. "Where is Peter? How could you assist in such an evil scheme?"

Elsie met Agnes's accusing look with one of equal rancor and indictment.

"Well," Agnes said, "why did you take my son?" In her heart of hearts, she knew the answer—Elsie must hold her responsible for her father's death.

By way of reply, Elsie shifted her eyes to direct Agnes's attention to the door she had just entered. Agnes recognized a soft tread behind her. Still clutching Elsie's arm, she turned.

A grimy figure loomed in the doorway. It was Grant, Pitt's henchman. His gaze seemed blurred and unfocused. His trousers were half unbuttoned, the belt undone. He was wearing the same filthy stained coat that he had worn yesterday. He gave a noisy yawn and belched.

"Mrs. Meadowes," he said. "What an unexpected surprise. Come to join us, have you?" As he approached them, Elsie pushed away Agnes's hand and sidled close to Grant. The stench of stale clothes and sweat emanating from him was overpowering, but Elsie looked up at Grant as though seeking reassurance, then fixed Agnes with a hostile glare.

Agnes stepped back. "Join you? All I want is to find my son. Some evil person has abducted him this morning and brought him here." She was wary of Grant, but not afraid. He had not taken Peter—she knew it was not his stocky outline she had seen. Grant belched again. Agnes caught fumes of stale beer, mingled with onions and other odors too noxious to contemplate. He gave her a leering grin. "Abducted your son?" he said, drawing uncomfortably close. "That is a most tragic occurrence. Whoever would do such a thing? I trust you do not accuse little Elsie or me?"

Agnes glanced quickly at the window. Somewhere out there, she thought, Thomas awaits my signal. She felt a ridiculous urge to throw open the window and call him. "No," she said, trying to disguise her revulsion and mounting unease. "I do not accuse *you* in particular. But I saw someone bring my son into this house here not fifteen minutes ago." Grant scratched his stubbly cheek. "I never heard nothing, did you, Elsie?"

"No sir. That's 'cos they ain't here," said Elsie in an expressionless tone. "You must've imagined it, Mrs. Meadowes."

Ignoring Grant, Agnes lowered her gaze to the girl. "Elsie, I know it was you that took Peter away. Perhaps you did so because someone told you I was responsible for your father's death. I assure you, that is not the case. Now tell me, do you know where Peter is?"

"Why should I believe you? Why should I tell you anything?"

"I do not know what you have been told, but, I repeat, I had nothing to do with your father's death. Nothing save finding his body after Mr. Grant hid it. And since doing so, I have been much occupied in trying to ascertain who murdered him, for it was the same person who killed Rose and the apprentice."

"That ain't true, is it, Mr. Grant? It were her what got my pa killed, you said."

Grant ignored the question. He came toward Agnes menacingly. "And what of Mr. Pitt? I suppose you had nothing to do with *his* apprehension, neither?"

"I was not responsible for his arrest, although I cannot pretend sorrow at his fate. But do not fret on his account; by his own testimony, his friendship with a certain judge will swiftly ensure his freedom. In any case, Mr. Grant, now that you are left holding the reins of his enterprise, you cannot be entirely sorry he's out of the way. This house will be very comfortable without Mr. Pitt ordering you about. So if Elsie won't help, why don't you reveal what you know and keep Pitt where he deserves to be? Think of the fruits that would then be yours to enjoy."

Grant shifted his bloodshot eyes. He scratched his groin and shuffled from side to side. Did Agnes imagine it, or had a flicker of doubt now appeared in Elsie's eyes?

Grant cocked his head, squeezing the fleshy folds of his neck into tight concentric rings. "What d'you wish to know?"

"Where is my boy, and who in the Blanchard household assisted in robbery of the wine cooler?"

Grant snorted. "Sorry, I can't help you on either count. I was just taking a nap and never heard a whisper. But if young Elsie says he ain't here, then he ain't. And as for your other query—I'm in the dark as much as you. Besides, I'd be for the noose if I said a word. Pitt'd find out somehow or other. He's too much hold on too many men of influence." Then, giving Agnes a farewell nod, he added, "I'll bid you good day now. I've urgent business to attend to," and shuffled out. Halfway down the hall, he called to Elsie. "And you, girl—how about making yourself useful and fetching us something for dinner? I'll be back in half an hour."

Grant slammed the front door. Elsie hesitated for a second and then, without looking at Agnes, made as if to follow. Agnes placed her hand on her shoulder. "Wait a moment, Elsie. Listen to me. Whoever told you I killed your father only did so in order that you would help abduct Peter. None of it is true. I don't believe you want Peter harmed, or me killed either. That is why my son has been taken—so that I would come after him and whoever murdered your pa would do the same to me. Is that what you want?"

Elsie regarded Agnes intently, then wiped her nose with the back of her hand. Tears glistened on her lashes. "I don't know his name. And even if I did, after what *you* done for my pa, I wouldn't let on," she said stubbornly.

"Why would I kill your pa? You only have Grant's word for it. And that is because he is afraid *he* might be murdered if he lets slip the real culprit. He knows who it is, though—you could see that as well as I. Did Grant tell you it was he that hid your pa's body in the chimney?"

"No."

"Then take a look at how dirty his coat is. The stains on it are your father's blood and the soot from where he hid his body up the chimney. And if you still don't believe me, go and speak to Mr. Pitt at the roundhouse. He knows the truth."

Agnes could see her waver as she absorbed the information. She waited. Give her time, Agnes told herself. She is under no obligation to help. Do not press too hard.

Elsie sighed miserably, "It were Mr. Grant what told me to take 'im to where pa's cellar were—he was going to take Peter there, down by Pickle Herring Quay," she ventured.

"Take who?"

"I dunno who he was—a man, tall, dark-haired, middling sort of dress."

Agnes nodded, eyes gleaming. "You are quite certain of that? You never saw him before?"

"Never said that, did I?" said Elsie, cross at being doubted. "He was all covered up in the carriage, but I fancy I did see him once before. Or if not, he were very like the man what chased after your friend by the river."

"I see," said Agnes, pondering. "But it wasn't one of the menservants from Foster Lane?"

"No."

She hadn't expected so firm a rebuttal. "I take it you know what Mr. Theodore and Mr. Nicholas Blanchard look like from watching the house. Was it one of them, or someone from the shop?"

Again Elsie firmly shook her head. "Anyway, whoever he were, like I said, I went in the coach with him. When I spun Mrs. Sharp the story, he stayed in the coach; he put on a glove and waved from the window to masquerade as you. I was meant to keep an eye on Peter for a few hours, until someone came and took him away. He said getting a bit of a scare was no more than you deserved and the boy wouldn't be harmed." She now was looking at her feet as she spoke.

"It's all right, Elsie. I don't blame you. He duped me just the same." But Agnes was puzzled. Why hadn't Elsie recognized the man in the carriage? But she nodded encouragingly, "And once you had Peter, what happened?"

"Him and me and the other fellow went in the carriage down to the river. I showed him where to come and ran ahead to make things ready. Only him and Peter never arrived, and when I came back up the steps to see where they'd gone I saw them both going off in a boat."

Agnes nodded. "What brought you here?"

Elsie blinked and turned away. "I don't like being in that cellar much on my own, now Pa's not there. Mr. Grant told me I might stay here. He said Pa's death and Mr. Pitt's arrest needn't make a difference. I could help him just the same."

"So Grant was never involved in the scheme to snatch Peter?"

"No. Only he told me to do what the man said." Elsie looked nervously over her shoulder toward the door. "I never told him nothing about all this, nor that they come 'ere. He was fast asleep just now, and never woke."

Doubtless his slumbers were aided by the bottles of ale, thought Agnes grimly. "Tell me, that night when you waited for the message and I asked you to come down to the kitchen, why did you run off?"

"I saw my pa standing there waiting in a doorway."

There had been a figure sheltering opposite, she recalled. "Waiting for you?"

"I thought so at the time, though it can't have been 'cos he never came after me. When I looked back he was waving his arms and making faces, but not at me." She stopped. "I'd better go fetch the dinner now or Grant'll be angry."

"One more thing. Was it you who let Peter and his abductor in just now?"

"Yes. He said it would only be a short while afore you came looking. He wouldn't stay long after that."

Agnes felt her heart pitch. Her arrival had been expected. Peter had been taken as a lure. "And where did they go?"

"Upstairs. Don't know where, though."

Agnes nodded. "Very well. Hurry off now. And on your way up the road, you will pass an alley where a friend of mine, Mr. Williams, a curly-haired man wearing a brown coat, is waiting. Tell him to come close to the front window of the house. I shall call him any moment now."

Elsie nodded as she marched off. Agnes sensed the girl's regret at what she had done, but could see that she struggled to find the words to say so. She followed her down the corridor, waiting for half a minute, just in case Elsie should say something more; but she went out in silence, and Agnes could wait no longer. She was just about to climb the stairs when she observed that the previously open door to Pitt's front room was now closed. Grant had been gone a half an hour, she remembered. She had heard him go out and shut the front door. Was someone else now inside?

Agnes looked in. A thin line of light leeched between the closed shutters. She was uncomfortably reminded of the ride in the carriage when Marcus Pitt had insisted the curtains remain closed. She had opened the shutters no more than an inch or two when she heard shuffling on the stairs and a heavy tread in the hallway. She spun round just as a head peered in. "Mrs. Meadowes," said a familiar voice. "Thank God I have found you."

Chapter Forty-three

AGNES WENT PALE. "Philip, whatever are you doing here?"

"Come to offer my heartfelt sympathy and, more important, practical assistance." He closed the door behind him. He was wigless and hatless, dressed not in livery but in his street clothes—a smart blue woolen cloak, black breeches, and leather boots, all of which were spattered with fresh mud, but looked new. "Mrs. Sharp told me about what happened. She came to Foster Lane and told Mr. Matthews that Mr. Pitt had taken your son. Mr. Matthews said we ought to offer you assistance. I knew this was where you would come since I'd accompanied you here before, so I said I'd come."

"I see," said Agnes quietly. "You are most kind. But I already have Mr. Williams to help."

"I know—I saw him outside just now. But he alone is no match for all Pitt's cronies. Furthermore, he asked me to tell you he has gone for the constable and will arrive directly."

Agnes took this in. Why had she felt compelled to resolve matters in such a foolhardy manner, without giving Thomas so much as a hint as to who she believed might be guilty? Was this a last remnant of the reserved person she once had been? Philip, meanwhile, showed little urgency about his commission. He examined the book-lined walls, then picked up items from Pitt's desk. A silver inkwell, a goose quill, a candlestick, a box containing sealing wafers. "Nice things, ain't they, Mrs. M.? Think he'd miss one or two, now he's in the roundhouse?"

She made no reply. She was conscious of his hands, flecked with dark hairs; of his long, strong fingers picking up the objects and turning them over. What else had those fingers held? "Give me back my son, Philip. It will help your case. You will never escape now, but I will do what I can to assist if you release him unharmed."

"What? Have you gone soft in the head? I told you, I'm here because Mr. Matthews sent me to help you find him."

"I doubt that. But Mr. Williams is waiting for my signal. I have only to cry out and he will come."

"I told you he isn't there. Come, should we not begin our search for Peter at the top of the house?"

"Why? Aren't *I* what you wanted? Or is it that you plan to dispose of me by shoving me off the roof?"

Philip's amiable expression vanished. "I told you, Mrs. Meadowes, I don't mean you harm. I am here to help. Why won't you listen?"

She had waited for this moment to confront him, but now she hardly knew what to say. She thought of Rose as Elsie had described her, running for dear life across the mudflats. She thought of Noah Prout's murder, and Harry Drake's decapitated body. She threw up the window sash and shouted into the deserted street, "Thomas! Come now and help me search for Peter!"

As she bellowed, a powerful arm wrapped about her neck. Philip spoke slowly in her ear. "Whatever are you doing, making such a spectacle of yourself, Mrs. Meadowes? Thomas isn't there. I told you, didn't I? And you have me to help you."

"You may kill me, but you will not deceive me. Elsie saw you that night chasing Rose—she will identify you. Where is Peter?"

Philip laughed bitterly. "Then if the girl betrayed me, I fancy some misadventure might soon befall her. Quiet, Mrs. Meadowes. No more questions. Let's go and look for Peter together. And remember, you brought all this on yourself. I am only here to help." He shifted his grip to her arm and began pushing her toward the door.

Agnes twisted to face him. "My desire was only to uncover the truth. A woman who worked for me, and of whom I was fond, met an untimely death—is it so surprising I should want to discover what became of her?"

"Fond!" cried Philip, spinning her back and pushing her up the stairs by the arm which he held in a firm grip. "There's a joke. You was never fond of anything save duty."

Agnes paused. Perhaps you were right once, but not any longer, she thought. "Then I have become fond of Rose since her death. She was not perfect, I grant you, but she didn't deserve to be killed."

"'Course not—a veritable tragedy, it was."

They reached the first landing.

"I'm not entirely green," retorted Agnes hotly, thinking of the pair of them in the larder. "I know you killed Rose in a jealous rage, and Noah Prout and Harry Drake."

Philip squeezed her arm tighter. "Now you're going soft again. Why would I kill Rose when I loved her? Why would I kill any of them?"

"Because the poor girl wanted no more to do with you. You don't like being turned down, do you?"

Philip pushed Agnes roughly up the next flight of stairs. "I was demented, was I? That's rich. I would've married her. Is that a crime in your book? There's any number of women want me, only not you 'cos you're cold as granite, and not her. Even with money I wasn't good enough for her."

"And so you followed her."

"I went after her to tell her I loved her. What I'd done for her, how rich we'd be in a week or two's time. But instead she shamed me. Treated me like I was nothing. No other woman ever done that. And she had money all along—she offered it to me to leave her alone. It was that that done for her. Trying to pay me to go— like I was her lackey."

They had reached the third-floor landing, a long corridor with doors opening on each side, dimly lit at the far end by a garret window darkened with grime. Philip shoved her to the window, yanked open the latch with his free hand, and flung open the casement. "Look out there."

Beyond the jagged black gables stretched the wide curve of dull gray river. Silhouetted against it, seated on a parapet like a frail bowsprit on a ship, sat Peter. His mouth was bound. A blindfold had been tied around his eyes, ropes about his ankles and wrists. But there was nothing to stop him falling. Agnes opened her mouth to call out to him, but found she could utter no sound. What if I startle him? she thought. If he moves an inch he will fall.

"Let me fetch him," she whispered.

"All in good time. I have told him he will be quite safe so long as he behaves himself and doesn't move. Of course he can't see, so he doesn't know where he is. So, Mrs. Meadowes, feeling less meddlesome now?"

"Ssh," whispered Agnes. "Don't let him hear or he might move."

He ignored her. "All I desired was Rose and the means to support her. You, of all people, should comprehend. Yet with every turn you obstructed me. You spoiled my scheme. I lost Rose and the money I was due from Pitt."

"My meddling had nothing to do with Rose spurning you," whispered Agnes hotly. "You might deceive yourself that you acted for love, but in truth you were propelled by other, darker motives—jealousy, greed, and fear."

On hearing this, he lunged at her and closed his hands around her neck. Agnes reared back her head, crashing against the window frame. From the corner of her eye she saw Peter move, as if he were straining for the source of the sound.

Philip increased the pressure about her neck and she tried to pry his fingers away. After a minute or two, sensing her waning strength, he let go with one hand and reached to his pocket. He gave a sharp flick of his wrist and a blade sprang out from its handle, gleaming in the dim light. "And now, since you are so very curious, I shall show you how I killed them so easily. Here is Mr. Matthews's spare razor; he leaves it in his pantry drawer, and never remarks when I borrow it. When you left the wine label in the drawer I knew I would have to silence you. But I presume that was your intention. To let me know you had found me out. Look how sharp it is."

Still holding Agnes firmly by the neck, he waved the blade in front of her face and sliced it down an inch from her cheek. A thick lock of hair fell onto her breast. Philip was speaking again, but his voice seemed to be fading. Somewhere below, she thought she heard the sound of voices, footsteps. She tried to wrench away and scratch his hands; she tried to say that of course she had not intended to threaten him by leaving the wine label in the drawer. But at every sign of resistance, Philip shook her, banging her skull viciously against the wall and laying the blade flat against her neck.

Agnes felt her eyeballs bulge and her tongue swell over her teeth. Blood pounded in her neck and forehead so she could barely hear him. She was aware only of echoing shouts, footsteps growing louder, pain, and fear.

He pressed his mouth to Agnes's ear and asked her which way she preferred to die. Which way? Blade across the throat, or strangulation? Which way?

"Philip! What the devil are you doing?" a voice boomed through the fog.

Philip gave a start and turned to see who it was. "Keep away," he muttered. "There's business here in which you are not involved."

"I prefer to avoid trouble where I can, but I am here to help Mrs. Meadowes, and I don't like to leave her in this disorder." Over Philip's shoulder, Agnes caught a glimpse of Thomas Williams as he drew his sword and ran Philip through.

For an instant Agnes was unsure what was real and what she had imagined. But as Philip's legs buckled under him, and blood gushed from his mouth, she came to her senses. She turned wordlessly to the window. It was no dream. Peter was still sitting there.

Holding her finger to her mouth so that Thomas would not call out, she opened it, and tried to heave herself through. But the sill was too high.

Thomas pulled her gently to one side. He jumped up onto the ledge and squeezed his way out. Silently he inched his way on all fours toward the parapet. All the while Peter remained immobile, straining to hear. When Thomas was two feet away, Peter must have heard a faint rustle behind him. He half turned his head and went as if to move forward. Agnes closed her eyes. She opened them again just as Thomas grabbed him unceremoniously about the waist and dragged him back to safety. "There now," he said, without removing the blindfold. "I've your mother waiting for you inside. Let's go and see her, shall we?"

Thomas lifted the shivering child through the window. Agnes carried him past Philip's body and down the two flights of stairs to Pitt's room before she untied his blindfold and bindings and embraced him.

"I went in a carriage with Philip," he said, his ribs heaving with sobs. "After we went in the boat, he said we would play a game and he would bring me to you, if I let myself be blindfolded. But why did he leave me out there so long in the cold?"

"It's all right," she said as lightly as she could, breathing in the scent of his damp hair. "It's over now. He has gone. He won't trouble you again."

Chapter Forty-four

"JEALOUSY," SAID AGNES, "is as cruel as the grave. It leads men and women to desperate lengths, to commit untold evil. Philip could not reconcile himself to the fact that Rose's affections had cooled for him. He was a handsome fellow, with an appetite for women of all shapes and sizes." She glanced at Doris, and then at Nancy. "And he was accustomed to having any girl he chose."

She was holding forth during the servants' breakfast, having arrived back too late the previous night to apprise anyone that Philip was dead. She was exhausted, her neck was bruised, her limbs ached. But despite everything, the Blanchards still had to be fed and the household was still a kitchen maid short, and now a footman. She had risen at seven as usual, but before beginning her duties had searched Philip's things. Secreted in a corner of his chest she had found a note from Marcus Pitt, arranging a meeting for the payment of his "commission." There was also a small leather purse containing fifteen gold sovereigns. The rest of Rose's money, Agnes presumed, had been spent on the new attire he had been wearing yesterday.

She looked around the table. Mrs. Tooley was pale-faced. In a minute or two, thought Agnes, she'll reach for her salts and want a lie-down. Curiously, however, Agnes no longer resented her weakness.

"If he had the pick of us all, why in heaven's name did he waste time on someone who didn't want him?" asked Nancy. She was brittle as ever, but she had a gleam in her eye. What was it? Agnes wondered. Anger that Agnes had not believed her story about the purse? Guilt at her involvement? Fear for herself and her unborn child?

"Because being spurned was new to him—and bothered him deeply. He convinced himself he loved her, and pestered her repeatedly to take him back. And Rose, as we all know, could be unkind on occasion."

"Unkind—that's putting it mildly," said Nancy. "She was a hard jade and I don't care who knows it."

Agnes sighed. Not very long ago she had harbored just such jealousy and bitterness. "Rose didn't care if she hurt Philip because she too had been hurt in love. She and Thomas Williams had become engaged when he came to London to work for Blanchards'. When Rose's father died suddenly, she was obliged to seek work, and found a post as a maid to Lord Carew. But Rose detested life as a servant. She begged Thomas to marry her early so she could stop working, and when he refused because he was worried about his own position, she broke off the engagement."

"Then she'd no reason to feel sorry for herself, had she? She only had herself to blame."

"Quiet, Nancy." Doris broke in with unusual authority. "Let us listen to what Mrs. Meadowes has to say before we hear your thoughts on it."

"She was a headstrong girl," said Agnes. "After the quiet of Newcastle, London must have turned her head. Like Philip, she enjoyed the company of the opposite sex. She thought that with all the eligible men in London she would not find it hard to persuade someone else to marry her. But then a month or so later she realized it was not going to be so easy, and asked Thomas to take her back."

"Then if she was after Thomas, why take up with Philip and Riley?" asked Nancy.

"Because Thomas was still uncertain about his position. And being determined and impatient, Rose couldn't wait. She set about trying to make him jealous. She flirted with Riley, and then she turned her attentions to Philip. But her plan misfired. After a few months, Thomas told her that he no longer trusted her and would never change his mind.

"By then Rose had tired of Philip. But he convinced himself he was smitten with her. So much so that he asked her to marry him. Rose laughed at him and told him he was an idiot even to think he could support a wife when he was only a footman, and said he knew as well as she that servants were not allowed to marry."

"And the man in the street?" said Mrs. Tooley, dabbing her eyes with the effort of taking so much in. "Was he another follower?"

"He was her brother," said Agnes. "He returned from abroad, and only then discovered what had become of his father and sister. He was aghast to find Rose living as a servant. After all, she was an educated girl. He suggested that she come and help him in a school he intended to open in France. I think that was why she cooled toward Philip. She wanted to tell Mrs. Blanchard—there was no other reason for her to have taken such an interest in her comings and goings. But in the end, possibly because she would never be listened to with sympathy, she decided against it."

"I don't understand," said Mrs. Tooley. "Do you mean to say Rose had nothing to do with the robbery after all?"

"Oh, no. She was the reason it happened. Somehow Philip got wind of her intention to leave. Perhaps he overheard you, Mrs. Tooley, ticking her off for talking to a strange man in the street. Then there was the letter Nancy found. In any case, he became desperate to change her mind. Remember, Rose told him they could not marry because he couldn't provide for her.

"He looked for a way to make money quickly. Being a friend of one of the apprentices, he visited the workshop frequently and knew what was happening there. He heard about the wine cooler—the most precious item Blanchards' had ever made. It must have seemed a God-given opportunity, and so he devised a scheme to steal it."

"But did he not feel disloyal for ruining the family that gave him employ?" said Patsy. "I always thought him such a deferential fellow."

Agnes nodded, remembering Philip dressed in livery, handsome, the perfect servant. "He had a capacity for deference, I do not deny that, but underneath he resented the restrictions of his position much as Rose did."

Agnes caught John exchange an uneasy glance with Mr. Matthews. Perhaps, she thought, they are worried I might let slip their plans for the celebrations to mark John's coming of age, and the pilfering that has gone on to fuel them.

"But how did he set about orchestrating the scheme?" said John.

"Unlike you, John, Philip frequently passed his evenings in the alehouses of this part of the city. He claimed he was in the Blue Cockerel on the night of the robbery. In such places Pitt's reputation as a preeminent thief taker is well known." Here Agnes was unable to conceal her disapproval. "The business of thief taking relies upon a vast retinue of informants. It would not have been hard for Philip to establish contact with one of them and then arrange a meeting with Pitt."

Agnes took a sip of tea. Disturbing images crowded her thoughts; of Pitt, holding her captive, pressing himself on her; of Philip's hands about her neck; of Peter blindfolded on the edge of the roof. She blinked, looked up again, took a breath.

"Pitt and Philip agreed that the reward for the wine cooler's return would be split between the pair of them and a fee would also be paid to Harry Drake, who would carry out the robbery. But

Harry Drake was a greedy man, and when he saw that Philip was employed in the house of a silversmith, he had the foolish idea of extracting further money from him. On the night that Elsie came to take the message for Pitt, she saw her father waiting in the street, signaling to someone at the house—Philip, who was in the dining room at the time, threatening to reveal his identity unless he paid for his silence. Philip pretended to agree.

"Philip must have taken a wine label from the dining room— I found it in Drake's pocket and returned it to Mr. Matthews's drawer. I fancy Drake must have protested that the wine label wasn't valuable enough to buy his silence. So Philip said he would find something more, and arranged a meeting later that night at the house where Drake was guarding the wine cooler. Only instead of taking more valuables to Drake, Philip decapitated him."

John glanced again at Mr. Matthews, who asked, "But why did Philip need to murder the apprentice? Why not simply incapacitate him?"

"I asked myself the same question. I believe it was because he had only just learned that time was short. Rose's plan to leave was more imminent than he had first realized. If the apprentice was not silenced, his scheme would be more perilous. The apprentice might overpower Drake, in which case the scheme might fail and Rose would be gone before he had made himself rich. He was unwilling to take that chance."

Nancy turned scarlet. "It was him what egged me on to take the letter that was sent her. I only did so to make him notice me." She grew suddenly tearful, one hand resting protectively on her belly. "And then I meant to put it back, only she discovered it was missing and flew at me. I thought he'd lose interest in her once he knew she was going. How was I to know he'd kill her on account of it?"

"You have no need to blame yourself," said Agnes gently. "He was expert at using charm and flattery to get what he wanted. I too was misled by him in a way. The truth was there all along, but it took me a while to see what it was."

"How did you discover it was him?" said Mr. Matthews, his gaunt old face resembling that of an Old Testament prophet. "I never would have thought him capable of such devilry. You must have probed in places you were not entitled to go."

"It was the boots that made me first suspect," said Agnes, avoiding his pointed remark.

"What boots?"

"The morning after the robbery and Rose's disappearance, I found a pair of boots on the kitchen table. Philip was in your pantry. Although he confessed to having been out that night, he pretended he did not know what had happened to Rose and said the boots weren't his.

"I thought no more of it, but when I found the gun in the cellar I decided that the culprit was most likely one of the menservants. Who else would have an opportunity to hide the gun there? And then I began to reflect upon what Philip had told me of his relationship with Rose. He pretended there was nothing between them when she left, but when Nancy confessed that she had taken the letter, I thought she would not have done so unless she had a purpose, and that purpose was most likely turning Philip against Rose. Philip said he had passed the night at the Blue Cockerel, but while the landlord recalled seeing him, he had no notion when he left.

"When Elsie told me she didn't know who had taken her in the carriage, but that it wasn't one of the menservants, I confess I was baffled. But then I realized that while she would have recognized Mr. Matthews or John, she had never laid eyes on Philip."

Mr. Matthews ran his hand across his venerable head. "But the time you went to Mr. Pitt's house, Philip accompanied you. And I thought you met Elsie there."

"That is true, but Grant insisted that Philip wait outside. Had he not, perhaps Elsie would have observed him and identified him sooner as the man she had seen chasing Rose by the river."

"I still do not believe that Rose was as innocent as you say," protested Nancy. "What of the salver I found her handling?"

"That was nothing to do with her. Theodore had established a duty-dodging scheme with Riley—cutting marks from one piece and putting them in another to try and save duty, in order to finance a move to the west of the city. I doubt it earned him much, but he yearns for a life free of his father's influence. But none of it had anything to do with Philip and his evil scheme, or Rose's determination to leave."

Mrs. Tooley took a noisy sniff of her salts. Her hands were shaking. "I have a replacement maid arriving this morning. I sincerely hope she's more manageable than Rose Francis."

At this, Nancy and Doris bombarded her as to the age, appearance, and background of the new arrival. Then everyone fell silent for a moment, and Mr. Matthews coughed and rose. The sternness in his eyes had returned. "I thank you for enlightening us, Mrs. Meadowes. When you have finished your breakfast, I should like a further word in private."

AGNES KNEW as soon as she entered the pantry what he would say. Rose's purse and a folded paper lay on his table. She was gratified to note that he could not meet her eye. "I am sorry," he said. "The decision of which I am about to inform you is not mine. Sir Bartholomew Grey came to call on Mr. Blanchard, Senior yesterday, and told him of your visit. Even had you not removed a letter that was not addressed to you from my office, I have no recourse. You will be paid a week's notice. To assist you with your child, I should like to add this to that sum." And he handed her Rose's purse.

Chapter Forty-five

THE BELLS OF ST. PAUL'S struck two as Agnes Meadowes, laden with a basket of provisions, her cloth-bound recipe book, and an assortment of cleaning utensils, unlocked the door to a small house in Watery Lane. Depositing her possessions in the dark hall, she made her way into a shabby front room, furnished with four tables and a counter, all covered with dust. Not for the first time, she remarked to herself that there was a great deal of painting and scrubbing to be done. Striding through to the kitchen, she surveyed a range that was brown with rust, a floor slick with congealed grease, and a blackened dresser, the recesses of which she had not yet dared explore. Upstairs was a warren of sparsely furnished rooms in a state of similar filth and dilapidation. Nevertheless, she felt not in the least despondent. She had used Theodore's five pounds and Rose's fifteen sovereigns to rent these premises, where she would begin a new enterprise as proprietor of an eating house and purveyor of pastries and pies.

She carried a bucket to the pump in the yard outside and filled it with water. She began to scrub the range, but was soon forced to stop. Rose's brother, in recognition of what she had done in pursuing his sister's murderer, had given her Rose's ring and silver box. The ring had caused a blister to appear on her finger.

Agnes pulled it off. She smiled as she remembered coming upon Rose in the larder, locked in an embrace with Philip. In the past, both she and Rose had been forced along unwise paths. But unlike Rose, fate had given her opportunity to set things straight. She slipped the ring into her pocket and returned to her work.

Sometime later, when the range was clean and the blacking of the iron well under way, Agnes heard a knock on the door. "Elsie," she said, seeing the thin-faced girl, still swathed in her rags and red shawl, and wearing Rose's overlarge boots. Without knowing why, Agnes embraced her. "You are here at last! There's a deal to be done before this house is habitable. Tomorrow, Sarah Sharp will bring Peter. This evening, Thomas Williams might call." She smiled as she mentioned his name, and thought of his hair spread about his head like a mane, his arms flung out like the spokes of a wheel on his pillow. "And suppose Mrs. Tooley keeps her promise and comes to visit this weekend. You have never known anyone so particular as she is. The smallest cobweb is guaranteed to give her a turn."

"Then why don't I make a start upstairs and you carry on down here?" said Elsie, her feline eyes surveying Agnes calmly.

"Yes. But first let us take something to eat. I am half starved, and I am sure you must be too. There's nothing in the place save an oyster pie, a piece of gammon, and an orange I brought with me." Agnes took out Rose's ring. "And since this is too small for my finger, I should like you to have it—for helping as you did, and joining me now."

Wordlessly, Elsie slid it on her bony finger and rubbed it on her shawl to bring up its luster. Then she cast her eye over the basket. Her hungry look reminded Agnes of the time not so very long ago when she had snatched the orange.

"Thank you, ma'am," she said. "Mr. Pitt could never have fed me half so well. Did you hear, by the by, that his case has been dismissed for want of anyone willing to give testimony against him, and he's back in Melancholy Walk? I'll set a table, shall I?"

Acknowledgments

A GNES'S COOKERY and the duties of other members of the house are based upon household guides such as *The British Housewife: or the Cook, Housekeeper's and Gardiner's Companion,* by Martha Bradley, 1756; *The English Housekeeper,* by A. Cobbett, 1842; *The Servant's Practical Guide: A Handbook of Duties and Rules,* Frederick Warne, publisher, 1880; and *The Experienced English Housekeeper,* by Elizabeth Raffald, 1997. Other helpful books included *What the Butler Saw: Two Hundred and Fifty Years of the Servant Problem,* by E. S. Turner, 1962; *Costume of Household Servants,* by P. Cunnington, 1974; *Life Below Stairs,* by Frank E. Huggett, 1977.

Descriptions of eighteenth-century silversmithing practices relied upon *Three Centuries of English Domestic Silver,* by Bernard and Therle Hughes, 1952; and *Silver in England,* by P. Glanville, 1987. Details of markings and duty dodging were taken from *Hallmark: A History of the London Assay Office,* by J. S. Forbes, 1999. I am also grateful for the assistance of the librarian at Goldsmiths' Hall.

As ever, my thanks are due to Sally Gaminara and her editorial team at Transworld Publishers; to my agent, Christopher Little, and his staff; and to Ruth Fecych at Simon & Schuster for her hard work on editing the U.S. edition.

Questions for Discussion

1. Consider how Gleeson reveals the book's society and time frame from the very first page. What are the social classes of the main characters? Share some examples of how the author establishes characters and settings with her language, tone, and cadence.

2. Why does Agnes keep herself separate from everyone? How does her relationship with the staff change from the beginning to the end of the book?

3. After Elsie steals from her, Agnes doesn't appear to be angry. Why do you think this is? Are there other instances of Agnes's compassion? If so, what are they?

4. Agnes suffered greatly at the hands of her husband. How do her past relationships with men impact her actions—particularly with Philip, Thomas, and Marcus Pitt—during the investigation? Do her feelings toward men change?

5. What are the most powerful instances of station and class affecting how people interact with each other (for example, Agnes and Rose versus Agnes and Lydia Blanchard; Rose and Philip versus Nancy and Nicolas Blanchard)? How does class affect Agnes's ability to investigate Rose's murder?

6. When Thomas explains the meaning of the stamps on the pieces of silver to Agnes, it casts doubt on the integrity of the

Blanchards. At this point in the investigation, who do you suspect as the murderer and/or the thief—Marcus Pitt, Thomas, Nicolas Blanchard, or one of the servants? Ultimately, were you surprised by the identity of the murderer? If not, what clues led you to suspect who the murderer was?

7. Theodore Blanchard promises Agnes twenty guineas—a veritable fortune for her—if she successfully completes her mission with the thief taker and the wine cooler is returned. However, though she succeeds, he cheats her. Were you surprised? Agnes knew that Blanchards' business did not pay proper duty. Did she have any other recourse to make Theodore keep his word? What would she have gained or lost from using this knowledge against the Blanchards?

8. After Agnes is intimate with Thomas, she discovers that Rose once had close ties to him. Why doesn't she ask Thomas directly about Rose? How do her assumptions about Thomas affect her behavior?

9. Rules were very strict for servants in the Blanchard household—they were not allowed to marry and, for the most part, had only one afternoon off a week. How were their lives similar to and different from slaves? Do the restrictions on their lives, such as the restrictions on marriage, shock you?

10. When Agnes is dismissed, what is your opinion of Mr. Matthews when he gives her Rose's money? Do his actions change your opinion of him? Why wouldn't he keep the money?

11. How might the events and characters in *The Thief Taker* differ if they had been set in the United States?

Questions for the Author

You are already well grounded in eighteenth-century British history. How much further research was required to write *The Thief Taker*? What means did you use (for example, books, the Internet, university professors)?

I consulted many books on eighteenth-century cuisine and on household etiquette. I also spent some time at Goldsmiths' Hall—the center of silver- and goldsmithing in Britain—where I researched the intricacies of assaying and duty dodging.

Where did you learn about the thief taker profession? Why is it called "thief taking"?

I learned about thief taking from Lucy Moore's book The Thieves' Opera, *which details the exploits of Jonathan Wild, an eighteenth-century thief taker who partly inspired my creation of Marcus Pitt. The term was so called because although many thief takers were highly corrupt, they often informed on the criminals they employed in order to receive rewards, thus enabling the thief to be "taken," that is, apprehended.*

Are any parts of *The Thief Taker* based on real events? What inspired you to write this story?

The story is not based on any real events. My inspiration came from my fascination with the strange process of thief taking that reflects the inadequacies of law making and policing at the time and also from a desire to write about a female protagonist rather than a male one, as in my earlier books.

Do you believe it's more difficult to write mysteries than other genres? How do you plot your novels? Do you know how the mystery will end and then work your way back?

All genres have their difficulties, but since I have written only historical nonfiction and historical mysteries I wouldn't dare claim they are the most difficult to write. What is certain is that mysteries depend heavily upon the plot; and without careful planning it would be difficult to place clues and red herrings and develop the characters and story line with any consistency. When I start plotting I usually have a sense of key characters and how the story will end, as well as a few key scenes in my mind. Then I work on adding more characters and joining the scenes together to build the novel.

The English class system plays a major role in *The Thief Taker*. As someone who lives there, do you feel that modern-day England is still a very class-conscious society?

There is a strong sense of class, but class no longer presents the barriers it once did—with talent and luck anyone can do anything in twenty-first-century Britain.

Are most of your favorite writers from the eighteenth century, or do you follow the careers of any current authors?

I have always enjoyed eighteenth-century and nineteenth-century literature, but I have very eclectic reading tastes and read widely on a range of subjects. I particularly enjoy and admire the historical fiction of Sarah Walters and the nonfiction of Katie Hickman, who wrote Daughters of Britannia *and* Courtesans.

You've worked at Sotheby's and were an art and antiques correspondent for *House & Garden*. What piece did you come across that impressed you the most?

I remember while I was writing for House & Garden *that the Badminton cabinet was sold. This was an incredible tour de force of baroque furniture making, covered with inlaid, brightly colored stone decoration, that was made in Italy for an English aristocrat—the Duke of Beaufort—when he was only nineteen years old.*

The Thief Taker is very visual in nature. Do you pay greater attention to the setting details because of your art background?

I do try to see what I am writing as I find it helps me get into the mood of the period and to conjure the atmosphere for the reader—an essential requirement if they are to believe they are in the eighteenth century.

You were born in Sri Lanka, but you currently live in England. Which do you consider your home? Do you visit Sri Lanka often?
I consider England to be very much my home, although Sri Lanka is very dear to my heart and a great place to spend a holiday. I last visited about ten years ago but hope to go back soon.

Tips for Creating a Memorable
The Thief Taker *Book Club Meeting*

1. Agnes Meadowes is an accomplished French chef. Experience the flavor of her kitchen by serving some of the dishes she describes: almond soup, boiled cod, jugged hare, roast venison, apple tart, and so on. For a simpler culinary experience, serve scones and tea, such as Earl Grey or Darjeeling. Delicious recipes can be found on www.joyofcooking.com.

2. *The Thief Taker* takes place in eighteenth-century England. Invite a historian from your local university to add historical nuance to your discussion.

3. We experience in intimate detail some of the restrictions placed upon the characters in *The Thief Taker* because of England's class structure. Enhance your book club discussion by watching *The Remains of the Day* or *Gosford Park,* which illustrate the restrictions on the servant class. Compare and contrast the lives of servants in both stories.

4. If *The Thief Taker* were a film, discuss which actors you would want to play the various characters and why.

About the Author

JANET GLEESON was born in Sri Lanka, where her father was a tea planter. After taking a degree in history of art and English she worked for Sotheby's, and later Bonham's Auctioneers. In 1991 she joined Reed Books, where she was responsible for devising and writing *Miller's Antiques & Collectibles*. She is the bestselling author of two works of nonfiction, *The Arcanum* and *Millionaire,* and three novels, including *The Serpent in the Garden* and *The Grenadillo Box.*